THE IMMEDIATE JEWEL OF HIS SOUL

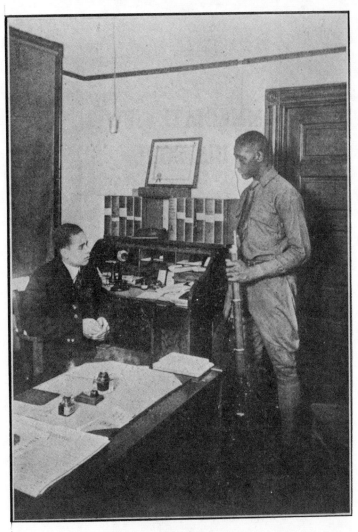

"None will barter the immediate jewel of his soul."

THE IMMEDIATE JEWEL OF HIS SOUL

A ROMANCE

By HERMAN DREER

AUTHOR OF "OUT OF THE NIGHT"

McGrath Publishing Company
College Park, Maryland

Reprint McGrath Publishing Company 1969
Reprinted from the copy at Fisk University

Library of Congress Catalog Card Number: 79-76101

Manufactured in the United States of America
by Arno Press, Inc., New York

To
My Wife
To the Pioneer New Thot Club
To All
Of Those
Who Have Passed and Will Pass
Thru
Virginia Theological Seminary
and College
That Monument
Of
Negro Achievement
I Dedicate This Work

PREFACE

In the wide sense there are three points of view from which novelists may write: the bizarre, the real and the ideal. He may portray life in caricature to produce laughter; he may depict it as it is or is likely to occur; and he may exhibit it as it should be.

This romance abandons caricature; it adheres strictly to the problems that actually face us now. As its philosophy is realistic idealism, it sets forth some of our immediate aspirations and ideals. It is a story of the earnest Negro, trying to rise unto great place.

To those of the inner circle, I hope these pages will be edification; to those without, I fondly pray that they will be food for thot and a stimulus to unselfishness and fair play.

HERMAN DREER

Saint Louis, Missouri
November 17, 1919

THE IMMEDIATE JEWEL OF HIS SOUL

THE IMMEDIATE JEWEL OF HIS SOUL

CHAPTER I

Be gone, my son, and greet thy way,
I cannot lead another day,
I've led thee to the heights I know:
Take now thy life and make it grow.

"Smith, you'll be leaving soon, won't you?" asked Henry Lee, a lad of eighteen and a classmate of William Smith, whom he addressed with an air of non chalance.

"Yes," was the melancholy reply, "and I feel lonely now. Think of the teachers I have learned to love, think of my classmates and friends. It is not easy to give them up. After taking many precious years to form these ties, at length they must all be broken. I go out into the night. And for what?"

"For the greatness that is yours, for the striving. You are young and if, as Reverend McCall says, our last days are often our best days, much that is good is merely waiting for you to claim it. Cheer up; the best is yet to come!" said Henry, trying to radiate some of his own sunshiine.

"That sounds fine, yet I deeply grieve that this time at last has come."

"Now, Smith, old boy, be serious, but not too serious Get some ginger into you. You know the pagan philosophy: Eat, drink, and be merry today, for tomorrow we die?"

(1)

"Yes, I know it well.   Our Sunday School teacher has mentioned it often."

"Well live it—to some extent any way.   This much at least we may accept from the ancients.   There must be joy as well as sorrow.

"You are doing no more than many a man has done, who was eager to rise.   To advance in any way, we must give up something we love.   It may be home, treasures, friends, or even life itself."   So history has taught us.   If we risk nothing, we gain nothing."   Remembering the event planned for Smith for that evening, Henry did not give William a chance to reply; but took the whole situation in hand, saying, "Well, old boy, I must be going.   You know why.   But understand my young man, tho this occasion is planned for you, if you do not watch sharply, I'll have more real fun than you.   You're putting on; trying to be serious.   Just wait till the girls get you tonight.   You'll be serious all right.   I know you."   Henry hurried off, excusing himself with perfect tact and decorum.

William Smith, who has just formed our acquaintance, even in this tilt with Henry Lee, behaved in no unaccustomed way. A proud son of Africa, whose blood had not been adulterated by the vicious stock of any land, he towered six feet, with a massive aphysique, a genuine black prince, a king of kings.   His broad shoulders were capable of any human task, and his hands, tho calloused by much gruesome toil, were equally ready to answer the call of ciscumstance.   A glance at his flowing, crimpy hair, his sparkling honest eyes, and his pearly teeth, at once commanded grave respect and lingering admiration.

As he moved along Randall Street of a cosmopolitan eastern town during the latter part of August, after his high school graduation, he thot of the deep mystery of human existence.

In the midst of this particular meditation, he met Henry Lee. What he said we already know.

Smith, like a happy connoisseur, surveyed the situation grandly. How well he knew that preparations would be elaborate! Did Pilgrim Tabernacle ever indulge in anything insignificant? He could not recall an instance of such. At last those willing members were making ready for him. Was he worthy of this care?

Call to mind what he had seen. All were eagerly bent on a merry occasion. Members, old and gray, had long finished appetizing cakes embellished with scrupulous care with many comely designs. Women of middle age so well prepared the choice meats, that even the most fastidious could uter no complaint. Nor were the younger set without their special tasks. They prepared the salads, decorated the dining hall, and scattered prophetic greetings of great joy. Smith knew that the bustlings of these cheerful souls was a wish; he wondered if he deserved it.

Then came another question provoked by the friendly intercourse with Henry Lee, "How can I repay them?" These questions and others crowding William, at some time face us all.

Upon the sea of life we all must sail, and whether we would have it so or not, our own pilots we must be. Friends and relatives will cheer us, near and from afar; but glory is before us, happiness within us, and victory continually at our side. And tho we founder, we will not fail; worthy of the strife, the gift, and hope, we cruise along successful ever more.

CHAPTER II

The guests are met, th feast is set,
May'st hear the merry din.—Coleridge

The dining hall of Pilgrim Tabernacle was sufficiently spacious to accommodate at its tables three hundred persons. On occasions of great significance, however, these did not suffice. Whether this particular evening could be so construed, few would categorically declare. Still as it was to be an affair of great moment with the young, who always patronized their social functions in great numbers, the committtee on arrangements wondered whether the hall was large enough.

William, who was to be feted by his church, was well beloved by all the members. Who did not know his interest in the old and young, especially his honored devotion to the little folk? What important event occurred there in which he had not taken part? Brought to Sunday School as soon as he could talk, under its spiritual guidance he had flourished and worked in a way that was highly gratifying. For four years he had been president of the Young People's Circle; from the age of twelve he had aided the choir, first as tenor and after his voice changed as leading baritone : and when the older members desired an impressive home missionary, he ended their predicament by offering his services—in short all the activities of Pilgrim Tabernacle had been touched and bettered by his personality.

Now that this excellent young man had graduated from Madison High School and was about to make preparation for his life work, the Church was honoring him with a reception,

(4)

as an expression of their appreciation of his manly conduct
and their hope for his constant achievement. The Church
also had said it would come. Confronted thus, the Committe
was considerably embarrassed as to how to meet the situation.

Here was a throng of honest, sturdy young folk, equally
ready to give and to receive. Remember it is more blessed to
give than to receive. Is that true? At least the ministers
have preached it. Yet when we think of the barriers of life,
we say, "Let the rich give and the poor receive." If this were
logically followed, where would the churches be? Among our
people, commonly the well-to-do withhold, but the poor give
their all. Shall we condemn their depths of zeal? "Judge not
that ye be not judged."

How excellently did they dignify this occasion with a sim-
plicity much in contrast with the elaborately decorated hall!
The ceiling was wrought with an intricate yet delicate bas-re-
lief, from the center of which was hung a chandelier with a
brazen circle of sixty lights. The walls were frescoed with
pea green as a border above and below for many carefully de-
picted, Biblical scenes. For this occasion, however, there were
added bunting, and runners of crepe paper in twirls and undu-
lations. This unostentatious adorning gave prominence to the
six tables extending almost the center length of the room. Yet
no less attracive was the virgin, white cloths and the vases of
roses and carnations equi-distantly placed, which rested beau-
tifully upon them. At slight intervals from the flowers there
were fancy dishes of after-dinner mints, salted peanuts, olives,
and dill pickles. Along the edge of these tables were dainty,
blue plates on the top of which were paper napkins containing
views of scenes presented in the poems of Paul Lawrence Dunbar. Finally on each napkin rested an embellished cardboard,
a star of triumph. In the center of the star was a tiny photo-

graph of William Smith. Here was being enacted no unimportant drama, but one of much consequence and great joy.

If you want to see our humble people, where they express themselves most freely, where they are determined to try and achieve, see them in their religious endeavors giving out unselfish love. See them testify in public to the abundance of God's grace. See them minister to the sick and dying. See them cling to the faith of their fathers, tho others in like circumstances "would take arms against a sea of troubles and by opposing end them." See them after they had been cheated and robbed, depprived of justice, lynched, scourged, or violated—at such a time as this, seeing them bearing no man a grudge, asking God's benediction upon all people, black and white, saint and culprit, rich and poor. Each race has some distinctive virtue. Ours is to rejoice at the pleasure of our fellowman, to enjoy ourselves and not envy someone else's enjoyment.

Just before the ceremonies began, the chairlady of the Committee onArrangments and mistress of ceremonies, Mrs. Lulu Castle, accosted Mr. Grant Stevens, the chairman of the deacon board, "Mr. Stevens, have we not reason to rejoice? Our church lays just claim to having fostered the most unusual youth Williamsburg has ever seen. Just think how he has climbed with the growth of the church, year after year taking the leading parts in our Sunday School programs, and when he became too old for that, producing concerts of the highest order!"

After a few moments of reflection, Mr. Stevens asked, "But is'nt that the very reason why we should feel sad? Don't you see that thru him we have gained such a reputation, as we may lose with his departure? Who is going to take his place?"

"No one, of course," was the prompt reply. He alone can take his place. None can fill it for him. You can't fill even your brother's place, nor can your brother fill yours. Tho many don't know it, we are all personalities; and we can contribute our greatest blessings by wearing our own shoes, not those of others. If each member will be true to himself as William has and not play the hypocrite, Pilgrim's reputation for attainment will not suffer in the least."

"I'm sure you're right, Mrs. Castle, as you always are," he said, jokingly. "My feelings, however, are mixed. You understand me, don't you?"

"Yes—look," she agreed, pointing towards the entrance. A sort of urbane hilarity and bustle were plainly apparent in that quarter.

At this moment, the boys and girls of the Young People's Circle formed a double line extending from the main door to the seat of the distinguished individual. The rows, in which each member seemed supremely happy, faced each other and formed as tho our young man was to run a gauntlet. As William entered, escorting Susan Lee, who of the young ladies of this thrifty town had impressed him most, the occupants of these lines clapped hands and cheered as homage to this uncrowned king. When he had reached his seat, he casually glanced at the wall before him. Seeing a curtain gradually being lowered, he gave more than scant attention. Displayed on this choice fabric was the following character appraisement: A MAN IN WHOM THERE IS NO GUILE!! WILLIAM SMITH—A KNIGHT WITHOUT FEAR AND WITHOUT REPROACH.

At a sign from the mistress of ceremonies, all sat down to a sumptuous repast, made more gracious and appetizing by superb orchestral music. As the courses were being relished, sparkling humor gave the spice to life. During these glad moments, it was difficult to discern whether Smith was the special company of Susan, for all of those within speaking distance had their distinctive claims to make. This evidently was not her day.

When the dessert was eventually laid, Mrs. Castle called first upon the visiting ministers to speak. We have often heard that our ministers can always speak effectively after an excellent meal. Whether this is true or false, let others prove. Every speech on this occasion, however, was eloquent. The feast certainly might have been a stimulus, yet not so potent as the grand theme—THE DEPARTURE OF A BLACK YOUTH OF GREAT ABILITY FOR A FAR COUNTRY. Each commended William's untiring church work, his enthusiasm to advertise and give strength to the Business League. Then, because of his many community interests, they hailed him the long expected Moses, a universal man.

Finally, the pastor was presented, Reverend Andrew Ross. His speech was a survey of William's entire life. When he at length announced that this young giant of energy had decided to prepare for the ministry, the satisfaction of the church was shown by long and loud applause. During this outburst, whisperings among the older members seemed to say, "I told you so. God's cause needs our best."

In closing, the venerable divine said, "Friends, we all have our 'ups' and 'downs,' but God who reigns on high is ever with us. This Negro race has suffered for weary centuries. But shall this always be? I think not. The night must end, then comes day.

"When I saw our brothers lynched in the South, circumscribed, rebuffed and scorned in the East, North and West, indeed I did despair. I believed that progress was only degeneracy, that civilization was barbarism, that love was hate. And just when I was about to vow eternal vengeance toward the white man, as Hannibal, the great Carthaginian, did to the Romans, I saw the light, I saw a man. Booker T. Washington sprang up almost in the night and entered securely the affections of black and white. He emphasizd economic freedom. Some wanted him to bring all things, but he was a specialist. He did one thing well. Yet since the economic by its very nature ramifies into the social, he raised his voice in immortal tones at the Atlantic Exposition and said that black and white could be together in all matters purely economic and separate in affairs purely social as the fingers on his hand. For me the problem was solved, for hope had returned. Then Du Bois kept hammering away with constantly increasing force for us to seek the paramount force in a nation, political freedom. Thank heaven, we are at last paying attention. Following in the train of these comes our promising youth. None but God can say that he will be as great as Washington or Du Bois. Yet the world can say that he will be our leader, our prophet, a man in whom there is no guile, a knight without fear and without reproach— William Smith."

Cheers at once filled the hall. How well Reverend Ross expressed their sentiments! Had not William penetrated their souls, as deeply as human beings could? His sacrifices had been unusual.

Resuming his remarks, the pastor declared, "Friends, we can not do too much for this lad. I have never seen his like. Besides the church in some impressive way should encourage each of its members that completes a school course. It should do something tangible for that person on each such occasion. We remember those who are kind to us. If the Church always receives and never gives, it is not doing God's bidding. These young people, we must remember, will be in our places tomorrow. In the case of Smith, you may be helping to prepare your future pastor, for you see I am withered and gray with the frost of many winters. If this lad's face were not black I should say without the least hesitation, "Some day he will be president of these United States. He is equal to it, he has in him all the possibilities: but, friends, his face is black."

Turning so that he could face the young man squarely, he said with full affection, "Smith, my gallant friend, the hope of our church, as an expression of our appreciation, different members will make special presentations in behalf of Pilgrim Tabernacle. In the name of the Lord, these gifts we tender you together with the continued support of the church for your schooling. Keep close to the cross and bear in mind his solace, 'Lo I am with you always, even to the end of the world.'

Since you have unstintedly given given your life to these your friends and to this your community, God speed you on! May endless years never cease to sing your joyous march to hard earned victory! Go with our prayers of triumph, go with our tears of love, go with our hope of blessing."

When this was done, William made his response. "Dear Christian friends, you graciously send me on, and I go. I have put my hand to the plow and will not turn back, for God is with me." There were many "Amens".

"Darkness is indeed before me. But is there no such a thing as endless night? No. 'The morning light is breaking. I know this, I know I have been bowed, I know I have at least touched the skies, if not in big accomplishments certainly in my dreams of race distinction. Yet I am not most happy. I wonder how I shall do without you, your hand shakes, your prayers, and your devotion. I am trying to imagine how my unknown friends will be. Will they grapple me or will they leave me?

I must take the chance. For Humanity I will hazadrd all.

'Man am I grown, a man's work must I do,
Follow the deer? follow the Christ, the King,
Live pure, speak true, right wrong, follow the King,—
Else, wherefore born?'

"With reverent thanks I accept your proffers of love, your gifts, and your devotion. They overwhelmingly humble me. You have given me a great responsibility, to prove to you during the coming years that my life will be what you expect. As I strive to learn the old and new of God, appropriately to enter His great service, happy recollections of this occasion will be a lamp to my pathway. I leave. I must. God calls me there; but I will return to you, my loving friends, and with you die, bringing in the sheaves."

CHAPTER III

America, I love thy name,
  Thou land of liberty.
Does he too love who brings thee shame
  By hell's hot savagery?

These sons who hang or burn are thine,
  And they have served thee best;
Guarded our President benign,
  When doubtful were the rest.

America, when we have died,
  To keep our country free,
Will hate for blacks fore'er abide?
  What will thir portion be?

The day following the reception at Pilgrim Tabernacle, found William speeding South. This trip brought him many novel experiences, the first of which he had on the train. Of course he had heard of some behavior which was peculiar to the South, but he did not begin to comprehend its full significance until this day. When he entered a coach at Washington D. C., he found himself facing this sign displayed in yellow and black: COLORED. At once he knew he was in a Jim Crow car in the very capital of the Nation. Why was there this distinction? Did it mean that he was criminal, vulgar, or immoral? It was simply because he was black. What a difference a color makes in America!

At once William began to ponder. He thot of Negro scholars who would be teaching in the best universities of the Country; their hair was sufficiently straight, but their skin was not white. Thereupon William questioned himself as to

(12)

whether the white people of the South were essentially different from those of the North.   An expression of Tennyson
quickly flashed itself before him—"Man is man."   He concluded then that the difference was only superficial, due probably
to custom and education, or to lack of education.   He knew
that great men had come out of the South; Washington, Jefferson and Lincoln.   Were no more to come?   He could not believe it.

These reflections called to mind an important circumstance
he had noticed in many cities of the east, particular at the national capital when the marine band gave its concerts.   The
national anthem which is "The Star Spangled Banner" never
brought forth as vigorous applause as did the sectional song, "I
Wish I Was in Dixie".   "Surely" surmised Smith, "that must
be a delightful place."   Now *he* was going to DIXIE.

With such musings, chiefly on the status of the colored
people in America, he arrived at Cassida, a typical Southern
town, teeming with the life of earnest people and wilful people alike.   Sturdy Negroes were the laboring folk and they
were masters of their toil, speedily carrying their merry burdens with many a merry tune.   Here and there a straggler
with jaunty pride casually looked on.   But the good work never ceased.   Porters, truckmen with ease, courtesy and grace,
and smiles that only colored men can give, busily made charming history, strenuously made a happy land.

While William stood outside the station observing this jolly atmosphere, he noticed two modes of address.   While he
was thus occupied, his uncle, Abbot Heywood, came up and
said, "William, I was just about to go home under the impression that you had missed your train. Give me your suit case.
Come, we must hurry home."

"I'm ready, Uncle Abbot," said the youth, turning from

his observation of the throng and giving the old gentleman a very warm handshake. "I'm happy to see you Uncle Abbot. I hope you're all well.   How is Aunt Carrie?   Are all well?"

"We're all in excellent health, I assure you."

"You must pardon me for a few days if I seem to be a little distant.   You know this is my first time South.   When I seem to have drawn myself almost into a shell.   I'm thinking hard, how I may adapt myself to what appear to be extrme artificial conditions."

"I   noticed   that you were   considerably absorbed with something, when I touched you."

"Uncle Abbott, I deem this an   excellent   opportuity to study our people, my people at close range.   I'm eager to see if the Negro in the South behaves as Dunbar and Chestnut depict him.   I have resolved not to let slip the occasion to know them, for these are the people who gave me my existence, among whom I must live, whom I must help to get their heritage."

"Boy, I tell you, you've got an old head on your shoulders."

"This should not be considered unnatural.   Reverend Ross, my pastor, regularly preaches concerning racial relations in the United States.   As he talked one Sunday morning, I recalled my study of history and I could not bring to mind a single colored face that it contained.   Upon going home I searched my histories from cover to cover.   Not a Negro varrior or statesman there!   I saw at once that we must write some books."

"Probably you're too reflective," the uncle interrupted.

"No uncle, some times I wonder whether I think enough. You call me a boy.   Grant that I am not a man in age, my sufferings and sacrifices have made me a man in experience. A Negro child one year of age is older by far than a white child born at the same hour; and by the time the white child is twenty-five, the colored child is forty."

"There's much truth in what you say."

Here his uncle took his suit case and started off. As they drove along, William askt, "Uncle Abbot, please explain to me this circumstance. The colored people call the white Mister and Missis, the whites call the colored Uncle and Aunt. Is this a mark of ignorance on the part of our people or of the white? Is it fear on the part of our people and arrogance of the white? If the relationship is so close as to admit of 'uncle' and 'aunt' under any circumstance, certainly the relationship is not one-sided. Our people ought to return the compliment."

"William, it's this way. You up North don't quite understand. Slavery has never been gotten out of the South. Before the war, there were the Mistress and Master; now the Mistress has become Missis and the Master Mister; but the colored man has remained where he was. If we started calling the white folks Uncle and Aunt, the Rebellion would have to be fought over again."

"Uncle," was Smith's interruption, "we shouldn't like for that to be; but this distinction must end. We must be addressed as we are."

"In the South," continued Mr. Heywood, "there are a few colored people called Mister and Missis by black and white alike. This few however are wealthy.

"Don't bother yourself about these matters at this time. Prepare for the happy moments you are to have with us." Then turning the conversation as much as possible, he askt, "Has your journey been pleasant?"

"Yes, uncle, just as pleasant as it could be under existing circumstances," recalling those character forming events which had veritably engulfed him at Pilgrim Tabernacle.

"But why do you say 'under the existing circumstances?'" inquired the devoted uncle. "Has some recent occurrence saddened you?"

Thereupon William related the details of the church reception. He was very fervid and enthusiastic.

"We all are glad when there is even the slightest indication of approval," put in the uncle.

"That was the greatest experience of my life," remarked William, who as he related the story, lived again through the entire festivities. "The devotion of those generous souls irresistibly wove my career with the hopes of Williamsburg. They are my friends. They believe in me; and I in them. This tie I know can not be severed by time. I was happy there.

"Such thots as these kept rising, as I journeyed here. I'm well aware when, absent from a friend. That's why I say 'as happy as circumstances permit.'"

"Well, here we are at last!" exclaimed the southerner, as he stopt his brown roadster in front of his resplendent cottage, suggestive of the colonial style. Stepping from the buggy, he called, "Andy, Andy."

A stalwart farm helper scorched by many suns hurried around the house. Approaching the vehicle, he said, "Yes, sar; yes, sa-a-r; right heah."

"Give Prince some water, and then hitch up the carryall. I want you to get William's trunk. You haven't met my nephew, have you?" the planter said.

"No, sa-a-r."

"William, this is Mr. Jones, my most reliable worker. Mr. Jones, this is my nephew, William Smith."

"Boy, I'se sure am proud to see yo'. Mr. Heywood talkt so much about yo'. We'd been terribly disappinted if yo' hadn't came," said Andy bubbling over with joy.

"Mr. Jones, I'm really glad to meet you," said the youth shaking the gentleman's hand vigorously.

Turning toward the planter, Andy declared, "Mr Heywood, dat ain't no boy a-tall, dat's a man. I tell yo' he sho did hurt my hand. Put him on my plantation and he'll work the socks off all my folks." He paused a moment and then said, "Well, I must be gone, be good to yo'self, and nothing can't harm yo'." With these remarks Mr. Jones hurried away.

That afternoon as William sat on the porch indulging in many delightful reveries, he noticed a green bungalow trimmed in white, in front of which extended an incomparable lawn bordered with a stocky growth of hedge. The summer chairs and benches scattered here and there and the tall oak tree standing guardian over all made a scene both unassuming and picturesque.

From the oak was suspended a swing, which was affording great joy to a girl of six. On the porch sat the mother and two of her boys, one eight, the other ten. Happy was this industrious family, whose members by sacrifice and toil had become the foremost Negroes of that town. Such as these America desires—energetic folk; and these were surely energetic.

The father, Christopher Loving, was president of the Union Banking Institution, which did a prosperous business with both black and white. He had risen to this distinction thru his plantation and his construction company. The farm was handled by tenant farmers, the construction company by his eldest son.

Having met all his relatives and gone over the farm to get an idea of the manner in which our people workt, William turned to the house and sat on the porch. He came there to read the life of Alexander Hamilton of African descent, a great

American statesman. The scene across the street had been somewhat distractive. This did not last long, however, for he was soon absorbed with that grand career.

When he had been thus occupied for a half hour, his attention was once more diverted. He scrutinized Mr. Loving's home again. Then he began to meditate, comparing what was before him with other residences he had seen, or imaged from his reading. Since this abode far surpassed the rest, he asked himself if he were not beholding the eighth wonder of the world. It was superb; indeed a masterpiece of architecture and landscape gardening. What loveliness! The mother and children made the scene complete. How happy they were!

As the young man now mused on and on, a rising noise caused him to look down the street. There he saw a crowd of turbulent individuals; men, women, boys and girls. Many of the children had just sprung from infancy. The men, however were in the majority. With cursing and profanation they advanced in his direction, down Staten Street, one of the main thorofares of the town. He beheld that a few were masked. These alone had pistols. Approximately a score who followed them had rifles. Others had pieces of pipe or bars of iron; the remainder carried staves, sticks, or ropes. William divined at once that this was a mob.

As these blood thirsty people approached, their defamations continued. They were not intelligible to William, however, at his distance. He learned later their nature, which was like this. Colored people who lived along the way were his busy informers.

"Damn these niggers," said one of the reprobates! "When they gits a little property, theys better'n white folks."

"Think of a nigger refusing to lend a white man money," thundered another.

"Keep the nigger down, he never was nothin', he ain't nothin', and he never will be nothin'." How paradoxical their behavior was!

"We, po' devils, have seen a nigger get rich while we stay po', even after we saw to it dat dey didn't hab no schools," remarked the first speaker.

"If we let dese niggers go on dis way, dey'll soon be running de gov'mint," came from another.

"Whiles we're at it, let's do a turnkey job. Clean up the neighborhood, run all these niggers out of town dat's got prope'ty. Dey's not de ones dat wuk fo' yo' no way." Many a remark of this kind was uttered by many an ignoble throat.

When William informed the household of the disturbance, there was general consternation. They wondered what to do, where to go. They bustled about a few moments in great anxiety but returned to the place where they were before. "Have mercy, Lord, have mercy," said one. Then followed groans, mutterings, and sighs.

Seeing nothing done to alleviate the matter, the visitor askt, "Is there no way to stop this, but who are they after? They must be very close now; and they are headed this way."

This utterance only increased the alarm. "Can't we stop this?" he repeated.

"Not at all," said his aunt resignedly. "There's nothing to do but take it. Oh, it's so dreadful to have to live thus!"

"It's a disgrace to us and to the Nation, particularly to us to tolerate such outrages," he spoke in great anger.

"You're from the North, William, you don't understand the South," affirmed the aunt, apparently trying to palliate the matter.

"If to suffer thus is necessary to understand it, God give me ignorance! No, I don't understand. I never will. Let me have a pistol or a rifle, and let me take several men and break up that mob. You told me scoundrels don't live on this street. They are after some one who deserves to live. Even if it is a Negro criminal, they have no right to break the law. They're just a bunch of cowards. A few brave men can end this. Give me a gun or a rifle," he demanded.

"William, we haven't any. Andy was saying we ought to have them in self-defense," she remarked.

"Well, Aunt Julia, I didn't think you'd try to live down here, where the lives and property of our people are not protected by the law, without a good supply of fire arms and ample ammunition. The honor of our women are not even safe here. The constitution of the United States allows a man to defend himself in his home. A man's home is his castle," he protested.

"Sam Halloway had arms, but the policemen went into his house and took them," she said.

"Auntie, if anybody respects the law, it is the colored man. And this talk of the proportions of Negro crime is all bosh, as long as white men make these criminals. Read some of the studies in the race question made by even white men and if you read between the lines as well as the lines, you'll see that many planters want Negro criminals. Many of them get their wealth from Negro convict labor. Such a system is profitable for them.

"The colored man respects the law, but the law does not respect him. He must now demand respect of the law. How can he do this? By being a man, by stopping this business of turning the other cheek. If the law will not protect him, he must protect himself.

"He must grasp the situation. No policeman is allowed even by the law to cross your treshhold and search for anything without a warrant. Besides that warrant should state exactly what he is searching for. If you have been living respectably, he has no business with a warrant to search for the means by which you defend your home. You shouldn't take them out into the streets but you should use them anywhere on your premises in self-defense. And I shouldn't let any policeman have them.

"I've been interested in reading what has been done when authorities surmised that the colored people were going to defend themselves. The policemen rush at once to disarm the blacks, and let the whites keep their weapons. As I know this they'll not get a weapon in my house unless I'm dead or dying."

"William, calm yourself," the aunt interrupted.

"Auntie, I mean it. If I have lived as a man should live and a policeman came to my house, I'd greet him courteously and seek his business there. If he said he came to search for arms, I'd ask for his warrant and read it carefully. Then I'd return him the paper and tell him I forbade the search, for I must defend my home. If he would rush in anyhow, he would go out a dead man. This is how I would act as a respectable citizen. Respectable Negroes do not keep arsenals. If I were a culprit I'd act differently, I'm merely saying how the honest, law abiding citizen of any race should act. When the law fails to protect, a man must protect himself."

"I hope somebody will do something," said the aunt pitiably.

"Well, I see this is work for all our people, to stop this humiliation," he remarked now, becoming calmer. He thot of following the course of the mob and started for the front.

"William, my boy," pleaded the aunt, "don't go out there. Aren't you afraid?"

"Satan himself couldn't frighten me now," he said and

left without more ado. The others remained within thru accustomed cowardice and scare.

William angrily stood on the porch, and watched the mob at work. The outlaws had stopt in front of his uncle's house. Large numbers of them were on Mr. Loving's premise. As the mob comprised about a thousand, the street and sidewalks were crowded for quite a distance. Smith had to resist the temptation of throwing a stone, but he conquered himself upon deeming it only foolhardiness. He wanted the persons leaning against his uncle's trees to move, but he held his peace.

He saw a colored man of very stately mien, already beaten unconscious, dragged to the lawn he greatly admired. The children had fled into the house. Mrs. Loving wanted to run too, but thinking that someone dear to her was involved, she stood upon the porch and faced the mob stolidly. When she beheld the haggard face, however, her spirit was broken. She shrieked and screamed: "My husband, my poor husband! Spare my husband, he has done no wrong! We'll give you all we have, but spare him. My poor husband, my poor husband."

The limp man with wandering eyes sputtered out, "No, dear, I worked hard for mine. The—rascals—shan't—have—one—penny."

Hereupon one outlaw slapped him in the face and shouted, "Damn it. Shut up. Why should I worry? He'll be quiet very soon."

"Chris, Chris," called the wife forcing her way to her husband.

Several ruffians pushed her back. Yet she tried to reach him, crying in the meanwhile, "Don't kill him, spare him, I'll give you whatever you wish."

"We'd rather put him quietly to sleep," someone answered.

"Oh, God," prayed the devoted wife, "save my husband, save him. We have served Thee always. If ever I need Thee, my Savior 'tis now."

"If you don't stop that damned hollering, we'll get you first," said one of the miscreants.

"Take me," she cried. "Do, but spare him."

"Here, John, gag her and leave her until we finish this job," commanded the mob leader.

That day the children saw their father lynched in their own yard, from their cherisht oak tree. They saw his body suspended and riddled with bullets, all because he would not make a loan to a white man of ill repute. They saw women and children enjoying this debauchery, as if it had been a theatrical show.

The family was not even allowed the body. Dimpled boys and lithesome girls took parts of clothing as souvenirs and danced with ghoulish glee. Then excelsior was placed about the body, and many staves were lit. The flames quickly did their work and the spectacle was soon at an end.

Where were the officers when one of their foremost citizens was suffering this disgrace? They were calmly looking on, not attempting or daring not to oppose. They even beheld photographers taking views of the scene, views to be sold the next day as additionals souvenirs. There was abundant evidence for prosecutions, but none were made. The next day, matters went on as if nothing disgraceful had occurred.

What happens to people who lose their sense of shame? They hasten to degeneracy. America beware!

William stood upon the porch thru the entire catastrophe. Several members of the mob lookt at him, but that was all. When they had finisht, they straggled back, whence they had come. The stranger watched them until they faded out of view.

Looking across the street he saw the wife gagged and tied, stretched upon the porch. The little girl and boy were trying to relieve her. William went at once to her assistance and freed her from her bonds. She thanked him, while she wept. Then suddenly she became stolid and wiped her eyes.

"This isn't the end of the sport. True, I'm a woman, but a woman can die bravely as well as a man. The devil must pay for this." Then recalling that she had never met her sympathizer, she said, "Pardon any untowardness on my part, you'll make due allowance for all unseemliness. I'm the wife —I was the wife—I'm the widow of the man you saw lynched —Christopher Loving."

"William Smith is my name. I'm the nephew of Mr. Heywood."

"He told me you were coming. I'm more than glad to meet you. Edward, my oldest son, will be delighted to see you. I'll see that he meets you. I thank you again for aiding me."

"Madame, I haven't done anything. The kind of assistance I wanted to render I could not. Just think there wasn't a rifle or pistol on the place! I wonder if they don't even have a shot gun. Well I hope our folks will get busy' and break this up. But where is your son?"

"He's directing a job about five or six miles from here, but he'll be in soon."

"Madame, you seem rather calm in view of this disturbance."

"My determination for vengeance makes me so. The law of this state punishes murder by death. I'm going to permit the state ample time to do its duty. Now that my husband is gone, life means nothing to me. If the state fails, I will perform the execution. I'd recognize the scoundrels even at night."

"But what of your children?"

"Benjamin, Lily," she called, for they had been standing in the hall. "This gentleman is our friend, he is Mr. Heywood's nephew." They bashfully came forward and greeted him. Then the mother said, "Have no fear, they shall be provided for The main thing now is this. I must not bear the insult alone. Those people who went from here do not feel that they have done wrong. They're rejoicing as if they had won a great battle. Some of them must feel as I have felt. They're going to be sorry for this."

Several hours after this, William sat down to supper. The signs of anxiety had not completely worn off; yet they were doing rather well at readjustment. During the course of the evening, William askt, "Uncle Abbot are our people doing nothing at all to end this or to prevent its recurrence? It used to be that our men were lynched for rape, but now they are lynched because they steal a hog or because they have acquired a little wealth. I'm not satisfied with auntie's answer."

"William," began Mr. Heywood, "we thot that if we lived right, respected ourselves and the white people, that lynching would pass away. But we seem to have been wrong. Loving has been called by black and white alike the town's 'most honest man.' Yet you see how honesty has been rewarded. God in his own good time will make the matter right."

"But, Uncle Abbot, what are we going to do in our own time?"

"Just wait on the Lord."

"Heaven helps those who help themselves. Furthermore, does the white man wait? Isn't the machinery even too slow for him?" inquired the nephew.

"Well, they do at times seem impatient. Things must

happen for them rather quickly. For intsance, just the other day, Uncle Parker, as faithful a man as ever lived, went to Jenkins' store to get some odds and ends. While he was there young Jenkins appeared—now a lad of twenty-three.

" 'Hello! Jack,' said Uncle Parker, 'Ise sho am proud to see yo'.

"The father took a block of wood and struck our poor brother such a hard blow on the head that he became unconscious. 'I'll teach you,' he said, 'to address a *white* man properly. That's not Jack; that's Mr. Jack, Mr. Jenkins.'

"The next day with head bound, Uncle Parker came back to the same store and said, 'Mr. Jenkins, you know I nursed yo' boy, till he went off to skule. An' Ise always called him Jack. I didn't realize that time done made a difference. I
" 'Well,' said Jenkins, 'thats all right. Just see that it doesn't happen again'."

"Do these crimes continually occur without being punished?" askt William.

"Yes, they do. And up in the country, sometimes called 'the back woods,' many of the atrocities never reach the press. I don't know what's to become of us" said Mr. Heywood very deeply moved.

"Uncle Abbot," affirmed William with unusual bitterness. "This day I consecrate my life to my people. I have decided to enter the ministry, but I shall not merely preach, I shall work among all sorts of people, only to bring protection and freedom to my race. What I saw today will last me a life time. For your sake I kept quiet today. Hereafter I respect nobody's feelings unless it is for the good of the race and humanity.

"One such Loving is worth more than all the members of any mob. Yet the worthless live and the worthy die. AND 'pologize. I'm sorry it happened. It won't happen no more.'
THIS IS DIXIE.

CHAPTER IV.

Doubt thou the stars are fire,
  Doubt thou the sun doth move,
Doubt truth to be a liar,
  But never doubt I love.—Shakespeare

Now Smith was gone! Williamsburg knew it. The Sunday School mist him, the Church mist him, and so did the community at large. Of those who had become fondly attached to this interesting personality, none treasured him more than Susan Lee. Her father was one of the most accomplished men of the town, whose efficiency was well known by virtue of his being president of the Eureka Shirt Factory.

His daughter's advancement was his great concern. In order that she might impressively begin the battle of the sexes, he spared no pain that her debut into elite society might be unexcelled. Nor did he in this prove a failure.

Susan, now eighteen, accomplished and attractive, resembled an Hawaiian beauty. She was somewhat more than five and a half feet tall, of excellent proportions, firm and robust. As she moved with stately grace, one would particularly notice her wealth of black, straight hair, and her delicately brown complexion. Nature had endowed her well, for even women who beheld her were entranced.

Many were her suitors, but many she did not desire. For her there was only one—the valorous William Smith. Often she plaintively askt herself: "How is he to know this?"

"Wait until he speaks," came the answer.

Will men thus always be favored in such artifiicial societies as our own—have numerous, excellent and superior chances of marrying, while the women have but a few? The woman wonders how long it will be before someone asks. Why should she wonder or wait for that which often never comes?

Within the brief few months that had passed since Susan became a debutante, many undesirables had long since askt; but the hope of her anxious nights, the pride of her noblest thot had not touched the exalted theme of love. This was not a pleasant recolection.

To prevent that mood, lest she should be sad at any moment, nature was doing its utmost to keep her well pleased. Rains not desired were kept in steady abeyance; sultry, stifling days somehow had dropped out of sight. The leaves seemingly nourished with an extraordinary refreshment, preserved their former hue, untinged with crimson or autumnal brown. Hitherto at this season of the year, many had already danced their dance of death and vanisht with a sigh. But now they all made merry with the magic breeze, whistling melodious symphonies.

Towards twilight, the day following William's departure for the South, as easily as a nymph, Susan stept upon the porch of her gothic home, expecting company. Her cheeks were promptly kissed by a welcome breeze which seemed to say, "Be composed, my goddess, somewhere a lover's true."

She started to arrange the chairs, then suddenly stopt to reflect. "Here I am," she mused, "with great social opportunities, excellent home conditions, luxury and coveted prerogatives; yet what I desire most, I fail to have. My soul craves William. Will the longing of my aching heart be satisfied?

"He and I have been casual friends at a distance for several years, but our intimacy is just about two months old. His occupation and my hesitancy have prevented a declaration. He did say that he admired me. He promist also to write. But as we haven't plighted troth, I'm a prey to much uncertainty. If I love him why may I not tell him so within a week instead of waiting for months of intimacy or even a year or years? Society considers such improper. Sometimes I wish I could give society a lecturing and then a genteel threshing. I may win him and yet I may not.

"So many couples are mismated that I blame society. If women keep getting the wrong men, something is wrong with the social order. Probably a revolution is needed. Some sacrafices the group may justly require, but to deprive a woman of her love is often to court death. Well, I hope to win and li-i-v-e." She sighed clasped her hands upon her breast, and bowed her head. Then she let her hands drop and thrust her head back in despair. A rustling of dresses caused her to turn and look. Her reverie had been interrupted. "Come up, girls," she said, welcoming Thelma Haskell, Catherine Staples, and Letitia Straus—all debutantes.

Quickly they greeted Susan and seated themselves comfortably on the imposing porch, happy to chat of the event at Pilgrim Tabernacle.

Before such a line of talk could begin, however, Thelma interfered. "Girls, watch me," she said. "Is this the way?" All became uproariously absorbed in the perfect pantomine she was executing to portray Susan's recent emotion. They laughed and clapped their hands. After assuming the attitude of despair, Thelma said, "Susan, you reminded me of Lady Macbeth and the merchant of Venice. What was troubling you? 'In sooth I know not why' you are so sad. It wearies me!"

"Thelma, you're a regular old tease," Susan remarked, enjoying the joke, even tho she was the butt of it. "I have my serious moments, sometimes impulsive ones. Just now I was obsest with both."

"But, Susan," exclaimed Catherine, the daughter of the

high school principal, "you were so dramatic!"

"Hereafter I must be sure, that I am alone within my room, when I give full vent to my feelings," protested Susan, now somewhat flushed.

"Don't you do it, don't you do it," urged Letitia naughtily, shaking her finger at her schoolmate, "don't you dare do it for the world. It would be a shame to deprive us of the show."

"Do be serious, girls," pleaded Susan, "let's think of other things." Yet she knew she would return to thots of *him*. "Tell me how you enjoyed the banquet."

"I know *you* enjoyed it," was the prompt thrust of Thelma. "You were afraid we'd take him from you, but we had to talk to him a little. We couldn't help it, could we girls?"

"No," was the quick response. It was somewhat annoying to Susan.

"You know he is so tantalizing, isn't he?" ventured Thelma playfully. Her friend was now completely disarmed. "Don't blame us," Thelma continued. "We all have our ambitions for the noblest. There is no sensible girl in this town who does not acknowledge him our best. It's a game to win. Be sure you play it well. If he wants you, why, you're his; if he wants me, then I am his. At present, however, we're giving you the right of way. The honor is all yours."

Aroused by this unusual demeanor of her friend, Susan said, "Thelma I appreciate your frankness. Many girls never would have said that; yet under cover they would have been doing their utmost to outdo me. Still I didn't think Kate was more than passingly interested in William. Girls, I am going to give you a little bit of information. Some time ago, brother and I used to go together to socials. That's impossible now because of a perpetual, previous engagement with Kate, Kate, Kate."

"Now, Susan," smiled Catherine, "Henry knows where he stands in my affections. Yet I may be interested in others and others interested in me. Do you think Henry's admiration for me would go far, if I couldn't arouse the commendation of his associates? Furthermore, if no other girl desired him, I shouldn't either. I—I couldn't be jealous. And what's the use of loving, if you can't be jealous?"

"A-a-ah, Kate, aren't you ashamed of yourself. I'm going to find Henry and tell him what you said!" ejaculated Letitia, rushing from the porch.

She hadn't gone far before she was overtaken. "No, you won't gasped Catherine, holding her friend firmly. "You're going right back on the porch, like a good, little girl." There were many outbursts of laughter.

"You know I shouldn't be so bold," said Letitia, taking her seat.

"But I had to make sure," remarked Catherine, now at ease. "Should you have told, how could I meet him after that?"

"It would be difficult, I know," declared Susan, glad that the joke had fallen on someone else. Then turning the conversation, she said, "Now, girls, let's be serious. We're all interested in particular young men, whom we hope to marry. I'm interested in William."

"Interested!" they said with surprise, "You're wild about him!"

"I was going to say crazy about him," Letitia declared

As if nothing had occurred other than a common interruption, Susan smiled and went on. "Kate dotes on Henry, Letitia claims Sinclair Young; and Thelma—Thelma worships

Beckett King."

Thelma stared at Susan, as if in amazement, laughed heartily and then said, "Girls, doesn't she put the case well?" She began to mimic her chum. "Kate *dotes* on Henry, Letitia *claims* Sinclair, I *worship* Beckett, and she is *interested* in William.

The bantering now ran high. All were quite happy. After surviving the storm she had raised by her careful delineation of the *les affaires d' amours,* Susan resumed what she had planned to say. "Often girls are so very much afraid that one will take their beaux, that they manage their own heart's troubles even without the advice of their parents. And when the dear old people become aware of the situation, the girl is either engaged or ready to announce her marriage. On the other hand, frequently for lack of advice, they lose or choose improperly. Because of this, since ours is an age of co-operation—so says Reverend Ross—I was thinking that we of the twentieth century should not be above advice, even the advice of one another."

"I believe you're right, Susan," said Letitia. "Consequently I'm willing to teach or learn."

"What do you think of the idea, Thelma?" inquired Susan.

"You know I'm strictly modern," was her terse reply.

"And you, Kate, are you with us?" inquired Letitia.

"Yes," she said, and paused, "for better and for worse."

Then Susan spoke again, "Of course we always have the counsel of our parents, but it'll be excellent for us occasionally to have our own experience meetings. What I'd like to know is this. What should a girl do to keep first palce in the affections of a young man while he is away at school?"

Merriment arose afresh. "Isn't she *interested?*" said Letitia.

At this point, a young woman and her escort passed by. The lady's dress at once attracted their attention. It was a pink georgette, elaborately trimmed and draped. "What do you think of that?" askt Catherine.

"For once let us not discuss dress," Thelma entreated.

The girls agreed. Then Catherine, very eager to get her friends' ideas on the question proposed by Susan, urged them to return to business. "I have a thot you might consider. In many cases I do believe it helps. If the young man in question is fondly attached to his mother, tactfully court her as well as the son. To win her is to gain half the battle. And whether the relationship between mother and son is unusual or not, to enter the mother's affection certainly makes the task easier.

"At last I understand you," came from Susan. "You sly fox, Kate, you're not satisfied to win the mother. You're courting the whole family. I see now why you call frequently." Catherine blushed.

"You mustn't embarrass her, Susan," Letitia interrupted.

"I just have to be naughty sometimes. If I had to be good all the time I suppose I'd soon die from congested emotion," Susan responded.

"Well, my suggestion," spoke Letitia with a somewhat staccato effect, "may be astounding, but you're under no compulsion to follow it. I'm perfectly willing to use Kate's sterling counsel; but I couldn't make a supreme sacrifice and lose. I think it would kill me.

"Knowing myself to have this temperament, I have determined during Sinclair's absence to enjoy myself with all the boys equally—that is, the desirable ones. This is my way of getting out of the dilemma. Having thus a great effection for Sinclair and a slight interest in many boys, I could lose Sinclair and yet live."

"I see nothing shocking in that," said Thelma with great firmness. "I have known many girls who have staked all on one and lost. Then they became overwhelmed with a grief that caused poor health or death. Isn't my sister Julia just such an example? All absorbing and disappointing love! This love all for one and one only may be romantic, but it's dangerous."

"Besides," said Catherine, "your choice must be between many, a few, and none. Who of us would say ,'Refrain from the company of all young men during the absence of the lover?' If we're to marry them, we should first know them; not just one, but many. To do this, contact is necessary. Now is the time to learn thoroly."

"Kate, I think I'm forced to agree with you; for if you have an exclusive few, one will very likely be preferred," said Susan, "and probably develop the strong possibilities of a rival. Whether this is true or not, the public will soon single out a specially favored one and conclude that the absent friend has been superseded. Before long, some officious person will be writing your beau that he hasn't a 'ghost' of a chance."

"Yes," remarked Letitia, "some people are very meddlesome. I, too, think it better to be about equally interested in all here, with a supreme affection for the one absent."

"One circumstance, however, we should not forget, for it is the staff of parted lovers—it's correspondence," Thelma declared. "Of course, all lovers write to each other; yet, judging by what I've read, I can not believe that they're aware of its significance. We can not make too much of this.

A few years can make a mountain of difference between us. During that time we should not let the boys get ahead of us. As they grow, we should grow. They go away boys, but come back men.

"Do you remember Wright's 'The Shepherd of the Hills'?"

"Of course we do!" they replied, and began at once to discuss different parts of it that they liked best.

As soon as she got the chance, Thelma continued where she left off. "You recall then that Ollie Stewart, who had been early betrothed to Sammy Lane, changed so much in the few years he was absent, that she could not marry him. The qualities that led her to love him were no longer there. This is human nature.

"What we must do is to discover thru frequent correspondence our lover's new outlook on life as it comes. Then we must go to the library, get some books and read along that line. We must do more. We must think along that line with thinking people. At length, when our young man comes from school with his new ideas, to us at least they will be old, familiar friends."

"Bravo!" exclaimed Susan. "Has Socrates come back again?"

"I hope you understand what I mean," she continued, not at all flattered. "So long as the natures of the young man and young woman blend in ideals, the marriage is likely to be a possibility. If it does occur it will very likely be a happy one. It is because girls have neglected this fact that very few early sweethearts marry; that men as a rule marry not the home girls, but girls where they pursue their life work —at least where they begin it."

"But if we write frequently," inquired Susan, "may we not be too forward? Mamma says we should write occasionally, and be patient and wait." Here she recalled the ideas that ran thru her mind, just before her friends appeared.

"My answer is this," was Thelma's impatient utterance: "If the mother is to marry the man, let her do what she wishes. When the time comes for me to marry, however, and I see the man I want, I do not promise to wait. Wait? Wait for him to choose someone else? I'll make the fight of my life to get him; there'll be no escape. If I lose, I shall certainly have the satisfaction of having made a good fight."

"How will you fight?" Susan inquired.

"Don't you know?" said Thelma. "I'll use all the arts of woman, and my own distinct accomplishments. I'll make a study of winning men's hearts and proceed accordingly."

Thus the girls went on until it was quite late.

When Susan retired to her boudoir that evening, she brot before her all that had been said. How could she win? She had seen the man and certainly she loved him. Should she follow her mother's advice or Thelma's? Unquestionably she would write; but should she risk all by making a disclosure and then launching the 'fight of her life?' or should she wait, striving in the meanwhile by tact to force a declaration from him?

"Susan, Susan," her mother called.

Then the tender maiden askt herself, "What did Milton say? 'They also serve who only stand and wait.'"

CHAPTER V.

We are in a world of changes; and to be perfect is to change. And that person is most perfect who changes most often.—Newman.

As very few of the members of my race have had a chance to attend a first class college or university, they can not understand how those who come from such institutions do not take the same attitude towards the Church and religion, as they did before they went away. These brave boys and girls have fought strenuously day after day in sadness, trying to keep the old beliefs. The trouble is this: Almost every professor in these schools put such ideas aside long ago. Even the ministers who come to them do not hold such.

These facts our people should know, for our present religious views may be making our economic freedom impossible. For once we come to know the difference between our religion and that of our white brother and the significance of each, we shall become more united in our struggle in this country to get all that becomes a man.

Sometimes an historian presents facts that we dislike. It is not his business to tickle his fancy nor our own. He should tell the truth. In this spirit I relate the events which worked signal changes in the religious views of William Smith. This chapter is not mere fiction. Every incident related herein actually did occur. Do not think William's experience exceptional. It is typical. I am relating the experience of the college man and the college woman. Reader, perhaps you will find it shocking; but these experiences have been none the less shocking to those who had them.

Three years at Henderson College, the pride of the North, had produced the College Seer—as he was called—the lad who in glory had left Williamsburg to find a broader glory in the exalted affections of the best sons America had produced. This school which could claim as its graduates some of our best poets and novelists, at least one of the presidents of our great land, could not help rejoicing at the career of William Smith, who excelled in all his endeavors. Peerless on the gridiron, in class, and in debate, who was this powerful son of Africa? Was he the promist emancipator of his race or should we look for another?

One thing was certain. He was black. About this there could be no mistake. Was his complexion a handicap? Color is almost invariably the curse of the colored man. His unpardonable sin is being black. If colored and white show equal fitness for a task, who is taken, who is left? Even at times when the Negro has arrived at eligibility for the captaincy of an athletic team, even tho he was the honor man, who has been given the distinction? Ask some of our all American men.

There are, however, many noble white people and there will be some as long as the world endures. These are intelligent people—staunch and generous, lovers of humanity. With them a man is a man. They have no time for prejudice, for prejudice is characteristic of ignorant folk. Their lives reveal this lofty ambition: FAIR PLAY, AND MAY THE BEST MAN WIN! This motto, fundamentally democratic, the favored utterance of General Joshua Chamberlain, had became the spirit of this institution. Here was a place where merit, and not color, courage and not color, perseverance and not color, decided the fates of men.

The Negro who wanted as his *summon bonum,* a jug

of molasses, forty acres, and a mule, was not the one who
came to that great institution of learning. Besides, that Negro
with such ambition is not typical of this stalwart race, which
has suffered most to make America. Regardless of innumer-
able closed doors, despite forbidden opportunity, notwithstanding peonage and gross humiliation, the typical Negro
today is not a prodigal pampered by the indulgence of a
doting father, not a profligate dedicated to Saturnalias, but
a man, an exploited man, a lily in a pool of slime. He asks
no favors; he seeks only an open field and a fair fight.

With this spirit, William entered Henderson College. In
this enlightened environment, while his Alma Mater shaped
him to her will, he brot her proud distinction. As he came
to his senior year, he realized that he had a new attitude
towards life. How different things must be from what he
had supposed! Who was right: the theologian, the poet, the
scientist, or the philosopher? Or did each have but a glimpse
of the truth? For quite a while William perused several
passages from Tennyson and a sonnet from Rossetti. The
passages follow:

> Flower in the crannied wall,
> I pluck you out of the crannies,
> I hold you here, root and all, in my hand,
> Little flower—but if I could understand
> What you are, root and all, and all in all,
> I should know what God and man is.—Tennyson
>
> We have but faith: we cannot know,
> For knowledge is of things we see.—ibid.
>
> Think thou and act; tomorrow thou shalt die.
> Outstretched in the sun's warmth upon the shore,
> Thou say'st: "Man's measured path is all gone o'er:
> Up all his years, steeply with strain and sigh,
> Man clomb until he touched the truth; and I,
> Even I, am he whom it was destined for."
> How should this be? Art thou then so much more
> Than they who sowed, that thou shouldst reap there

Nay, come up hither. From this wave-washed
   mound
Unto the furthest, flood-brim look with me;
Then reach on with thy thought till it be drown'd.
Miles and miles distant though the last line be,
And though thy soul sail leagues and leagues be-
   yond,—
Still, leagues beyond those leagues, there is more
   sea.—Rossetti

These passages and many like them William studied carefully, trying to arrive at the truth.

William reasoned somewhat thus. Are these passages
false or true? Is the preacher right and everyone else wrong?
Does each profession but get its portion of the truth? The
preacher says the world is six thousand years old, the scientist
gives the age of the world as being millions of years. The
preacher says the world was made in six days, the scientist
says it was millions of years in the making, and that creation
has never ceased. The preacher says Adam was the first man,
but science says that even Egypt had men before Adam; that
Adam is a creation of Babylonian mythology.

To get these ideas in his sociology was very disconcerting,
for William had been reared in an orthodox church. Accordingly his religious views were strictly conservative and dog-
matic. He had been taught for years that the Bible was a
perfect book, a flawless revelation of God. The Bible was
the whole truth—telling all that had been and was to be.
Persons disbelieving the infallibility of the Bible or rejecting
Christ as the son of God, he was convinced could not be
saved.

Now that he found himself instructed by individuals who
did not hold these dogmas, but believed in God and the Bible
in a different way, what was to become of them? Where was
he to find an anchorage? These people were not scoundrels;

but some of the noblest people he had ever met. Not satisfied with contact in class to thresh out these soul problems at close range, he called upon his professors in physics, biology, sociology and philosophy for conferences. They encouraged his inquiry, and suggested to him many books for further reading. As these were assuredly, admirable men, ready to instruct or advise, strenuous workers to uplift humanity, he could not persuade himself that these men would be forever lost.

One day while he was in the class in ethics, a question arose concerning punishment. Soon the discussion turned on an appraisement of everlasting punishment. Almost as soon as it began, one student askt if punishment by hell fire was just.

"Let's work it out," the professor said. "Is it lawful for a mother, for any offense her child might commit, to throw it into fire even for a moment?"

"It's certainly wrong," the student replied.

"Is it just then, for God to burn his children not for a day, a week, or a year, but forever?" the professor askt.

"The two acts are identical. Yet I thot God could do as He pleased," said the student.

"So he can," the professor admitted, "but is it just? Which is the Superior Being? Which would you expect to be the nobler, God or man? If man burns his child, he is a criminal? Is God different, if He burns His? If man will refrain from such punishment and try to reform his child, will not God do the same?"

"Is there such a thing as hell fire any way," another pupil inquired.

"I don't see how it can be possible," the professor calmly responded. "If there is such it can not burn souls, for these are spiritual."

"Professor Young," remarked the student who began the discussion, "I think the trouble is this: our ministers, by trying to carry us back to the middle ages when the church burned and tortured, because God, so some said, would torture. In medieval history I learned that the Bible was written centuries ago with no thot of us in mind at all, and now we have outgrown much of its morality. We must write our own Bibles and construct our own morality, and so must every age. No previous age can do it for us."

"Then what are we going to do with this Bible?" askt Smith.

"Reinterpret it in light of present day thot, as it is exprest in all branches of knowledge," the professor replied. "There is enough good in the Bible to inspire the noblest in any man. Accept the good, reject the bad."

"But we have been taught that all is good," William declared, "that nothing is to be added and nothing to be taken away: that God is the same today, yesterday, and forever."

"To reinterpret is not to take away, nor to add. You merely re-evaluate what is there. Besides, the Bible does contain such statements as you mentioned," remarked the venerable instructor. "As to whether God changes or not, that is a point we might reconsider. If you conceive of God as being the universe, you are immediately aware of many changes. Various species come and go. Creation really has never ceased. Even if you conceive of God as personality, you must admit changes; for sometimes God is calm, sometimes angry, and sometimes jealous. These are changes of moods. If you think of God as a Spirit, He changes with the spirit of the people who worship Him. With the warlike Jews, He was terrible in His acts, One who never lost a battle, a mighty God of war. With civilized people, He is not a God of war, but Love—the Prince of Peace."

"But professor," inquired William, "I'm planning to prepare for the ministry. Can I preach what we have discust to the people? Would I not be called an infidel and my career as a minister finisht with its beginning?"

"Smith, I'm glad you askt that question," the professor replied. "I hope my answer will help you."

"It is the duty of every minister to preach the truth, not only the truth in the Bible, but the truth in nature, in man—in brief, anywhere it is to be found. Only the truth makes a man free. Ministers have too long condemned such men as Voltaire, Rousseau, Paine, and Ingersoll. These intellectuals have not contended that they were right and everyone else wrong; they have merely called the attention of the ministers and of the world in general to the fact that there was some truth that some persons had neglected. And they have rendered a valuable service to our age and all subsequent ones by reminding us that this other side of the truth should get a hearing.

"No one has a monopoly of truth. Let the ministers in their Sunday schools consider the Bible and also what these men have to say about it. The Church will always be behind the schools if it will not permit both sides of the truth to be aired at its meetings, especially in the Sabbath Schools. Under no circumstances should it shirk this responsibility.

"The minister necessarily mut proceed with tact; but the minister must tell the truth, even if it costs him his pulpit. You can minister to the needs of man even out of the pulpit. A man of your resourcefulness need have no fear of making a living. The world doesn't need men absorbed with the idea of making a living; it wants men absorbed with a determination to tell the truth. No matter what the outcome, do your duty."

Professor Young, of reverent memory, certainly won many disciples that day. The boys reluctantly left him at the toll of the bell, to attend their next recitation. As William reflected upon what had occurred, he knew that he was changing rapidly—he saw life anew.

Was it good for him to change? He could not answer. Knowledge was sweeping him on and he could not stop it.

He went about his studies now with even greater zeal. He read many more texts on sociology, anthropology, religion, and the Negro, among which were the writings of Wallis, Spencer, Boas, Von Luschan, Chamberlain, Ripley, Sergi, H. H. Johnston, Finot, Ripley, William Wells Brown, and George Williams. Since he was going to work chiefly among black people, why shouldn't he try to know them well? Very little was said concerning them in the American histories he read, which could be regarded as an inspiration to the colored youth. Accordingly he plunged into source material, documents and periodicals contemporaneous with slavery.

In his study of sociology, he became particularly interested in this discovery, namely: that there are no pure races. Greeks, Romans, Jews, Germans, Frenchmen, Hottentots, Kaffirs, in brief, all races, have been formed by intermarriage and miscegenation. Yet in the South many politicians ride into congress on Negrophobia. They say, "Keep the white race pure." They have laws forbidding the intermarriage of the races. Yet they are permitting amalgamation to take place faster in the South than in any section of the Country. What valuable information this was for him! Why should it be presumed that America today has the finest men that time can produce? Has progress ceased?

We should not be doing justice to William's intellectual and spiritual growth, should we omit a talk he heard one Sunday afternoon in chapel and an address he heard under the auspices of the college Y. M. C. A. It was the custom to have at Henderson College the foremost ministers of the Nation to stimulate the religious life of the youth. To hear these men would force one to conclude, "The old order changeth, giving place to new, and God fulfils Himself in many ways."

On a bright Sunday afternoon, a distinguished minister from Milwaukee, in addressing the students in College Chapel, made the following statement: "I don't care whether you have ever gone to church or not; I don't care whether you will ever go to church or not. That is a matter of slight importance. I do care, however, as to what you resolve to do with all your being. If you have been a liar, a murderer or a thief, if you have been the meanest man that ever lived, but have formed unshakable determination henceforth to help uplift your fellowman, to give him a drink of water when he is thirsty, a crust of bread when he is hungry, to give him shelter when he is houseless, you are bound to become good in the process. If you neglect doing this, but go to church, you can not see the kingdom of God.

"On the other hand, if you pursue this course with all your soul, though you never go to church, you will live daily with God.

"Yet I would have you to go to church and become active members. The Church represents organized religion. And you know that organization accomplishes more than spasmodic efforts. I want you to join the Church not because of fear of God, but because you love Him, because you love your fellowman. You can do good out of the Church, but the largest amount of spiritual renewal can be accomplisht thru the Church, which is a specialist in this activity. And this is an age of specialization."

William reflected long on the entire discourse. Did every

minister talk like that? What of being justified by faith? Was it a noble life like Christ's that would save men from themselves?

Another minister of liberal disposition, a preacher and scholar of great repute, was requested by the President of Henderson to address the students in the Y. M. C. A. auditorium on "The Ministry as a Life Work." This was one of a series of talks. Business, law, medicine, and music had already been discussed as vocations. Now came the Christian ministry. That evening an enthusiastic group of budding leaders was thrilled by the eloquence of this eminent divine. During the course of his remarks, he made a significant utterance which caused Smith to be rapt with wonder. The speaker said, "Young men, ministers frequently mystify and terrify men with declamations of heaven and hell. We get caught up in the spirit and say these things. When we come to reflect, we feel that probably we do wrong to make such an appeal. For after all, we do not know whether there is a hell of torture and a heaven of golden streets. In our saner moods we regard them as being figures of speech to describe the extremes of joy and bitterness that we experience here. Within you is the kingdom of heaven or of hell.

"I avoid making appeals from hell fire, as also do my colleagues. Inspired by Christ's personality, I anchor upon this statement of his, 'I go to prepare a place for you, that where I am there you may be also.' I do not know its nature, hence I dare not try to describe it. This is a matter about which the minister needs to be very particular. I'll tell you why. When the members speak of hell, they mean one thing; when the minister speaks of hell, he means something else— wasted opportunity, unsatisfied desire, lack of comfort, extreme poverty, or the like.

"Another difficulty you will experience in the ministry

will be with reference to your conception of God. If you speak of God as actually having eyes, hands, and feet, you deprive Him of one of His chief attributes—omnipresence.. The conception of God as spirit is the more logical. We bow and kneel to this Existence, as if he were far away, yet the attribute of omnipresence has Him always with all men. Our problem is to make the people conscious of His uninterrupted presence."

After hearing this talk, William askt himself what he should do. Should he enter the theological school or choose some other calling? He had promist Pilgrim Tabernacle that he would enter the ministry. At least he had said he would. And his word was a promise. The church of his youth, those devoted friends, whose means were constantly coming to Henderson to help him continue to be a man—these people had kept their promise. Should he not keep his? It was difficult not to do so.

His friends expected him to return home as the same William Smith that had gone away. How impossible! How could he be unaltered? Could a man see a fellow being who was innocent lynched in his own yard before wife and children, and be unchanged? Could he hear that wife pray and see her petition unanswered without questioning his faith? Could a man be impervious to the teachings of such men as Professor Young and the great divines that visited Henderson College? Could he be unimprest by these individuals of international repute? Impossible. William was born again and he knew it; at this cosmopolitan institution. he had had many rebirths.

"Will the people understand?" he askt himself. "Will they regard me as an impostor? I have been sincere in all that I did there and I am just as sincere now. Moreover, I shall be sincere in all I do when I return. But I can't proceed exactly as I did formerly. Of what service would my college training be, if I did?

"Is it for this that parents send their sons to college? Do they want us to get such ideas as I possess, many of which are diametrically opposed to those by which they have lived? Certainly they send us here to change, to be different, to reject the false and grasp the true; to abandon ignorance and superstition, and become amenable to all that the College or University thinks will make a liberal and noble man.

"Professor Young says, 'You can be a minister even out of the pulpit. No matter what the outcome, do your duty.' This may be the kind I'll have to become. Anyhow, I know now what to do. I said I'd prepare for the ministry; so to the theological school I will go."

CHAPTER VI.

The night with lingring shadows is all the day I've known,
  The greatest treasures others wait, and scorned am I alone
America, my mother, I've not failed thee in the least,
  And yet what other son of thine's unbidden to thy feast?

No other native land thou want'st to flourish on this spot,
  Yet in the South, East, West and North some maketh
    this thy lot.
Thy dusky prince unto himself must build a seperate race,
  United with his foren folk, to rise unto his place?

America, in making worlds safe for democracy,
  Thou'lt not forget thine own fair house where color flat-
    ters thee.
Our wrestling with the scorning, to do each fond behest
  Will win at least not frowns, but joy and loving at thy
    breast?

With great distinction and impressionableness, as one of the most scholarly and forceful characters that ever finisht at Excelsior Theological Seminary, the Reverend William Smith was called to pastor Sinai Shrine at Seaton, a little town eighty-five miles from Williamsburg. Thus he was not entirely disassociated from his Pilgrim friends. He would meet them in conventions; he could preach for them occasionally; and often make a flying trip to attend social events or make more secure expectant ties of love.

The beginning was fascinating. Should it not rather be so? Should hurricanes with ruin rampant, give us battle at the start? Sometimes it is thus. Sometimes the turmoil arises with our birth to be our constant companion in life and in death. We prefer, however, the calm and serene. If this we may have, we are willing to accept all else; if such a gift

49

is too costly a boon, we will get it some day anyhow.

How William rejoiced that he was again useful! He was shaping for the better many who had never seen the light. In commencing his great effort, he knew that he had to hold himself in leash, for his congregation, tho ambitious, to be called progressive, was not quite ready to accept all the "progress" at their young pastor's disposal. There remained with him, however, this decision: "Since, no matter where I go, I shall find the hosts of my people conservative in religion, no larger peril awaits me here than elsewhere. Therefore I am resolved, I will not sacrifice my personality. Tho the whole universe condemn me, I will not temporize, I will not truckle, I will be myself and speak my thots. The world has nothing to give me commensurate with my manhood. I will suffer or grieve, I will laugh or rejoice, and I will be a man.

Altho the Reverend Mr. Smith entered upon his pastorate just after leaving Excelsior Theological Seminary, he had been granted as a special token of esteem six weeks for a vacation. What better use could he make of this boon than to supplement his agricultural knowledge with a course at Cornell University? He had had years of practical farming. If, during the summers, by attending school and by study thru correspondence at leisure moments, he could equal his rich experience with the best theory the world could afford, he would make of Seaton—a rather unpromising rural community—a great commercial center. Accustomed to see all things thru, he did not relax until he had become master of the art.

The former pastor of Sinai Shrine to a great extent had lived away from his flock. The *esprit de corps* had been that the minister was to be fine appearing, to call on the members occasionally for a social chat, to marry the lovelorn, pray for the sick and dead, and preach rousing sermons. Such had been Reverend McCauley's ministry. His successor, however, did not follow the predestined course; he strove to promote a kindlier fellowship and touch all lives for greater usefulness.

Accordingly, on Monday—always—and often during the week, he was clad in overalls, busy among the farmers, showing them improved methods, whereby they might obtain larger and better yields. Seaton was peculiarly blest by his presence.

One year past happily. William had won a permanent place in the hearts of many of the fellow townsmen. He attended to his own business, he was always launching something new, which strengthened the community life.

Because of these endeavors and of the great commendation which spread abroad, the State lookt toward Seaton and then set its pace. The adjoining states were also followers. On account of this recognition, who but Reverend William Smith should make the address on "Church Extension" at Pilgrim Tabernacle, his home church, in behalf of the Tri-State Convention? He was chosen without a dissenting vote.

When the fall came on with its glory, emphasizing the approach and departure of all things, the convention assembled on the appointed day three hundred strong and set a record by its rapid, yet thoro dispatch of its business. The delegates were highly satisfied with what had been done, when they came to the last day of the session.

That morning the Reverend Mr. Smith arose to speak. Glad were the faces, anxious the hearts. On this great occasion, a product of Pilgrim, the Pride of Pilgrim, was to have on the program the place of honor. Most of the members, old and young, who had half willingly and half reluctantly permitted their fond associates to leave them, were again cheering and welcoming him to othes victories. The opportunity had come!

"Dear Christian Friends and Fellow Citizens," he began easily but firmly, "I am fully aware of the distinction you bestow upon me. This is a great occasion demanding great utterances. Whether I am equal to your expectations, I leave you to judge. But I thank you for your favor, accept the task, and render an account of my stewardship.

"The European nations are engaged in a great struggle, striving thru blood and brains to make it impossible for any group of people to be goverened without their consent and participation in the government. This is a basic law of all democracy! Consequently I wonder why Almighty God permits America, a land dedicated to the principle that all men are created equal, to look silently on. Can she permit the great issue to be solved without taking part? If I correctly read the signs of the times, America will decide the day." There was great applause.

"These people are fighting for liberty. Can this priceless boon be gained in other ways? Probably. But how has it been gained? How did the English gain it? Tho they were not so passionate as other powers, someone had to shed comely blood. I am thinking particularly of the rise of the protectorate under Oliver Cromwell. What caused the passing of the Old Regime and the establishment of the French Republic? Was it not the shedding of blood? How awful is this truth! Someone had sinned and atonement was long due. At last the purging came. Countless lives were laid upon the altar of Freedom. Woful day! Yet this has been the history of all nations. Without the shedding of blood there could be no remission of sin." There followed a grave silence.

"God has spoken. Who will combat His word? Is the

shedding of blood for the remission of sins an eternal law? Is this the only way? Will man never cease to oppress his fellow man, till he has poured out his precious blood? Must there always be civil wars, rebellions, riots, strikes, and barbarous conquests? Why have throbbing intellects, if we will not think; why have hearts, if we will not love? Why should rigth be establisht only by the arbitriment of arms, O Father, when Thou hast advised us to attain all grandeur not by Might, nor by Power, but by Thy Spirit?

"I am thinking of my people, the climbing black folk of America, opprest for centuries and throttled even now. In the South we may accumulate but not enjoy, in the North we may enjoy but not accumulate. Who are responsible for this calamity? Friends, both black and white. Since the white people, however, are in the majority and have had more centuries of favorable environment, theirs is the greater sin. They have sinned in not requiring the education of the South. We know the South has some excellent universities, but the masses of the people remain unlearned.

"The summer I went South to visit my uncle and stopt at other points, I met hundreds of young white men unable to read and write. Moreover, there seems to be a desire on the part of some to encourage this condition; for tho there are illiteracy tests for voters, the whites are not required to pass them. Since the South, furthermore, is agricultural and the masses of the people live on the farms where schools operate only for a few months, what else can exist other than bitter prejudices expressing itself to the disgrace of our glorious Nation in Jim Crowism and Lawlessness? If, as we believe, prejudice is a gift of little minds, whenever you meet an educated man, you meet a man without prejudice.

"Our sin has been, not to demand our rights; even if to demand were to die. Can the exalted utterance of Patrick

Henry, 'Give me liberty or give me death,' if lived by us as it was by our forefathers, bring other than one of these two: liberty or death? Even for us there probably may be no remission of sin without the shedding of blood.

"The utterance of eloquent Miss Nannie Burroughs, the sage of Washington, D. C.—'We've fought every race's battles but our own' must cease to be true. Greeks, Romans, Jews, Germans, Spaniards, English, and others, have fought their own battles. Shall we of all peoples, forgetting the spirit of our ancestors, wait for others to fight ours? God permit no such shame to come upon us! Let us struggle ever, and cry out with might, tho we may be the dying voice of an immortal cause, a voice crying in a wilderness.

"There is too much to do to remain silent and inactive. Why have we delayed? Is it not because we have been waiting on God and God has been waiting on us? We have been admonished since the dawn of slavery on these shores, 'First seek the kingdom of God and his righteousness, and all these things shall be added unto you.' Here is the thot preacht thru the centuries which, with other conditions, has made us a contented people. It has caused the masses of us to say with religious fervor, 'You may have all this world, but give me Jesus.' True, we have Jesus and the white people have the world. Who is the happier?

"Friends, I want you only to face facts. Have we not first sought the kingdom of God and His righteousness? I believe we have. A few observations, which you can parallel in almost any city, will suffice to prove this. Many districts in Washington, D. C., have five and six churches within a radius of ten blocks. Within an area of half a square mile in Saint Louis, I counted eighteen churches. This congestion is characteristic of our people. We have more churches than the white people, tho they are more numerous than we. Are our schools and business institutions thus multitudinous? If our people had been directed to put about one-third of their energy into business, our Nation would be quite different. This is our departure for church extension, not to expand by numbers of edifices, but by influencing many activities. Far better would it be to have a few first class churches than swarms of second class ones.

"The attitude of some pastors prevent this. I heard one in a neighboring state say that the members of a colored church must always have something to do. Who would contradict him? All Christians, white and black, must have something to do. Why should the Church ever stop, while the world moves on? What was this pastor to have his members do anyway? He said, 'Our church is paid for. If I don't put these folks to work, they'll soon be fighting me. So I'm going to have them build a new church.' In this instance the members did not fill the existing substantial edifice; yet they must have a larger and newer church. This man assumed that the only thing Christians could do was to build churches. With mortgages out of the way, with an inspiring group following him, tho a large opportunity had come to remould the lives of his people thru careful and regular pastoral endeavors, to lead them into new enterprises of moment, he did not see the kingdom of heaven was at hand and that he was to lead his people in.

"Let us not err in this direction. We can have too many church edifices; but we can not have too many ministers. Not every minister need pastor a church; let him pastor the people. A minister does not exert his greatest force in the pulpit. He is most influential in making his word flesh, to dwell among the people.

"Our numerous and excessive churches, and our unparalleled devotion to them certainly show that we have first sought the kingdom of God and its righteousness. Does not the world call us a distinctly religious people? What other race offers the other side of his face when slapt? The meek shall inherit the earth? Do the meek inherit it? Have they ever inherited it? Will they now? God knows we are meek. We have first sought the kingdom of God, now have these other things been added unto us? What things? JOY! PROTECTION! EQUAL OPPORTUNITY! LIFE! There have been added DISCRIMINATION, SEGREGATION, JIM CROWISM and LYNCHING!

"Is the God of those who oppress us our God? Pray to remove these abominations. Do you get an answer. They tell us God will answer in His own good time. Why not in ours, that we may enjoy the good fortune?

"The attitude of two great men may help us take a proper stand. The lamented Gregory Willis Hayes, President Emeritus of Virginia Theological Seminary and College, used to say, 'First go into your secret closet and pray. Pray as if it all depended on God. Then come out and work. Work as tho it all depended on you.' The other celebrity, Sir Rabindranath Tagore, says, 'When gods fail to help their sons, men must come to their assistance.'

"Has the time come when we should consider the suggestions of these men or must we wait longer? Must the Negro not look more and more to himself for the activities and comforts he deserves and desires? What else did Cicero mean, when he said, 'Every period of life is burdensome to those who have not within themselves the resources for a virtuous and happy life. On the other hand, nothing that the necessity of nature brings to pass can be a hardship to those who seek all good things from their own ability?' If the kingdom of heaven is within you, if God is everywhere—and hence within you—then within ourselves should we look for all we may do or become. I believe that the idea couched in the words of these philosophers is true not only for individuals, but also for sexes, races, and nations. We do not know the will of God and probably can never know it. It is hardly worth while trying to find it out. We can guess it and work out what we think it is by studying the Bible. But some of His will is yet to be exprest by those who live now and others that shall live. We do know, however, the desires of our own hearts, to have the rights of man. Let God continue to inspire us, but let us not err in thinking that service to God does not mean service to man.

"Recently I heard an orator say, 'God shall fight our battles for us.' Patrick Henry said the same, but he took good pains to urge the patriots to take arms in their defense. I still have in mind the utterances of the celebrities. God is not going to fight our battles; He has His own to wage. 'Our thots are not His thots, our ways are not His ways,' hence our battles commonly are not His battles. Why did Christ say, 'My God, My God, why hast Thou forsaken me?' If God would forsake His only begotten son in the crucial hour, is He not likely to forsake us who are less worthy? Friends, the fight is on; the conflict is ours, to win or lose. God will inspire us, but after all, man will be saved or ruined by man.

"In view of this realization what is the mission of the Church? It is to see that the other things shall be added unto us. Does this mean that the Church is to become a participant in politics to the detriment of religion? Must the Church become the field of worldly disputes and subtle malice? It must not. Yet it should not remain within four walls. It ought to expand. It should preach that Christ came not that we might have death, political or otherwise, but that we might have life and have it more abundantly. It must promulgate that religion is not a one day affair, but a matter of every day of the week; that religion is not separable from business, politics, law, medicine or any pursuit; that religion is life. Hence I contend that no person is a Christian who fails to live the life of Christ. It is not so much a believing as a living.

"We are to live the life of mutual helpfulness, of being our brother's keeper. We must not sin nor must we permit our white brothers to sin. A glance at our condition arouses amazement. If our white brothers are religious, then we are not. If we are religious, they are not. We must become like them or they like us. The difference must pass away.

"The problem of Church extension, therefore, is upon us. Since the world says that we live the exemplary life, we have much to teach our white neighbor. How can we do this while we meet him so seldom? We must meet him more, that he may learn of us and we of him. What shall we say? Declare that God is no respector of persons, that Christianity is not segregation of races in any way, but the universal brotherhood of man.

"This idea of interdependence of all races and all nations must pervade the world, the United States included. Since we are by choice or otherwise an asylum for weary peoples, tendering them the torch of liberty, no one group has made this Nation what it is. All have had a share. Is this a matter to be spurned? Now when the world is in a death grapple, agonizing to bring men together, shall we by supineness, quiescence, and cowardly submission retard the victory by clannishness, by living unto ourselves, by developing within the land a distinct civilization? Not unless the white people make us do so. We shall be only so mean as they force us to be. Desperadoes here and there, unscrupulous profiteers, myopic and biased schoolmen would lay this weight upon us. They have establisht ghettoes for Little Chinas, Little Italies, Little Africas and the like. And we, unprotesting, silent and docile, accept the slander. God forbid!

"The Honorable Mr. Roosevelt, seeing that this attitude is developing a national disunity, has, with his accustomed far-sightedness, begun to call for a manifestation of pure Americanism. He believes that the German-American Alliance is establishing a Little Germany, creating a propaganda which will make the burden of the United States extraordinarily heavy, should we be drawn into the war. Accordingly he is the apostle of one hundred per cent Americanism—'no hyphen, no this or that, no qualification whatever, but simply Americans.'

"If any group of people deserve to be called one hundred per cent Americans, it is our colored men." The applause was vigorous. The delegates carefully followed every utterance. "Some have called us Negroes, but we are not," he continued. "So much white blood was mixt with ours during the two hundred fifty years of slavery and continues to be illegally mingling in the South, that the Negro among us is to be found only after years of patient search. So few there are. Some have called us Afro-Americans, reminding us of our African descent. This, however, is not the only source of our existence. Many of my brethren have in their veins some of the proudest blood of Anglo-Saxons, French, and Germans. This is a matter of triviality. I grant that some other land was the abode of our fathers; but we were born in America. Thus we are Americans, nothing else.

"Since the Federal Constitution vouchsafes to those born upon these shores the full rights of citizenship, our due is all that this land affords during our sojourn. And here we shall abide forever.

"Some say, however, that we must have patience, that we must be long-suffering. Great heavens, what do men expect? All tolerance from the colored, but none whatever from the white! Who have been more patient than we, who upon this continent have suffered longer? Those advocating long suffering say, 'Wait, a crisis will come and we shall reap its joys.' In every crisis of American history, they urge, we have been benefited. Yes, we always get the crumbs which fall from the table. Why not like other folks, for instance, the suffragists, produce a crisis and receive the first fruits of them that slept?

"Some are afraid, others are indifferent, and still others are ignorant. If our people were alert to their opportunities, why would they permit an organization like the National Association for the Advancement of Colored People to struggle for existence. Why is not every adult black man a contributor to its weal? This society, as it stands for upholding the Constitution of the United States without equivocation, contending for a democracy not on paper, but in the lives of men, is the most patriotic society in America. A friend tells another friend his faults and tries to help him amend them. Such is the business of this group of individuals. It is the one organization in which all Americans should enroll, black and white alike. It is not a theory, but the greatest example of this concretion of thot ever witnessed by the eyes of man. As we might expect, it appeals for a democracy which begins at home and spreads abroad. The idea is tangibly demonstrated. Here black and white love and think together. Here there is no color line.

"When I recall the accomplishment of this society, when I think of the sacrifice of Christ, when I see that Europe is fighting for our ideals, I wonder why we say no more than we do about the brutish malice, the degenerate littleness which is doing its utmost to foster here a separate civilization, separate ideals, separate ambitions, but mutual hates. Has Lincoln labored and died in vain? Must there be another War of the Rebellion? We hope not. We cry, 'Union and Liberty Now and Forever, One and Inseparable. One Language, One Country, One Flag.' At the same time the hosts of the Nation, by oppression or quiescence, are doing all they can to split the Country. Pray God that this shall never be!

"Our ancestors came to this Country accompanied by white men. We have gone with them shoulder to shoulder, from Bunker Hill to the North Pole. After all these years of comradeship, shall they leave us now? Shall we leave them? We shall ever march together; for our language is their language, our Country their Country, our flag their flag." At this moment William had his audience thoroly within his grasp. He had taken the convention by storm.

"Since our white brother has retarded the progress of the Nation," he continued, "by finding time to be prejudiced, God Almighty calls us by the good in our hearts and in those that scorn us, by the thunder and by the lightning, to demand universal brotherhood. Tho white favors white, we must favor only merit, truth, and right. We must preach the end of segregating movements. When wars are upon us, black and white die together. When peace comes, why can they not live together?

"Think of separate schools for a group of people in a democracy! What a paradox! Democracy means mixed schools with mixed faculties. Why are we blind to the fruits of this: the stratification of society, schools for the rich, and schools for the poor, but not American schools? It has been the hope of our greatest men that the College and University would be purely democratic. Somehow, these institutions in unmistakable numbers, have either been unaware of these hopes or as a matter of course ignored them. What college or university in addresses and leadership has made it positively clear to the students that such was expected? The matter is left entirely with the students. These promising young men and women are not interferred with in their racial antipathies. They bring them to the schools and carry them away as they came, or accentuated by biased professors. These are scholars who set out to prove a contention and prove it. Of course some men can prove anything. Thus the hope of democracy is crusht.

"Since this is so; let us never ask for separate schools. Let us enter these strongholds and by character and scholarship show our selves the equal of all people. If the cleft school must come, let it be forced upon us, for it tends to increase racial separateness and thus undermine our government. How can there be a democracy based on color rather than upon the inequality of merit? The ideal is the mixt school. Why run from a goal we have reacht with hope of returning to it some day? Why not use the ideal while we have it. We can not deny that the masses of our educated people, if they had been dependent upon mixt schools, would still be illiterate. The fact still remains, however, that a democratic government should have democratic schools, if it is to continue as such. Aristocratic schools perpetuate aristocratic government, with a hope that democracy will never rise. So the Church should contend.

"A further activity needing church help is politics. The Scriptures say that the powers that be are ordained of God. The corruption which exists with many of them, however, almost persuades us that they were ordained of hell. As soon as they find the colored man about to get an important office they arrange a gerrymander or get a new charter and thereby shut him out. If proportional representation were in vogue —the form which is certainly democratic—we should have in the United States Senate at least four members and thirty-six in the House of Representatives. This is just an inkling of the injustice we bear. What hosts we should have in the state and city assemblies!

"This condition is a concomitant of any policy of racial separateness. I shall mention but one example. In several states I have visited around election time, I have observed signs to this effect: THE REPUBLICAN CLUB, THE DEMOCRATIC CLUB, THE NEGRO REPUBLICAN CLUB, THE NEGRO DEMOCRATIC CLUB. Only white people attend THE REPUBLICAN CLUB and THE DEMOCRATIC CLUB. The colored people attend something else. May these Jim Crow organizations die forever! The fatlings of plutocracy! The corrupters of the public weal. If white and black worked together in politics in all their meetings, corruption would pass with the night. God open the eyes of the whites to this some day!

"Another work the Church may well perform is to spread good tidings, intelligence to all people. Consider how one-sided has been our life. I touch upon the press. Newspapers edited by colored men circulate freely only among colored people. Newspapers edited by white men circulate freely among both black and white. The consequence is easily discerned. We know the whites much better than they know us, with the additional advantage of knowing ourselves. We know how mean they are and how good they are! We are aware of their basest and their noblest thots. Most white people take the colored man for a joke. They believe us all minstrels, ready always for a jig, a slice of watermelon, or to bow and scrape. The black man who never laughs, the one who is always serious, this type they do not know. Equally ignorant are they of what we think of them, what we think of ourselves, and what we think of life. Our points of view as exprest in newspapers, magazines and books of our men commonly do not reach them.

"Papers of all groups should have a wide reciprocity, especially those of a group that is circumscribed. A democracy can not afford to be ignorant of the ideals of any of its groups. For ignorance keeps people apart, intelligence brings them together.

"Preach the gospel to all people, 'but go rather to the lost sheep of the house of Israel.' Begin with those about us, our white brothers. If they will not hear, if they will keep up the bars, if they reject the brotherhood of man—to live in a realm of equal opportunity for all—like other nations that rose on the enslavement of man, political and otherwise, America, too, will fall. Keep off this doom, preach that out of one blood God made all peoples that dwell upon the face of the earth, that we are not enemies, but brothers in sacrifice, love, and honor.

"Bring to their minds incidents like this which I am about to relate. An East Indian, who might have been regarded as the twin brother of a boy in the Sumner High School of Saint Louis, matriculated at a university located in this town. Yet the Sumner boy of the same build, with the same complexion and bewitching hair, whose fathers suffered and died that this Nation might be free, must keep without. He would not even be accepted as one of its janitors. Those who gave their lives that their Country might be free surely have died in vain, since they who have not suffered and bled for the Union, are more highly honored than those who did. Shall the undeserving continue receiving blessing, while the worthy are crusht under foot? No! These things shall pass away!

"To hasten the process, let us remember that God is no respecter of persons. We must be JUST like HIM. If a black man commit a crime, see that he is punisht. If a white man commits a crime see that he is punisht. If a black man performs a noble deed praise him; if a white man performs a noble deed praise him. If a white man marries a colored woman or a white woman marries a colored man, let us remember that before God there is no difference. Both black and white are His. Persons so matched have braved much, have assumed greater responsibilities than others who marry. They dared unite with the one they loved.

"I know that I am walking on fragile ground, but let us keep stepping until we reach more solid soil. Commonly when these marriages occur, we look down upon them with scorn or dismay. The white person is ostracized and the colored nearly so. This condition, too, must change. Is it not the democratic ideal? If we are to have one country, must we not also have one morality. Can we have a united country with one morality for whites and another morality for blacks? Would human beings be little valued if white men who impregnate colored girls under age were prosecuted; if other white men who cohabit with colored women could marry them if they chose? Too long this practice has been characteristic of our land. When will man learn that justice is even-handed?

"If two persons of good health love and wish to marry, who should gainsay them, be they white or black, or white and black? I have met in my travels happy marriages of both sorts: the white woman and the colored man, and the white man and the colored woman. Seeing a mutual attachment being fondly exprest in the careful toil and sacrifice on the part of both for their children, whenever this democratic couple proves itself in a community, the neighbors should endeavor to break down all barriers and make these stalwart people their own.

"Let our reproach for the marriage between white and black vanish like a mist. Rather reproach the union of unequals, be they white, black, or black and white. On the other hand, when persons of relatively the same spheres and accomplishments choose to marry, our part is to make the union last. Some say these people quarrel. Not all do so. Yet how few marriages of any sort are without some differences? How many marriages of our peoples are absolutely without quarrels? Having seen many of these nuptials followed by unparalleled devotion, I can believe that before I taste of death that America will have one morality.

"Do not mistake that I am advocating intermarriage as a group ideal. Nothing is further from my purpose. I am merely saying that, if it happens, that is the affair of those two. I am simply indicating the evils which arise by forbidding by law intermarriage. The base miscegenation of slavery and another sort has not ruined us. Can a noble miscegenation do worse. At least it has not where it has been practised. What the Nation needs to become conscious of is that the government is an aristocracy, and no democracy at all. And as long as societies are aristocratic, morality is impossible.

"Our Heavenly Father, may we know that a man's a man; may we treat a man as a man; may we love a man as a man; and may we marry a man as a man!

"This is the test of our religion: our thots must be thots of love for all; our lives must be lives of love for all.

"A final consideration, a very important consideration, I now present. This, I hope, will set aright all particularities out of joint. Despite the pleasantness of romance, the basis of happiness seems to be economic. Poverty, we know, is the mother of vice, crime, and most uncleanness. Yet the adage says, 'Money is the root of all evil.' Not so. Rather the lack of money has been the root of most evil. I call this to mind because of what the Scripture tells of 'filthy lucre.' We must realize that not all lucre is filthy! We must lay up treasure not only in an imagined realm, but even on earth, where moth doth corrupt and thieves break thru and steal. How otherwise can we prepare for our children's comfort in case we die prematurely, or prepare for old age?

"We must accumulate. To do this we must more and more enter those branches where money grows. Let us go extensively into the trades and business. If we want to get together, let us put our money together. This is what the Jews have done. If we have not the experience of financiers, let us get it as we got our churches and schools. Just tread the wine press. We shall not tread alone. Here and there our people are ready for a big enterprise. If these people having the desires of our hearts will not come close to us, let us come close to them. All need to march together.

" 'No man liveth unto himself, and no man dieth unto himself.' If this thot we carry with us, our religion will extend iself into all phases of our community life.

"The white man has been deluding himself by thinking he does not need us. Similarly we have resolved to let him alone. But how can we do this? We need his business experience. He needs us at least to fight his battles. Besides, each will always have something to teach the other.

"Zangwill well portrays the spirit of America, to assimilate all people, in his play, 'The Melting Pot.' However, it lacks one element: America's most loyal folk, the colored people. The broth will not be right, unless these colored masses also simmer in that crucible.

"When then is the ultimate goal? The answer is simple. If we can live the life of Christ, the Church will extend its influence to every man. Our battle will be won over night. When we become like God, no respecter of persons, we have life, we give life, we save life. Thus our building can never fade away."

CHAPTER VII.

Society is in a conspiracy to keep persons from
being individuals.—Emerson.

The Reverend Mr. William Smith had made a good
speech. Good? So some said, but others thot it heretical.
What could have happened to the 'prophet of Sinai Shrine?'
Who expected anything like this? Despite the consternation
he had caused, no one left the auditorium during the course
of the address. No one even dared interfere; for just when
ire was aroused by a statement seemingly irreligious, the Holy
Spirit seized the speaker and his hearers, thrilling them with
sacred emotion. No one called the speech ineffective; all felt
that the racial issues in the main were sound. The greatest
difference of opinion bore upon the apparent atheism of the
clergyman.

"What could have possest Rev. Smith? We lookt for
one of the good old sermons to take us out of self and lift
us upon the rock of eternal ages," said Reverend Caldwell, the
president of the convention.

"Yes," agreed Reverend Williams, secretary of foren mis-
sions, "I lookt for something different myself. I admit tho,
that we have been edified, baffled, and mystified, and have
considerably lost our bearings. Mr. President, for this reason,
while I'm on my feet I want to offer a suggestion. Suppose
we depart a little from our usual way of closing the convention. Let us dispose of some of our afternoon work, as the
committees are ready to report and close the afternoon session
with a discussion of Reverend Smith's address. You know

(68)

we must discuss it and then take action on his suggestions. We should have our dinner hour for reflection upon it. Mr. President, I move that we do this." The motion carried.

At the close of the morning session, the delegates did not go at once to dinner, but divided themselvs almost automatically into three groups, the better to discuss the young minister's remarks: conservatives, progressives, and radicals. Such a spontaneous arrangement was a natural prognostic that theological belligerency was in the air. Each group aglow with enthusiasm and determination to carry the others was untiring in effecting a thoro organization. These groups were maintained at the tables and continued up to the time of afternoon meeting. With plans definitely arranged, the groups lost their identity in the general assembly. As the members assembled with unusual promptness, devotionals suffered no interruption. The president then declared the convention ready for business.

"Mr. President," began Rev. Monroe, leader of the conservatives, properly to discuss the address of our dear brother, we should be strictly parliamentary. We need a motion more definite than any that has as yet been proffered. I therefore offer the following. He read his motion and forwarded it to the recording secretary. It ran thus: 'Resolved, that the Convention withdraw the hand of fellowship from Reverend Smith, pastor of Sinai Shrine, thus depriving him of all privileges and distinctions which accrue to a member of this organization. This shall mean that he can not represent here or can his church send delegates, that no minister enrolled with us shall preach in his church, nor shall he preach in any church as a pastor enrolled with us; that our members may not attend his church, and his members may not commune with us. This withdrawal is to be effective until he is removed from the pastorate of Sinai or until he renounces the main

tenets of his address which conflict with our articles of faith.'
The motion was seconded and at the call for unreadiness the
discussion began.

The radicals had hoped to get in a resolution first, but the
conservatives had been the more alert. Now each group tried
to get recognized. Eight or nine speakers arose simultaneously, appealing, "Mr. President." As recognition under these
circumstances was utterly impossible, Rev. Caldwell said, "Gentlemen, you are about to be disorderly. Please be seated. Remember that order is heaven's first law. I know that we are
assembled in extraordinary session. I am aware that all are
eager to handle the order of the day; but let us proceed aright.
Rise one at a time, proportion your speech so that every one
may have a chance, and move on with dispatch. I'm ready
to go on."

Again a conservative won the floor. It was Rev. Stone,
pastor of Shiloh, who remarked, "Mr. President, in this matter we want to be fair. In requesting a withdrawal of the
hand of fellowship, we need to state the charges, and have the
accused brother make his defense. For that purpose, I rise."
He stroked his grizzled beard, nodded his head several times,
and then cleared his throat.

"We feel," he continued, "that the dear brother has forfeited his place among us, because he has not respected our
traditions—doctrines which we have cherisht and reverenced
for many decades. Some of his utterances hark back to in-
fidelity. The notorious Robert Ingersoll could not have said
worse. For instance, the young man said, 'God is waiting
on us and we are waiting on him.' Thus he tries to impute
to the Holy Father idleness—He who started light to dazzle
in the sun, to sparkle in the stars, to flash in capricious lightning, He who poured the waters forth from His radiant
throne to make the fertile earth—my God began His work

in eternity and has never stopt." He spoke with great emphasis.

"Amen, amen," was an uproarious response coming from
various parts of the assembly. "Hallelujah, hallelujah, praise
His name!"

"Mr. President," Rev. Hillard, a radical, appealed.

"Rev. Hillard."

"Mr. President, I rise to ask the speaker a question."

"Rev. Stone," askt the president, "do you permit a question?"

"I do," was the reply.

"My dear Sir," sought Rev. Hillard, "have you not yourself by your utterance just now overstept the margin of these
same traditions for which you seek to withdraw the hand of
fellowship from Rev. Smith? You yourself just said that
God has never stopt His work. Did not Brother Smith say
the same. The Bible has us to understand that God rested on
the seventh day. This, you even deny, tho Christ himself
said, 'Tis finisht.'

"Furthermore, when we are trying to have sinners to decide to follow Christ, don't we say that God, that the Spirit
is waiting for you to repent; that God, that Christ stands at
the door patiently waiting?"

"Mr. President," remarkt Rev. Stone, the learned gentleman knows that tho I may err in some of my remarks, our
conception of God is as one prompt to act, industrious, good
and just. Rev. Smith has implied that God neglects His children, that God is unjust. Did he not say in quoting Tagore,
'When gods fail to help their children, men must come to
their assistance?' What does this argue but the negligence
of God, what but His injustice? Thus I lay before you the
charge that Rev. Smith is wholly unorthodox. If I am wrong,

let my reverend chatechizer or 'the prophet of Sinai Shrine' himself prove it."

"Mr. President," began Rev. McVicar, another conservative of the most uncompromising type, "we must sustain our co-worker in his charges." He almost roared with his heavy bass.

"Amen, amen," came back many responses.

The distinguisht pastor continued, "Rev. Smith today has been as heterodox as a Turk reeking with Christian blood, and as ingratiating as a hog in a lady's chamber. He challenges God's answering in His own good time. If a human being can not wait for the All-wise, for the everlasting Father, the Prince of Peace, to answer his prayer, not only is he unfit to preach, for the salvation of men, unfit to be a doorkeeper in the house of *my* Lord, but is unfit to claim allegiance to the Christ."

"Verily, verily I say unto you, Rev. Smith, you must be born again."

"Hallejujah, praise the Lord," the delegates shouted in various parts of the assembly.

The enthusiasm flowed profusely with violent inundations, as is the custom, when tense religious fervor is provoked. Nearly every representative wanted to speak at once. Many arose, but like a meteor flashing unawares to vanish and give way to orbs of more lasting grandeur, they spoke and were admired for their brilliancy, but the gaze of all was fixt upon the men of great renown with hope as for a coveted light. The meeting surged with cheers for each respective group, but how could one doubt the leaning of men untouched, unseasoned by the lives of diversified thinkers, trameled by the radiation of one clime, and, therefore, hostile to new truth?

Then came forth the Rev. Stamford, a man of somewhat progressive views, "Mr. President, the dissention evoked this

morning may have some just basis I do believe. The clamor
of metallic tongues, however, and hearts brazened with
duplicity, and coated with envy for a man who has turned his
back upon the night, needs scant consideration. Yet those
who love the truth, who believe that even the Church must
step ahead, value the many contributions of our distinguisht
young man. Who can deny that we must reshape our ideas
to adjust ourselves to this complex life? Must we not rethink
our attitude towards the great issues mentioned by Reverend
Smith: social equality, intermarriage, mixed schools, newspapers, and business? Consider, for instance, the prevailing
conception and denial of any desire for social equality, hark-
ing back to our ancestors of recent generations, suffering in
indecent slavery. They desired not to live in the cabin, but in
the big house, they desired not to have corn meal all the time
but an occasional taste of magic flour. Life was not merely
the fiddle and the dance, but labor and rest, leisure and travel,
and schooling. All these our forefathers desired. What was
this to them other than social equality?

"Since we, however, have had advantages of school, have
lived in other years, and other climes, our conception of social
equality can not be theirs. We include the right to vote and
hold office. We go even further than that. If we shall have
democracy here, we must not be many nations, but one with
liberty and justice for all.

"To this extent I agree with Rev. Smith; and with him I
contend that the laws of the South preventing intermarriage
of individuals of different races, is autocratic and therefore
subversive of democracy, that it prostitutes not only our women
but the women of our white brother, increases crime and moral
degeneracy. So far am I with my noble and able friend.

"When he says, however, of my Redeemer, of Him who
has cast countless worlds into space, that we do not know
the will of *our Father* who is in heaven, and that it is not

worth while trying to find it out, we meet at the parting of the ways," he spoke with great fervor.

"Amen, amen," the responses arose and continued for quite a while. Rev. Smith sat still, almost stolidly thruout all these remarks. He did cast, nevertheless, a casual glance at the various speakers.

"Do we know the will of God?" Rev. Stamford seemingly askt his entire audience.

"Yes, we do. Praise His name. Yes, we do."

"Do we not know that out of Chaos God formed the universe, that by making plants and beasts and man He willed us life? Do we not know that before he created man, according to His *holy and everlasting will* he determined that Christ should come, that the word should be made flesh and dwell among us? Was it not His will, that Christ should teach 'Love thy neighbor as thy self?' Is it not God's desire that we should love one another, that we should love our enemies? Is it not worth while to try to learn more of this, that our light may shine?"

"Amen, amen."

"Rev. Smith," concluded Rev. Stamford, "I love you. I want you to succeed. And tho some of your utterances seem untimely and apostatic, I know that you are sincere. I am fully aware that not a word was spoken to disrupt this convention, but to spur it to larger usefulness. I look upon you almost as a lone star on a gruesome night, almost as a beautiful flower in a tractless desert. We must admire you because you are rare. I will not vote against you. It takes a brave man to do what you have. You have said these things because you believed them. Now if the hand of fellowship should be withdrawn, do not be dismayed, God is ever with you. True we have a covenant, but if we were to question every minister here and each would be as frank as you, we should find, I am afraid, as many different interpretations of that covenant as there are ministers present. Let anyone deny that we do not differ as to our fundamental doctrines!" The conservatives squirmed. They wanted to speak, but Rev. Stamford would not yield.

"The matter, however, which you need to rethink is your categorical, that we do not know the will of God and that it is not worth while trying to find it out. In your defense, I should like for you to touch upon this." Thereupon, the speaker sat down.

Now for the first time a radical gained the floor. He had been sitting nervously trying to get recognition. When the chance eventually came, he arose and said with the air of a braggadocio, "Mr. President."

"Rev. Gaston."

"Dear Christian Friends, members of the convention, you know what I am going to say. For several years you have called me an extremist and said that my folks have no religion at Mount Horeb. Well, if we don't have much religion, we do have something. We have the largest and most beautiful structure in the state as well as the biggest congregation. Besides, my people are doing the most missionary work at home and abroad. Friends, my folks have religion; I have a little religion myself. I certainly burn with love for Christ." The delegates smiled.

"I have no speech to make, I merely rise to commend Sinai Shrine. I will answer, however, the preceding speaker. Rev. Stamford, is not God unknowable? The history of the world has assuredly been a search for God. Each generation learns more of Him. And in that great day, or thru the ages, when it is our pleasure to see Him not thru a glass darkly, but as He is, shall we know Him?" He almost shouted. "Friends, we shall not, but we shall become better and better acquainted. If we were to find out all about God, I am afraid we should become tired of heaven and leave it in order that we might go to some place where there would always be something new to learn. If we can not know God, we can not know His will, we can approximate, but we can not know."

"Mr. President," exclaimed Rev. Monroe excitedly, "I appeal for the vote, if Rev. Smith has nothing to say. There has been enough discussion. Let us vote."

"Mr. President," said Rev. Ross as the preceding speaker sat down, "Permit me a word." The request was granted. "I rise as the father of this young giant. For many years I nurtured him with teachings of the Christ and you know his phenomenal youth as well as his ministerial career. How strange life is! From this very church with loving pathos, we heralded Reverend Smith into prosperity and success. Here he was ordained to preach the word and here he is accused. Gentlemen, it is strange.

"Let us be careful how we judge. The ideas of this young man to many of us may be new. We were always told that we could not have too many churches, but did we think that out for ourselves? No! We just accepted it. If now we are honest, we must admit that our religious growth is not determined by the number of churches, that it is better to have a few first-class churches thoroly up-to-date than a host of second-class churches behind the times.

"If this is followed, however, then what? Not every minister has a pulpit literally. Some are evangelists, others are college presidents, some are teachers in seminaries, others are publishers.

"The question 'Where do I exert my greatest influence?' had never occurred to me. Unquestionably it is not in the sermon I utter, but it is in the sermon of my daily life—in laying hands on people, in fully sharing life not from afar but at close range.

"I do not agree with all our youth has said, but we need such a speech as his: frank and earnest. We need the Truth."

"Rev. Smith," remarkt the President, when a consensus of opinion had been exprest that the pastor of Sinai Shrine make his statement, "what do you have to say?"

With his wonted composure and equipoise, Rev Smith addrest the chair, surveyed his audience and spoke thus: "Friends, now there is little need for words. As men your minds are fixt, you know how you will vote and so do I. Then do not think that I hope to change you. Not at all. I have enjoyed working with you, it has been a pleasure to preach in your churches; but I have not desired to be an unwelcome guest. I weighed my words before I spoke and I said them because I believed them. Whether you think my presence pernicious to the faith or wholesome, vote according to your conscience. I can afford to sever our fond relations, I can afford to resign my pastorate, but I can not afford to leave this community. I can not *afford* to be less than a man. I have no defense to make. I have done my duty. Now may you do yours!"

The president having commended Rev. Smith, exprest his regret that the convention had to close thus, but he hoped that, whatever the decision, they would act with the Spirit of Christ. They had prayer. Anxious were the hearts devoted to Rev. Smith while the ballots were being collected, and more anxious during the counting of the same. Whispers of tenderness, sighs of love strongly imprest this upon the assembly. When all the votes had been tolled and checked, by a slight majority, the hand of fellowship was withdrawn.

CHAPTER VIII.

Here how we bathe in sweetened rest,
　　Or spring to joys the lovers make!
We think man but a passing jest,
　　Yet warm friends seek, and friends forsake!

Condemned by the Church! Scorned by upstart time-
servers! Abused and misunderstood! Persons who yesterday hailed him an uncrowned king, today keep anxious space
between. Fond only of those whom all the world admires,
worshippers of those who court the crowd, considered him
stricken with a contagious malady. "Poor young man! You
know that I am sorry, but I must keep away. The Church
demands it." Thus the manners of those who dwelt apart
forcefully spoke to Rev. Smith.

When we have long been nurtured by the attention and
counsel of many acquaintances and these at last suddenly slink
away, our souls still hunger and thirst for the accustomed
care, ignorant, mayhap, where to find it. We ponder, mind-
ful of what has been, and wonder should we covet its return
or something like it. Then promptly we are flooded with a
vision proudly dear, and tho we stand alone, we should exchange it never for the old—for what had long outlived its
time and should have passed away. We ourselves have died
with these old glories; but now we live again. How we hate
to die, either in the flesh or in the spirit! Yet we all must
die. We who live must give the life, that they who die may
live.

Such were the thots crowding Smith for recognition, as
he sat with his mother one pleasant evening enjoying the old
home place. It was several days after he had returned from

a flying trip to Xenia. He had left immediately after the convention and had accordingly given very little time to his friends. At last his vacation had begun. This was the one day of the year, when his mind might follow any fancy. Whether he would go back to his pastorate, he was uncertain. Probably the members would not have him. At this time, however, being in Seaton was not a matter of importance. He should lay all thot of former activity aside and be thrilled by the rapture of vacation. His friends and those of his mother, particularly the younger set wanted to see him. Now he was at their shrine. Hosts of charming memories, of good well done kept him facinated with the spot. Now he realized why his mother would not leave Williamsburg to be with him at Seaton. He himself was so entranced, he began to wonder if he could leave. He had come and gone often, but could he now?

After a while, William left the porch and went within, to obtain a pencil, in order that he might make a sketch of the sunset. So variegated were the hues with unusual tints, that the artist in him could not resist the alluring scene. Then he thot of his sketch book, which would be more convenient than a mere piece of paper. A brief search brot him upon it. Thus prepared for a feast of beauty, he started to work. He had made only a few bold lines, when he felt that black and white would not do justice. He decided therefore to get his crayons. He desired most his paints, but these he had left at Seaton.

He had hardly more than gone upstairs, when two fair guests arrived, Susan attired in Alice blue and Thelma in russet. At the request of Mrs. Smith a saintly old matron who had never lost her winsomeness, the girls nimbly tript into a medium-sized room, the modest but commodious parlor. They askt the mother not to announce their presence. She consented. The callers then closed the door and made themselves at home. The pianoforte, which they noticed immediately upon entering for a few moments was the chief attraction. Indeed it was a great temptation, but they did refrain from touching the keys. They whispered about the music displayed, then went to the well curtained windows, from which proceeded abundant light, to see if he had come. *He* had not. The young women now ran lightly from here to the opposite side of the room, where they found a divan loaded with oriental pillows and a few that were strictly suggestive of college life. Tho they had handled and admired the room before, it seemed not less interesting now. The massive chairs cushioned in blue with mystic designs were the next attraction. The belles were thinking of some of their own artistic work and wondering if theirs was equally grand. After musing and chatting about these, they glanced at the landscapes placed here and there. One seemed to be faithfully representative of the vase of fragrant magnolias before them. They were flowers of rare beauty.

Finally William appeared on the porch and rapidly began to make a sunset that he hoped would be true to that of nature. He was enjoying his occupation immensely when a sweet voice called him. He turned to see the owner. "Where are you, Susan?" he answered, recognizing her at once.

"Here I am," she replied, rushing upon the porch, laughing merrily.

Thelma followed and said with great satisfaction, "Making a sunset?"

"Yes," William responded. "The effort was irresistable. You know well that I am a dilettante in this phase of art, but yet an ardent lover of it. I wish I could give more time to it. Public life, however, prevents me."

"Still you're showing considerable talent in this sketch," said Thelma. "It seems that this is going to be just as excellent as some of your landscapes we were just admiring."

"I may be able to get the same results with crayon; but I'm not sure."

"I know you will," remarkt Susan with emphasis. "You can do anything."

"I appreciate the compliment," he assured her. He rapidly workt on. Upon pausing for a time and seeing them standing over him, he requested them to sit, but they preferred to stand. "Girls, you so quickly overwhelmed me with surprise that I so far lost my bearings, as to be inconvenienced in spontaneous hospitality. Of course set words conventionalized are not always necessary to express a cordial greeting. Yet I need indulge in no lengthy harrangue to have you feel welcome." He left off sketching for a while and then said, "I seem almost in fairyland; so delicately sweet and cheery is the air because of your presence."

"We are indeed glad to come at any time," said Thelma with a smile.

"Thelma," he resumed, his face flusht with the tint of the setting sun, a face which showed the calm of a conqueror, "I was confident that you would act your own thots unsolicited by anyone; for such as you we masculines call the assertive type, the feminist."

"Well, you do understand me in part," came from Thelma, smiling with her accustomed good-naturedness. At once there was exhibited a set of teeth, charming and perfectly designed.

"Susan, I was not so sure, however, as to what your attitude toward me would be after the convention. I am fully aware," he said as his hand moved the crayons almost automatically, "that my remarks to some were very startling; but what I spoke should have been uttered long ago. The Church as constituted is suited to the older generation. These will soon be dead. What will happen then. Will a new Church suddenly spring forth to satisfy the new people? Not at all. The changes should be gradual. It is these I am trying to start, to encourage directed evolution instead of a violent revolution, or the extinction of the Church."

"True, I was shockt, but I believed in you, William; hence I never once feared," she declared.

"I did not once think that you would consider me a renegade," he affirmed. "The hope that has arisen in you from my avowal of endeavor was not yesterday betrayed. It was merely set on with unusual momentum. Feeling, however, that because you are a 'mother' child, willing oftimes to sacrifice your own idea and act upon hers, even tho your better judgment desired another course, I wasn't sure what you would do."

"William, you've spoken discerningly," came from Susan, striving to adjust herself to this sudden expression of what was one of her fundamental characteristics. "You understand me well; but you know the first commandment of promise, 'Honor thy father and thy mother,' With the reverence of that ancient holy people, almost with adoration, I have esteemed my mother. I could defy my father; but as yet, I fear that I might yield to any wish of hers."

Thelma followed the completion of the sketch, at the same time listening to the conversation, ready at the proper suggestion to make her contribution.

Turning the talk a little, for the purpose of trying to convert her to a different manner of procedure, he askt, "Has not your judgment frequently proved superior to your mother's. I'm aware that Mrs. Lee is a lovable woman with a valuable experience gained by contact with the hard, hard world. Grant her all this, yet can she equal you in view of your having largely shared that experience, read more widely than she, and traveled more extensively?"

"Occasionally I do devise better plans," she admitted, "Yet I can't say that in matters of great importance, I have ever excelled. Up to this time, no circumstance of honor has been able to draw me from a friend, no matter what has been said. Still our relations might be in a measure altered by some suggestion of my mother."

"You see then that I was right," remarkt Rev. Smith.

"Pardon me," put in Thelma at this point, "but may I interrupt you a wee bit?" She had been about to invade the kitchen to call upon the mother, for once it seemed that the conversation between Susan and Smith was about to become extremely confidential.

"Why certainly," Susan replied and William added his assent.

"Thank you," she remarkt. "I have often told Susan that she must solve her own problems, she must see her chances and not leave such immediately personal affairs to the dictation of others. Her parents have lived their lives; Susan must live hers. Since life was less complex for them than it has been for her, they can merely suggest. They are just as powerless as we to portray a detailed future. When Mr. and Mrs. Lee married they thot they knew each other well, but, if you just question them for a moment, they will assure you that many modes of behavior not at all glimpsed during courtship, gained expression later on. They will tell you that even now, tho well acquainted, they don't know each other thoroly They believed their love to be genuine and even themselves to be so; and life has been according to their faith."

"Thelma," said Susan, somewhat abasht that she had become the topic for discussion, "there is much truth in what you've said. As evidence of my appreciation, let me assure you that I will reflect upon it tonight. I will try to be more self-propelled.

"But have we not neglected the chief purpose of our visit, in going thus astray?" came an utterance more atune with her eager nature. "Reverend Smith," she pronounced it with firmness, "we have come to offer you congratulations on that extraordinary address, extraordinary in its bold heroism and in its heralding the dawn of a new era."

"Yes, Reverend Smith," said Thelma with the firmness of Susan, "accept our hearty congratulations. We treasured every word you spoke. I think you know that the zeal of the young people of the Church is not so great as that of the old. It is due to preaching to a new generation— as you said —wisdom suited for the past. You come with a frank statement of the matter, bringing to your command the philosophy of the East and the West. And we enjoyed it, tho Susan was at times shockt. We can't merely live in the past, we must have a part of the present and the future. Besides, provincialism must pass, to let cosmopolitanism have the day. The learning of our fathers or of all America is insufficient, we must learn of all people of all the earth."

"This is well said, but what are the utterances of the people generally?" askt the divine. "Tho I dared to face the Convention, I have not visited a home. That may be quite a different experience."

"The older people," Susan affirmed, "are almost a unit against you. Still some of them believe that such thots as yours must have a hearing. These merely wonder whether the time is quite ripe for such. They do say, however, that the untrained and the narrowly trained ministers have too long swayed our people, that now, since the great issues of our great national life require unusual thinkers for their solution, the educated minister must be heard."

"It is needless to say," interrupted Thelma, "that the younger set is with you fully."

"Many of the younger set, however, are not in the Church," Rev. Smith said, "Consequently I don't have their support or I may say that their good wishes amount to little right now."

"If you were here," remarkt Susan, lowering her eyes tenderly, "don't you know we should crowd your church? Your appeal was for life and we need life."

"Probably you're right, for should I keep hammering away, I'd get them eventually any way." He changed the conversation a little, holding up the completed sketch. "Well, what do you think of it. It is yours to condemn."

"I think it truly exquisite. Then to think how quickly you have done this! You're more than a dilettante," said Susan.

"Yes, it is a remarkable sketch," was Thelma's remark.

"Let's start an art gallery," Susan said in jest.

"Yes," responded Thelma, "my collection will be at your disposal."

"And mine."

"And mine."

"But let's return to the point," requested Thelma, "Smith, I'd like to know if you preach at Seaton as you did at the convention."

"Yes, I do. However, I don't touch so many issues in one discourse, as I did at the Convention. With one issue before me calling for advancement, I speak with vigor; and as I do so I point to the new, I point forward," was Smith's reply.

"I so much wish that you could be in Williamsburg regularly," declared Susan with a melody of tone that generally compelled conviction. "How we should appreciate all your work."

"I may come," said Smith laughingly, resigning himself for any happening. "I may be forced to some other field."

"Who would be so bold as to try?" inquired Thelma, fully aware that William would not be bullied about.

"Ministers." William replied. "Because I know this, I have been trying to conclude whether I sould enter another field or not."

Here he met distinct opposition. Both young ladies were firmly against his leaving the ministry completely. They felt that he might give most of his time to something else for a while, but not long. They wanted him never to lose an opportunity to preach, to do pastoral work or enter biblical discussions.

"William," said Susan with an impressive look, almost with a plea, " remember that you are specially trained for the ministry. Remember that you are better qualified to do this work, I believe, than any man in the state. Pilgrim is with you, God has called you, and you can not turn back."

"Yes, William," said Thelma, "Susan is right. You can't forsake your calling. An educated man can do more than one thing as a means of livelihood. So you need no defense. If Seaton doesn't want you, return to your home town and go to work. Do anything for a living. We'll think no less of you. The truth is we'll admire you the more. Start a mission of your own. Hundreds are waiting to follow you."

The conversation went on until dusk. When it was about time for the girls to go home, William said, "Girls, I hope you have spent a pleasant evening and accomplisht the purpose of your call. You have heartened me with inspiration. You have shown the way. Now I know what I shall do.

"Your coming is indeed a compliment."

"Under ordinary circumstances, we should have waited. We could not talk with you long on the day of the last session, because you had to hurry away. As some were against you, we thot it should not be necessary for you to seek your friends. We thot your friends should come to you. So we are following our philosophy."

William walkt with the girls to their homes that evening, throbbing in his every vein with new life. He had the freshness of a first spring morning after a weary winter, and the gladness of a soul set free. What a blessing, he thot, that we have women! What a joy to be a part of them! Trials might arise with the morning, but women force them soon to take wing.

"God bless them," said William as he strolled homeward, "there is just one course for me to pursue."

CHAPTER IX.

Be still sad heart and cease repining,
Behind the dark cloud is the sun still shining;
Thy fate is the common fate of all.
Into each life some rain must fall;
Some days must be dark and dreary.—Longfellow

"Must I be carried to the skies
    On flowery beds of ease,
Whilst others fought to win the prize
    And sailed thru bloody seas?

"Since I must fight if I would reign,
    Increase my courage Lord.
I'll bear the toil endure the pain,
    Supported by Thy word."

News of the ouster of Rev. Smith by the recent state convention came to Seaton as an astonishment. It was difficult at first to make the people understand why their idol had fallen; but when some of William's utterances had been communicated to them, apart from their setting and with bias, the people concluded that the convention should be sustained. Since the markt gentleman was popular and magnetic, they knew that spasmodic and scattered efforts to remove him, however indignant they themselves might be, would avail nothing. Accordingly the foremost among them fomented designs to force the prodigal to depart or return as he went out. Apparently the pastor of Sinai Shrine was resolved to let them have their way, for he did not return to his pulpit until the second Sunday after the convention. Thus he took all the time allowed for his vacation.

When he reacht the thrifty, little town, his sermon was already prepared. In order to avoid contact with many of the people, he arrived on the midnight train. Thus he was able quietly to go home and obtain a good rest before the ordeal of the next day.

Shortly before time for the service, he started for Church. He became interested on the way in surveying the passersby. What were their thots? What did they think of him? There was certainly no change in the words of greeting, no lessening of the vigorous handshake. How could they be Christian and act otherwise? If these same people could lay loving hands upon the wicked, those who had not pledged themselves to follow Christ, how could they withhold this consideration from one truly born of God and specially set apart to do His work? There was, however, a difference in their countenances. True Rev. Smith was to be chastized but it was to be the chastisement of God.

Preparations had been made for his home coming. Each minister of the convention pastoring at Seaton, being almost ultra-conservative and therefore unanimously opposed to William's views, to let the town know in a formal way that they were a unit, had decided to preach on a designated Sunday from the same text, "Beware of false prophets." This was to be one week before Rev. Smith's return. The following Sunday they preacht the text, "Dust shall be the serpent's meat." They argued that God the same yesterday, today, and forever never deserted his own. He had been their dwelling place thru all generations and lo, he would be with them always even to the end of the world. Thru the darkest days of slavery, thru the perilous reconstruction, they had walkt with God and God with them. How could He desert them now, when they believed in Him. Furthermore, the ministers urged that, since Rev. Smith had departed from the old doctrines, he had forfeited his right to leadership. Thus they were resolved to wrest it from him. At each congregation the majority of the members voiced the approval of the united effort.

Tho unaware that this sermon was being preacht from the pulpit of his colleagues, yet somehow divining such, Rev. Smith uttered the final one. Pervaded with the opposition of the state ministry and with the cooling inspiration of Susan and Thelma, he sensed what was going on elsewhere. He chose, therefore, the familiar text, "He shall be like a tree planted by the rivers of water, that bringeth forth its fruit in its season." He told his members what had occurred at Williamsburg and that probably while he was giving his remarks, he was being denounced in the neighboring churches. He had always had a good attendance, but on this particular morning, large numbers were standing. The surplus had come not to worship, but merely to observe what would happen.

Notwithstanding the fact that they had come out of curiosity, William was happy to see them. Since they had very likely heard only one side, he thot he owed it to Seaton to present the other, for they were all followers of Christ; and tho they might go in different directions, they would finally assemble at the same place.

The gist of the sermon was this. "Trees are of various sorts; and even trees of the same species differ. Of even the commonest trees abut us, the maple and the oak, you can find no two alike. They differ because the environments of these are not the same. A tree near a stream is bound to be richer than one away from such.

"The tree near the rivers of water is likely also to be long-lived.

"It gives fruit not prematurely, nor when it is too late; it bringeth forth its fruit in due season.

"Finally, drought will sometimes reach other trees, but the leaves of this tree shall not wither. God has said it and it must be so.

"In applying the text, I have in mind all people, but because of recent momentous events particularly all ministers. I do not even exclude myself.

"The tree is man. The water is thot. The river is immensity. Like trees we differ because of different parents and different associations. If we are planted: that is, established so as not to be moved, if we are grounded in the immensities of thot not only of the few men who wrote the Bible, but the thot of men of India, of Egypt, Persia and other lands; in the thot that not only of the past and of the present, we are richer than they who have only the thot of one land and that of the past. We communicate the thot we have thus received inspired by God. Those having little give little, those having much give much.

"Remember the rivers move on and no one can bathe in the same stream twice. Thus the tree by the water ever has fresh food and gives luxurious fruit. So it is with man; a life fed on stale food naturally stagnates."

In closing, Rev. Smith became very personal. His hearers had been deeply swayed, for tho they had harkened to some machinations of the throng, they had to commend a personality. "On Tuesday night," he said, "the Church will meet and decide as to whether I am to be re-elected or not. May your judgment not fail you! Nothing will change my attitude toward you. I have served you faithfully in the greatest and I will serve you equally in the least.

"Because I have ever lookt for better things even before I was called to the ministry, and before I came here, I can not now use the other thing. I may not have brot forth fruit recently in its season, but the fruit hitherto was always strictly on time. I am, have been, and ever shall be a tree planted by the rivers of water. I stand for progress; I will move abreast of the times. I will always bring forth the new that is worth while, if I can find it. And as the years change, so will I. This may mean that you will not want me, but God does. I can go elsewhere. I am a minister not only in the pulpit but out of it.

"This is a serious moment, but serious moments must come and with them defeat or victory. However, I can not believe that I was born to fail; my mother has suffered too much to give me birth. She came of a tribe of African stock, that knew nothing but ultimate achievement. What one may now call defeat may eventually be attainment. Does not defeat often prove to be real success? Of course. Today we fail, and so tomorrow and tomorrow. But do we yield? Not at all. Cloud and fog fast fall upon us, we pine and grieve, we languish amidst forgetting folk. Still we try. At last when we have nearly despaired, convinced that our efforts were in vain, we have achieved the coveted renown. Sunshine came after rain, rejoicing after sorrowing. What seemed defeat was a glorious victory."

When William left the pulpit at the close of the services, he noticed some of the older folk who had usually lingered to shake his hand, did not stay this afternoon. The faces of many showed signs of disappointment, for these expected denial or retraction. Since neither came forth in his discourse, here and there disapproval was strongly exhibited. Strangers could not have discerned it; but the members could. The deacons omitted the social chat and merely attended to the business of the day. This added to the omission of an invitation to dinner from the elderly people distinctively indicated what should be. The younger people were for him, but not the others. But in William's heart there was malice towards none.

CHAPTER X.

It is not prosperity, but adversity that proves the man—
Bacon

Several months after William had resigned the pastorate
of Sinai Shrine, the ministerial conference assembled in extraordinary session. The divines thot they had played a trump
when they swayed the members to vote not to re-elect the
young pastor. The battle, however, was far from being won.
Smith had taken a more strategic position, as it were. He had
found employment in the public schools. To discuss this was
the business of their meeting. They had approacht the principal and superintendent in vain, now they desired to find a
way to reach the members of the School Board.

At the appointed hour the conference opened and proceeded with dispatch. Having finisht the preliminaries with
unusual expedition, the president called for the new business.
All faces were resolute, radiant with an understanding of what
they were to do. Tho devotionals had been greatly curtailed,
the more energetic ministers seemed restive. They were happy,
however, in their responsibility, happy in their confidence.

Acknowledged leaders of the community, they were very
eager to keep and get all possible distinction. With this in
mind, Rev. Canty, pastor of Christ's Church, arose and said,
"Mr. President, you know our business. We are here to decide upon ways and means of removing a great annoyance.
We succeeded in effecting Rev. Smith's resignation, but that
is all. He is yet in town and worse than that he is teaching
in the public schools. There he will get the children of all
our churches and with his heresay lead them to destruction."

Rev. Matthews, pastor of Hebron here interrupted, saying, "Pardon me, Rev. Canty, I'm just as desirous as you to re-

move any nuisance; but I'm not here to throw mud. If we speak the truth, we must admit that Rev. Smith is at least a gentleman. A man like him is not going to lead anyone to destruction; he will undoubtedly teach doctrines incompatible with our faith, but he will not ruin a life."

As this wsa a round table argument, the President allowed them almost absolute sway in determining who should speak and what should be the time permitted. This was a fortunate circumstance for those of the opposition, when Doctor Matthews made his startling remark. Thus there followed considerable heated discussion, for the prevailing feeling was that Smith should not be in the schools. True the schools were undenominational, yet the pastors strongly believed that the man of their condemnation was too good a preacher, too thotful and inspiring, not to win a following among the youth.

"Didn't he make of the poorest young peoples' meeting in town the largest and most interesting?" inquired Rev. Young, impressive of voice and bearing, and long pastor of Saint Johns.

"We must concede that he understands youth, being much nearer to them than any of us," remarkt Rev. Canty, pained by the truth of it. "Hence we are compelled to remove the menace. As a plan of carrying our point, I suggest that we preach a special sermon to our people in order to have them, in continuous streams, voice their disapproval to the principal, who I am sure, would then suggest that Rev. Smith would go elsewhere. If we get him out of the public schools, that would be enough. We should have accomplisht our aim and should be willing to stop there."

"Would you stop there?" said Rev. Lester, the venerable pastor of Seaton, a man loved almost equally by all the groups; radicals, progressives, and conservatives. "I should like to know anyhow why you are bringing up this action against the

young man. For he has acted like a prince. I defy anyone to
mention an instance of his reproaching or rebuking us. Mention his utterance against us." All were silent.

"Why preach a sermon against him?" he resumed. "To
act as we did some months ago would be shameful and in-
famous. Think of all the ministers preaching from one text!
What a disgrace! How bitterly I have regretted it ever since!
We all say that we are inspired by God. Then tell me, pray,
how often has he inspired any two of us to preach the same
text on the same Sunday. As we are different, we are inspired
to different thots, altho by the same God. If we should repeat that act, where would be the inspiration? God would not
be in it. It would come from Satan, from malice and not from
love. But what is the basis of your complaint?"

"This is our grievance and a sore one," said Rev. Young,
who like Rev. Canty felt that something should quickly be
done. "Rev. Smith approved a dance in school."

"What can we charge concerning that?" inquired Rev.
Lester. "What you have just said would be a just reason for
unfrocking a minister, but you've already done that for a
less sufficient cause. Rev. Smith is no pastor. You know that;
he's simply a teacher. Besides, if you are going to take from
the public schools all those teachers who either dance or approve of dancing, you wouldn't have anybody to carry on the
work. In many of the high schools of the country, boys and
girls dance together without offense. I remember having seen
such in Washington, D. C., Chicago, and New York.

"Gentlemen, you are well aware that I'm ready to attack
vice without delay; but I do believe in meeting it properly. In
the case of dancing that is vicious, I'm ready to attack it now;
but is the dancing which is conducted in public schools vicious?
If it is, we have been asleep for many years. We have allowed it to become a part of the curriculum of all first-class

public schools and many private ones. It is in the kindergarten, the grades, and the high schools. If this is our grievance, it is not Rev. Smith we should attack, but those who are responsible for its being a required feature of the school program.

"Let us injure no *man,* especially one who has been true to us under our machinations. Some day he'll be among us again. He's coming back. I have the faith."

"Probably that is not a just ground for complaint; still I felt that one called of God should not approve a dance," resumed Rev. Young. "One other grievance, however, remains. Rev. Smith is calling our childrens' attention to love, whereas we should like for them to postpone it as long, as long as possible."

At this point there was universal consternation. Some opened their mouths and kept them so for a while. Others uttered excoriating sighs. Some rose. Others sat in uneasy chairs. The president at once proceeded to get order. In the midst of this confusion, to the dire astonishment of all, Rev. Smith came in and greated them good morning.

Why had he come? That was the question. When certain that our plans are well laid, that they are the consummation of hours of patient reflection, there rises within us the certainty that, come what will, they can not miscarry. Since they were contrived in secret, they would continue in secret until the time deemed convenient for their execution. For the inconceivable to happen, for premature opposition to get the right of way, our ministers were not prepared.

Rev. Canty, who had been most tenacious in his contention, at once revealed the greatest loss of self-possession. He was wholly taken off his guard. Under such circumstances, if some one else acts first and then the stern aggressor is given a few moments to himself for reflection or a thrust, he would come back with another almost irresistable onslaught. So the chief accuser was placed. Rev. Canty hoped that just for an instant Rev. Young or someone else would take the initiative. He could not recall when he had been so much disturbed as he was then. Why did not some proper utterance or event detract his thots from himself? Why could he not continue to think out a resistance? Had he been basically wrong, had he been unjust? What spell was this? Why could he not speak? Why was the moderator tongueless? Why did Rev. Smith just await the ministers' bidding?

The young man whose career had been challenged stood a master diplomatist, silent to the dismay of all. Calmly and patiently he surveyed his accusers, as if thru telepathy striving to divine their purposes. Not a face wore a welcome, and distant were the smiles. Since he was flayed an incongruity and labeled a malefactor, let those with just complaints lodge them in his presence.

Rev. Canty wondered how William learned of the meeting. He soon dismist the thot tho. It was not a question of how the young man came there, but how ought they dispose of him. The arch-aggressor, because the others failed to act, knew they were waiting on him. Any dereliction on his part, he felt might be positively detrimental to his designs. After a few moments of unnerving silence, Rev. Canty, to get his bearings went to a window near by and raised it as far as it would go. The place was not in need of ventilation, as any one present would have testified. Not the body but the mind was ill at ease. Just as the sash went up, a woman, jubilant and robust, passed by with a basket of clothes upon her head. And as she walkt along, with a voice of overwhelming sweetness, she sang this old familiar tune:

> "Must I be carried to the skies
> On flowery beds of ease,
> Whilst others fought to win the prize
> And sailed thru bloody seas?

> "Since I must fight if I would reign,
> Increase my courage Lord.
> I'll bear the toil endure the pain,
> Supported by Thy word."

The ministers listened rapt on every word. Rev. Canty beckoned for the ministers to observe the singer. Thus the spell was broken. "How remarkably God consoles even the worst of us!" he said. "We never have greater burdens than we can bear. But let us return to business." The pastors soon returned to the conference, eager to bring it speedily to a close. When all were seated, Rev. Canty said with much spleen, "Mr. President, this young man, a markt individual, has overstept many proprieties by coming here. Brother Moderator, I demand an explanation."

The President, having no desire to delay the crisis, without ado askt Rev. Smith to make a statement.

"Gentlemen, since you desire it, I will make a statement," said the former pastor of Sinai Shrine with a smile that bespoke an unconcern as to what had been planned against him. "I have come to be at your service." Then he sat down.

This was another surprise, for very few were satisfied. Rev. Canty, now himself again, became persistent. "Doctor," he contended, "the distinguisht gentleman conducts himself rather obscurely. What does he mean? He has convinced us that his sphere is different from ours; and yet he comes among us. What effrontery some men will have! When will they learn that some conventionalities are sacred? Gentlemen, it is almost impossible for me to understand it."

As he spoke, Rev. Smith lookt at almost everyone present, trying to grasp unspoken thot. He was certain that the ministers were not neutral, that either they were for him or against him. When Rev. Canty paused, William arose with his accustomed grace, positive and assertive. With his clarion voice that easily filled the assembly room, he said, "I was not aware that you held secret meetings. Hitherto, not only ministers but laymen of any denomination have been permitted to come. Then why should I be unwelcome?" The situation was fully comprehended by him.

"Rev. Smith, our meetings are not secret," put in the President determined at all hazards to lay the matter bare, "yet when we go into extraordinary session, until our plans have been well formed, we prefer not to clash with opposing forces out side of our group."

"Yet, often the clash might be indefinitely posponed, if the individual likely to confront you contrarily would be with you at least awhile," interrupted Rev. Smith.

"We have assembled to organize plans to have you modify your teaching. You have disturbed us, annoyed us, bored us. Not satisfied with making many of our members disgruntled, you seek to make fickle all our young, or lead astray the conscientious." Rev. Canty was angry and made the young devine feel it.

"Something of this nature had come to my ears, as I visited some of my former members. I learned that some parents were told by their children that I had discussed love affairs in school. Some probably thot that I was urging their children to marry prematurely, when nothing was farther from my purpose. They evidently did not understand me. You do not understand, yet ignorant of the situation, you seize upon this as a basis for having me removed from my position.

"Do not for a moment be deceived. If you can get me out of a position, I hope you will enjoy the accomplishment.

I am not here to ask you play hands off. As I said at first, I came to help. Gentlemen, do not forget that you are God's chosen. Do not debase yourselves. Do only what is right. My business in the world is to make people happy by being good and helping them to be the same. Since even ministers are sometimes mischievous and you may be so now, I have come not to make you uncomfortable, but to serve you."

"Well, let us have the service," thundered Rev. Canty very impatiently. "And don't be long about it. Our time is valuable."

"I'd at least be courteous," replied William with his accustomed grace.

"Rev. Canty, be silent," said the President. "I think I have charge of this meeting. Let Rev. Smith proceed."

When the President, gained control once more, William resumed his remarks. "I was teaching Tennyson's 'Idylls of the King.' Have you read them, gentlemen?"

Of twenty pastors present only four knew of the book.

Here the young divine related the story and proceeded to discuss it as he had presented it in class save for the literary merit. "The idyl which has occasioned the present altercation is called 'Lancelot and Elaine.' Lancelot, the favorite knight of a noble king, by several remarks incited Elaine, a beautiful, simple maiden to love him—a man of fifty-four, a girl of eighteen. She askt him do her a favor—to wear a pledge as he fought at a tournament. This request was equivalent to asking him to wear an engagement ring. After he was wounded, she nursed him back to health. To reward her, he instructed her to speak the wish nearest to her heart. Since he told her that in wearing the pledge, tho to disguise himself, he had never before done so much for any woman, she naturally thot she was preferred above all. She spoke her dearest

wish, which was to become his wife. When he rejected her
love, she askt to follow him around the world. He said 'that
could not be.'

"Then he offered her land. This she would not accept.
At length he left her without saying goodbye.

"Whether this classic should be taught to high school pu-
pils, I am not prepared to judge. Superiors in making the
course of study have deemed it a proper work. As a member
of the teaching staff, I am pledged to teach it."

"But what was your interpretation," inquired Rev. Canty
with a jerk, for he wanted the good or ill done quickly.

"I said that if a young man had made overtures of the
same kind as those of Lancelot to one of our young women, she
would have spoken the wish nearest her heart. Very likely.
If this request to be the wife had been rejected, however, our
young lady would not have askt anything else. Why then did
Elaine entreat it? Why did she have to die? This was my
answer."

The ministers were intensely interested. "Elaine lived not
in a great city nor one of middle size. Society was rural, thus
the houses were far apart. She lackt a mother and all that
such possession implies—motherly counsel and else. Reared
apart from girls and deprived of association with many young
men, she clove to the first she saw, with affection for no one
else. If she had had the privilege of our girls of today as in
public schools, to be in class with boys, to see them in the halls
and talk with many, she would have been forced to make a
choice and her love would not have been of the dangerous
sort that cannot survive a refusal. Elaine's was purely a case
of unguided love. Such was my interpretation to try to prevent the occurance of Elaines."

"Doctor, you have a silvery tongue," said Rev. Canty with

a slur, "I'm glad you've come. We shall consider your explanation for its worth."

"Gentlemen, as I have already said," responded William, apparently unaffected by the sneer of Rev. Canty, "I live not to injure but to help. Is your life purpose the same? Are you trying to help or to injure me? If my being at Douglass High School, retards the progress of the community or if it must prevent my aiding the people as I deem I should, I can leave. But do not think I will leave the state. My career has been determined by this vicinity and until I have spent an equal number of years in service as payment for my debt to those at hand, my ear is deaf to other fields." His attitude was a challenge. He arose once more and lookt about the assembly. Then he concluded thus, "I hope I have been of service. May God bless you!" He departed almost as unexpectedly as he had come.

The latter part of the next month found Rev. William Smith practicing law at Seaton, yet not unharrassed by many pastors. Since few of the members of the churches brot their legal problems to his office, tho he had been well recommended by the State Bar Association, he thot that the Ministerial Alliance had not acted exactly right. They opposed him as minister, teacher, and lawyer. Could they not distinguish between the man and the office? Must personality enter in? Regardless of all ill feeling, he would continue his practice at least until spring, when he would decide upon a permanent work. Then it would be a plunge into a weltering flood, to sink or swim, survive or perish.

One day in January—several months after the conference —when the blinding snow was reminding the improvident of their follies, Reverends Smith and Canty met in front of Sinai Shrine. Tho it was rather cold, William removed his glove.

Rev. Canty did the same. They shook hands vigorously. Many happy recollections and bitter memories forced themselves to view. "Rev. Canty," said William calmly, but with a pleasing defiance, "you have now exhausted your devices—at least against me. I have decided to return to the ministry. Tho at first a great portion of my time will be devoted to pastoral work, I shall preach regularly. I will rise among you and *you* shall hear from me." The lawyer would not stay for a reply.

CHAPTER XI.

All that is wrong concerning him is paraded before the world in such a way as to involve the whole race, irrespective of merit or demerit, while his worthier acts go unnoticed—the heroic efforts of thousands of them to render aid and benevolent assistance to yet other thousands on the inferior planes of life; the daily industry of millions in domestic service, on the fields, in the varied vocations of business, in the schools, churches, and on the fields of missionary endeavor; the Negros' ambition shown in the purchase of lands from earnings eked from the most exacting economy, in the establishment and maintenance of libraries, in the founding of publishing houses, and in the establishing of good homes—who knows of these things?
—Riley.

The issue will be settled in the Spring. The birds will come again in the Spring. Smith will attain a grandeur he can not see, in the Spring, the jubulant Spring.

The months that lay before William were passing slowly, weary months of anxiety. He had before him ambitions which could not crystalize, until the long nights had past away. This by no means meant that he was not working; for he well proportioned his time for systematic endeavor, interspersed with timely recreation. Like a general amassing a wealth of munitions and supplies, numbers of men, and bounteous information for many days before launching a campaign, William zealously planned his preliminaries not only for an effective organization, but for sure success.

During these days he wondered how he might spend the bulk of his leisure moments. Should he break other customs or should he for the interim permit the right of way to any who sought to enter it? Was there now or had there been a demand for strict conformity? Did the wavering of the masses or the bigotry of the clergymen taking advantage of his seeming indifference expect a departure of any sort that would prove them right and him wrong? The ministers, rigid

104

as they were, were in a state of flux. The people mobile and fickle, awaited the dominant will which would sway them to pleasure or to ruin. Was he the posessor of that dominant will?

Such were William's thots one wintry morning as he lookt from his abode upon the hurry of busy folk, enroute to the factory a few miles off, to get the fruits of honest toil.

The day was cold but not offensive; for tho worn countenances exhibited many cares, each face was bright with the gleam of morning. The younger folk, smiling and buoyant, were as free as the bare trees bidding the skies good day. Yet coats were buttoned snugly; scarfs tho wantonly flying in the sportive air kept themselves about the necks of the willing workers. I can not say that there was a cadence, but there was a regularity of movement indicative of resolute people. Here were comedy and melodrama galore. Was there also tragedy?

Turning towards the table our lawyer noticed "The Williamsburg Post," which had come in the night before. He scanned the news of the previous day until he came to the society columns, for he was eager to know not only of those in places of potency, but even of the plainer folk. The events were not out of the ordinary. There had been the accustomed number of births, deaths and marriages. In brief, all was going well. Yet one announcement engaged him especially, that of a party to be given at the home of Mrs. Annelle in behalf of her goddaughter, Letitia Strauss. It was the linen shower, the happy precursor of Letitia's marriage. William wondered why he should be so obtuse as to have forgotten it, the opportunity to see and greet many old friends anew. The welcome of many now might be cold, rigid, or rebukingly artificial; yet they would be glad to see him. He belonged to them, they belonged to him—each had contributed freely to make the other what he was. At this party he would find them, some with antipathies born of his religious breach and others with adoration for his courage. Should he go? There was his place, there was his treasure, and there was his heart.

Since Susan, Thelma, and Letitia were upon the most intimate terms, he became promptly aware that he would be expected. "If I'm going," he said to himself, having reflected a while, "I must obtain a worthy gift. To make a proper selection I should start now rather than wait until I arrive at Williamsburg. I have so much business to adjust today, that I can leave only on the late train. This would not allow sufficient time for a choice in Williamsburg. I must, therefore, make the purchase before going to my office."

Laying the paper aside, he turned again towards the window. The workers steadily moved on. This time he noticed particularly groups of men and women conversing with evident hilarity. Besides, girls and boys were following in their train. Were they equally happy? The frequent, zealous glance at each other, the hearty laughs, and the equipoise with which they passed assuredly reflected a satisfaction, which is one of the joys of life. Here *certainly were comedy and melodrama*. Was there also tragedy?

Wrapping himself securely, with an air of calm defiance, William stept into the street and joined the happy throng. Before him was the work of the day, together with thots of the following evening. However, he had not gone far from his home when he noticed in the street a little urchin of three years, a child of poverty. Hatless and almost shoeless, for several toes had burst their prisons to get an icy freedom, without a coat, with ropes for suspenders, with jacket and trousers tattered and unkempt, this lad was running directly down the street to obtain a rubber ball that seemingly would not stop. Rapidly approaching not far away, swerving from side to side with reckless speed, came an automobile. Two young men, easily recognized as the reprobate sons of the chief manufacturer of Seaton, wantons who put no premium on human life, occupied the front seat. Neither said anything to the other, yet with the same momentum, the car came on. They evidently failed to see the child. If they saw, they did not care, for no signal was given by horn, bell, or voice to warn the joyful, little lad.

Several persons saw the danger, among this number was William Smith. He shouted at once to the driver to avoid the boy. Did he hear? Evidently not, for the automobile now was speeding faster than ever. Suddenly the child stopt, waved a good bye to his mother, who was on her way to earn his daily bread. It reminded our lawyer of the gladiatorial greeting. "We who are about to die salute you." Upon hearing her name called the mother turned. At once she saw the danger and shriekt.

What should be done? Would not some one with great courage risk his life for the child? For attempt or rescue meant death or just bare escape. Quick must be the decision and quick the effort. The mother started for the merry lad but was restrained by several women at her side. She struggled to go, but fortunately they held on. They knew that at her home there were two daughters who needed a mother living, and not dead. Which did the community need the more, the mother or the child? With these gallant women there was but one answer.

Faster and faster came the vehicle. Now the young fellow stoopt to pick up his ball; then he sat down to toss it. Shouts and cries from many troubled breasts sought to warn both child and driver. Yet neither seemed to heed it in the least. How in a crisis we may be entranced to defiance or indifference!

When William observed this combat between reckless-ness and innocence, convinced that action must be speedy, he wondered whether he was sufficiently quick of foot to make the rescue and escape. Then came the thot that this was a white child. Should he be willing to die even for it? Well trained as he was to lead a slighted race, should he give his life for this one child of the race that scorned him or save it for the millions of his race who loved him? If this had been his child, and if a white man, filled with the hope of millions, hap-pened to pass that way, would he sacrifice his life for a little black lad of poverty? He quickly reacht his conclusion. He was living his life for man. It was not a question of white or black, but where could he serve humanity. Here was a chance.

He remembered that he had been a sprinter in college, having won many a hundred yard dash. He had always run as if it were a matter of life or death, in order that his alma mater might have the glory of splendid achievement. Once he had fallen at the finish, exhausted; but he had won. Now, however, he was out of practice. Still this could be no de-termining factor. Before him at last was his first actual race for life or death. The others had been races with human beings; this was a race for a human being—the greatest prize that all the world could give. Because it was an unusual race, many of his college tactics were of little avail. Upright he was to dash with his greatest rapidity until within a few yards of the little lad: when he must stoop and run low without lessening speed, seize the child and carry him to safety.

As the automobile had not been heard, the same should be true of him; lest the child frightened by a sudden and un-expected approach should run towards the vehicle to certain death. Like a flying meteor, this stalwart, black prince dashed ahead. Faster and faster he speeded on, faster and faster came the demon. How could a human being outstrip a miracle of mechanical ingenuity? Nearer and nearer they came to each other. Finally William reacht the lad and seized him, without the little fellow's having been aware of his approach. The automobile was just a little more than a yard away when he graspt the tender boy. He made one step to escape with his prize. Then the vehicle struck his hindmost leg and whirled him round. He fell and the car hurled by. Shrieks and curses rose from the anxious and horrified onlookers. They grieved to see their champion fall. When the dust had settled, there could be seen death's challenger, lying on the ground—unconscious and bleeding. The tattered child, however, stood calmly at his side wondering what had occurred.

The mother took her child and fondled him. Speedily she sought to thank William, but he was motionless. She put her babe aside, then lifted the head of the gallant, young man and began to apply her handkerchief to staunch his blood. By this time many workers were about her. "Take him to my house," she urged. Most of those present wanted him carried to the drug store, but she insisted that he be given a soft place to lie and that a physician be called. Her request prevailed. Thereupon she dispatched this message to her employer, "Tell Mr. Davenport that I shall be late today. Let him know of this accident. I'm sure it will be all right."

It was not long before a physician came. A few minutes were sufficient to revive William and dress his wounds. His injuries were a wrencht ankle and several severe bruises, almost cuts, along the side of his head. As soon as this had been done, the mother thankt him because he had braved so much. She took him in her arms to help him sit, ministered to him in various ways, and enlisted the willing service of those about her. Here the barriers of centuries were broken down. True, he who had dared was black; but he was a man for all that.

Slowly he regained his strength. About a half hour after he had been brot to the house he felt that he was himself once more. Then he askt if anyone had seen his overcoat. It was handed him, neatly brusht. The lady of the house tried to have him stay longer; but he informed her that he had much to do that day. She wisht he might rest. Now about to go, he askt for an old cane or a stick, with which to support himself. A stick was quickly put into his hand. A few minutes later, he donned his overcoat, thankt those who had attended him, and limpt away.

Tho the mother entreated his name and address, he would not tell. However, when he pulled out his muffler a tiny case fell on the floor. When he had gone, the gentle lady picked it up. She could not tell how it came there, nor could she guess what it was. Upon opening it, she saw several cards. She took one and read it. It ran thus, "Rev. William Smith, Attorney at Law, Room 391 Booker T. Washington Building." She rejoiced to know who had rescued her child.

CHAPTER XII.

The fountains mingle with the river
And the rivers with the ocean,
The winds of heaven mix forever
With a sweet emotion;
Nothing in the world is single,
All things by a law divine
In one another's being mingle—
Why not I with thine?

See the mountains kiss high heaven,
And the waves clasp one another;
No sister-flower would be forgiven
If it disdained its brother:
And the sunlight clasps the earth,
And the moonbeams kiss the sea—
What are all these kissings worth,
If thou kiss not me?—Shelley.

The guests assembled promptly at the home of Mrs. Annelle, to inspire and make happy one of the most genteel girls of Williamsburg. As they stept into the spacious hall, specially designed for social functions, their smiling countenances bespoke the praise of this stately maiden, Letitia Strauss, who had determined to know the best of life. Her rhythmic gait enhanced by a silk of old rose commanded the attention of all.

The people there were truly joyous. Magic ditties which seemed to come out of Fairyland, dances old and new, alluring games, and intermittent feats elicited praise for the jollity of life. How excellent it was to live!

After the second dance, Henry Lee called his sister to one side. Thelma and Letitia, thinking that it was not a matter requiring privacy, came also, merely to gather the news. They were following a basic instinct, and in this they knew they could not err. When they had reacht the drawing-room with its brilliancy and oriental trimmings, the girls seated themselves about a table, embellisht with artistic carving. Henry placed before them a newspaper, "The Seaton Post," nointed to the article he wanted them to read, and then stood opposite them to enjoy divining their thots by observing their facial expression.

"I had meant for it to be a secret," he smiled, "but since you all have come, I'm willing that it be an open secret. What do you think of it?"

"Yes, what must we think of it?" said Thelma. "Don't crowd. Give us all a chance to look. No, it will be better for just one to read. Susan you can do this very well. Read for us all."

Susan read, "A DARING RESCUE BY A NEGRO, REV. WILLIAM SMITH, BARRISTER OF SEATON. He riskt his life for a child of one of our poorest families—a lad of two years. When we think that this man, so dear to his race, should take the chance he did for a member of that group which commonly looks upon his people with scorn and spite, we hope that there will come out of this adventure a closer relationship between the white and darker breeds of men. Rev. Smith is no common man. Had he been killed, his race would have suffered a great loss; for look where you may, you will not find in our environs one who has accomplisht so much as he in developing a lasting friendship between the two racial groups." The article then went into detail concerning the whole incident and commended the stand of the mother. The young people listened almost breathlessly.

There was not intermittent comment. When they had finisht, they first lookt at each other. Then Thelma said, "It is just like him."

"I, too, am not at all surprised," came from Susan. "I hope he isn't seriously injured."

"The paper informs us that he finally went to his office. If this is true, I'm confident that he is much better now," put in Letitia.

"Since the incident occurred yesterday morning," said Henry, "and as William has a vigorous constitution, within a few days he will be perfectly well anyway."

"We were hoping that he would be here this evening," quickly spoke Letitia, slyly glancing at Susan. "He has never missed anything like this."

"Yet," said Susan coyly, "We did hope that he would come."

Henry then displayed a yellow journal, "The Seaton Gazette." At least it was "yellow" on the Negro Question. "Girls," he remarkt with much vivacity, "here is an editorial in another paper on the same incident. You will be interested in following this, I know, for this periodical generally heralds our faults and keeps silent concerning our virtues."

They read, in this instance, with more fascination, but interspersed their perusal with spirited comment. Before they could come to the end, a familiar voice said, "Good evening, girls! How are you?" They turned and greeted William Smith. "I'm glad to be with you, once I thot I couldn't come —Why, hello! Henry, I didn't see you when I came in." Each shook the other's hand vigorously.

"Im so sorry you have to use a cane," said Susan, deeply moved by William's limping. "It's bad enough to have to wear head bandages. Doesn't your ankle pain you more than your head?" There were many smiles.

"Yes, it does. My head wounds are rather slight, even tho several stitches were necessary.

All exprest their sympathy.

"Well, old man," said Henry, "I'm glad you escaped, for we have much for you to do. I know you didn't purposely come to see me, so I'm gone. Enjoy yourself with the girls. Of course, I'll see you many times this evening and at least once tomorrow. You'll not be leaving for several days, will you?"

"I go back tomorrow night," answered William, "but as you said we'll see each other many a time before then." Henry went to find Catherine Staples, the woman of his choice. As a matter of course, she had been informed first. Her absence from the group was due to the fact that she desired to disclose the secret to others. About the first young person she met was Sinclair Young, the prospective groom and the gentleman of the evening until William came. After she had told a few, these did the rest. They were willing informers.

The news of the exploit was soon known thruout the house; and tho Smith had quietly come in, fearing a demonstration—for he knew that the events of yesterday might have got the speed of him—the people everywhere were aware of his presence. Crowding the drawing-room, they heapt upon him an avalanche of congratulations. William tried to slink out of view, but he could not. When the orchestra gave the signal for a quadrille, those who had commended him proceeded to arrange for the dance. Soon all had gone except William, Susan, Thelma and Letitia. Sinclair came for Letitia, for the dance was on. Then Beckett King came for Thelma. At first she lookt at him haughtily, as if he had been a transgressor of her peace. Then she started for the hall. As she reacht the door, she turned and said, "William, your achievement now is certain. Had any one else attempted that rescue, death would have claimed him. But you were spared, spared for us. And we are spared for you. This is the blessing of Providence."

"Why had Thelma said this?" thot Susan. "This congratulation was quite different from all the rest. It contained an appeal that went to the soul. She had noticed that Thelma was no longer deeply interested in Beckett King, and tho she would go out with him occasionally, her utterances of him no longer told of a hero-worship which was constant the summer William went South. Was that speech a challenge? The words were such as any acquaintance might have spoken, but the air with which she pronounced them was very portentous. Susan recalled the conversation on her porch the evening after that spectacular feast at Pilgrim.

Thelma had said with great frankness, speaking of girls and of William, "We all have our ambition for the noblest. And there is no sensible girl in this town who doesn't acknowledge him our best. It is a game. Be sure you play it well. If he wants you; why, you are his. If he wants me, then I am his. But at present the honor is all yours; and I am giving you the right of way." Then flashed before her another potent utterance of Thelma spoken that same evening, when she informed the girls that her mother had said, "Be patient and wait." Thelma had affirmed as a reply, "If the mother is to marry the man, let her do as she wishes. But when the time comes for me to marry and I see the man I want, I do not promise to wait. Wait? Wait for him to choose someone else, I suppose? I'll make the fight of my life to get him; there will be no escape. We'll fight it out if it takes all summer. If I lose, I will have made a good fight." The whole scene came before her like a panorama. Evidently Thelma had come to the decision that now was the time for her to marry. Probably at last she had seen the man she wanted and had resolved to fulfill her prophecy of several years past.

If Susan understood any woman other than herself, it was Thelma. She knew that the belligerency characteristic of Miss Haskell in her childhood was even with her now. The words spoken on that momentous evening were even at this time very important and prognostic. Thelma by her utterance made as she arrived at the door of the reception hall had apparently, so far as her friend was concerned, cast a bold defiance. Susan was quite aware that she must pick up the gauntlet and enter the lists. Accordingly she thot, "William *must speak tonight*."

Susan tried to analyze the feelings of the man she loved, but he was not one to wear them on his face. Then she remembered that while Thelma was speaking, she herself had not lookt at him; she had been regarding her friend, Thelma.

When all the others had gone, and at last she and William were alone, Susan led him to the divan. She desired not to be disturbed. When they were seated, she said tauntingly, "Pardon me, please, but I brot you here, taking for granted that you didn't plan to dance. Had you made any arrangement for such?"

"Susan, do not mock me. You know I'm a minister," he pleaded.

"But how liberal you are, William!" She pronounced his name with great affection. "Most ministers would do away with all laughter and enjoyment."

"People do call me liberal. I am probably, however, more practical than liberal. I see that it is instinctive for people at times to give vent to their feelings in rhythmic motion. They do this even in their religious services. Those not possessed of a strong religious fervor will dance. Such at least is my conviction. Yet I can not subscribe to unrestricted dancing. I oppose public receptions, because the people dance indiscriminately and without supervision. I have nothing to say, however, against a supervised, private dance, where one knows or may become well acquainted with all the others.

"Furthermore, if I were not a minister I—I'd ask you join me in a quadrille."

"Then, William, you think it all right for the masses to dance but not for ministers. Why shouldn't right be the same for all persons?" she inquired in the spirit of twentieth century impatience.

"So it is, tho some believe it to be otherwise. To be frank, I'd dance here tonight, if I did not believe it would interfere with some work I aim to do in the spring. Sometimes in my efforts to aid the younger folk, I see them practicing so much vulgarity with their dances, that I feel like calling upon the ministers and their wives together with other earnest church folk, to learn to dance, open a dancing school and teach our generation the beauties of rhythmic motion.

"If ministers would do this service, they would get a firm hold on their young people, such as they have never had. But for me to suggest this to them even ten years from now would be an aeroplane's dropping a bomb on an unfortified city. Yet if I enter an assembly like this two years from tonight, I will hardly miss a dance, and I will be a minister still. Bishops used to train people to dance without any lowering of their religious dignity. The same can be done today."

At this utterance, she smiled. "With eagerness I'll be waiting for those years to pass. I certainly want to see you on the floor. With whom will you take your first dance?" she inquired playfully.

"With my wife I hope."

Susan paused, questioning whether she should ask what crost her mind. Would the boldness be a sacrifice of modesty? Her mother had said wait, let the man take the initiative. She had waited long and so had Thelma. Susan delayed no longer. "Pardon me for being bold, but do you have any idea who the lady will be?" Tho she smiled again, William began to feel the sure charms of a noble woman enmeshed by many conventionalities.

"I have not decided that as yet. I do have an idea as to whom I should like for it to be. That's my principal reason for coming here tonight. I'm old enough I think at least to begin to settle the question of marriage." William had never been so confidential. Whom could he have in mind but her? But hadn't she led him on? Still if he did not mean to consider her, why did he not tactfully turn the question, to discuss some other subject? He continued confidentially. "Do you think you could dance with a minister?"

Susan somewhat bow'd her head. "If you were to leave the ministry, I'd dance with you at any time upon any occasion. Scruples would go to the winds. If you were to ask me to dance with you tonight, I think I could not. I'd beg you not to insist, and you would yield. Wouldn't you? However, if the minister, two years from tonight, should ask me to dance with him in public, I could do so. I should have prepared myself for it."

"Would you require that much time?" he askt sportively.

"I'm not sure, but I certainly could not bring myself to do so tonight, even if you were ready."

"Is there present any young woman who would do so?" Now he was teasing.

"Thelma would be so defiant, I believe." Why did she say "defiant?"

"Now tell me why you would not."

"Mother and some of the older members of Pilgrim wouldn't like it. They'd accuse me of making you fall from grace. You know I desire their benedictions."

Then turning the conversation somewhat, he said, "Susan, we met during my years in high school but casually. Towards my graduation, we did find time to establish a close friendship. The summer before I first went to college, I saw you by appointment, but not frequently."

"That was because I followed strictly the counsel of my parents. When I had made my debut, however, I became more self-propelled; but by that time you had to go away."

"You know, however, that I admired you," he spoke fondly.

"But the heart craves more than admiration."

"Then came our letters, ceasing to be formal, vividly announcing a mutual love. Since I have finisht my schooling, I have had ample opportunity to study you closely. I do not say I know you thoroly; for we can become better acquainted."

"I understand."

"I came here this evening to ask you to be my wife. Very unconventional isn't it for a minister to make a proposal of marriage at a dance?"

She admired his frankness and directness; even tho he had made it difficult for her to reply. At length she said, "And you're not going to ask?" Of course she meant the opposite. Her entire being indicated this. Her eyes spoke worlds of entreaties, to say nothing of many graces.

"I was wondering if we could be happy together." He held her hand tenderly. "Susan, there is no question in my mind about my love for you. I certainly love you more than any woman I've ever met. It is because I do love you truly that I could give you up, if by so doing I should make you happier or not less happy. I'm trying to decide whether we'd be good companions. I think the dispositions of the man and wife should be such as to make capable the blending of ideals. None will injure the object of his affections.

"My ambition is to lift my race, regardless of all opposition. I am ready to defy any organization which obstructs my way. I'm practically a reformer, as such I must from time to time change. And I will change too rapidly for those about me; consequently I may occasionally be ostracised. Could you bear this, could you share in this work, or have you been educated to stay aloof from society? My work will frequently be hazardous, indeed, at time perilous. If forced to protect your home, could you do so? Of course, I should supply you with abundant arms and ammunition.

"I mention all this, for I would not have a woman marry me for one thing and get something else. I believe in letting her see the worst of it as well as the best. You know I'm able to give you a living not in the least inferior to that you now enjoy. There will be romance, but also stern realities. I do this because I believe in marriage as a contract. As such the terms should be fully known to both, and a breach of faith should make divorce speedily obtainable."

"William, I have thot, and I believed we could be truly happy. You are indeed more radical than I, but wouldn't my love offset that?"

"Susan, I'm ready to give my life to make you happy, but I will not give it to bring you sorrow. Thus I love."

At this point, he was interrupted by someone who had just come. The stranger did not tarry long, but went promptly to the dancing hall. He had not gone many steps, before the orchestra stopt. Fearing another disturbance, he withdrew to the parlor. As soon as he reacht the place he said, "Come to the piano, Susan, and I will tell you how I feel." As he

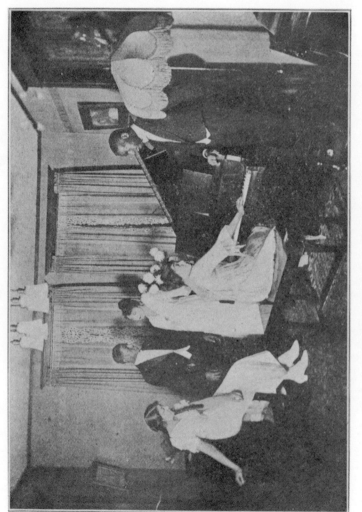

"Before he could finish the parlor was being invaded"

could not move freely among the guests, he decided upon the parlor as the place where he might be most free. He felt like singing and entered into it with zest. He lookt at her lovingly and then requested, "Play your favorite, my favorite." It was "The Rosary." Upon hearing the delicate strains, most music lovers would have felt certain that a professional was singing. So full and clear were the tones. His closing was truly a climax.

Before he could finish the parlor was once more being invaded. Mr. and Mrs. Lee had now arrived and proceeded at once to find William to congratulate him. They were glad to find him singing for Susan. Conversations flowed along variously, but ever, now and then came hints of another announcement—that of William and Susan. When the orchestra began a minuet, however, the disturbers were gone once more.

"Susan," said William, "I have told you my feelings in speech and song. I will sing you another lyric which will tell the same. You see I love you. You see I will marry you, if our temperaments are not so diverse as to prevent genuine companionship. If you think we can, let's decide now."

Why did he not positively ask her to marry him, and take the responsibility of making her happy? She would have assumed it for him, if he had only spoken as she had desired. Why did she not say anyhow, "William, we can be perfect companions; our rearing and education are not so widely diversed as to make ideal companionship impossible? You will be the best husband in the world. I will be the best wife. Isn't that enough? Let's seal it with a kiss." Society said the man should take the initiative. "Probably it is better to wait awhile," she thot. She waited.

When the music in the dance hall ceased again, William offered to sing another song—"Then You'll Remember Me." It thrilled the souls of both.

At the close of the linen shower, William walkt home with Susan, but he made no more formal proposal than that already spoken. At the door, he took her hand to bid her good night, but he did not kiss her. She wondered if he would. She hoped strongly, for she was well aware that had he kissed her, he would have proposed according to *her most exact desire*. This he did not do, but with a solemn expression and head somewhat downcast, he went home in deep reflection.

As for Susan, she feared that she would lose him, if she did not act quickly. Within three days he would return. She would claim him then.

In her chamber, almost thru the entire night, she mused upon Thelma's momentous words: "If he wants me, then I am his. But at present the honor is all yours; and I am giving you the right of way. * * * But when the time comes for me to marry and I see the man I want, I do not promise to wait. Wait? Wait for him to choose some one else, I suppose. I'll make the fight of my life to get him; there will be no escape. 'We'll fight it out if it takes all summer.' If I lose, I will have made a good fight." Had Susan made a good fight?

CHAPTER XIII.

Love, now a universal birth,
From heart to heart is stealing,
From earth to man, from man to earth:
—It is the hour of feeling.

Some silent laws our hearts will make,
Which they shall long obey:
We for the years to come may take
Our temper from today.—Wordsworth

Sixteen months had past since William attended the linen shower. During these days many signal events had occurred to make more potent the life of Seaton and Williamsburg. Letitia had married Sinclair, Catherine had married Henry, but Susan had not been able to obtain the kind of proposal she desired. She was waiting. *Probably* he would come *some day*. William had not called regularly as previously. Susan had not inquired into his reasons, but lookt to herself to discover the reason for the failure. Was her temperament against her? The handicaps of nature were the hardest to offset; but she would make the attempt.

She lost no time. She estbalisht THE COLERIDGE-TAYLOR CONSERVATORY OF MUSIC for instruction in piano, organ, violin, violoncello, mandolin, and guitar, with five assistants. As she desired to test her initiative, she kept her plans secret until she was ready to mail her dedication announcements. The conservatory had from the time of its inception been carefully advertised, but the prime mover was unknown. Because of the location mentioned, many persons wondered who was the promoter. The affair, however, was so tactfully managed, that the public was completely sur-

123

prised. Because the enterprise was carefully planned, the institution was a success from its very opening. William and Susan were both satisfied. Since even her mother had not been consulted in this endeavor, she had an argument for her efficiency.

Thelma was yet teaching in the L'Ouverture College, but she was devoting most of her spare time to community welfare work. She had reclaimed a number of girls from houses of ill resort, and having taught them the arts of the home, had them become industrial factors and makers of citizens. In this activity she had been aided by the Y. W. C. A., which rejoiced that she had started a work long neglected, but very necessary in our multifarious lives. That institution had vainly tried to reach the abandoned girls. The coming of Thelma was thus a providential favor. Since she had succeeded in an unparalled way, the workers of the Young Womens' Christian Association were glad to co-operate both in initial and follow-up work. The mistake had been made in the manner in which these persons had been approacht. Before the administration of the present Secretary, the Young Womens' Christian Association was an exclusive club for the wives and daughters of the best women in the town. The masses were approacht but only with an extreemly long handled spoon. Fortunately the last secretary was a woman of the people. When she explained her plans to Thelma, she found a willing missionary. Thelma had gone to those fallen human beings, not as their superior, but as their equal—one prone to err. Her attitude was veritably that of a friend.

So well had she conducted her work that she was hailed by the ministers as a palpable apostle of practical Christianity. She was deemed the making of the Young Women's Christian Association.

The spring following the party at Mrs. Annelle's William purchased a farm of six hundred acres, situated about eight miles from Seaton. On this tract of land he placed six five-room cottages for his croppers, whom he expected to work fifty-acre tracts. Near these houses he placed the necessary barns and stables, that his helpers might concentrate upon their special work, being able to start with the best advantages. This was a great advance because on the surrounding farms the people lived in cabins. About a half a mile from the rail-road he built a brick house and furnisht it like a house in the city among the well-to-do.

For the home site he used five acres, which he had designed by a landscape gardener, that it might have the appearance of a suburban estate. Across the entire front of the house he extended a porch in steel gray, colonaded with Gothic pillars. Various plants which would bloom thruout the season arose before the porch; roses, rooster cones, hyacinthes, lilacs, snow-balls, crysthanthemums and others. About fifty yards from the house in every direction extended a neatly trimmed hedge, which appropriately set off the evenly cut grass. Here and there was placed shrubbery to add to the charm of symmetry. Leading to the house were graveled walks which connected with the main road and that to the garage.

About a quarter mile from this site he had built a church with a seating capacity of three hundred. Tho a frame structure, it was beautiful, both within and without.

About a quarter mile from the home site in the opposite direction, could be found the farm buildings which would come under William's immediate supervision. Directly to the rear of his house was a fifty acre tract given over equally to an orchard and an experimental farm. The rest of his land was for staple crops.

Here William spent most of his time, assuredly changing the status of farmers about Seaton, preaching a progressive gospel to an increasing congregation, and commanding the attention and respect of the entire state.

Thelma had been deeply imprest with the news of William's attainment and, like the Queen of Sheba dissatisfied with the report, she wanted to see for herself.

The truth is Thelma had never had for Beckett King the deep affection she cherisht for William. As she had said on Mr. Lee's porch that autumnal evening, she had given Susan the right of way. While Smith was in college and the theological school, she had shown Susan how to win. Up to the night of the linen shower, she had not placed an obstacle before her friend. What had caused her to change she would not reveal, but evidently she was bent on marrying the young clergyman, if she could; and Susan seemed to know it.

To speak justly of Susan, none could call her narrow; she had always been above little things. Not only would she refrain from speaking ill of Thelma, when she discerned the change of attitude; she actually praised her. How noble is the soul of woman! If she and Thelma now were rivals, such they had not always been. Thelma had never written William a line, tho he had written her once from college. Whose advice had been the most pointed in her gaining the clergyman's affection? Thelma's. She was fully aware what should be done to marry the sometime prophet of Sinai Shrine.

Sixteen months had elapsed since that eventful night, eight months more remained, at the end of which time he would dance with his wife. Would it be Susan or Thelma? She feared if she did not act quickly, it would be Thelma. At last she accepted her friend's advice. She would make the fight of her life.

That evening when Thelma came in, after having supervised a club meeting at the Y. M. C. A., contrary to her wont Mrs. Anderson with whom she lodged was not on the porch; but was in the parlor with her mother—Mrs. Haskell—and Rev. Ross. Thelma knew that her pastor admired the summer breeze with an appreciation more uproarious than her own. Altho the day had been unusually hot—it was the first week in July—there he was within doors.

As soon as she had removed her hat and gloves, she returned to the parlor and shook hands with Rev. Ross once more. When she had seated herself in an arm chair, he spoke of her community work which had received practically all her time during the vacation. He commended her for it, hoping she would draw even more women about her as aids.

Thelma had the highest admiration for her pastor, because his every activity was guided by a conscious purpose. Thus she discerned at once that he had not come to discuss her service as a social worker. She decided therefore, to make him state his business.

Mrs. Anderson, however, prevented this by interrupting thus, "Pardon me, but what do you think of the work of Rev. Smith?" she was about to answer her own question, but hesitated, when she saw that Rev. Ross was going to speak.

"I think it really phenomenal," put in Rev. Ross. "Each time I think of it I regret the fiasco which occurred at the Convention. If ever there was an apostle of Christianity, William is the man. Like Christ, he has been misunderstood, but he is in spite of it reaping a harvest of souls."

"I'm glad he has risen regardless of the opposition from those who should have helped him up. In their hearts, I know they are sorry, for they see that some day they must bring him back and apologize. Don't fight against God," said

Mrs. Haskel, deeply moved. She was a Christian of the old school.

"Somehow it has seemed queer to me," remarkt Rev. Ross looking pointedly at Thelma, "that there isn't a Mrs. William Smith on that estate. What's the trouble, Thelma?" All who had grown up in his church from infancy he continued to call by their first names. "I hope the girls of this town won't let him escape, to be seized by a lady of Seaton."

"I think we'll take care of that," said Thelma smiling and did not blush at all.

"I suppose some of the girls will be wanting to see that splendid estate. We'll have to get up a party that they may go, won't we?" he said to Mrs. Anderson.

Thelma now knew that Mrs. Anderson had spoken to the minister of the conversation of the previous night. "What a delight that would be!" she exclaimed, "but I have decided to go tomorrow."

"I'll try then to arrange for a party to go with you," was the minister's tactful remark.

"Rev. Ross, I am going on business and will make the trip alone." She spoke with firmness, her tone distinctly indicating that she desired no company. She was almost angry, but was doing her utmost to keep composed

The minister was somewhat unprepared for such a direct thrust. Accordingly he had to pause for thot. While he reflected for a reply, not a word was spoken. Thelma was waiting for his next remark. The others felt themselves unqualified to take the initiative. At length, after a few moments, he said pleadingly, "are you aware of the risk you take?"

"I am aware of everything," was her interruption.

"You must remember tho you are a woman. If you do this, your name will become common gossip. When this happens to a school teacher in this town, it is not long before she is compelled to do something else," the minister argued.

"Rev. Ross, if the Board of Trustees wants my position, it is welcome to it. I lived before they employed me, and I'll live when I have left them. You say I am a woman." She emphasized the word. "Because I'm full grown, I feel that I can look after myself. If I should tarnish my character by making this call, I have womanhood enough to offer my resignation without any outside request; if I thot I could not make it without being sullied, I never should have accepted the position. Such is my confidence in the Board of Trustees, that I believe they would never have employed me, if they thot I could not make a trip like this, and end it as I'd begin it. You are impugning not only me, but those discreet gentlemen who placed me here.

"You don't know what you're saying. I went into ill resorts to save abandoned women and came out as I went in. You know how long I have been doing this. You and your entire brotherhood have praised me for my courage and moral strength. Now when I go to call on a *man*—the noblest character in these parts, the most lovable individual *you've ever met*, and you *know it*—you infer that my character will be besmirched."

"Don't you see I'm trying to guard your good name?" Rev. Ross replied. "I believe in you fully, but it is not so with my associates. If you go unchaperoned, of course I will defend you. But I do not want to see you out of the schools, your influence over the girls has been most wholesome. So well do you know how to guide."

"The irony of it! Yet I can not guide myself. If I go, I suppose I shall be treated as was William. Well, I'll give the Holy Church a chance." She paused to observe the effect of her bitter utterance. As no one spoke, she continued, "since I have reacht the age of discretion, I can manage my own affairs. I never let others attend to my business. It is proper for William to board a train to come to see me, yet it's improper for me to board a train to go to see him. Men can do as they please, but women must not suit their fancies. Fie upon your double standard of morality that requires good girls to marry trashy men, fie upon conventionalities which permit men to sow wild oats, but deny the same to girls; fie upon your society women who will kick out one of their own sex, but will hurriedly embrace the scoundrel who ruined the girl they scorn. Such is the church, such is the home, such is society." Rev. Ross wanted to speak, but she stopped him. "I defy you all. If I hadn't thot of going alone, I'd certainly go now. I've made up my mind. It would take all the powers of heaven to stay me, so it is useless for hell to try." She almost screamed.

Mrs. Haskell was much embarrassed, the others were greatly surprised. "Thelma," said the mother, "it seems as tho you have no respect for your pastor."

"Mother, I honor him in the highest. I appreciate his counsel, but I can not follow it now. I have there in Seaton a work of my own to do and nobody can do it for me. I will leave tomorrow at eight-thirty. Even at this time all is definitely arranged. I will remain here, however, only on one condition; that is, if nature opposes: if tomorrow the plains become mountains and touch the skies; if the streams I must cross become shoreless seas; if the lights of heaven and all artificial light fade into mist."

"Thelma, I must admire you," said the pastor. "Your strong will moves me irresistibly. Let me shake your hand. You have done too much for the Church for it to forsake you now. I can not speak for my brethren, but I can speak for myself. May the peace of God be with you always! God speed you on!" Turning to the other ladies, he remarkt. "Thelma is true blue. I'd trust her with anything, even my life. Have no fear. She is able to take care of her self."

Thelma started towards the door, then turned and said, "Thank you, Rev. Ross. But will you excuse me now? I must be making ready for my journey."

"Certainly," he said. Thereupon, she left the room.

CHAPTER XIV.

He is the living light-fountain, which it is good
and pleasant to be near,. The light which enlight-
ens, which has enlightened the darkness of the
world; and this not as a kindled lamp only, but
rather as a natural luminary shining by the gift
of Heaven; a flowing light-fountain, as I say, of
native original insight;—in whose radiance all
souls feel that it is well with them.—Carlyle

Tho William had been on his estate just a little more than
a year, he had greatly changed the life of his environs. Can
a man be born again? Who could doubt it now? Had not
the cabins for ten miles around given place to cottages and
weatherboard houses? Had not many who had left for the
cities returned to the farms? Were there not more independent
farmers just out from Seaton than anywhere in the state? And
what had made possible the building of the new station but the
new impetus give to farming?

William had attracted considerable attention by experi-
ments of various sorts at his demonstration farm. For instance, he showed the effect of different feeds on hogs, having been able to market the heaviest hogs on an extremely
economical, concentrated food. Since his stock always topped
the market, other farmers began to seek his methods. Furthermore, from the most uncompromising land, he had by careful treatment of the soil obtained the greatest yields of corn.
Wherever his land was simply as good as that of a neighbor,
he produced almost twice as much as his fellow farmer. He
had exhibited also unusual skill in intensive truck gardening.

William's specialties were hogs and small grains, but since
he was more than well versed in the many aspects of agricul-

ture, his experimental station became a frequent rendez-vous. Here flockt both white and black to learn of this wizard of the soil.

The morning following Thelma's conversation with Rev. Ross, William began the day's work in his orchard. As it was likely that the threshing machine would not arrive until late in the afternoon, or the next morning, he would discuss with his croppers there some essentials of spraying and tillage, also to contrast certain features of his orchard with those of several unprofitable fruit farms nearby. One of these was on a well drained spot, an excellent site for a lucrative orchard. Its failure to bear had been due to the fact that it was planted in sod. The owner of that plot went with William to be informed along this line and observe the effect of cultivation on the delicacy of pulp and texture, and the vigor of the new wood.

While in the midst of his discussion one of his helpers handed him a special. A glance at the familiar handwriting told him at once that it came from Susan Lee. He was eager now for noon to come when the demonstration would have been concluded, the visitors gone, and leisure present. Since he had to wait he resigned himself without more ado. From this point, the farmers promptly noticed, however, that there was a change in their instructor. His speech was rapid with a quivering tone. Yet the demonstration went on.

How the time lingered! How perplexing the weariness of waiting! Once he colored with the flush of vehement emotion. Almost as frequently as he put thots of Susan aside, they returned with greater vividness. Thus he was stirred till noon when he could have sweet moments of undisturbed reflection, when he could think of all she had been and all he hoped her to be.

Fearing interruption by casual visitors, William did not

return to his house but went to his forest reserve at the farthest extremity of his farm. As he stretched on the ground, he noticed flitting and playing two humming birds. So happy they seemed that he envied them. He drew the letter from his pocket, opened it, then said to himself, "I wonder what she has to say now. What does she think of me? She trusted during these years in my sincerity. Háve I been false? I can not feel that I have. But she has waited alone for me. Sometimes I think I should go at once to Williamsburg and ask her point blank to marry me. Then I wonder if I can be the type of husband she desires. She wants me to find my comfort in satisfying her desire for a home life created and sustained with equal enthusiasm by us both. She loves the home, I love a public career, with a radicalism that may take me so frequently from her that I should almost have the status of a boarder. If I can not be indeed a husband, to furnish the companionship a mother and children should have, if I lead a life which would soon make my wife a widow and my children orphans, should I marry? Is not this the very thing she would oppose? And would I not pursue my present way of life, which is the result of years of thinking in spite of her opposition? This would create between us a gulf which might become well nigh impassable.

"I love the girl I know better than my dreams of heaven. But when the question arises of spending days, weeks, months, and probably years with another, I should have in mind her good fortune rather than mine. If I can not make her happy I will not make her miserable, even for her own sake." Then he paused in his revery and wiped his face, for it was quite warm. At length the decision came, "Let me see what she has to say. It may be possible yet."

He read carefully and with deep feeling.

"William, my Dear:

"How are you? Since we said we should be permanent friends, you will not think it presumptuous for me to ask about your health and welfare. For a month you have not called or written. Tho you know the reason, I am in the dark and dare not call for light.

"Another month and another might have past without my writing, for tho miles may keep between us, our souls may touch with or without the aid of pen or voice. Tho there, I know your heart is here by your very silence; and all the world is aware—the world in which I live—that my heart is happily with you. You love me, William? Am I wrong? I believe you because you have proved it; you have said it, you have sung it, you have lived it. You love me more than any you have met. If I err, tell me so; but for this you have no tongue, for if we live I have written truly.

"Long has been my pondering and long my hesitation, you know I was taught to wait. However, the last few days have given birth to events which may greatly alter the lives of us both. I shall not here state what they are, but let it suffice that they prompt me now to act. My dear, you are a man, and being a man who has loved one woman, it is impossible for you not to have varying inclinations for all my sex. I laugh to scorn his utterance who says of several women that he cares as much for one as for another. Such affection I consider wholly impossible. I agree with Canouib when he says,

> "Beauty must be scorned in none
> Tho but truly served in one'

These lines reflect your personality.

"Almost a year and a half have past since you gave me hope of woman's greatest joy. True to my sex, I have feasted on it, desiring always its immediate realization. In this you have made a conquest, but I have not, tho yet I have hope. Tho still I think you love me best even now, during these sixteen months your admiration for my friend, Thelma, may at this time border on the beginnings of passionate love. All this while you have been wondering whether to marry me. Have you not had sufficient time? I am ready to hear the best or the worst; but please end the suspense.

"It may happen that you will not marry me, but you will not find a woman who'll love you more than I. Nor will there come the man that I shall love more than you. Yet we may not marry; that is a matter for you alone to decide. I say this because our artificial society makes it possible for individuals not to get their choices. Even during my brief existence, I have met women who say they did not marry the man they loved best, because these men did not propose. Moreover, father tells me that my mother was not his best love, but that his choice jilted him and married someone else.

"When I think of these conditions, I drift at once to Milton, who expresses in the lines I shall quote a great truth, if we consider them as applying not only to the man but also to the woman baffled in love. He says:

'For either
He never shall find out fit mate, but such
As some misfortune brings him, or mistake:
Or, whom he wishes most shall seldom gain,
Thru her perverseness; but shall see her gaind
By a far worse; or if she love, withheld
By parents; or his happiest choice too late
Shall meet, already linkt and wedlock-bound
To a fell adversary, his hate or shame;
Which infinite calamity shall cause
To human life, and househould peace confound.'

"William, light of my life, the barriers to your realization vanisht long years ago. And I thot that mine had vanisht, but here they are.

"During those days you were in college how I cried and prayed that you would finish and come back to me. At last you did return and I claimed you for my own, then you were mine and I was yours.

"Love, think of the nights of anguish, think of the days of weary waiting. Your soul has so mingled with my own, that I am yours and you are mine for ever. You may wed someone else, but as for me, never. Do as you think best for me and for you, but our spirits cannot dwell apart.

"I am that type of woman that loves one and once. To be disappointed in love will cause me unutterable langour; but, William, I will not die. I shall suffer, but I will not die. If I should go, you would soon follow; but I must live, my love, that you may live. Your work has just begun and you need womanly counsel; for the good of your work, for the good of the community, for your own good. Decide this matter without delay; I will make any sacrifice for you. You need my advice, come, let me give it; or I shall come to you.

"Sixteen months ago you intimated that two years from that eventful night you would be married. That same night Thelma began an intimacy with you which since has forced you to take notice. I am extremely frank now, because I feel that we should understand each other thoroly. If ill must come of this, may it be speedy! If good, I can wait forever.

"William, I have tried to be frank and specific. Surely you understand me. I do not know what your answer will be, but as you love me truly, you will act for the greater happiness of us both. True, eight months' life before you, and as you have always kept your work, I know you cannot do less now.

"Hearts everywhere are beating for their lovers; yours is beating and so is mine. Nights and days of anxious waiting, for you my heart beats every hour. My hope of ages rests upon you, my childhood dreams I longed to come true. Do you not hear me faintly calling, calling to you, heart atuned to love; in the distance, can you not hear the call of love? Dearest, oh dear! I am seeking, seeking the one man for me. Love, my soul is calmly pleading. Love, you will come to me?

"Do not deceive yourself. You are my friend, you are my all in all; and I am

"Yours in the past, the present, and the future,

Susan."

When William had finisht, he started homeward full of the emotion Susan had aroused. The curtain seemed to have been lifted and he saw what he was and what he hoped to be. "I see the way. I will answer," he thot, "today. Then as soon as the wheat harvest is over, I will go to her. She shall wait no longer."

CHAPTER XV.

O saw ye bonnie Lesley
  As she gaed o'er the border?
She's gane, like Alexander,
  To spread her conquests farther.—Burns

William, bent on making himself wholly subservient to the gladness he had just found hurried onward suffused with the glow of the coming achievement. The wild flowers now took on a grander aspect, the trees were now brighter than ever. The squirrels frolickt with great glee, peculiarly thrilled with glee. The birds made soothing harmonies. Would you believe all this was a part of him? The sun of splendid happiness had given him a new birth, for he became aware that with this awakening his soul could sleep no more. No more was it good for him to be alone. He knew that before the close of summer he would marry. There was no other way.

As he came towards the rear of his garage, he was met by one of his helpers who had been seeking him for some time. "Rev. Smith," he said, rejoicing that his effort was now successful, "a lady wants to see you at the house. She wouldn't give her name. She's been there now more than an hour. Besides, my madame says she fears she must scold you; for dinner has been ready almost as long."

William wondered who could it be. Was it possible that Susan had come anyhow? She had said if he did not come to her she would come to him. How would he receive her? He would receive her as she deserved.

"Mr. Brown," he said, then paused a moment for reflection, "tell your wife put on an extra plate; we shall have com-

139

pany for dinner this afternoon. Just as soon as I brush up and wash, I'll be in. I'm glad I didn't come from the front."

Mr. Brown, proceeded to deliver his message and William prepared to meet his guest. When he had finisht, he came to his parlor in his khaki trousers, and khaki shirt, from the neck of which suspended a knitted black tie. This habit together with his tan shoes and leather puttees gave him the appearance of an American soldier of 1918, Sometimes visitors upon seeing him thus attired, askt if he was in the service of his Country, meaning of course if he were a soldier. He would reply, "Yes. I've been in the service of the Country all my life; however, I'm not a soldier, tho if necessary, I'"! fight. I'm not a member of the standing army, but I do belong to the working army, which is to help, according to our President's phrase to make the world safe for democracy." His dress was always impressive.

William lost no time in his preparations. As he neared the arch leading from the dining room to the parlor, his soul felt a yearning. It was trying to burst the bonds of present experience to grasp at others more profound. He sought to fathom the impassable, to know and yet be not known. Mr. Brown had been unable to describe the visitor with the distinctness with which he had pictured others; in such a way as to cause William to be fully aware who the person was; that is, if the two had ever met. Why had the gentleman failed in this instance? Was it because he did not look fastidiously, due to the lady's being of the common place or to his being face to face with such an extraordinary presence as overawed him before he could become self-composed? How for once he wisht the impossible; that intervening doors might vanish without ruin, that supernatural sight transcending all clairvoyants might serve him at this hour! Then he realized the wish was vain, that happiness arises from the natural; that it is not good always to know what is hid, to know what each tomorrow will bring. It would take away all the surprises, most of the laughs, and much of the joy of life.

He was satisfied at last not to know, until he would see her face. He took a step forward and paused; in his heart there was great rejoicing. The new day had come at last. Each thing he toucht seemed spirited with the benevolence of an Aladdin genius, so that it would ever now be different with a splendor intrinsic and ideal. The brush he used was lighter, for with each movement to make himself suited for the tête-a-tête, visions arose of home enchanted, of Williams and Susans yet to be. He walkt now with better grace, for the call of youths unborn was lingering with him; and as he moved on, the old world had past away, and he saw a new heaven and a new earth. As garments which have long kept us company till other fashions seem more worth the while eventually pass for the more novel to bring a long awaited joy, William left old thots behind, to cling to those which Susan had conjured up. His dream of dearness now was tangible. One goal at least he had reacht at last.

On other occasions, when visitors had been announced, William had had no trepidation; the coming of strangers was entirely a matter of course. They were welcomed, feasted, and entertained with the characteristic southern hospitality. But he had felt no depth of passion, no unusual desire to see his guest. In this instance he had already delayed too long. If it were only Susan! He hoped that it was only she. He rusht into the parlor to greet her who had called. He was face to face with a woman almost peerless, with a queen of beauty and of love, heiress of great princes of Egypt, of a people great in every land. He came forward astonisht, he bowed as a plumed knight, and with a cheery smile shook hands with Thelma.

She was the first to speak, for William was too firmly besieged with amazement and consternation. Thelma understood in advance that her coming would be a surprise. How great this would be of course she did not comprehend. "I'm glad to see you, William. How have you been? How are you? You have indeed a wonderful establishment here; I hope to view it more minutely. As the train flew over the trestle just out from Happy Forge, a stranger to me, but a friend to you—a Mr. Trundle Hope—askt me if I had seen your estate. When I told him I had not, he said that I was just where I could obtain a fine view of it, if I only had a field glass. When I produced one, he took great pride in indicating and explaining the various parts of your land of heart's desire. Would you believe me if I told you I saw a group of white and colored men in the north western section of your farm, but their features were not plainly distinguishable."

William was glad that she had some idea of the place, because he could pass over many details and dwell upon the aspects of chief interest. He continued silent. As a consequence, Thelma went on, "That view of course since it was largely panoramic, was seen from too great a distance to reveal some features which should leave with me a kaleidoscopic impression. In this I need have no doubt, you will place everything at my disposal. You will want me to speak to your friends in Williamsburg with authority; for they are desirous of all they can learn of you."

"Yes, my whole farm shall be at your disposal," said William, now gaining his equipoise. "I'm glad you've come and hope you will not regret having called upon the humblest worker of these parts. But," he gave great emphasis to the word, "you have come alone. Why didn't some of the others come also. The more the merrier our party would be. It seems that Susan would have been good company." He hesi-

tated before pronouncing Susan's name, then uttered it with
noticeable feeling. Thelma was not daunted by this outburst;
she had planned well and was consequently ready for all surprises.

With wonted frankness she said, "Susan, I'm sure, didn't
know I was coming." He thot of Susan's statements concerning his fair caller, of the letter which had given him a
new birth. At once he discerned that another battle was on.
"To those who were eager to come I said nothing. I wanted
to see you alone," she admitted. William now saw that Susan
divined aright. Was not Thelma's last utterance an avowal
of love? When a woman tells a man she wants to see him
alone, or if the man has so told the woman, is it not because
of something admired, is it not because of love? Thelma continued by saying, "Rev. Ross, mother and Mrs. Anderson
suggested getting up a party; but that would have required
probably several days. As I was in the spirit of coming, I
would not wait. I might have told Susan, but thinking I should
not, I have come alone."

William found himself at once in a quandary as to what
could be the purport of her excursion. He listened almost
breathlessly, for as she spoke, his thots went back to Williamsburg, where clustered in romantic musing and temporarily resigned satisfaction was one who had come out of Dreamland,
Fairyland, or Eldorado to make a conquest of his heart. Could
there yet come another?

As he wanted Thelma to relish her visit, he checkt that
flow of thots and askt if she had brought baggage and whether
it had been properly cared for. "I brought simply a bag with
me," was her response, "which I left with Mrs. Johnson, in
town. She says that you have helped her much by sending
to her visitors to spend the night or to remain several days.
I was referred to her by the secretary of the Y. W. C. A., as

the rooms there had all been taken. As she is both winsome and congenial, I have no doubt that we'll become bosom friends. Besides, she commends you highly."

"Mrs. Johnson is one of my dearest friends. I'm glad you're well situated. Now I can be composed. Come have some dinner," he said incoherently, extending towards her his hand with a gentle bow. "I'm sure you must be hungry, since you arrived this morning at ten o'clock. Your subsequent time must have been given to adjusting your affairs. But how long do you plan to be here?"

"I don't know," was her quick response. They started tor the dining room absorbed in several big ideas. "I may go back tonight or tomorrow, or I may remain several days. All depends upon how much I can accomplish."

William found himself once more wondering what she could have in mind.

They sat down to a well spread table, as only one is spread where there is loving and rural abundance. Both were thrilled with the opportunity to enjoy a good repast and showed such by hearty application. While thus engaged she thot she would make an excellent first impression by showing a deep interest in the work he dearly loved. She was testing this philosophy—to be sure it was some of her own—for a woman to win the affection of man she would profit by being deeply interested in those activities which interested him. She might have in some instances different views, but his interests needed to become her interests. Thus she knew definitely where to begin. "William," she said, commencing the conversation, "The very fact that I have come this distance alone, despite thunders of criticism, indicates that we have at least something in common, namely, the success of your experiment here. I have frequently heard from afar that you are engaged in a great work. Well, that's nothing new to me; for thru all these years I've known you, so far as my intelligence permits me to observe, a great work has alone been able to attract you." Somewhat abasht, he thankt her for her compliment. "True I've heard something from others, but should like to know at first hand from you, what is the nature and scope of your endeavor. You know that during vacation I devote practically all my time to community work. My specialty is to reach the girl who has fallen; yet I give some time to other girls and even to boys. Since you yourself are naturally magnetic and radiate inspiration, I am here to catch even the faintest gleams of incentive and carry them to persons almost devoid of hope. Tell me, therefore, what you are doing and what is the ultimate attainment you have in mind."

"I am engaged in an experiment, Thelma, which I feel should succeed; yet I can not be too certain, tho I may realize many great accomplishments. Ordinarily, when men engage in experimentation, they have their equipment so well under control, that a large amount of success is rather sure. I am speaking of course of the best scientists. Mine, however, is an experiment in democracy; I am trying to convert the prejudice against races into an hostility against particular individuals, who wilfully neglect to make the best of opportunities and who expect to reap tho they have not sown; to see to it that he who sows shall reap; to place in public office the man who is most efficient and unselfish; to give every man an equal chance to rise, no matter whence he comes or what he has been."

At this point Mrs. Brown seated herself as would a proud hostess, to eat with them until all were ready for dessert. William introduced Thelma to Mrs. Brown, in order that all might participate in informing not only his guest, but, as he said, their guest. Mrs. Brown sometimes would join in, also her husband; on this occasion, however she preferred to listen and not to speak.

"William, you have indeed a great task before you, one which may require many generations for its completion. It is more than a life work."

"That's true. Still we may be able to speed it on its way."

"But you have located here in the South amidst a people, committed not to democracy but aristocracy, an ideal which has been with this section since the importation of the first slaves, probably even earlier. Here prejudice goes rampant; true a few of our people vote, but the many are shamefully disfranchised, while white men more ignorant than they go to the polls. Here you are faced with the so called Jim Crow cars on railroads and street car lines; partial courts; and frequent manifest humiliation." She wanted him to feel the bigness of his undertaking.

"Thelma," he said with assurance, "I feel the weight of all you spoke. But do you think I can find democracy anywhere in these United States?" She shook her head. "You're a graduate of one of our best northern universities. Tell me if you found democracy there."

"Tho I went shoulder to shoulder with the first in my class, not for once during my entire stay did I feel that I was not colored.

"Of course my effort here is more strenuous than it would be in Pennsylvania or New York; but if the proper relations can be realized in the South between black and white, the battle, practically speaking, will have been won."

"You're not doing this alone tho, are you?" Thelma inquired with a dainty smile.

"No, not now. I have five croppers to aid me, aside from the co-operation of three white farmers who specialize in tobacco. Then there are others who have aided me by mentioning my endeavor in their addresses before white audiences. Especially has this been true of editors and ministers."

"Give me some idea of an instance wherein you have done something to break down prejudice," she implored wanting to be satisfied.

"In this country," he began firmly, "for about five years farmers believed it unprofitable to grow white potatoes and onions for the market. They never ceast to grow them for their tables, but had left off producing them for sale.

"Seeing that the soil in this country was particularly adapted to the growing of these two vegetables, I thot the failure to hit was due to the preparation of the soil. Accordingly I askt Mr. Brown, who had planned to grow only tomatoes, to plant onions and potatoes instead. He was reluctant because he is a specialist in tomatoes, but I gave him a guarantee of four thousand dollars, the amount he expected to realize from his tomatoes. In addition to this I had him put in an acre for each of these crops at the demonstration farm. I told some farmers what we were doing and askt them to visit us, when we could show the plants, the cultivation, and results. We invited both white and black. When the season closed, we had attained signal success.

"In the same way, I suggested to my other croppers what they should make their staple crops. Since our products became preferred because of lusciousness, texture, marketing and storing qualities, demands have arisen thruout the state for the privilege of attending our demonstrations and obtaining suggestions as to the most economical way of producing a quality, maximum yield."

Thelma wanted to see him thru, but as she was speedily brot to an appreciation of the magnitude of his work, she felt compelled to interrupt. "You know, William," she said with interest, "achievement is not unaccompanied by other things.

We must pay the price of success. Some, I doubt not, envy you, and by your own words, many already seek to learn of you. True you are young and vigorous; but are youth and health everything. I fear you may work too hard. I do not mean to be inquisitorial, but are you doing all this without advice, without well qualified helpers?"

Smith was somewhat disconcerted, for he had not been greeted hitherto by thots of his own welfare. Now that they had been spoken, they brot reflection. This did not last long, so he replied, "My croppers are my helpers, particularly Mr. Brown, and Mr. Wilson, my specialist in orchard gardening. When we decide to launch a movement in the interest of a particular crop, we meet in conference, arrange plans and detail the work. Thus no one needs to do too much."

"But you are the prime mover; besides you are a minister, are you not exhausting your strength to the extent that you need a counsellor to restrain you?"

"Nothing worth while, Thelma, is accomplisht without much work. As for my being a preacher, you know you and Susan both opposed my forsaking my chief calling. I am merely keeping my promise. My preaching now is more effective than ever, for not only in trying to spur others to get a thoro education and achieve, can I point to the success of others, but I can indicate very forcibly the attainment of those about me. They understand what I mean, when I preach, 'The word was made flesh and dwelt among us.' "

"I was wondering tho if your sacrifice were not too great. Your work instead of obtaining the good-will of the ordinary white farmer may merely aggravate the evil you are trying to stamp out? Haven't you really excelled him? Pray tell me what white man wants to see a colored man outdo him?" Inquired the fair guest.

"They may not desire it but in many ways they ignore

it. They ignore it. They allowed Booker T. Washington to outdo them. They allow our boys in college in many instances to forge ahead. They just can't help themselves. If I haven't said enough, this I know will suffice; the white man everywhere allows his dark brother to excell him in unselfishness, religion and loyalty." William protested with firm assurance.

Thelma responded with her usual complacence. "In this you are right, but won't the southern demagogs, the products of color prejudice, or rather to some extent, the makers of color prejudice, do you great wrong? Your intentions are strictly logical; but are you not trying to alter conditions which in themselves are so mighty, that they may ultimately engulf you?"

"That is true," he admitted, "but wrong must be righted. Truth and right must prevail. As the apostle of truth and right I'm ever ready to pay the price—even to die. Kelley Miller, our great chieftain, a calm thinker, reminds us when we would be rash that the pen is mightier than the sword. He says that almost invariably it has required shot and shell to knock wrong doctrine out of the heads of some white men, as is instanced by most of the wars of history. At last has appeared a lover of peace, the colored man in America, a man who can fight, but a lover of peace, devoted to peace after 'principles purely pacific.' The speech of Edmund Burke on 'Conciliation' with the American Colonies, with very slight modification is our plea today. The principles therein embodied are applicable to all backward and opprest peoples. Right never changes. The English colonists stood oppression for a hundred and fifty years and gained their political freedom by the sword, and not by the pen. We hope that what Kelley Miller informs us has been true thru the ages, will not be true in our realizing liberty. We've already shed blood for the liberty of others. May that also suffice for our own!

"But man was born to die. So I have no fear. Socrates could die for a cause; so could Cicero, Julius Caeser, Abraham Lincoln, and our boys at Houston, Texas; and even Christ. More than this, I know I have the courage of Christ."

Thelma was considerably thrilled by William's frank outpouring of his feelings for she knew that he had uttered the sentiments of his people, East, West, North, and South. She herself was an individual desirous of a greater emancipation. Accordingly she sympathized with him profoundly.

"Now or never," he continued, "white and colored must come together. As soon as the white man is educated as he will be, hoaxes will cease. From the beginning white and black have been played against each other. For instance, in antebellum days, the white man who did not own slaves but complained of his lot, was played against the colored man by the planter's saying, 'You're always complaining, tho you forget that you're free. You're better off than the nigger.' Then the colored man was played against the poorer white by the planter's saying, 'You niggers grumble because you're not free. but look at my neighbors who are free. They're just poor white trash. You're certainly better off than they because you are always sure of your meals.'"

"Yes that condition continues even now," said Thelma, who was well informed of conditions in present day society. "Today that old idea occurs between capital and labor. The capitalists plays the white laborer against the colored laborer. Not until the white man takes the colored man into his unions will he be able to get the proper wage. He can not see if all laboring men were to strike simultaneously, white and black, that the capitalists would be compelled to yield. But thru some peculiar hocus-pocus of color prejudice he cuts off his nose to spite his face. He wants all for himself and none for the colored man; but such can not be. And when these two groups do come together, we can look for a new order of things."

"At first," put in William, "we seemed to differ. But aren't we on the same vantage ground? I admit that the work is strenuous, and at times perilous. Yet it is a work that must be done. The barrier must be removed, for it prevents our national life. It has made our justices, our morality, and even our education one-sided. Everything is out of joint. When I think of it, I lose patience. This game of politicians and fanatics must cease." At this point William felt that he had been thinking too much of his own problems, having done hers scant courtesy, consequently he turned to her and began, "Thelma, now that you know the plan of my work, let us turn to Williamsburg. To be sure I obtain the newspapers of that grand, old town; yet there is much they fail to mention of a strictly personal nature, that you can disclose. Tell me all the news, tell me about all my friends, about yourself —anything and everything."

Thelma was not surprised at this turn the conversation took; the fact is she had expected it. She congratulated herself tho on having been able to restrain the outburst until this time. Her purpose was to have him make a complete revelation of what he aimed to do, in order that the activity which absorbed his life might also absorb hers, thus they would have much in common. This realized, her task could no longer be desperate, for she would have made a way to his heart. Yet another device offered some gladness, strongly prophetic of success. She might win him thru his mother. This was her chance for another mutual interest. Since he was indeed fond of Mrs. Smith, by far more devoted to her than most men are to their mothers, Thelma was happy to say most of this venerable lady while discussing Williamsburg. "Nothing unusual has occurred, William; you know it is too hot for receptions. Pilgrim, however is planning an excursion to Seaton for the express purpose of allowing the members to see just what they have inspired. They have never forsaken you. You are theirs now even as you were years ago. When the convention closed its pulpits to you, Pilgrim continued to say, 'Come,' as you will recall. They did not understand all you said; but they trusted in your sincerity. They love you, because you always loved them."

"If they had forsaken me, I should not have disliked them; for I knew some of my utterances shockt them. Now that they have been so liberal, as not to allow the old love to cease, I cherish them all the more. I shall be happy to place my farm at their disposal.

"But how is my mother? I wish she would come here, yet I appreciate her reasons for remaining where she is. Well do I remember after that eventful convention. I myself was so enrapt with the past that I preferred to linger there. How I wisht to stay! Yet I had to leave, an important work awaited me. I had to rise unto my place." By this time they had finisht their dessert; so William escorted her to the parlor. She was well imprest with her experiences and was confident that her trip was not in vain.

Once she started to mention William's mother, but believing that her end would be better served if he suggested the theme, she waited until he had given her the cue. Then she said, "Your mother is quite well. I suppose you're unaware that I go to see her almost as to a shrine. I go so frequently. I went just before coming here, as I wanted to come fresh with news of her. She had thot for some time of visiting you, but learning of the plans at Pilgrim, she thot she'd wait for Mrs. Green. Isn't it remarkable how your mother seems to take no account of time? She might easily pass for an elder sister, yet her life has been strenuous to aid you in realizing your chief aims."

"I have much to prize in her, for tho she would have preferred my settling in Williamsburg, she was broad enough to see that like a prophet of old, I had to seek honor in a distant country. I have been unable to bring her here; yet if my success depended upon her presence in Seaton, she would have been here long ago." Thelma had not erred in her judgment; for the tie between mother and son was unusually strong.

To make a master stroke and prepare for subsequent effort, she would become personal. She had to gain time, or as some would put it, she had to make up for lost time. No letters had passed between her and William. Never had they met alone except to pass the conventional greeting. This was their first tête-a-tête. Thelma planned that this should not be their last. Furthermore, she intended to write. Whether he would answer was not the question, but she must somehow thrill his soul. Since she knew William had commended her with an admiration which might involve great promise, she was always optimistic. She could not, however, construe it as the love that makes man and woman one. There was Susan, whom she knew William loved. She also knew that his calls had recently been markt by long intervals, a sign of the estoppage of love. But as she had ceased regularly to call on Susan, she felt sure that Susan suspected her. Ordinarily Susan would wait. It was her temperament. Would she wait now? Thelma was afraid to take any risk. She said therefore, "Certainly you miss your mother and probably others who have cheered you much."

"Yes," he replied, "I do miss them, so much, that I rejoice when anyone comes from those parts."

"For sometime that has been my belief," she affirmed, looking at him bashfully and then lowering her head. "It seems your work, tho well organized, needs one other helper."

"And, pray what is he to do?"

"To give you constant counsel, to keep you from working too hard. A great man needs a wife. I've wondered why you've waited so long. I can say this because when we were quite young, we said whatever we pleased to each other; but when you stept into manhood and I into womanhood, Susan came between. Since then we have kept apart. I have said this reluctantly, but I am speaking only for your good." She knew she was playing with fire.

"Thelma, I have been thinking of it and have about reacht a decision. I have not, I fear, dealt fairly with Susan; but I will do so now. By the way, let me show you the farm, Brown is coming with the auto. I will tell you more of what you suggested as we go over the farm." William had spoken before he was fully aware of the significance of his words. The idea came to him that Thelma might be interpreting his remarks for her own contentment. Should he speak freely? Certainly it was best for her to know. Susan had hinted that Thelma was her rival. William held both women in high esteem and he would have both happy; but he made up his mind that rivalry would have to cease.

At present Thelma was his guest and as such she would receive hearty welcome. He helped her into his Chandler and started over the estate. "How beautiful it is to have such pleasure! I think I must make Seaton my home," she remarkt.

He replied, "Thelma, Seaton would be glad to have you."

CHAPTER XVI.

My boy stept over the hills,
    A master of the night;
He seized the morning in his hand,
    And darkness changed to light.

He met a star that rose
    Out of his brother's brest,
It fell upon his rainbow soul
    And hailed him to a quest.

He lookt where giants claimed
    The mastery of the world,
Advancement o'er all other folk;
    With glories e'er unfurled.

They marched to conquer love,
    And sink it with the night,
But tumbling with this hate
    They died, eclipsed by light.

My boy stept o'er the hills,
    Awakened by the cry,
"The veil is lifting with the star.
    Who scorns but waits to die."

Thelma and William were kindred spirits. Born anew this day with visions bright, they sailed on and on. For a time they said nothing to each other, because there were elfish voices skipping thru the air that had a language lovingly their own. The breezes, pure and serene, told of journeys over seas to distant lands, where God's folk, just rising unto place, wisht civilization would embrace the world. The laughing birds scouting on wing suggested the nobility of companionship. Yet they had their foes. Many perisht each winter. Some hastening on the return of spring, were stopt by the bullet of civilized barbarism. For all this, they could not help singing the gladness of the time. To fashion a Dvorakain symphony like unto that of "The New World," the trees joined in with measured bows, gracefully gesticulating to the strains resounding full and free.

What need of speech, when all else was talking; the whispering birds, the lowing cows, the bleating lambs, the capricious calf, the prancing horse? For quite a long while Thelma and William could only be silent. But their souls were not quiet at all. Great idealists like them could not be near and at the same time distant. The glance of an energetic eye, a dynamic expression of profound interest and astonishment, and the understanding of a purposive personality conjured up avenues of communications inexpressible in song or speech. Each thus soared in imagination, surmising the beautiful in the other, dreaming of the grandeur of being together, making noble the common place.

They stopt at all buildings, for this was the courtesy shown all visitors. Tho there was the temptation to be personal and use the time for intercourse touching the crystalline experiences of childhood and youth. William thot of the reason why Thelma had come. Her trip should realize that end. With this in mind, he showed her the cosy homes of his croppers.

When he had completed the tour, promptly with the world before her in panoramic view, she wondered how he could afford this. His answer was "Capitalism of today is wrong. It does not eliminate classes, rather it fixes them. A wage earner gets hardly a tenth of the wealth he produces. The bulk goes to the enterpreneur. I might within fifteen or twenty years easily accumulate a million. But a millionaire is an anachronism in a democracy. I am striving to give the worker all he produces, at the same time to keep a minimum for my counsel and guidance. Thus I never have any trouble getting workers. Furthermore, I run my farm on the eight-hour plan except ·during seed time and harvest, when we go far beyond this. During these seasons the laborers are given double pay for all extra time."

"I've been thinking that you're making trouble for yourself. How do neighboring farmers take this?" Thelma questioned, rejoicing that she had come alone.

"They are rather complaisant. They've come to regard my estate as a university of these parts, a sort of rendez-vous for the inspiration of progressive methods in farming. My ambition is primarily not to make money, but to show others how. Consequently I am no competitor to arouse their envy. My position is that we must not pull apart, but strive together. As an example, I go as readily to aid a white farmer as I do to aid a black one. Besides both black and white frequent my place, probably the whites more than my own people. The immortal words of Mrs. Dickinson in her "Assault on Fort Wagner" are my inspiration. She says, "Black and white were buried together, black and white in a common grave. Let liberty see to it then that black and white are raised together in a life better than the old."

Thelma, thru whom spoke generations crying to be born, stood like a stature, firm and still. She was thinking of what she could do to help bring together two peoples equally misunderstood. She took a dainty memorandum, and jotted down a gem. Looking away from a cottage to the West, she discovered a beautiful knoll. She moved in its direction and William followed almost automatically. "Come," she said with her voice as magic as the chimes of Christmas morning, "come I want to recite a poem which I recently composed."

He listened attentively while she read the following idyl:

O cabin dear,
Dost thou not hear
Her faltering voice?
Thy gloried choice
'Twas once. Dost not remember well
How sweetly to her songs we fell?
A mother fair,
O'erwhelmed with care,
Tript to the field
A hoe to wield,
The buried treasure there to reap,
Her babe forsaken, fast asleep.

The fleeting wind
Oft too unkind,
Takes holiday
To sport and play.
Refreshing greetings, sweet and long,
It fashions in a cradle song.

While baby sleeps,
The mother keeps
Beside her mate
Early or late.
To bid their poverty goodbye,
The two must slave, or fall and die.

When the weary sun,
Blushing for fun,
Shoots from the view
And bids adieu,
That evening shades might fall
And sport in the slumbering hall;

The mother stands
With welcome hands
At the cabin door,
Love's shower to pour
On him who unseen trophies brings,
Her lord, her saint, her king of kings.

The tattered shirt
With honorable dirt
And sweat, ne'er stains
The soul that rains
A flood of twilight, mirth and joy,
That hearts unchain and griefs destroy.

"Come, come, my boy,
Naught can annoy:
The white man's hate
Or a curse of fate,"
She said, with loving arms entwined,
To bring a star to his troubled mind.

"Our souls run true,
Our lives renew;
God makes the strife;
God crowns the life.
Tho riches' gulf we may not span,
Our babe shall pass, for he's a man.

"Come to your meat,
My noble sweet,
The day is done
And joy begun.
As heaven and earth are blithe and true,
You live in me and I in you."

"I'll work for a song,
I'll suffer wrong,
But where'er I be,
My spirit's free;
The darkest hours are filled with light,
The stars e'er shine tho out of sight.

"With you as bliss,
I naught can miss.
Our rising race,
Has set the pace.
Love, flowers are gay and skies are blue,
You live in me and I in you."

"Thelma," William began just as soon as she had finisht,
"I like your poem. Yet in a way it comes as a surprise; for
I've been under the impression that you're so fully occupied
with public service, that you had no time for the Muses."

She smiled and whispered sweetly, to be the more en-
trancing, "I have to continue scribbling to finish my appren-
ticeship. I hope some day to sing the deeds of the sage of
Seaton. Would you like that?"

"To be sure, it would be par excellence," he jested merrily.

Thelma moved somewhat closer to him, lookt away a moment, then lookt toward him and smiled. To be mischievous, she artfully took his hand and speedily let it go. That was long enough, too long; for in the instant Seaton had vanisht for the land of pure delight, for the joyous trembling of mate for mate, for the rapid heart-beat that hurries us to love, for the thrills that herald the approach of heaven. William wanted to retain her hand, to hold her against his heaving bosom to assuage the tempest there. His hands moved involuntarily towards her, and as he glanced, her lips quivered with soft emotion, her eyes spoke depths of love. Then smiling with the radiance of happy sunlight, she called in pleading tones of dainty melody, "William, William," and as if he had been naughty sprang from the knoll and answered back, "my William."

He followed, replying, "Thelma,"—his voice was all entreaty--"Thelma, don't."

Turning towards him, she said, "What do you wish William?"

The prophet stood, silent and dismayed. He recalled his days of romping with the Thelma of the past, he recalled her passing into womanhood, he saw a loving personality. How his soul cried out within him! How he longed to break the silence! Why could he not clasp her hand and be himself again? He moved nearer to her and she towards him, then leapt before him Susan's words, "William, you love me; and tho you may not take me for your wife, there is not born the woman who will love you more than I."

"Of what are you thinking, William?" laught Thelma to end his meditation, but would not wait for an answer. "This is a beautiful retreat. Who could not be happy here? The birds of paradise have never ceased their ditty since here we paused. They sang, 'Be dear, my friends.' And the

breeze whispered a pleasing lay, 'Young people soon grow old!'
Besides, yon gay stream purled along saying, 'I hope to see
you when I return.' At the same time the trees which form an
admirable screen, lisp, 'I'll see that none disturb you.' Even
my home companions, the flowers speak; they promise, 'We
shall be your garland against a very welcome day.' "

With arms outstretched, he rapidly goes to take her when
a whistle hoarse with sounding, announces the approach of
the community threshing machine and the laborers on surrounding farms. This was followed by a sharp outburst of vigorous singing, faintly first, then loud and louder:

> Pack up your troubles in your old kit bag
>   And smile, smile, smile;
> While you're a lucifer to light your fag,
>   Smile, boys, that's the style.
> What's the use of worrying?
>   It never was worrthwhile;
> So pack up your troubles in your old kit bag
>   And smile, smile, smile.

Finally appeared the man and the voice, a young, white
planter from a neighboring farm. Finding Rev. Smith vis-a-
vis with a young woman of great charms, he was much embarrassed. To make, however, the best of the untoward circumstances, he brusquely began to perform his duty. "My
name's Fred," he spoke. "What's yours?"

"Mine's William. Is there someone you're trying to
find?"

"Yes," responded the new arrival. "I'm looking for Mr.
Smith, the elder who owns this farm. I've just lately moved
into this section and have not learned all the folks."

"I'm your man," said Rev. Smith, "and I think I know
why you've come. How soon will Mr. Davis begin threshing?"

"Within half an hour."

"Tell him we'll be on time." In an instant the planter had gone.

Thelma, because of the dignity he showed, a dignity somewhat unusual among rustic people, inquired whether his attitude was typical. "He showed no hesitancy in properly addressing you. Where we are, white people dislike to call a colored person Mister or Miss. That's social equality, you know. Furthermore, you must not call them by their first names. The gentleman who just left considered us human beings like himself."

"His attitude is typical, Thelma," was the response. There may be the traditional southerner on outlying farms; but on this and neighboring plantations and even in the towns, my co-workers and I are addrest as we should be by anyone in New York City." He paused a moment, reflected, and then continued, "Thelma, come witness a novel sight. I believe you have not seen a wheat threshing?" He spoke inquiringly, yet in a mood which was almost care-free.

"No, I have not. I have so much longed to see one. How fortunate I am in having come in time for this great occasion! I am almost overjoyed." Thelma thot of the excellent tete-a-tete ended, but decided not to resume it at this time.

A few moments later they stept into his car and soon were on their way to his palatial home.

After the croppers and their helpers had been notified of the appointment, William and Thelma started for Mr. Davis' farm. As they rode along, greeted by fields of swaying corn on either side of tar oiled roads, they noticed men going in the same direction with pitch forks on their sturdy shoulders. The white workers were talking merrily, the colored were either whistling or singing. Then came occasional pranks accompanied with vivacious outbursts of "Oh, boy!" Next, a caper followed a strut accompanied by this merry tune, "Going to Halloway with my *Amanda Jane*." At once hearty peals of laughter all about the salubrious performer rang happily.

Lord and lady soon reacht the designated place and parkt at a point from which there was a full view of the coveted activity. Whereupon Thelma and William left the car to meet a group of women about whom tots were frolicking. After being introduced, Thelma made herself a friend of all the little folk; and they were trailing behind her to share an envied caress. The women were happy too, for they noticed at once that this urban personality had none of "your city airs."

Having placed the visitor in good company, William proceeded to organize the workers so as to expedite time. He himself chose to feed the bundles of wheat to the harvester. Daniel Martin, a white farmer, was to take the stand with him, cut the bands and hand him the bundles. Andy Clarkston was to receive the grains in the bushel baskets and empty them into barrels nearby. Mr. Davis' laborers were to haul the bundles of wheat from the stacks to the harvester. Henry and James Mitchell, both white, were to hand the bundles to Daniel Martin. All other laborers, white and black, were to handle the straw.

Here was a joyous scene. About sixty people, as many black as white, were about to perform a miracle for humanity. The field, where once countless blades of wheat stood, now showed everywhere a stubborn stubble. This however, was no barrier to the urchins who ran wherever they desired, in their bare feet. They lookt at the seven large stacks of wheat faintly visible in the distance, products of arduous life. Then they lookt at the large oil engine panting, ready to make the harvester go. Particularly did they eye the long pipe, which they thot would make some melodious sound. One little fellow bolder than the rest moved near to examine this magic worker, whereupon Mr. Davis shouted, "Boy!" The lad speedily took to his heels.

The colored laborers, who were to dispatch the straw, took their places and, as if beginning a ceremony, started to sing "The Hoeing of the Corn." This was followed by "Thresh Dat Wheat and Pile Dat Straw, Folks Git Tired of Corn Bread." Such robust strains of matchless harmony filled the air and thrilled all hearts, that all were at once exalted.

The whistle sounded for the task to begin. All were in place. The work was on. The harvester was fast, but Rev. Smith was faster, also were the other busy folk. Each tried to outdo the other, to show himself a man among men. This master man, however, could not be found. To get a greater inspiration, from time to time, individuals sang to the accompaniment of their own rhythmic souls, such songs as, "I'm Going Back to East Colorado" and "One More Time, Eh, Lord."

At sunset, the toilers ceased and went to the "big house" for the evening meal. Having washt, white and black sat down to the same tables and all were served at once. Heartily did they eat. Joke followed joke, hilarity ran high; most were highly pleased. A few of the white, Thelma noticed appeared at rare intervals somewhat choleric or disgruntled. Whatever their inner thots were, spleen never once was uttered. When

all had finisht, the guests left for their homes.

It was not long before a wonderful harmony again arose. The men were singing on their way home the following air:

Thresh dat wheat and pile dat straw,
   Folks git tired of corn bread.
Thresh dat wheat and pile dat straw,
   We folks want some white bread.
Ha ha! Ha ha! Ha ha! Ha ha!
Ha ha! Ha ha! Ha ha! Ha ha!
   We're goin' home dis ebe'ning!

When de sun pops in de sky,
   Airs itself and says goodbye,
We air fightin' wid de dust,
   Because some must, some must.

Thresh dat wheat and pile dat straw,
   Folks git tired of corn bread, etc.

Tho de rich folks laugh, and spend
   All our life blood to de end,
We can live at least oneday;
   We can be gay, be gay.

Thresh dat wheat and pile dat straw,
   Folks git tired of cornbread.
Thresh dat wheat and pile dat straw,
   We folks want some white bread.
Ha ha! Ha ha! Ha ha! Ha ha!
Ha ha! Ha ha! Ha ha! Ha ha!
   We're goin' home dis ebe'ning!

When the strains ceased to be audible, the heavens were veiled with purple twilight. Thelma said, "Can this be a dream? Do miracles now occur? What is this but a miracle? How did you bring this about?"

As he answered he moved towards his car. "I first won the confidence of my people. I told them their power when acting as a unit; that as they were the laboring force of the South they could compel fair treatment. I instructed them to refuse as a unit to be employed unless they were regarded as human beings. The work you saw done this afternoon was given freely. When a man gives his labor, he can not afford to take insults. I would not. As soon as this was learned, the others followed in my train," William spoke with great earnestness. He had by the time he finisht come to his automobile.

When they were seated, Thelma said, "Indeed this is truly wonderful. I came here liking this vicinity, but now I adore it. How long do you think the bliss can last?"

The prompt response was, "Forever."

Chapter XVII.

Do not, as some ungracious pastors do,
Show me the steep and thorny way to heaven;
Whilst, like a puffed and reckless libertine,
Himself the primrose path of dalliance treads,
And recks not his own rede.

*   *   *   *   *   *   *

This above all: to thine own self be true,
And it must follow, as the night the day,
Thou canst not then be false to any man.
—Shakespeare

When Thelma reacht Williamsburg and found no one at her home, she left her bag where her mother might readily see it and thereby know of her daughter's return. Attacht to it, she left a note, saying that she planned to make several calls, after which she would be at home for the evening.

She first saw Rev. Ross and told him of her trip in great detail. He was deeply imprest. Before she left, he told her that the party of which he had previously spoken would make an excursion to Seaton on the following day. Would she go? No! She preferred to go later. She called next on William's mother, then several other dear acquaintances; but she consciously avoided Susan Lee.

This done, she returned home amidst a shower of her mother's tender embraces. For quite a while, Thelma spoke of Seaton and William, then of William and Seaton. Mrs. Haskell interrupted with this remark, "My child, come, have some supper. Surely you are hungry."

"Mother, I'm not in the least," she said with great fervor. "I'm so full, that I just must talk. I have room for nothing else."

"Now I know what has occurred. You're in love with

167

William Smith. What will Susan say? I see why you have
not been close friends recently. Until a few weeks ago one
could hardly turn for the other."

She spoke pointedly, as she was disillusioned. "You have
been friends from infancy, but now—"

"Mother, I'm so hungry."

Mrs. Haskell laught. "How has it come so suddenly as
this?"

"I didn't feel thus a while ago; I do really crave something now," Thelma pleaded.

"Is it bread or is it William?" her mother taunted.

"Mother, mother, mother!" she laught. "Please let me
have some supper."

After a few exertions, Thelma sat down to an appetizing
meal and attackt it vigorously. How vehemently she tried to
dispel all thots of Seaton! Yet they 'would not down.' Mrs.
Haskell permitted her to eat without interruption. Then when
Thelma had finisht, she brot a letter which had been there
for several days.

"A letter from President Harper at this time—what an
unusual circumstance! He has never written me during vacation until the early part of September. Why this letter now?"
she mused. Without more ado, she opened it and read thus:

My dear Miss Haskell:
    The members of our trustee board waited upon me several
days ago and discussed your visit to Seaton. They feel that,
tho in all matters pertaining to Sojourner Truth College and
the community you have acted with tact and great discretion,
in this instance you have been most unwise and rashly impetuous. When I was importuned by our worthy officials,
you had already been in Seaton ten days, during which time
your name had become a synonym of evil suggestion.
    Not only have the trustees opposed you, but petitions con-
taining the names of fifteen hundred patrons have askt for

your removal, stating that your continuing on the Faculty would lead them to send their children elsewhere. The public is one in saying that your attitude is the expression of ideals that they wish their children not to acquire.

It is quite a calamity that our dean of girls has brot this odium upon her. For parents and girls both loved you well.

Yet I am constrained to ask that you tender your resignation. I know that many girls will not return, because your great affection made you a part of them. Since my constituency, however, demands this, I act.

Yours sincerely,

Thomas Harper.

"Mother," began Thelma, as soon as she had finisht, "President Harper has written me a very entertaining letter. Read it."

Mrs. Haskell eagerly began to peruse it, but when she had come to the end of the first paragraph, she frowned and said, "Thelma."

"Read it thru first and then put me on the wrack," the daughter spoke as if in jest.

When Mrs. Haskell had concluded, she remained silent for a while and then said, "You've just made a perfect mess of it. My premonitions pointed to something disastrous. Now the catastrophe is at hand. Thelma, why have you done this?" She sat down in anguish, then tears began to flow. "I cautioned you concerning this, yet you would go. I know you've done no wrong; but I dislike the ill feeling and unpopularity you have brot upon yourself."

The daughter lovingly embraced the mother and attempted to console her with these words, " 'As a man thinketh in his heart, so is he.' It is not what people think of me that is of prime importance, but what I think of myself, what I am, what I know I am. Many who walk and flaunt themselves angels of mercy are veritable devils infernal. I try to let my life be as a book where all may read. I am truly myself. Out-worn creeds and customs have no power over me. In my life I smash them all. I'd rather be myself than ape the powers that be! I'd rather be a beggar than crush the soul within me! Why have I done this? It was my desire. I did it, because I am a woman. I did it, because woman must be as free as man. I did it because neither heaven nor hell shall keep me from the man I love."

"Thelma, dear," the mother pleaded, "be calm. I believe in you, but I would not have you suffer. I fear that you'll have now few companions; that you'll be very lonely."

"Mother, do you realize that it's possible to be lonely in a crowd? This was often true of Christ. Similarly it's possible to be by one's self and yet have ample company. In attending some of the receptions of Williamsburg and con-versing with some of its so-called 'best people,' I've found them so empty, that I felt as if I were in a desert, plodding forlornly. These people don't think, they pay others to do their thinking for them. They scorn me now, but soon they'll give me tender embraces. As for the women, they've always murdered one another. Then why should they spare me? Notwithstanding this, be undisturbed. I have to depend upon no one occupation for my livelihood. I can now give all my time to those in the slums. I rejoice to go to those who need me," she spoke with great persuasiveness. Thus the mother was won.

"How can I break the news to your father?" Mrs. Haskell askt.

"Just permit me, mother. You know father and I get on very well."

"What a relief!"

"Mother, I see I have much business before me. Help me this much, please. While I make ready to go out again—

contrary to my former arrangements—do call up President
Harper and ask if I may have an interview within half an
hour."

Mrs. Haskell proceeded at once to the telephone. A few
minutes later she returned. To her surprise Thelma was
writing. "Thelma, President Harper will be expecting you.
What are you doing now, my child?" she remarkt.

"I'm writing my resignation, I'm trying to glorify you.
This night you will be proud of me." When she had completed this, she went upstairs to get her hat and scarf. As
she stept upon the porch, she said, "I've had a vision. I've
found my place. Have no fear. Goodbye, just for a while.'

Chapter XVIII.

All our friends, perhaps, desire our happiness ; but, then
it must invariably be in their own way.   What a pity that
they do not employ the same zeal in making us happy IN
OURS! —Lytton

President Harper, a man of forty-five, a giant in bronze,
with a bearing which at once commanded attention and respect, was seated this luxurious evening in his simple but alluring study.   It was a room of about ten square feet with two
modestly curtained windows that afforded ample light.   Resting
irresistibly in the center on a rug of beautiful but plain design
was a mahogany table supporting a vase of red roses.   In
one corner was a couch loaded with historical pillows, a
veritable summons to sit, inquire, and love.   In the opposite
corner was a case of books, to transport one to many storied
lands.   In the corner which would last be seen upon entering,
was a rolling-top desk.   Before this, making an excellent appearance, was a commodious, revolving chair.   Here and there,
yet well placed, were several chairs for visitors.   This study
with all its suggestiveness did not suit Mrs. Harper, until it
furnisht the biography of the spirit that staid there longest,
by athletic pictures and pennants of the schools that had inspired.   So carefully had the furnishings been selected that
to enter was to become a prey to the temptation to scrutinize
every detail, to stand captivated.   How attractive, how bewitching it all was!

At seven-thirty, the bell rang.   The distinguisht educator
who had been in his study for an hour, put aside his book
and went to the head of the steps to greet Thelma.   To his
surprise, he did not meet the lady, but shook hands with Mr.
172

Charles Tucker, president of the Board of Trustees. "Mr. Tucker," he said, "I'm happy to see you. How have you been since last we met?"

"First rate, Dr. Harper, first rate. Your pleasing countenance tells me at once that all has gone well with you."

"Not quite all, but I've been feeling fine." He moved a chair near the table and askt his guest to be seated. Then he himself sat in the revolving chair, with his back towards his desk, but his face towards his visitor.

Mr. Tucker, to whom long years in heading a construction company had made abstemious about the use of every minute, lost no time in stating his business, once greetings had been exchange. "Dr. Harper," he began pleasantly but seriously, "Have you as yet decided upon your new dean of girls?"

"No, not yet. A matter of such moment as this needs much reflection; and not even one week has past since you took action."

"I was thinking that Miss Kelley at the Nathaniel Turner Industrial School would be most satisfactory."

"Since I do not know her very intimately and since it is my duty to recommend, have her present her credentials and call to see me. I was hoping that we might do something to reinstate Miss Haskell. You are well aware that she is the best teacher that has ever entered the walls of Sojourner Truth College. Her spirit strongly reflects that of the great leader, after whom our school is named. I believe if our people were educated to this conception, they would make of our staunch citizen not a reproach but a providential satisfaction. I meant to leave within a few days for Buenos Ayres. If, however, you and your colleagues, will at least reconsider your action, I will forego my vacation and conduct the campaign for Miss Haskell's continuing with us."

"Dr. Harper, that is unthinkable. Once I've put my hands to the plow, I never turn back."

"Mr. Tucker, you are a business man," remarkt the educator. "Being such you have not never modified your plans and policies. Many an undertaking you have estimated at a particular price, only later to go over the whole account again and make your bid at a different figure. Besides, in doing so you know you have been wise. If the furrow was crooked, you turned back and made it straight. Why not do so now?"

"A woman who would so lower herself as has Miss Haskell, deserves no consideration," he replied irritably.

"My dear sir," said President Harper, with his eye well alert to the inconsistencies of modern society, "you are a deacon in one of our most progressive churches, a church whose business is the salvation of the people. Accordingly, after your faith in Christianity, if Miss Haskel has erred, you must consider her. If she has sinned, you must help save her. Does the attitude you and your colleagues have taken tend to save her or ruin her?"

Growing impatient, Mr. Tucker rose to go and said, "Let her come to church and there be saved. But what about the salvation of the young who would come under her instruction? It is better that one should suffer than many."

At this point the bell rang again. "Be seated just a moment longer, if you please," spoke Dr. Harper with great composure. So inured was he to the choler and phlegm of patrons, that Mr. Tucker's outburst was like a zephyr of spring.

A voice called, "Miss Haskell wishes to see you, papa. May she come up now?"

"Yes, show her up at once."

"I must be going, Doctor," said the trustee who now had become uneasy. "I have some other business needing attention."

"Doctor Harper spoke for time, and before the conversation could end, Thelma greeted the gentlemen good evening. Recognizing Mr. Tucker, she sat between him and the door, then said to him very affably, "Surely you're not going to let a woman run you away.""

He frowned and twitcht, "No, I can spare a few minutes. I suppose you want to ask me to keep you on the Faculty," he sneered. "Well, say your say—"

"Mr. Tucker, don't insult me," she uttered with calm defiance. "I've always respected you. Don't take me for a child, for you will be grievously mistaken. Let the lion within me remain asleep. Before I'd ask you to use your influence in my behalf for any position, I'd curse God and die." She was very positive. Her voice rang like a silver bell. Turning to President Harper that she might change the conversation and thereby not lose her temper, she said with her accustomed dignity, "Pardon me, Dr. Harper. When I entered your house I had no intention of making a scene; but having been trained to defend myself, I had to answer the distinguisht gentleman."

"Miss Haskell, no apology is necessary. You were entirely within your right," was the educator's terse remark.

"Do you still wish me to remain, Miss Haskell?" inquired the trustee, partially wishing to remain and partially to leave.

"Yes, Mr. Tucker, since what I have to say is concerning my relation to Truth College, as one of its chief executives you should hear me thru," came forth almost spontaneously. Turning more directly to her adversary, she requested goodnaturedly, "Tell me please why you didn't dismiss me, but preferred to ask me to resign? There was no need for ceremony. Whether I wrote the resignation or not, I could not teach at Truth College."

"True the request is a formality. Yet we did not want to injure your career. Years hence some one desiring to employ you would not consider you, if our records read 'dismissed,'" Mr. Tucker affirmed, mopping his face with his favorite blue, bordered handkerchief.

"What oddities occur in life!" Thelma ejaculated, producing her resignation from her bag. "You'd cast the undesirable on others no less desiring her."

"Not that at all," the trustee said, with a grimace, squirming almost at every word, "there might be others who'd accept you regardless of anything we might say. We'd have to acknowledge your efficiency. Still we can not condone your recent impudence."

"Pardon me, but what was my impudence?" Thelma requested.

"You went to Seaton alone and spent most of your time on the estate of Rev. Smith, a man who has not the good graces of the minister of Williamsburg, nor of many of the people—a visionary, a radical, a fanatic. Hence we believe that you are of the same type," Mr. Tucker resumed now with more vivacity. President Harper decided not to interrupt.

"A person with original ideas has no place in society?"

"Those ideas are not to be incompatible with the welfare of the majority of the group."

"Mr. Tucker, have you ever visited Dr. Smith and surveyed the work he's doing? Do you realize that he is bringing white and colored together upon terms of increasing familiarity. Aren't you aware that such must be done, if we continue here? Can't you see that to serve God, you must help your fellowman?" Thelma broached him fervently, for she now had no need of diplomacy, but only for straight forward thrusts.

"No, I haven't been there and do not wish to go. I've heard enough of it to keep me away." The trustee was very impatient and unreasonable.

"You let your prejudice get the better of you, and condemn a cause of which you are ignorant. You are just like most white people in this country. They see the Negro only from a great distance, most of them never meeting our best; yet they assume most intimate knowledge."

"That's neither here nor there. To be brief, Rev. Smith's ideas, which unfortunately have seized you too, are not welcome here. Furthermore, you went contrary to the advice of your pastor. As dean of our girls, you were to them a model. Your life we regarded as the tangible ideal which our girls should achieve. Since you've ceased to be that, your place is naturally elsewhere. Aren't you quite different from most of our women?" Mr. Tucker spoke rapidly, desiring the matter soon to end. Yet in doing so he was somewhat brusque.

"Yes, I'm different from many of the women of this town. I've tried all my life so to be. If I'm regarded as being of another variety, my labor has not been in vain," she admitted with meek sedateness. "Mr. Tucker, I'm always changing. If you meet me tomorrow, you will not meet the woman of today. Thus I've taught these girls to be; not fossils, not models for such are merely samples; not ornaments for ages the same, but plastic creatures ever fresh and new with a grandeur unique, that will not only attract men, but make even women pay them adoration. I should have them so moulded that their spirits would never grow old, that even after they marry they might always show their husbands new charms, something in them for further conquest. Once a husband knows his wife thoroly, he is likely to seek another woman who can entertain him. A wife needs to be very resourceful. She should always have a surprise."

The trustee became exceedingly interested in her train of thot. However, as he did not wish her to know to what extent, he turned his face somewhat, lest she would observe the emotion.

At this gesture, which Thelma interpreted as an effort for reflection, she renewed her remarks with Dr. Harper. "When I finisht reading your letter," she said, turning toward the educator, "I thot of ignoring it. Certainly I could only construe it as a dismissal. But having workt with you for two years and shared your joys and sorrows, sure that tho you penned the letter, the request was not your own; out of great respect for you, I have written the resignation. Here it is." She handed him the letter and went back to her seat.

At this point the other personality broke in. His tones were rather sonorous. "Miss Haskell, I'm hoping that the Trustee Board will reconsider its action and not accept your resignation. You've been an invaluable co-worker and I dislike much to lose you. Of course, a Faculty should be mobile, otherwise it can have no life. We can not always keep our workers; but when they do go, we want to lose them for important considerations, not mere caprices."

"Doctor Harper, do you think we have acted merely upon impulse and not for the interests of the community?" Mr. Tucker interrupted impatiently.

"I can regard the action as being only the result of a public storm, not of quiet deliberation. As one who for twenty years has been selecting teachers and passing upon their usefulness to the school under my charge, I was the one to dismiss Miss Haskell. I determine the policies of the institution; I see that they are carried out." The president was very impressive.

Here Thelma interrupted. "Dr. Harper, I couldn't remain now, since the majority of the people do not want me."

"Miss Haskell, you'll do, I know, what is best for the community," the president affirmed. Thelma nodded assent. "All this is the work of a few irascible citizens. There were several mass meetings, stirred by explosive oratory. My presence was not desired at any of them. I attended the last, however, and forced an opportunity to speak. I askt the people first to hear you, Miss Haskell; but so much venom had already been dispersed, that they chose a hasty course, to the disgrace of Williamsburg." He paused a few moments and then continued. "Mr. Tucker, do you know anything about Sojourner Truth, her whose spirit we try to emulate?"

"I know only that she was a great Negress who was freed before the Civil War and lived quite a while after it," he replied.

"Then read this chapter concerning her, in Mr. Cromwell's 'The Negro in American History.' Meanwhile I'll glean from Miss Haskell many particulars concerning her recent trip," he requested very politely.

"May I take the book home and read it? I'll have more time to do the task justice," Mr. Tucker remarkt rising to go.

Treating him as he would a school boy that studies only under the task master, Dr. Harper said, "It's important that you read this now. We have a serious matter to decide, which can only be handled after knowing all the facts." The president urged his request because of the influence of Mr. Tucker with his colleagues. As went Mr. Tucker, so went the other trustees.

Assenting to the entreaty, he withdrew to the farthest corner of the room, Thelma and Dr. Harper to the opposite. Tho Mr. Tucker wanted to know what was being softly spoken in the interview, he was finally able to concentrate sufficiently to be entranced by the life of that great woman. After an interval, he read voraciously. Having completed the sketch, he went to his former seat and said, "Dr. Harper, I'm ready."

The president turned in his chair, opened the envelope on his desk, and said, "Miss Haskell, read this. It's your resignation."

"Dr. Harper, I object," Mr. Tucker put forth impatiently. "That letter should be placed before the Board. This is no time for its consideration."

"I see no grounds for your objection. The lady knows its contents, for she wrote it. Moreover, it is addrest to me, I may hear it. Finally, since resignations are filed in my office and are never read at Board meetings except upon request, and as no such request has been made up to this time, the reading is entirely apropos," he uttered with great passion.

"Well, I don't like it," protested the trustee.

"Read on, Miss Haskell," said the educator.

President Harper,
Dear Sir:

I resign. I resign the girls to your wise counsel and to her who comes to be your dean. I resign the Board of Trustees to their proper sphere, champions of better days to be. I resign you and your loyal teachers to a work much better than the old, instructing adults as well as children, for all have much to learn. I resign myself to my own world of hope, love and youthful endeavor. I resign the shackles of woman, forged by superstitious conventionality, and hurl them to their destined place a thousand years behind Time.

What care I for the scorn of thousands? This world has its millions. I am living not for today, but for all the tomorrows. I go. Goodbye. I resign.

Yours respectfully,

(Miss) Thelma Haskell.

When she had finisht, Dr. Harper said, "Do you still feel the same towards our dean? Haven't you really made a mistake? Don't you feel that you should see your co-workers and arrange for a reconsideration?"

Mr. Tucker was convinced of his error and the very fact that he was wrong irritated him immensely. Unwilling to admit that he had made a mistake, he spoke vehemently, "Miss

Haskell is an imposter, a regular snake in the grass. She performs acts, which we vigorously condemn, then puts herself before us as a martyr. She's a devil incarnate." Suddenly inflamed with an almost unconquerable hate, he lost complete control of himself.

"Be careful as to what you say," came passionately from Thelma. "I have this evening given you my greatest respect, not because you deserve it, but because you're in the home of one whose character is faultless."

"Mr. Tucker," Dr. Harper interrupted, to have his guest resume his equipoise, "temper is powerless where reason fails. Miss Haskell has done you no wrong. As she has treated you most kindly, your vituperation is entirely out of place. If I were as sure of the honor of the majority of the women of Williamsburg, as I am of that of this young lady, I should know that the future of my race is secure.

"Women can deceive some men, but I know them well. This woman is a vampire. Get out of my sight!" he shriekt.

"You forget that this is my house, Mr. Tucker."

"Well, I can leave it," responded the trustee, as he started to go. Thelma stept to one side to let him pass. "Woman, don't look at me. I'll crush the life out of you," he said, rushing to her with hands outstretcht to grasp her by the throat.

"Stand back, you demon, you reprobate, you scoundrel. Put your hands on me and you're a dead man. Shame on you," she shouted, flashing a revolver in his face, before the president could place himself between them. "Thank you, Dr. Harper, but I can take care of him myself. I bought this companion for the white and black toughs who assault colored women. I'd expect to find them occasionally in the slums, but least of all here. This place should be sacred; only those with the highest sense of honor should enter it." The trustee cowered. "Mr. Tucker," she continued, after scrutinizing him a while, "if I thot you were ready for heaven, I'd send you there. You are not fit to die, and yet not fit to live. Sir, remember *I am a woman.*"

Then Dr. Harper interrupted to make the master stroke, "Don't you in your heart admire Miss Haskell?"

Before the trustee could answer, sounds of children's joyous singing came beneath the windows:

> Miss Haskell is a lady
> She's always sweet and shady.
>   We'll take her to the bowling green
> To be our fairy queen.

When these sweet sounds could no longer be heard, the trustee proceeded to leave. As the guest past out of the door, Dr. Harper said, "Mr. Tucker, I am going to recommend that Miss Haskell continue to be our dean." In a moment the trustee had gone. When the door downstairs closed, he added with great satisfaction, "Gallant lady, I believe we've won a victory."

CHAPTER XIX.

A little leaven leaveneth a whole lump. —I Cor. 5: 6.

It is like leaven which a woman took and hid in three measures of meal, till the whole was leavened. —Lu. 13: 21.

He hath put down the mighty from their seats, and exalted them of low degree. —Lu. 1: 52.

When the party which included Rev. Ross and Susan arrived at Seaton, William Smith was standing at the station, ready to give them every hospitable consideration the South could afford. After he had arranged for the conveyance of all the others, he placed Susan by his side. Rev. Ross and the mothers sat in the rear. Within a few minutes they were at the celebrated estate and seated for breakfast.

After the morning meal, the eager visitors made a tour about the farm. William took unusual pains to see that no phase of his enterprise escaped the attention of his guests. Furthermore, as each detail was considered, time was taken for a brief discourse, in order that all might have a comprehensive view of the entire plan, which would be both educative and highly enjoyable.

When they had made thus a complete survey of the property and witnessed several demonstrations, they assembled for a fête on the lawn. It was now late in the afternoon. The sun had gone down. Besides, a welcome breeze came upon them in a shady nook, where all was charming and delightful.

There the people rejoiced and reveled, singing, dancing, romping, and gaming. All were happy and gay. Why should they not be? Refreshments were free and in great abundance:

cake, ice cream, punch and various soft drinks. Everyone was enraptured that he had come and regretted the absence of his friends.

While the gayety ran high, William tried to find a secluded place where he might talk intimately with Susan; but as all had apparently laid claim to him, up to this time he had not succeeded. He might have gone off in his car; but as this was a party, he felt that he should always keep within reach.

At last, as the best he could do, he went quite a distance from the others but never out of view.

Susan was as fine and dainty as ever, sweet and good, like a robust girl ready for tennis. Her dress of white and her canvas oxfords bewitcht the gazer at once. Add to this a glance at her russet face, demure and fair, and her waving, dark hair, the spectator would not be charmed, transported, or allured, but completely overawed.

They sat upon a wicker seat facing the other guests, hoping not to be disturbed. "Susan, I'm glad that you have come. I've been hoping that you would have appeared earlier; since I could not leave because of the wheat harvest in the neighborhood. Within a few days we shall have finisht, then I'll have considerable time to myself," said Smith.

"I wanted to come, William, so much; but I thot it best to wait until today. When I learned that Thelma was here, however, I became almost furious." Her face showed it. "I wonder should I tell you this," she continued. "Well, it's all right. I had started, had really reacht the station, when mother overtook me. She pleaded and cried so bitterly that I decided to go back. She was sadly happy to tell William of the fullness of her heart, dedicated wholly to him.

"Yet I do wish you had come alone. We should have

found time to thresh out all uncertainties. As it is we may be disturbed at any moment."

"Suppose I had come. What would have occurred in Williamsburg? Do you know what the community did for Thelma? They held indignation meetings against her. That wasn't all. I met her, as she was coming from President Harper's.

"Just think of it. Mr. Tucker was so rude as to make a scene in the president's office. I'm glad he found his match tho." For a while Susan's jealousy was gone. Her face showed a smile delicately sweet and captivating.

"What did she do?" inquired William, very eager to know all the details.

"Ask me rather what she did not do. I have to admire her even tho she is my rival."

At this juncture, Lewis Brown appeard accompanied by another gentleman, of rustic mien but simple grace, a loyal citizen of the land. "Rev. Smith," said Brown a bit embarrassed, "pardon this intrusion, please. But Mr. Houston—" he pointed to the gentleman—"wants to see you on some very important business. If it hadn't been urgent; I'd forced him to wait until tomorrow."

"Is the business private?"

"I can say what I've got to say right heah. Dis all 'tis. Mr. Martin wants to rent me his farm dis fall for four hundred eighty dollars. What mus' I do. Ef you says, 'Tek it,' it's a bargain. Ef you says, 'Let 'er go,' I don' want it," he spoke with great directness, fearless and unshamed.

"It'll be all right, Mr. Houston," responded William very courteously. "You must draw up no papers tho; don't sign anything until I go with you to Mr. Martin."

"You bet yo' boots. One oder thing Rev. Smith. Dan'el Martin told me ef I sed 'Yis' today, I could buy rations dere and pay after I'd made a crop. Should I do dis?" the visitor inquired with a simple faith that showed almost worship for our young man.

"Pay cash for your rations. You have enough in bank to do this. If you start working a crop to pay a grocery bill, you may never get out of Martin's debt."

"I'd git out, but Ise gwine a foller your advice. I'll be heah early tomorrow mornin'. Thank you, good bye." He bowed and turned to go.

William detained him for a while. "Mr. Houston," he said, "you haven't met my guest, I'm sure. This is a dear friend of mine, Miss Lee of Williamsburg. Miss Lee, meet Mr. Houston."

"My spec's, my complemints." He did not tarry long. He soon said, "Be good to yo' self. Good bye."

Within a few minutes Brown and Mr. Houston were soon out of sight. Almost immediately loud outbursts of laughter now came forth near the house, as a result of the fall of Mrs. Castle. As it was merely an incident of merriment, the party was not disturbed in the least. Susan had started in that direction, but since order was very quickly restored, she returned to her seat.

"William, how I wish I could remain here several days! I've had a good time, a good time. I've been almost in a continuous state of ecstacy. I'm going to ask mother, if she won't stay longer. Papa can spare us. He'll do anything for me."

"Do ask her."

"I'll do so at once." She hurried off. When she had gone quite a few yards, she was accosted by a white farmer of middle age in working attire.

"Madame," he began, "can you tell me where I can find Mr. Smith? I want his advice on a very serious matter."

"There he sits. He'll be glad to see you." Susan found her mother with practically no difficulty, took her aside, and made her request. Her effort, however, was rather arduous because there were many interruptions. There were inquiries of "How are you enjoying yourself? Isn't the punch delightful? This is truly a wonderful estate, isn't it?" They rarely expected an answer, for before the person questioned could make reply, the inquisitor was gone. By persisting and constantly renewing the broken threads of speech, she was able to get a definite answer.

When she reacht William again, she saw that his visitor was about to go. He turned to him and said, "This is the young lady who pointed you out. I haven't seen her before; is she a stranger in these parts?"

"Yes, she comes from my home town, Williamsburg. Mr. Nailor, this is Miss Lee, daughter of one of the largest manufacturers in that town."

"Miss Lee, I'm glad to meet you. I hope you'll have a pleasant time here."

"So I am. I find this country almost a paradise." Susan was perfectly natural.

"Well, I must be going. We'll see Davis Monday. Good day, Mr. Smith. Good bye, Miss Lee." Susan lookt at him in amazement. For the first time she had met a southern white man who did not place himself above colored people. She stood entranced, almost as if hypnotized, watching Mr. Nailor move slowly over the stately hillocks of William's farm. She herself eventually started in that direction, sighed, and peered. Then she returned to her seat.

"William, I want some information; and you must give it. Since I've been in your company today at least twelve persons have sought your counsel. I have counted five white farmers among the number. What has come over this place? It was not thus before you came." Susan tossed her head bewitchingly and awaited an answer.

"A better day is dawning. That's all. The South, you know, is aristocratic. Once you grasp the significance of that, progress becomes rapid. The typical southern gentleman wants someone perpetually to do the laborious tasks of life, particularly his farming. Regarding the black man as his inferior, he seizes upon him to do this work perpetually."

"I know the colored share little in common with the whites. We do come together in a few stores, but not as equals. William, why is this?" she pleaded, breathing deeply the breeze which then passed gently by.

"It is simply the white man's ignorance. Booker T. Washington has well said, 'To keep a man in the gutter you must stay down there with him yourself.' The South has been staying in the gutter, while the North, East, and West have gone on high.

"I came here accepting two callenges: first that of my fellow minister, according to which I should not preach. The other defiance was the white man's; namely, that my place is down South on the farm. My people can not all become farmers, for many of us have the genius of merchants, or of mechanics, or of the professional men. All these we need and shall have. To dignify farming, however, and cause even many of the whites to consider it honorable toil, I launcht this big experiment."

"I've seen your building and several of your demonstrations given by use of equipment stored in them; but I'd like for you to tell me of some of the influences which do not lie at the surface."

"Well, this was my inspiration. Seeing that the colored

outnumbered the whites and that I was in the midst of a traditional aristocracy, I at once became aware that we were being even forced to work, while a few enjoyed idle ease. Not only were my people hardly making expenses, but even large numbers of the whites. We've been held back by the endless grocery bill. That's why I told Mr. Houston to obtain nothing on credit."

"I remember the incident."

"Another important fact you yourself mentioned. The two groups rarely meet. I do believe, however, they meet more frequently in the country than in the town. It's no uncommon sight for white and black farmers to help each other, both during planting and harvest. Both groups have been and are oppressed, and need each other's help to throw off their economic slavery. Of course the groups are closer together now than they were, when I came to establish here."

"Anyone can vouch for that whose life can touch both extremities. Tell me tho, what you did to help on the change." Susan's eyes were riveted upon him. The occasional laughter did not disturb her in the least. William paused merely to look at her and be made anew by the magic of her sparkling eyes. Would the day might never end!

"I put in a small crop," he began," and askt different members of my own race to let me help them produce theirs. Many were at first reluctant, but after a mass meeting in the school house, I had them all. There I askt how many owned farms, how many rented, how many meant to buy soon, and how many were not going to buy at all. I advised them if they had not bought, to see me before discussing the matter with any one who wanted to sell. The following day I lookt at the deeds of those who had bought. Most of theme were deeds fee entail and not fee simple; which means that those persons holding such were owners until death, after which time the property reverted to the man who sold or to his heirs. The possessors were furious. Several of the deeds were made out properly, but most of them were not. It was this incident that gave me my people."

Susan was not satisfied. She knew that he must have angered many of the whites, even tho he had merely done his duty. To learn the other phase of the issue, she askt, "How did you win the white farmer?"

"I pursued the same policy and found that many of them who thot they owned their land were merely renting for life. All their deeds, however, were rewritten, so that those who had been beguiled would have such a title as would permit the property to go to their own descendents. In addition to this, I showed many of them how to prepare their own fertilizer and how to test their soil. I have given myself equally to both groups as far as they would permit."

"You surely have done wonders. Yours is the work that counts." At this, she lookt away and within four feet of her, there skipt and played two squirrels. She called them. At once they stopt, turned in her direction and capered to a tree near by. She called again and they turned merely to notice; then gracefully scampered away. Susan stood enraptured, forced for a time to be speechless.

Seeing her thus absorbed, William askt, "What is your meditation? Permit me to share with you." Susan had gone to the tree where the sinuous creatures had sought refuge. She lookt up, in order to follow their movements; but she lost sight of them, as soon as they leapt to another tree.

"They are indeed happy. Would I were so! I wonder if they are mates." For the first time that day her brow was clouded. She was thinking of her own situation.

"I thot you were happy. At least you have said so several times today. Why are you otherwise now?" he questioned as he went to her side. He wanted to take her hand, but as there was no privacy in that spot, he contented himself with a look that spoke great admiration.

"I was happy until I saw the squirrels," she remarkt with an emotion so deep as to thrill his entire frame. "I was thinking how near they are to each other and how far we are apart."

"Aren't we near to each other, Susan? My soul goes out to yours and I do believe they oft embrace."

"I'll agree to all that; but do they go out to each other as the only possible refuge, as the only port in a storm, as the only oasis in a desert? You understand?" came the query, with a passion that revealed a determination to have an answer. The circumstances were not to send her empty away. Thelma, she knew, had made an impression. She must know of any change.

William reflected a few moments before making reply. The interruptions had been so many, as to prevent his being occupied only with Susan. The image and grace of Thelma kept looming before him; thus he found himself all day contrasting the two. He had resolved within several days to make the choice, which was recently forced upon him.

"That is the point I must reach soon," he continued. "My desire is not to make you miserable but happy. The life I pursue is one which may incite strong currents of envy. In a lawless South, I've declared war on prejudice, on fraud and all injustice. You recall the lynching of Mr. Crawford, one of the most worthy citizens of his state. What was his crime? The acquisition of legitimate wealth," he recalled too the lynch-

ing which he had seen, the summer he went far South. BRU-
TALITY! BARBARISM! SAVAGERY!

Now Susan became somewhat nervous, for she was about
to ask a question which had long been lingering on her mind.
She wanted to hear what he had to say concerning it. "William," she askt, "do you like Thelma?" As soon as she had
spoken, she moved a step or two away, for she partly believed
that she had acted improperly. Yet she was bent on standing
her ground, because she wanted to remove all uncertainty.

"Yes, I do," he admitted. "I like her very much. You
know how we used to romp together in early childhood."

"I remember," she said plaintively. "I wish I could tell
you how I feel at times especially at night as I lie in bed just
before going to sleep, I have tried to send you a thot. I think
of all I should like to have. Indeed strange presentiments
come before me. I fear, I fear—"

"What do you fear?" he broke in to retard her rapid emotion. Realizing the burden of her soul, he wanted to help her
to dispel it.

The guests in the distance now became rather uproarious.
The cessation of the music gave occasion for many peals of
laughter; for at this time George Brown, the son of the chief
cropper, passed by on a goat that was trying its best to throw
him.

Susan thus found time to become more composed; for the
attention of all had to some extent been disconcerted. When
the hilarity abated, they saw Rev. Ross coming towards them
leisurely.

"Susan, you failed to tell me your fears," he persisted.

"Sometimes I fear some great harm will befall you, and
I'll not be by to aid you. I fear also—William, I can't tell
you."

"Susan, you must," he persisted. "You can confide in me, can't you? If it's a secret, I'll carry it with me to eternity. I answer all your questions; surely you will answer mine."

"William, I can no longer hold out, you know my heart is yours forever. Oh, that yours were mine! That's my dread. I fear that I shall lose you," she almost whispered. Yet she was conquering the manly heart. What bulwarks can we raise againt sweetness, what defense against beauty, loveliness, and constant devotion! Love conquers all things.

"Try to remove the fear. A 'ew moments of privacy will settle it all. If I thot I had t ie promise of ten more years of life, I could make answer now," he said going towards the house.

"To know that you were mine even for a day would be bliss enough for me," her soul cried out with the admission she had made. For a while she trembled, because she felt as if the night winged horrors of disappointment to her.

"Think of this tonight," he urged to avoid rashness, "and let us decide tomorrow, after a soul to soul talk alone. You're going to remain over another day, aren't you?" At this time Rev. Ross was almost upon them. Already he had called to them saying it was time for the party to prepare for Williamsburg.

Susan sorrowfully replied, "No, I go back tonight. I ought to be stubborn for once. I ought to rebel." That night she went back to Williamsburg.

CHAPTER XX.

Fify years ago you doubtless would have rankt Japan among the benighted nations. *** But since the happenings at Mukden and Port Arthur, I suppose you are ready to change your mind upon the subject. *** In the proud days of Aristotle, the ancestors of Newton and Shakespeare could not count beyond the ten fingers. —Miller

While the party from Williamsburg was taking a full measure of happiness, while William was entertaining Susan under difficulties, twelve white men assembled at the home of Robert White, a hard worker strongly obsest with the idea of white supremacy. Tho biased, he was liberal enough to call in men of different occupations.

In the modest front room of the weatherboard dwelling, illuminated with a simple kerosene lamp, the gentlemen discussed miscellaneous topics till all those expected had arrived. When the last was seated, Robert White promptly began, "Gentlemen, we're here to decide what's to be done with niggers round here—especially this smart darkey, Parson Smith."

Mr. Davis, whose wheat was thresht the first day of Thelma's visit, rose promptly and interfered thus, "Mr. White, pardon my interruption but let us not speak of niggers and darkies. When we talk in that way we lose our presence of mind. Call them colored people. If we are to act justly, we must be calm."

"Davis, I'm just talking as I feel. To me they're just downright niggers, if to you they're different all right. Gentlemen the meeting is open." He spoke in utter scorn of a loyal race.

Fred Dean then arose. He had not been long in the vicinity and, therefore, was somewhat unwilling to lead the way. Having developed a keen appreciation for Smith he was ready for a defense, but thot he should first have a thoro knowledge of the facts in the case. "Gentlemen, as I'm a newcomer, just tell me what all the noise is about. What harm is Mr. Smith doing?"

Tom Howell, reporter for the "Seaton Gazette," robust and boisterous, was on his feet in a twinkling, "There's the trouble," he shouted, brandishing his first in the air and looking quickly from one to the other. "Mr. Smith," he sneered. "Mr. Smith. Before that coon came here nobody called a nigger Mister. Now all those darkies on his farm have to stay in their place."

Mr. Nailor, who had gone there directly from William's estate, broke in at this point, "Tom Howell, I know you. What have you done for this town? You've only gotten drunk off Crabtree's liquor, with that political bunch, and stolen the labor of ignorant colored men. If our courts weren't crooked, you'd been on the chain gang long ago. That's where you belong." This was too much for the biased men.

Luke Crabtree and Tom Howell began simultaneously to abuse Nailor. Pandemonium almost followed. The alertness of those not involved in the altercation alone prevented blows.

When quiet again prevailed, Nailor resumed his remarks as if no turbulence had occurred. "I call the Reverend 'Mister' and properly address all members on his estate. Because they are gentlemen, I treat them as such. Besides he and his helpers have made this community thrive more than any one I've seen here in the last fifteen years. I'll take off my hat to him and as many more as will do as much."

"They'll be wanting to marry your daughter, too," interrupted Newton Young, one of the brokers of Seaton.

"Newton, I call you 'Mister.' Yet if I thot any one of my daughters was bent on marrying you, I'd kill her before she'd have the chance. I'd rather marry her to any of those colored men on that estate, for they are honest."

"Gentlemen," came from Silas Jones, who had kept silence only with great constraint, "I believe Bob made a mistake in calling some of these folks here this night."

"No, Silas, it's better to have all sorts of folks in this meeting; for tho I feel that the niggers have taken some of our rights, I want to hear what some of our best men think of the matter," he put in, desiring to have all be tolerant towards each other. "Probably we can't never agree with 'em, but it aint goin' to hurt us to listen."

"As soon as a white man starts doing his duty towards his colored brother, men who want something for nothing begin to throw up the question of amalgamation. Want to marry my daughters," said Nailor with a jeer. "That's their business. The women will take care of that. If my daughter loves a black man, and he loves her; if they decide to unite, after having considered all the consequences—all I have to say is this. What God has joined together, let no man put asunder."

"You talk like that," said Sandy James, a pettyfogging lawyer, "because you've got your property, but these men who see the nigger going ahead, see that something must be done to keep the darkey down. If they don't wake up, the niggers will be running the country." Turning to Mr. Davis, he continued. "Davis, you're a fair-minded man, you're the biggest of us all. Answer one question for me. Do you think it safe for us to follow this high sounding talk of Nailor?"

Mr. Davis did not care to answer at this time, for he

felt that some of those present might purposely distort his words. However, as he was not a man to stand on the fence, he very soon made reply. "I may not agree with all Nailor says, but I do agree with him in this: treat a man as you find him. If he's honest, industrious and keeps his word, treat him on the square. There are some colored folks I don't want around me; but any time I can get one of Rev. Smith's force, I hold him tight." He struck one hand in the other, to be the more impressive. "I have to pay those men more than I do other folks, but they stick to the job, they do their work better and even show me how to make more money."

That's what we're complaining about," said Silas Jones, stamping his feet. "That nigger's running our folks out of work."

"On the contrary," went on Mr. Davis, "he's making work for them. He's showed them how to keep fruit upon the tree until it ripens. He's showed them how to treat their hogs for cholera. He's shown them how to raise other staples than cotton. And Silas, you know he came to show you how to handle your bottom lands, that would have meant work for many of our people. What's been the result? The land's idle —no good to you nor anybody else."

"I ran him away. I don't want a nigger to show me nothing," came from Silas with a scorn even for those who brook such consideration.

"Why don't you go to the University then and have some white man teach you something about improved farming?" remarkt Fred Dean, who was moving with the spirit of his age. He chewed vigorously his quid of home cured and offered some of the same brand to all present. "We folks have believed the professors were just dreamers, but these days, if a man means to go ahead in farming, he must keep in touch with the Agricultural Department of the United States and with the agricultural schools. Smith wouldn't be able to do these wonders, if he hadn't gone to one of those schools. He's done this community a whole lot of good. We're going to be glad to go. Having seen what this one man has done in spite of the prejudice against him, more of our people are going to stay on the farms and not run to the cities."

The tide had drifted too favorably in Smith's direction for several present, who had ambitions which they deemed it unwise to disclose at this particular time. These put their heads together, as it were, to make their case strong. Of this group, Luke Crabtree, the saloon keeper, who had listened attentively to all that had been said, arose to put in his contention. "Friends, this nigger's almost running me out of business. The darkies used to drink almost their entire week's earnings with me, now they're becoming scarcer and scarcer than ever. Instead of spending with me, they're carrying it to the bank. Even old Rufus Childs, that trifling nigger, almost never comes now. If this keeps up, there won't be anybody on the chain gang to work the county roads and some of the big plantations. Something's got to be done mighty quick."

"You ought to be glad the darkies are behaving themselves," spoke Daniel Martin for the first time that evening. "When they're good, you get more work out of 'em. Then you can depend upon them, for they work every day."

"That may be all right," came from Sandy Janes, "but when niggers get a little money, they begin to think they're just as good as white folks. I don't fear the nigger who hasn't any sense. You're not going to have any trouble keeping him in his place. It's the educated nigger I fear."

"You gave me the impression awhile ago," said Henry

Mitchell, the harness repairer who had been trying to edge in a word but somehow had been prevented, "that the Negro is inferior to you, that he is inferior to the white race."

"Yes, he's inferior," was the lawyer's quick retort. "He never was anything, he's nothing now, and he'll never amount to anything."

"If that's so," replied Mitchell, "the white man needs have no fear. If there's nothing in the Negro, then our discussion is out of place. Give him time and he'll die out. Nothing you do for him can save him, if he's inferior. Besides if you're superior, you have no cause whatever for worry. Everything is in your favor; success was yours before the world began."

"Well, they say there's nothing in him," rejoined the lawyer, not to be outdone by the good sense of a non-professional man. "Yet when we see one do the work of that smart darkey and his helpers, there may be a mistake. Hence we must be on the safe side. I might probably be speaking differently but for the 'Birth of a Nation,' the moving picture which was shown here six weeks ago. Did you see it, gentlemen?" All had seen it. "What do you think of it?"

All agreed that reflection was necessary. The attempted rape by the lustful, blood-thirsty scoundrel stirred the passionate natures of them all. The suggestion was enough to move to action and produce the effect that several had all the while desired. They seized upon it as the crux of their whole design. Vituperation poured upon vituperation, then many ebullitions of pusilanimity. The lawyer spoke now as if in a political campaign, and used all the tricks of the experienced "fire eater." He recalled the scene in the southern senate, which Griffith and Dixon have made disgusting and nauseating in the extreme. He followed this with a vivid sketch of the

Lieutenant-Governor's effort to force the Governor's daughter to marry him. Then he closed with praise of the Ku Klux Klan, representing it as the savior of the South. He sat down amidst great applause of half the assembly.

Those who had spoken in behalf of fair play, tho imprest by the lawyer's rhetoric, maintained their presence of mind. While the others went to Sandy James and shook hands with him firmly, congratulating him upon his magic eloquence, these gentlemen remained calmly seated, as if mere spectators of a drama. Eventually Mr. Nailor interrupted, "Gentlemen, pardon my disturbance, I call upon you now more urgently than ever to be composed. After a storm, we need to look to our moorings. This is a new South, and Rev. Smith is the new Negro. The scoundrel shown in the 'Birth of Nation,' tho later than the Uncle Tom type, is also passing. You know as well as I that in the last ten years not a colored man has been lyncht in this state for rape. The educated Negro never commits this crime anywhere; the guilty man is the culprit we permit to loaf in the streets."

"I don't trust none of them," put in Bob White. "I wish I could, but it just goes against the grain."

"Why can't you trust them? Your fathers did, and your mothers too? When the yankees came upon us and stript us of our parents and of their possessions, when filthy soldiers would have done them violence, who kept them pure, who died to preserve their chastity? It was the Negro slave. Bob, your own mother often tells how the slaves fought and died to keep her inviolate," affirmed Mr. Nailor with abundant gratitude for their unstinted love.

"That was the old nigger," was Bob's response. "They never gave no trouble. We like that kind of nigger even today, but we can find only a precious few of them. They're

dying out fast. If all the niggers were like those, we'd not
have no complaint. They always staid in their place."

"I see the trouble. You want a New South but an Old
Negro. The combination is impossible. Old things have
passed away. If you have a New South, you must have a
New Negro. And I don't bite my tongue to say that Rev.
Smith is the kind the South wants," Mr. Nailor again took up
the gauntlet as the contestant for the new order of the day.
He wanted these men to do nothing rash, so he held them in
abeyance.

"We'll see about that," interrupted Tom Howell, fully re-
covered from the rebuff given him at the early part of the
meeting. "Tom Dixon has as much blue blood as you, Mr.
Nailor, and we believe he knows his business."

Before there could come a reply, Mrs. White and her two
daughters brot in a service of cake and wine. As their energies had been well consumed by the day's work and the evening's discussion, they welcomed the refreshments with unusual
zest. Their minds relaxed, the tension lessened, then followed
an animated jollity that seemingly dispelled all differences.
Each had to be served several times.

When each was ashamed to ask for more, Bob White
again called the meeting to order. "Gentlemen, let's return
to business. I think we've had enough discussion; now let's
decide on some sort of action. The question, is 'What's to
be done with Parson Smith and his niggers, and others who're
taking on his ways.'"

The question was certainly perplexing, for White's manner of putting it included not only the colored people, but the
white who had profited by William's friendly counsel. Those
who had been swept away by Sandy James' invective, tho ready
to take any course against the Negro, were not inclined at all

to act against the whites. "Gentlemen, what are you going to do to these folks?" he repeated.

"I say, 'Let them alone,'" spoke Mr. Davis, representing the progressive element of the South, who tired of the turmoil produced by the lawless and the impetuous, were eager for the economic life of that section to take its proper place. "Gentlemen, we've been thinking too much about ourselves. We must stop it. We must look to the interests of the Nation. She has a proud name that should not be tarnisht. To do this we have always been aided by the loyal blood of our colored brother. If you knew the honorable place he has held in American history, you would aid him, and not throw obstacles in his path. Free Negroes and slaves were with Washington at Valley Forge and endured all the hardships of the Revolution. They were with Perry at Lake Erie, and with Old Hickory at New Orleans. Not a war have we fought on this grand continent which has not been made successful by the help of Negro slain. For the sake of our country, for the sake of dear old Dixie, let us be law abiding." The passionate plea made an appeal to reason and to the pride which has been the great force in solidifying the sentiment of that section. Davis loved the South, they knew. When the tears were trickling down his troubled face, they were enthralled in silence, they were captivated by his personality. For a moment all wanted to do right.

It was only for a moment. The tricksters' hearts could not relent long. They were too admantine.

"Gentlemen, I have all respect for Mr. Davis," came from Lawyer James. "I honor him as the great son of General Davis who fell in the cause of the Union—an unpopular cause in these parts—a man so courageous as to bear the odium of his neighbors, to follow what appeard to him to be right. I

honor Mr. Davis because of his whole-hearted support of every
activity launcht for the welfare of this town. Yet for the
life of me, something must be done to save the South. We
can't afford to let these niggers get such a hold on our people
as has this one. Already he has most of the well-to-do folks
on his side, and we poor devils grovel in the dust."

"I've listened to you attentively. I took you all to be men.
You don't want to do right. If the plea of Mr. Davis didn't
move you, why should any of us try," remarkt Mr. Nailor,
trying to force a decision. He stood with a hickory in his
right hand. "Gentlemen, nothing should be done to terrify
our colored population. You know we need their labor. Thousands of them keep going North because of just such men as
you. When they've piled up dollars by honest toil, you find
all sorts of ways to steal them. When they have laid by
luxurious crops, you take them as your own. You give them
poor schools, you insult their women. Now you're asking
what are we going to do to them. Haven't we already done
enough? He raised his cane aloft, as if ready to strike anyone who would disturb him. "I think I've heard enough," he
said impatiently, taking his hat and starting for the door. "I
lost enough by this kind of efforts of you scalawags. Crops
which should have been harvested long ago, have rotted because of just such foolishness. I've heard enough," he
screamed. "If anyone bothers any of my hands, hell is going
to overtake him. And that before judgment day. Good
night." He slammed the door.

"Just leave him to me," said Tom Howell. "I'll bring
him round. I've more power than you think."

"Others also rose to leave, who stood only for fair play.
There were many entreaties that all would remain until a
definite decision had been reacht. The lawyer, however, know-

ing that there were others present whom he could not trust with his plan, had no apology to offer, no entreaty to make. He desired only their speedy departure.

"Bob, I must go," insisted Fred Dean, shaking hands warmly, "I promised the old lady I'd be back long before midnight. So I'd better be on my way. Bob, I aint' goin' to do anything wrong, but because I love Old Dixie, you can count on me to do anything that's right. Good night."

"Good night, old pal," was the exchange.

The discussion waxed warm to bitterness; not against any there, but against a rising race. Seeing that villany was uppermost, one by one those for justice left; for they regarded a longer sojourn there as merely wasteful. Mr. Davis lingered until they formally dismissed and all were supposed to go home. When he was starting away, he observed that Young, James, Crabtree, Howell, and Jones lingered behind. Evidently there was to be an extra session. Feeling that he was not wanted, he mounted his spirited bay and galloped homeward.

When he had gone a mile, he decided to turn from his way and go to Nailor's, in the bright moonlight. When he reacht the main house, every place was dark. He called for quite a while without getting a response. Finally Jefferson Nailor, the eldest son, appeared at the door and said that his father had not as yet returned, that probably he had gone from the meeting to the station, to meet number sixty-five. The engineer was to bring him a message from Dallas. In an instant he was on his way.

When he arrived at the station, he found Mr. Nailor placidly walking up and down. After tying his horse to a tree, he went to greet his friend. "Well, this is a surprise," said Nailor, divining, however, what had caused his neighbor to seek him.

"Nailor," said Davis, "I couldn't go to bed tonight until I congratulated you on the spirit you showed against those rascals. We can stop these outbreaks that disgrace our country, if we only act soon enough. Are you willing to stop them?"

"You bet your boots. When will you make the start?"

"This very night."

"I'm with you in life and death. By the God who made us, who brot us to this land not to debase, but to exalt mankind, I dedicate myself to this holy work, to free my country."

CHAPTER XXI.

To be or not to be: that is the question.
Whether 'tis nobler in the mind to suffer
The slings and arrows of outrageous fortune
Or to take arms against a sea of troubles,
And by opposing end them. —Shakespeare

The morning following the excursion from Williamsburg, Rev. Smith went early to his tasks. He sang a merry tune. How woman impresses man! A goddess of beauty, a queen of love, a paragon of adoration. She sinks him in hell; then thru pity or sport and most often love, exalts him straight to heaven. Once man has toucht her saintly person, he has tasted food fit for the gods alone. He has sipped ambrosial nectar. Having once enjoyed rapture, how can he live but at this celestial board?

William had lately drunk the best of life. No day now could be dreary. Affronts of any sort were opportunities to be noble—to scorn hate, to love the sublime and true, to make the night like unto the day.

As he was eager to read the newspaper, before starting the demonstration arranged for the forenoon, he lingered on his lawn beneath the exuberant shade of a stately elm. There he thot of his recent happiness, particularly the ecstacy of Thelma and Susan. What a joy to have lived and laught during those golden days of immediate recollection! Some other changes, because of these soul benedictions, would have to come to his estate. How soon, he dared not say.

While contentedly overwhelmed by these musings, that set his heart afire with tenderness for all things, Andy Clarkston came to him hurriedly and left the "Seaton Gazette" and the mail. As the work on the farm was very well systematised, Clarkston had no time to tarry. He proceeded at once to put the material in order for those expected at the experimental plant.

Automatically, William scanned the first page of the newspaper. Tho he had planned to let his letters take precedence, eagerness for news forced a glance at the daily. His most immediate observation was the following headline: THE DAUGHTER OF TED NAILOR, OUR GREAT TOWNSMAN, MAY MARRY REV. SMITH, THE SMART NIGGER, The Father Says He Has No Objection, MEN, RISE FOR THE SOUTH. William was determined, now that the letters should wait. Thereupon he directed himself to a careful study of the article and, as far as possible, all its ramifications. Unaware of the meeting at Whites, he could not fathom it. He read it several times, then ceased to puzzle himself further.

Tom Howell had prepared a biased, sensational article, distorted in the extreme, to put the public against Nailor, one of the foremost business men, and prepare for instant action against William. The aim was to throw a match into a barrel of gasoline. The reaction was of such nature. The white people were about as dumfounded as William. For they had thot that the reputation of the editor of "The Seaton Gazette" was such as to prevent any yellow journalism. There was no reflection about the non-appearance of an editorial based upon the news item. The important consideration was the fact that the statement was in the newspaper. As a natural sequence a rapid discussion of the matter occurred in various groups.

William hurried to the house, only to find no one there.

Promptly he went to the garage, obtained his motorcycle and rode with greatest possible speed to the experimental farm. Generally these demonstrations were attended by both white and black; but on this occasion only colored farmers were present.

When William dismounted, Jim Turner, a young man of twenty-six, said, "Dr. Smith, you're late this morning. This is the first time I've know it to be so. We were all discussing it when we heard your 'bike.'"

"Gentlemen, I had something to make me late," he spoke with emphasis. "A scurrilous, a damnable article appeared in this morning's 'Gazette' concerning me." He read the item, then handed them the paper to survey. Smiles now gave way to melancholy, scorn and anger. They were as greatly disturbed as if they knew an unavoidable avalanche was sweeping upon them to utter ruin with no chance of their escape.

To remove their distraction, to bring them to a common end to assuage the horrors which brooded upon them, Lewis Brown broke the suspense.

"You stand here like frightened sheep. You say you're men, now show it. What are you going to do about this? You see what the white folks have done already. They've read this article. Don't you see there's not a one here, whereas generally we have as many white as colored? The white folks have acted, they're together. Where are you?"

"Gentlemen," interrupted William, who showed entire absence of fright or purturbation. "Andy, put away the experimental material and come by the house as speedily as possible. As for the rest of you, come by the house too, and I'll suggest what you're to do. I'll ride on ahead and by the time you get there I will have read my mail. I ask for this brief interval in order that you may be properly guided. As this is a crisis, every precaution is necessary."

"But what about yourself?" inquired Moses Lampkins, a middle-aged farmer, whose skin showed the weathering of many storms, whose shoulders were broad enough for any burden.

"Have no fear for me," was the prompt reply. "I can take care of myself, rest assured. However, should any misfortune come to me, I'll see that there'll be someone to guide you. Gentlemen, I'll see you at the house." The motor responded promptly, as if aware of the importance of every second. With equal readiness, William started on his way, smiled and waved adieu.

All were astonisht, the men older than forty were dumfounded. Previously when a colored man was about to be assaulted in their neighborhood all were cowed. The man assailed did not show signs of courage until placed at bay. To see one of their number calm before a brewing storm, which they thot would have a momentum greater than that of a cyclone or hurricane, to see him smile in the midst of grave danger, and act almost as if nothing untoward had occurred to disturb the even tenor of his way, was sufficient announcement that grim night had rolled away.

Another circumstance heralded the dawn. Formerly when a member of the race was being attackt, or if persons thot him liable, they shunned him, as if he were a contagious disease with power to create a fatal epidemic. On this occasion, it was not so. Every man was bound for an interview with the markt individual. No one thot of doing anything else.

A few minutes brot William home, where he would await his sturdy folk. Leaving his cycle before the door, he went at once to his desk in a very alluring study. There with expedition he proceeded to examine his mail. He had received four letters. According to his custom, he noticed the post marks and the chirographies before perusing the contents. The survey revealed two letters from Williamsburg, one from Seaton, and the fourth from Washington, D. C.

His attention was particularly attracted to the letter from Seaton, which had in the upper left corner the letters "K. K. K." and beneath them a skull and two crossed bones. With almost prophetic insight, he divined the contents. Unceremoniously he tore it open and read the curt missive. It ran thus:

Parson Bill Smith, Nigger, your days round here are numbered, if you don't leave this town within twenty-four hours. Be sure you make your git away quick.

> Signed in blood,
>> THE KLAN.

William smiled as he read it, and when he had finisht, he laught almost uproariously. It was not the laugh of merriment, but the laugh of fierce resolve. "I wonder what they think I am," he mused. Without more ado he read the letters from Susan and Thelma. As he expected, they contained an inspiration. He read them twice, then said to himself, "Before God, in the name of these two, I resolve to do at this decisive moment only what is right. I hope to survive the awful trial, but I hope to have my honor unstained."

Finally he read the letter from Washington. For the first time that day he seemed troubled. The contents of the communication follow:

Dr. William Smith,
    Denmark Vesey Estate,
        Seaton, ——
Dear Sir:

The fame of your endeavor has spread thruout the country. We have studied the work for some time. As proof, you recall probably the visit of Dr. Francis Keats, whom we sent there to make a survey of the community in which you live as it is related to your spirited undertaking. His voluminous report shows that you are engaged in the proper work to make America safe for democracy. You have succeeded in producing greater harmony between the races, where their members exist side by side in large numbers, than any one in the last fifty years.

We have been particularly interested in the news items and editorials inspired by your enterprise, articles which have appeared in the dailies and the magazines. You are a national character, whose name is on the lips of all our people, not as the Moses, but as the Joshua to take us into the promised land.

Finally, as you are a minister, with a tongue, veritably able to set worlds on fire, we feel that you should reach larger groups of people thruout the Nation. We learned that you were ousted at Williamsburg because of an address delivered several years ago at your convention. We have studied your discourse painstakingly and found ourselves in hearty accord with it. If you become one of us, you will have a clientele of fifty thousand willing listeners. The new times need a new gospel; and we behold in you its chief apostle.

We, the members of the American Democracy League, an organization formed to preach the new gospel of freedom, work, responsibility, and aggresiveness, see in you our logical leader, the chieftain able to carry out our great dreams. There-

fore, we offer you the position of national organizer with headquarters in Washington at a salary of five thousand dollars
for the first year, after which time you will receive an increase
of a thousand a year until you reach the maximum of twelve
thousand.

We are depending upon you. Answer, please, without
delay.

Yours respectfully,

HENRY SLATER, Pres.

EDGAR YOUNG, Sec.

For a while William was in a quandary. Should he go
to Washington for the larger work and at a later date return to Seaton or should he offer the malefactors of race a
firm resistance? "I'll reply at once," he decided. Whereupon
he typewrote the letter in duplicate, as was his wont in business transactions, placed one copy in an envelope and dispatched it at once. Then he placed the letters from Thelma
and Susan in separate pigeon holes, and lowered the top of his
desk. He had now in hand the letter from the Klan, the
call from Washington, and his own reply.

He placed his hands behind his head and leaned back
in the big revolving chair in quiet meditation. He was planning the activity of the approaching moments with great delib-
erations. He had not been thus occupied long, when Mr. Wilson knockt and informed him that all had arrived from the
experimental plant.

"Have them come up," William requested. Soon the
room was full.

"I have three letters I want you to hear. Read them for
me, Wilson. Take them in the order in which they occur,"
he urged. He was interested in studying the countenances of
the men, hence he askt Wilson as a favor to read for him.

When the orchard specialist had finisht reading the epistle of threat and warning, Moses Lampkins askt, "What have you decided to do? What do you want us to do?"

"Hear the other letters, then I'll make some remarks." As the letters were being read, William glanced from listener to listener. The expressions on their faces were most satisfactory. He rejoiced in silence.

"Gentlemen, you've heard my doom," said our great character with a smile and a laugh, that his hearers were baffled to interpret. "That letter from the so-called Klan is no surprise. The South is rather peculiar, it's perfectly willing to have trifling colored people to do the drudgery and all sorts of dirty work. Of course someone has to do it; but it could be so much more willingly and thoroly done, if the workers were specially trained for it. The South has yet to learn that not the ignorant, but the intelligent worker produces efficiency. Because of this very sentiment, as soon a colored man acquires a good, substantial bank account in many parts of this section, it is time for him to find new quarters.

"You see already what I've determined to do. Now I want you to make your decisions. I'm glad there's present at least one man from each of the farms owned by colored people; for we can save much time. Gentlemen, have you rifles and revolvers?" Everyone was well supplied.

"We bought them shortly after you came here. Don't you remember?" said Turner, ready for any worthy enterprise. His willingness to follow the great chieftain was characteristic of them all. "You said we might need them some day."

"How's your ammunition? Do you need any? If so, let me supply you now," spoke William to be doubly sure. Since during his presence among them, he had made constant inquiry along this line, they had taken pains to have ample quantities on hand. Renewal was necessary because of target practice for the rifle tournaments which our young divine held on his estate. Thus Rev. Smith had inspired among them an unerring marksmanship, important at this particular time.

All had sufficient ammunition. "Gentlemen, this letter has been sent only to me. Probably you're not to be molested; but once a mob has seized its victim, it does not stop there. It vents its passion upon others. You're as innocent as I, yet they seek to do me injury. Then may they not come to you? Since I believe they will, this is my desire: prepare to defend your homes. Let injuries come to your property and your families only after you have died for them gloriously. Follow the spirit of that great American, Theodore Roosevelt, who in a speech in the coliseum of Saint Louis made this statement: 'Some people have said that they would fight, but that they would not hit the first lick. I used to be that way. Now I have changed. When I see a man about to strike the first blow, I hit first. Then there is no second blow struck. When you hit a man, always put him to sleep.' Do you understand what you're to do?" now inquired Rev. Smith.

"I b'lieve we've got it, Elder," replied Houston. "If we sees anybody prowlin' round our farm, don't wait fo' him to shoot us, but we shoot first. Ain't dat it?"

"That's the idea," rejoined the young planter, glad that the instruction had gone home. "One further advice. If you have to shoot, be sure you're barricaded within your house in the day and barricaded on the outside at night. I've already told you how to dispose of your families."

"But, Rev. Smith," inquired the discontented Mr. Lampkins. "What are you going to do? If it had not been for you, we wouldn't had these farms. You stood by us, now we're going to stand by you."

"Don't worry about me," calmly remarkt William, who

had in his heart longed for that spontaneous remark. He knew now that his experiment had been a success. "Tho the persons who sent me my notice are dirty scoundrels, they will grant me a respite. I've twenty-four hours in which to leave town. Within that time, if I had to, I believe I could conquer the world. My men about me will look after the estate. Meanwhile I'll transact some other business. I can take care of myself."

They disliked the idea of his going about by himself, but as they believed he would do nothing rash, they made themselves contented and went straightway to their homes.

When all had left the study, William came to himself after a pleasing reverie which closed with thots of Susan and Thelma. Suppose he had married, what a trial this day would have been for the young wife! The more he reflected upon it, the more he became convinced that he had made no mistake by waiting. Of course he meant to keep his word, to marry within eight months. Yet he rejoiced that he was single now. A wife might object to some of the things he meant to do at this time, but as the matter stood, in all events he was sovereign lord. The will of the wife he would have chosen would have been strong, one which would require great persuasiveness to bring his way, if once she thot the best solution to his problem lay in a different course. Other wills now would have little power over him. He could go directly to his mark.

A married man will tolerate more offenses than the single one. It is not that marriage makes him a coward, but he feels that the demands of his family require him to keep alive at almost any price. In this case to die is easy, but to live is hard. Yet if the honor of the home is attackt, tho married, the man promptly defends it. If he dies in the effort, he rests in peace. Tht question was not to live, but how to live.

Such was William's reflection. As he was single and his mother well provided for, his life was in his own hands. If he wanted to go to Washington, objections were unimportant. If he preferred to stay and risk his life, it was his privilege.

At this point he thot of writing his mother, but almost as speedily as the idea came, there followed the decision not to do so. To communicate with her would only cause worry. Besides she might come there and be a hindrance or expose herself to injury.

What should be done would be done quickly. Within two days, all would be over. He would be in Williamsburg, Seaton or eternity.

"Well, I've been here long enough. 'I must be about my Father's business,'" he remarkt and went to the kitchen, to see Mrs. Brown. He instructed her to tell Clarkston as soon as he arrived to see Mr. Wilson, who would tell him what to do until it would be time for him to go to post office for the next mail. Plans had to be changed to meet the crisis. He then folded the three letters, placed them securely in his pocket. Then he took from a corner his automatic rifle.

He went directly to his range, set up a target and practiced. As he made fifty hits out of fifty attempts at the moving objects he thot it unnecessary to try the fixt ones even at different angles. Thereupon he lockt the targets and went back to the house. His cycle ready, he set the motor going and darted away.

His business was to interview white farmers, who were indebted to him for instruction and advice. He approacht one after another and had them read his letters. Their attention, however, was first drawn to the rifle he carried in his hand. "What would you suggest that I do?" askt William in each instance, not for advice, but merely to get the farmers' point of view. The suggestions varied. All regretted the predicament, but only a few deplored it. Accordingly some were non-committal, saying that he must decide for himself, others urged him to take the offer at Washington, trying to persuade him that it was the only thing to do.

A few, however, like Dean and Martin, insisted that he stay and fight the matter out. Then they told him of the meeting at Robert White's and requested that he see Mr. Davis, who remained after many of the others had left. William hurriedly departed from them to find this influential citizen.

When he had gone two miles he had a blow out. This did not delay him long, for being prepared for all except extraordinary emergencies, he adjusted the difficulty quickly, and was on his way once more. Within a few minutes he was at Mr. Nailor's. When he inquired he learned that Mr. Nailor came in late the previous night and left early that following morning.

"This is Rev. Smith, isn't it?" inquired Mrs. Nailor.

"Yes, this is he. I understand your husband came to my defense last evening in a meeting designed to work me harm," he replied very graciously.

"Sometimes I become so very much ashamed of my people," remarkt the grand matron. "Some of them do such foolish, mean things. To think of Tom Howell's reporting that you were going to marry one of my daughters, and you've never even met them! They've seen you only from a distance, not that they would be discomforted in meeting you."

"Some people will do anything," he answered. Then with the courtesy and grace of a prince, he bowed and askt to be excused.

"You can depend upon Ted, she replied, as he bade her

good day. "He's going to stick by you to the last drop of his blood. And I hope he'll teach those rascals a lesson.

He then hurried along to find Mr. Davis who lived on the adjoining farm. No one could tell where he was. The wife there gave encouragement also and William was overjoyed. "Mrs. Davis, if I do not meet your husband, tell him I'll be back this evening. Good day!"

"I will," she replied. Then William darted away.

As it was just about time for a number of men to assemble about Henry Mitchell's store, he determined to go there, as his last stop before going to town. To his surprise he found his enemies absent. Approaching the storekeeper he said, "Mr. Mitchell, I'm in for it. You need no explanation. What do you think I should do?"

"Kid," he remarkt, "you've given me more business than I had in ten years. I was just about to go under when you came; but you stood up for the little business man, and by gad, I'm goin' to see you thru. All I say is 'Stick on the job.' What do you say, fellows?" William gave him the letters to read, as he had the rest.

"Mitchell, we stand by you," they replied.

"Men, I tell you the boy has plenty of sand. Read this letter, Patrick," he said, turning to the district school teacher, "you're better at it than me."

Thereupon, he submitted to him the following communication: it was William's reply to the offer from Washington, D. C.

The American Democracy League,
  Crispus Attucks Hall,
    Washington, D. C.
Gentlemen:
  If you desire an immediate categorical response, my answer

is I can not accept your offer. I should be happy to extend my influence in accordance with the plans of your organization, but to leave Seaton now would be abject surrender, and deprive me of the dignity I should bring to your exalted work.

This morning, I received in the mail, which brot your kindly consideration, a notice from a Klan of these parts telling me to leave town within twenty-four hours at the peril of my life. With me, life is so insignificant in comparison with my privileges, that I have decided to play the fool and die. Not all the armies of this world, nor all that have been, and will be, can drive me, while I live from anything that is rightfully mine.

I do not believe in stirring insurrection unless as a last resort; I do believe in individuals not abandoning the rights they have won, but defending them as long as blood courses thru their veins. If when this crisis is over—I dare not say how soon that will be—you wish to consider me for the place, I will be able to give you a more favorable reply. When a challenge like this is offered, I really accept. I must show the Klan that I can live here if I so desire If after that I accept the place, my headquarters will have to be in Seaton.

If I survive, you will hear from me next week. If you do not, you will know that I have died in the South, to make America safe for democracy.

Yours respectfully,

WILLIAM SMITH.

How astonisht were all to hear that communication! Could any good thing come out of Nazareth? Here was one with skin so black, but soul as bright and pure as sunlight. Why could such a man who had veritably placed Seaton on the map not be permitted to enjoy the fruitage of his labor?

"I was late getting here, but was in time to hear that

letter. Let me shake your hand. That's the kind of stuff we want in this country." William turned to see the speaker. It was Mr. Davis and with him was Mr. Nailor.

When he had finisht an interview with them, he started off.

"Which way are you going now?" inquired Mr. Nailor.

William replied, "I'm going to see the mayor." He left without delay.

CHAPTER XXII.

"Those friends thou hast, and their adoption tried,
Grapple them to thy soul with hoops of steel.
. . . .
"Since my dear soul was mistress of her choice
And could of men distinguish, her election
Hath sealed thee for herself; for thou hast been
As one, in suffering all, that suffers nothing,
A man that fortunes buffets and rewards
Hath ta'en with equal thanks." —Shakespeare.

When he had reacht the edge of the town, William decided that he would walk to the mayor's office; he determined
upon this as a precaution, which would permit more freedom
for self-defense, should it be necessary for him to use his
rifle. Thoroly familiar with the conditions of Seaton and the
environs, he knew that white people in the country were almost entirely for him or were neutral. Either they were
going to aid him, or they were not going to oppose him. Accordingly his enemies were chiefly in the town. The machinations of the council of six included the bringing of a mob
from the urban throngs, he thot, to be composed chiefly of
persons who did not know him. How otherwise could he
account for the scurrilous article in the "Seaton Gazette?"
Tho cognizant of these conditions, he would go thus far into
the camp of the enemy. For the satisfaction of his own heart,
for the edification of his race, for the arousal of admiration
and respect among the reputable people of the town, William
concluded that this was necessary. He must see the mayor.

Reaching the garage and repair shop of his friend, Har-
vey Allen, he left the motorcycle there. The entreprenenr questioned him concerning the newspaper attack and his attitude

towards it. The planter replied, "When the enemy comes, he'll receive a warm reception."

"I'll be there to help you entertain him," remarked Allen.

"I'll be delighted to have your service."

At this William started upon his important mission. Persons who had not come much into his presence, casual passers-by, would have paid him scant attention; however, those who had observed him closely on other occasions, in this instance would have noticed a departure from the accustomed stride, the erect bearing, and the direct, quick pace. Our hero moved circumspectly with an occasional glance to the left and to the right.

When he reached the Union Station, whom should he meet, full of smiles and captivating graces but Thelma Haskell? After a brief exchange of greetings and other conventionalities, there were expressions of surprises at seeing each other. Of course Thelma had hoped to see him shortly after her arrival; but she was not expecting the good fortune which presented itself immediately.

"Why have you come at this particular time?" inquired William, as thots of his predicament thrust themselves crowdingly upon him. "I wish you had waited a while; I fear I can not entertain you, as I should like."

"I did not come to be entertained at all. I'll look after that was her assurance; I am going to return the compliment. You see I enjoyed myself so grandly last week, that I had to come again, I'm going to show you the time of your life." Such were the joyous outbursts which fell upon our great character like hail in a summer cornfield. "But where are you going?" she remarkt with a sudden turn of thot. "You appear to be on your way to a hunt."

"I am en route to the mayor concerning a little business. This morning the 'Seaton Gazette' published a scurrilous ar-

ticle concerning me, I cannot show it to you, as my paper is
at the house. Furthermore, in the same mail which brot your
letter—by the way since I think of it, you said nothing at all
in your letter about your coming. Why don't you let a fellow
know your intention? I should have had some one to meet you
and see that you were properly cared for." William spoke
thus because he felt, especially at this time, that some harm
might befall her.

"Don't you know by now, William, that a woman can't
tell a man everything? She must to some extent keep him
guessing. Society says that the men must seek the women;
if the man understood everything, you know he'd never run
after her. We have to do something to keep them coming,"
she remarkt with unusual affability. Then realizing that there
was yet to be obtained the information she desired, she pressed
a question to bring him back to what certainly was of immediate interest to him. "You haven't told me why you have
that gun." As he was not afraid to tell Thelma anything, he
explained the matter in detail, likewise all that he had done
that day as preparation for any outbreak. "Here's the letter
demanding that I leave within twenty-four hours," he said with
great emotion.

Thelma quickly scanned its contents and then spoke with
some degree of alarm and dismay, "What's the matter with
these white folks? The President has said that we are to
help make the world safe for democracy. How can we even
have democracy in America with such disrespect for the law
on the part of the so-called superior race. What are you going to do? You're not going to leave, are you? I don't see
yet what you're aiming at?" She had in her zeal for justice
and respect for property rights become bold and defiant. "I
know what they want and I'm ready to let them have it. I
don't see what you want down here tho. Why aren't you on

your farm organizing your friends to resist these insults? You've organized them for peace and they are with you. I saw that during the few days I was among them."

"I can protect myself, Thelma, I have no fear," he affirmed in his effort to assure her that all would be well. She lookt at him a while and then became silent, charmed with his princely aspect. Soon the spell was broken and she was returned to the foreboding of her soul dreams. "You can protect yourself, I agree. You can protect yourself against individuals, man for man, and even at great odds. But you know the seething South as thoroly as I; you know," she spoke louder and more defiantly as she proceeded, "the cowards; you know the black-hearted scoundrels come against one colored man by hundreds and thousands. So superior are we to that common refuse that one of us strikes such fear into tens of them and even fifties, that they must needs oppose us in hundreds and thousands. They pay us a great compliment. Yet when they come, a hundred or a thousand against one, the chances for defeating them do not exist. Under these circumstances your attitude is follhardy."

Thelma, my ambition is to be strictly law-abiding. The nation is engaged in war for world democracy."

"For all the world except the Negro. When American statesmen, politicians, and scholars engage in argument concerning demrocracy, if you think they mean a democrácy in which we are included upon equal terms with other races, you're sadly mistaken; we're on the outside."

"Probably they don't include us, but their statements are so far sweeping that they can not exclude us. We must be reckoned with. We shall enter this democracy whether they want us or not. The only government that will offer ages of peace is a democracy; it's right, and he who seeks to stop the course of right is by its very momentum crusht to insignificance and degeneracy. I mean to be right, I mean to do right. I'm going to perform no disloyal act. I'm going to lay this matter before the mayor." This was in accordance with his plans or as the soldier would say, it was a part of the day's work.

"What good will that do, William?" she inquired, at the same time trying very arduously to see some advantage in that action.

"It will probably teach the lawless that they should not permit the colored man, who receives very little from the country, to love, honor, and respect it more than those who receive mainly humiliations. It may teach them to be loyal to America in this great crisis and not embarrass the administration. Certainly I shall win the respect and admiration of white and black alike, who love the South. If I die, my death will be a monument to the loyalty of my people," he spoke with resolution.

"That sounds well," remarkt Thelma, showing by the intonation of her voice that she did not approve the sacrifice. "I admire your stand, yet this is not what a white man would do under these circumstances." Recalling his people on and about his estate, with whom he was almost a god, she askt, "What have you done as to the security of your friends—your helpers and your neighbors? You are too far-sighted not to be aware that this animosity will not stop with you. Harm will fall to your friends. Innocence should exempt a man from violation: but has it exempted you? And aren't you as innocent as those people? Are they not as innocent as you?"

"Yes, I am. You are speaking truly," he replied. Those were almost his very words.

"Hence you owe it to these people to organize them for their own defense. Forsake your own estate if you will, but do defend these helpless toilers," she pleaded earnestly, her bosom heaving as she spoke, and tears about to flow.

"It would seem too much like an insurrection," he remarkt. "Yet if our country were not at war, it is the very thing I'd do. But if there is only one person in the Nation to respect the law during this awful cataclysm. I am determined to be that one. I have advised my neighbors to defend their homes to the last drop of their blood. A man's home is his castle, and none can hold him lawless, if he kills the man who assaults it. I mean to have the law on my side. The twenty men on my estate when properly distributed in ambush, will be a formidable offense against any mob. Be sure I'll take care of that.

"Furthermore. do not think I shall forsake my people. If they have received letters of warning, if any of them has received one, my duty will be in their midst, and not on my estate."

"William," she returned with a conviction equal to his own, with equal emotion and firmness, "your life is dear to many of us. You must not throw it away. We can not live always, we may die by violence, yet we should do our utmost to see that our assassin falls with us; your mind, I see, is made up, and so is mine. Good bye, I'll see you this evening." She started away at once.

"Where are you going? What do you plan to do?" said William, calling her back. She turned and smiled with a wealth of love and devotion, "I'm on my way to Mrs. Johnson's, after remaining there a few minutes, I'm going into the country."

"Don't think of it," he urged. "You are putting your life

in danger even to be in the town   Really you don't know what you are contemplating."

"I do not know?" she uttered slowly. "I do not know your danger? I do not know the peril of your neighbors? I don't know? Yes, I do. Consequently my business is not in the town but in the country. I go to help save a loyal people. I go to save those who suffer most and yet serve most. Good bye, William, I'll see you this evening. I shall expect you. Remember. Good bye." She hurried on to the home of the gentle lady, with whom she lodged during the previous week, with an air of great importance.

William watcht her for a moment and then reflected, "How I do admire her. She is true gold." He went directly to the mayor's office.

While William was engaged in an interview with the chief city official, Thelma was busy ascertaining the preparations for resistance on Smith's estate. With despatch, she saw both Brown and Wilson, and learned what had been done. Men were already on guard, with proper instructions. Satisfied with this arrangement, she began at once what she regarded as equally essential for maintaining the peace of the entire community. "Mr. Wilson, I think that you are rather well protected on this estate, but what about your good neighbors? Here you have several natural ambuscades and redoubts, but what have our other kind friends? I was thinking that I can help them, if I can get just a little assistance from you. Since you know them all, can't you bring them together at one place for me to speak to them?"

"Miss Haskell, what would Reverend Smith say, if harm befell you in your effort? If I were even indirectly the cause of bringing you woe, I fear he would not forgive me," was the sturdy affirmation.

"I've talked with him in town already, and he knows I am determined to do something. I ask your aid merely to expedite time. If you refuse me, I'll find these people myself and see that they come together. I'm resolute. If you desire sincerely to keep me unexposed to affront and injury, you will at least do this little." Thus Thelma put her case tersely, for this was no occasion for parleying. With her it was a matter of life or death. And she was leaning we know towards life.

"Give me a moment to reflect," he said, trying to avoid too hasty a decision.

"How much time do you wish," she inquired.

"Five minutes," was the prompt answer.

"Take them," she rejoined with a glance that cautioned celerity. "As you use them remember that five minutes tardiness may be the ruin of hundreds of human lives."

He withdrew from the sitting-room and sought Brown who had just gone to look at the outposts. After having gone a hundred yards, he called. Promptly Brown appeared. When they had had a brief conference, Wilson speedily returned and found Thelma patiently waiting. "I have been following the seconds and the minutes, thru fear and anxiety," she spoke showing the watch fastened about her wrist. "But you are on time with a few seconds to spare."

"Miss Haskell, that is a circumstance concerning which Dr. Smith is extremely abstemious. Thru him we have learned to be prompt in all our engagements," was the proud asseveration. Then he went on, "I return to your business. Mr. Brown and I have decided to help you carry out any plan you have in mind for aiding our neighbors."

"I appreciate that so much," she remarkt with a full flush of happiness. "You can not imagine how my spirit rejoices. Thank you, Mr. Wilson, thank you."

"I'm happy to be at your service. Now what are your plans?

"Could the people come to this estate for about a half hour?"

"That cannot be. Dr. Smith's instructions interfere with that. For special reasons, which I do not care to divulge, he prefers that they do not come here."

"I know his reasons, now that you call his wish to my mind. But may they not meet at the school house? I want to speak to them assembled."

"That's possible," he replied. "That is the way out. Since there is no work in operation on the plantation, I'll notify several who will see that the rest are there. When are they to assemble?"

"Immediatly."

"Come let's be off." He obtained his rifle and went to the garage to get his car. When all was ready, they sped away to the home nearest the school house. There he left Thelma in congenial company and hastened to notify the others. He found all the farmers on guard. When he had explained to them the purpose of the meeting, they set their sons or wives or both to the task and started for the school house.

Within less than a half hour all expected were there, ready for the great undertaking. "Gentlemen," said Mr. Wilson, opening the meeting, "you will recall that the lady before you was present during the wheat harvest. She needs no introduction. I present to you Miss Haskell, who will give you all details. I ask you to excuse me now, as I must return to the house; but I'll be back as soon as Dr. Smith returns. I know you will want to hear what he's been doing. Well, I'll tell you then. Miss Haskell is an able young woman, strong and brave, a hard worker. She can give you good advice. Hear her. Good bye. I'll be back shortly." Hereupon he departed.

"Gentlemen, American citizens," Thelma began, with her voice full of melodious sweetness. "For years many of you toiled and toiled, yet never forged ahead. Each planting season found you deeper in debt than the one which had past. Still you workt on, merely existing, hoping that some day the yoke you could not remove would be smashed by your children."

"Yes, you're telling the truth. I never could get out of old Halloway's debt until about two years ago," remarkt one of the farmers, who was strongly corroborated by many others.

"It did not, however, happen that way," she continued. "It was not your children who showed you how to buy tools, implements and groceries, how to buy land, how to improve your land by its cultivation. It was not your children who brought you this freedom, who caused you to win the respect of your white neighbors. It was not at all whom you expected; and it came sooner than you thot. This happiness was brot to you by a minister, a farmer, a man of business, a gentleman— Rev. William Smith."

There followed great applause and approbation. Happy in the response she received, she resumed. "This friend of yours has been notified to leave this country within twenty-four hours. Tomorrow at ten o'clock he is due to be far away. You know, I suppose, he has decided to remain. This means that a mob is coming against him, as soon as knowledge spreads that he is here.

"Dr. Smith has been a friend to every one of you, will you be a friend to him? Will you love him with the greatest love that can stir the human heart? 'No greater love hath a man than this that he lay down his life for a friend.' Even at this moment he is in the midst of his enemies exposing his life for yours, for your glory and that of your children.

"He has done no more than you, yet he has been ordered to leave these accumulations of his young manhood. If innocence would not exempt him from reproach and violence, do not believe it will exempt you. When your leader has been overthrown, the mob will come in force against you. If Rev. Smith survives, you shall live; if he perish, with him you fall. Where then is your place in this great hour; scattered like dandelions in a lawn, or united like the streams of the mighty river?" She pointed to the familiar waterway in the distance. "Your place is on your friend's estate under one leadership. You did not acquire your lovely homes until he came; will you be able to hold them, if he falls and dies? Let there not be thirty different guards, but one. I mean that all the farmers should keep in communication with one another. In this way, if any farm is attackt all can quickly go to its defense. This is how the battles are being won in Europe, this is how you must win yours."

"We'll do what Rev. Smith suggests," interrupted Jim Turner.

"He has already suggested," Thelma broke in, "but he is just neither to himself nor to you. Human life must be protected, hence I appeal to you. Dr. Smith has not askt me to do this, he's entirely unaware of my plans. He said he would have done this, however, had the country not been at war. He feels that such united resistance as I have outlined would be misunderstood and interpreted as a rebellion or an act of war."

At this point some were disconcerted, and began to wonder whether they should combine against the prospective foe. To prevent such thots having much force, the gentle visitor soon turned to utterances that always sway the hearer. "You think of hesitating? Men, you must act, for your friends, for your own lives. During slavery, the Supreme Court of the

United States gave out this decision, 'The Negro has no rights which the white man is bound to respect.' The masses of the white people act in accordance with that statement today. Here in this district you do have much respect. Why? It is because you have wealth. If the white man does not respect he admire's you.

"If you desire even greater respect from them, earn your rights and be willing to die to defend them. Liberty has been gained by bloodshed. Do not fear to pay the price, you, he does respect your dollars. You are thrifty, that's why white and black alike will honor you, and sing your praises always. Who fears to die, preferring to be enslaved, is not fit to live."

There followed shouts and acclamations. Those, who wavered a while ago, were now bent on pursuing a common aim. Let's do something at once," cried one.

"Let's go at once to the estate," said others.

"Gentlemen," continued Thtlma happily, "I thot you would be noble. I was sure you stood for right. It may happen that we shall not even be approacht, but I regard such a prospect extremely doubtful. Rev. Smith has gone to see the mayor. We may get the news at any moment, but we cannot wait, we must be prepared. Human life, I repeat, must be protected. If the government will not, human life must be protected.'

"How may we organize?" put in Moses Lampkins, who believed in expedition.

"What man here can all follow, and obey at the slightest suggestion?" she inquired to help remove the delay.

"I can follow Jim Turner, like a chick following a hen," said Lampkins.

"I know I can," said many others.

"Mr. Turner," said Thelma smiling, I appoint you leader of these noble men. Their lives and all their possessions are in your hands. Be a matchless leader." Then turning to the throng she continued, "Gentlemen, excuse Mr. Turner a few minutes, I should like to talk with him individually." The honored farmer promptly went to the front of the room and heard the fair lady. He thot of his overalls, but as a crisis was at hand, he had no time to stand on conventionalities.

During their conversation Thelma and Turner planned the resistance: they were not to attack. They decided upon scouts, outposts, sentinels, and guards, also upon a line of communication. When all had been assigned they started for their posts. Hereupon they heard the report from the combustion of a motor; they knew it was Rev. Smith. He had seen the mayor and had returned to them. Such cheers and plaudits as are given kings and queens, advancing in the midst of holiday throngs were showered upon the prophet of Sinai Shrine, the man of business. He lifted his hat in grateful acknowledgment and dismounted in front of the school house.

"Thelma, Miss Haskell," he remarkt upon seeing her, "what are you doing here?" He was uneasy about her. "It will soon be dark and you will have a dangerous trip to town, I fear."

"Rev. Smith," she said. She was conventional because of the crowd.

"I am preparing to protect you, to save you; if not for yourself, or persons in Williamsburg, at least for these people." She lifted her hand to stay interuption and continued, "I don't know when I shall go to town."

"Thelma, this must not be."

"William, must not? I shall lodge at Mr. Turner's. Isn't he, and his wife all right?"

"Yes, but—"

"I belong to myself, don't I, William?" she smiled

"Yes, you do."

CHAPTER XXIII.

As for me give me liberty of give me death. —Patrick Henry

The waiting room of the mayor's office was very much crowded when William arrived to have his interview. According to the custom, he trailed the line and waited his turn. The other visitors who were all white first noticed the rifle, then the khaki, and finally his complexion. Here they lingered long, for they wondered why a colored man would come thus accountered into the office of the chief magistrate of that town, only to change their appraisement, when they beheld his portly bearing and pleasant demeanor. William took out a note book and began to write, while they continued to steal occasional glances. He appeared wholly absorbed in his work, but he never failed for a minute to take circumspect glimpses of his enforced companions.

The visitors gradually were successful in their business and speedily left for the next tasks. William soon began to feel that the office would close, before he could discharge his mission. He kept noticing the clock and comparing it with his watch, apprehensive lest one chronometer would deceive him. The whistle sounded for the close of civic work and brot him to his feet. All had seen the mayor except two who were ahead of him, two elderly gentlemen, and himself. Tho somewhat disturbed, he waited with his accustomed patience. Then the idea flasht upon him that he was not making the most of his time. Many details of his venture or of his contemplated resistance could be workt out. To this meditation, with stolen glances at the other persons in the waiting room, our brave character proceeded at once to apply himself. Sure that his prospective assailants meant business and that there could be no sparring for time, he thrust book and pencil into his pocket, and began to think of devices for getting an interview before sundown.

While William was thus anxious, the messenger came into the sitting room and said, "The office is closed. Only those in the sitting room will be heard." William sat down and resumed his writing.

How calm a man may become when he knows a life struggle is before him! How undisturbed is an intelligent soul when brot to bay! We sometimes feel too proud to fight, thinking that in so doing we stoop to baseness. We believe at times that it is wrong for individual or state to force a man to exchange time for eternity. We decry war, violence, and rapine, and look for the ages of peace. And to be consistent, we censure the taking of human life for any crime. Yet when a fray is forced upon us, when we regard it ignoble to flee, we fight and kill. Is this right? Shall it become the universal law? As long as it is sweet and noble to die for one's country, it is stately to die for one's honor.

Such was William's reflection just before facing the mayor, a rather chubby man of forty-seven, slightly grizzled, and adorned with horned spectacles. He placed himself back in his chair, scrutinized the dignified visitor, and then offered him a seat near his desk. "This is Rev. Smith, I'm sure. Make yourself at home." Did the speaker mean that? Was he not after all an exalted instrument in the hands of unscrupulous people? William sat down. "What can I do for you?" came a customary question.

"I don't know, Mayor Goodrich. You can better answer that question yourself, after I have explained my business," replied William smiling. He placed his gun across his knee and handed the magistrate the letter from the Klan. "Read that, please," he requested. The mayor read. When he had finisht William presented the letter from Washington, which he followed with his reply. Mr. Goodrich ruminated, after having perused the epistles, and waived for William to break the silence. He did not wait long. "I came to you, Mayor Goodrich, because I love this town, the Nation, and my people. As this is a very serious consideration, one which may not only disgrace your administration and the town, but even humiliate the Nation, I came to you with all possible facts, that you may act wisely and quickly. What are you going to do, Mr. Goodrich? What do you suggest that I do?"

The mayor aswered hesitatingly, "Dr. Smith, I don't see much that I can do. I can have the governor call the militia, but what good would that do? Instead of firing upon the mob, they'd aid it, either by joining it or by depriving your colored brothers of their weapons and then leave them to the mob. You recall what the papers stated concerning East St. Louis. That militia is typical of the South."

"Mayor, I know," said William, agreeing with the magistrate, "that the black man has practically no protection in the South, and very little in many other parts of this great Nation. That is why I have this rifle. Tho the constitution grants me paper protection, I cannot trust my life to it. Before Almighty God, I wish I could! But I must protect myself. The colored man who does not protect himself is dead already. You see I do not ask for protection, because I know in advance I can't get it."

"However, let nothing rash be done," put in the mayor, trying to use diplomacy. "Your people are loyal, I know you are loyal. I've watched your coming here, your influence among white and black, and your development of industry here. I've gone so far as to suggest that a group of the best citizens give you the same token of appreciation. Now that this trouble has risen, I thot out a possible solution. Why not accept the offer coming from Washington? Furthermore, I have a large estate in Tennessee, which I'd like for you to develop. I'll offer you ten thousand dollars cash as the gift of the townsmen, of course it's not as yet subscribed. I'll give you a large farm from my Tennessee estate and pay you two thousand a year to do there the work you've done here. It would be well for you to leave now and return later on. After several years, all would be adjusted. Here are two offers. Surely for the sake of the Nation, you'll go."

"Mr. Goodrich, permit me to relate two incidents," came the calm response," and then I'll give you my decision. Have I leave?"

"Yes, go on."

"At Ebbit Seminary, in Kelston was a very learned, colored man, Dr. Kemper, its president. The school he administered was located in the far South, where our people live in great numbers. Some misfortune caused a mob to come against the school and fire thru the windows. As this gentleman was a minister, his first thot was to seek divine aid. He despatched a messenger to the governor, asking for troops, and had the chapel bell rung for the gathering of the students in extraordinary assembly. As they came together in the chapel, the pistols without—in the language of the president—continued to bark like dogs. So well do I recall this, for I heard him relate it in a church in Saint Louis. Not to digress, I conclude. This great educator had those seven hundred students kneel in prayer. He himself led the petition.

While still engaged in that service, a message came from the governor that troops would soon be upon the scene, with ammunition and a gatling gun. The troops came in time and the mob did not storm the buildings. President Kemper mentioned this in a very important speech to prove that when in danger we should pray. He offered it as proof that prayers are answered on time."

"That is a rare incident," remarkt the governor. "It is very interesting; now mention the other."

"As you say," William went on, "a rare incident. Such happens in this country only in one case out of ten thousand.

"The other incident," he continued, "is like the first in many respects, but yet it has fundamental differences. Kendell Seminary at Harmony had at its head Dr. Wade, who was also a Christian minister. His school has the unique distinction of rejecting the offer of $75,000 for the building of a school for colored youth, because the donor, the Home Missionary Society, wanted to control its policy. It returned the money with interest. Today President Wade operates that Seminary which is controlled and supported solely by colored people. It is indeed our greatest monument of Negro self-help.

"Let's return, however, to the incident. One class in preparing to produce the 'H. M. S. Pinafore,' found it necessary to have special rehearsals for the principals. To expedite the opera, the professor in charge had the leading characters to rehearse in town at the home of the professor of music. The Seminary was located just outside the city limits.

"One evening, when the boys and girls were returning from such a rehearsal, three white ruffians accosted and confronted them. One of them pulled at one of our girls and insinuated, 'You're a fine lookin' nigger gal. You'll do me.' As he tried to kiss her, the captain of the football team, a strong, robust individual, struck the scoundrel in the jaw, broke the bone, and felled him to the ground.

"The other ruffians came to the rescue, but were rebuffed by our gallant, young men.

"The professor, a man of a very heated disposition, said, 'It's well I left my pistol behind; for I surely would have shot every one of them, the dirty dogs.' He would have done it. Turning to the young ladies, he resumed, 'We'll take the matter before Dr. Wade, he'll adjust it.'

"As the incident occurred at the foot of the hill on which the school stood, it was not long before all reacht the dormitories. As they climbed the hill, one of the culprits remarkt, 'We're going to bring all cotton town against you.'

"'Let them come on,' went back an answer.

"As soon as President Wade learned what had occurred he called the girls and boys into the chapel. This minister was just as conservative about his doctrine as Dr. Kemper. When all had assembled, he explained the situation and said, 'Boys, our girls have been insulted. What shall we do?'

"One promptly arose and declared, 'Dr. Wade, there's only one thing to do—defend them and die for them. What do you say, boys.'

"'Die for them,' was the unanimous acclamation.

"'Girls,' the president continued, 'we cannot assure you that you will live to see tomorrow.' Many were weeping bitterly. This, however, was no interference. 'We cannot vouchsafe you even your honor. There may be some base enough to violate your chastity. We do, however, guarantee this, that if even a hair on your head is troubled, it will be over our dead bodies. So go to your rooms and take your ease.'"

The girls promptly withdrew.

"One rule of the school was that firearms were not to

be kept in the dormitories. Yet the President askt if there were pistols or rifles about. He received an affirmative answer. Whereupon, he askt them to bring arms and ample ammunition to the chapel. Never before had I seen such an array of fire arms among my people. There were automatic colts, Smith and Wesson 32's, many shot guns and Winchesters. When it appeared that all had returned, Dr. Wade himself came in with seven Winchesters, which he distributed among the male members of the Faculty. Then he sent a student to his home for his own rifle, saying, 'Take this note to Mrs. Wade and tell her I'll not return until late, probably till morning.' Thereupon addressing himself to those ambitous young men, he continued, 'I'm going to instruct the professors as to how to repulse any manuever. You are to obey them without questioning. Most of you are to remain without arms; these are the only ones to leave the school grounds. They will watch the movements of the evening and form our first line of communication. Boys, this is dangerous work, yet our effort is valueless without it. I cannot, therefore assign it, I must call for volunteers.'

"Every youth volunteered boisterously, I want to be a scout."

"I'm glad of this unanimous response. I know now we shall succeed. Promptly, scouts were selected and dispatched to perform their work. Then the teachers were posted as captains. They posted their groups about the campus, so as to cover every approach, and awaited the attack of those who threatened.

"The night this occurred, the stars were faintly shining in the refulgent glow of a luxurious moonlight. Shadows of trees and houses—in short, all objects in the landscape were strongly visible.

"An hour after the school force had been on watch, the scouts sent back word that a hoard of about three hundred men were coming from Cotton Town." Cotton Town was the seat of a cotton factory, surrounded by the frame dwellings of the workers. It lay about half a mile from the school limits.

"When a hundred and fifty yards from the campus, one of the gang shouted, 'We're coming, Niggers, say your last prayers.'"

"'Come on,' went a robust answer, 'we can take all you can give, and pay you back with interest.' Our scouts were called in and armed. Thus we awaited them.

"'Remember,' came as the President's final advice, 'since we have a good number and most of you are in ambush, let the enemy fire the first shot. If they unload a weapon, follow your professor's commands quickly,' and there muzzles flasht outrageously in the quiet moonlight. The leaders came within twenty-five yards and started at the glare of those rifles, ready for blood. The one, who apparently was chief, called ten together for a conference, then messages were sent thru the ranks. This was followed by a retreat to their homes, with yelling and cursing.

"Mayor Goodrich, this happened eight years ago. The school still stands as a monument to Negro Self-Help, Negro Courage, and Negro Manhood."

"That is interesting, I suppose I had to listen as the Wedding Guest to the voyage of the Ancient Mariner. But what is the point of the incidents?" he parried, fully aware of the purport of it all.

"I promised, when I had related those stories to tell you my decision concerning your offer." William spoke rapidly now, tho not so rapidly as passed the currents of his emotion. "I mention the deeds of those men to point out the attitudes of my people. Dr. Kemper represents the manner of the new Negro. In the New South which is at hand the old Negro is a misfit. You cannot have a democratic South until this new Negro represents the majority of his race. 'The old order changeth, giving place to new, and God fulfills himself in many ways, lest one good custom should corrupt the world.'

"Mayor, I had thot of marrying sometime ago. I was sure that I would have been married by this time. I should have been married by this time. Now I don't know if I'll ever marry. I'll give my life for democracy here. I'll give my life for my race. I've scented blood, my fighting spirit is on fire. Mayor Goodrich, Mayor Goodrich, down in your heart do you really think I ought to go?"

"Certainly, because it will save trouble."

"Who made this trouble?"

"In a way you did, Rev. Smith, by taking hold of the affairs of the farmers."

"The man who stops robbers, who sees that workers are not only worthy of their hire, but actually gets it causes trouble?"

"You know those stock jobbers are envious of a colored man's rising to wealth and power. Probably after the education of a few years, this violence will cease.'"

"More and more, Mr. Goodrich, I believe that this is not solely a white man's problem. If every colored community would take the stand of Kendall Seminary, the problem would be solved over night. Those ruffians who vaunt and prowl like fiends infernal do so only because they are sure that their lives are secure. I do not believe in insurrections. As evidence of this, I call to witness my neighbors whom I sent to defend their own homes. My estate will be defended only by those who resided there.

"I have already mailed my reply to Washington. Your offer, too, I must reject. If you were to offer me the whole of South America, and India, and Africa—if such were yours to give—I'd have to refuse them. I must stay. I'll sell a farm, I'll sell a horse, a house, an automobile or the like; but Mr. Goodrich, 'none will barter the immediate jewel of his soul.' I'd sell my life for fifty cents a day, if it would benefit humanity. But worlds on top of worlds cannot offer me the price of liberty.

"I workt for the farmer, didn't I?" inquired William. The mayor nodded assent. "I purchased from honest toil those buildings and implements I use. Nobody in Seaton gave me one cent. That farm represents my life's blood. The land was honestly got, the buildings were honestly erected. The title to all is clear, isn't it, Mayor Goodrich?"

"Assuredly," the magistrate admitted faintly. "They are yours, so they are duly recorded."

"No man, Mr. Mayor, has ever been able to run me from what was mine. My reputation and honor cannot go down now. I have not had the proud privilege of going to France to die for world democracy, but I do have the privilege of falling for it in America. I have spent some rather joyous days with books and young women; but never have I rejoiced as I do now. The opportunity has come for me to die not in France, but in America, to help make America safe for democracy. This is the happiest moment of my life.

"You need not offer me any protection. I have but one request: Tell your friends, I'll kill every man who sets foot on my estate after sundown."

The mayor lookt in amazement at this man, this black man,

comely and self-possest. Tho desiring no harm to come to his fellow townsmen, he could not help admiring this attitude.

"Good day," said the mayor, shaking his hand, "I hope all will be well."

"Good bye," said William, "I may die, but not in dishonor. I will not sell the immediate jewel of my soul."

CHAPTER XXIV.

Ask and it shall be given you; seek and ye shall find; knock and it shall be opened unto you.   Mat. 7: 7

Behold he prayeth. —9: 11.   Men ought always pray. —Luke 18: 1

We shall not fight our battles alone.   There is a just God who presides over the destinies of nations; and who will raise up friends to fight our battles for us.   —Patrick Henry.

The morning following William's call upon the mayor, just before sunrise, the colored people who lived upon farms bordering on our hero's estate or who had been directly influenced by his operations, started for the home of Wendell Hill, to hold a prayer meeting.   Men, women, children—all assembled.   The work of the previous evening was almost undone, for there was not aman at his post.

Believing every detail would be well carried out, Thelma finally went to sleep at a very late hour.   She deemd it proper to seize a few hours rest, as she might have to stay on her feet forty-eight hours or more, after the dawning of the next day.   She wanted to have a maximum of energy, for she knew she had much work to do.

Tho the watch was faithfully kept during the night, yet every man had been able to get about three hours' rest.   This happened because of the careful arrangement and alternation of the guard.   Long after our lady had gone to sleep, however, the idea occurred to Hill, a man of unusual religious persuasion, that before entering upon any serious undertak-

246

ing, there should be prayer. His mistake was not in having prayer, but in having a prayer meeting in a crisis and leaving all the possessions of these people exposed to an unrelenting foe. Thinking that the lady from the city was accustomed to rising late, like other townspeople who had visited her, Mrs. Turner had not informed Thelma what was about to occur, but left her undisturbed.

She hurried to the assembling place, because she dearly enjoyed prayer meetings. Others were just as interested as she. So many came, that the leaders were at a loss where to place them. They finally left the matter with the people.

As the front room would not hold all the guests, many assembled on the outside—all firmly bent on serving their God, whether they were within or without. No unusual preparations had been made to appear in one's finest, everyone wore working attire. As they tript along chatting and smiling, one would not have thot a storm was rapidly sweeping on.

Wendell Hill opened the meeting by saying, "Trouble is brewing. The devil is mighty busy, but God can make him stay in his place."

"Amen, amen," burst forth vociferously from many mouths.

"It never hurts a man to take God with him, for God's a Captain that never loses a battle," continued Hill swaying the throng.

"No, he don't. Talk on, Hill," said one of the women. Hill would not wax eloquent, he merely said, "We'll open the meeting with scripture." He read as follows, from the tenth chapter of Matthew. "Behold, I send you forth as sheep in the midst of wolves; be ye therefore wise as serpents, and harmless as doves. But beware of men: for they will deliver you up. to the councils, and they will scourge you in their

synagoguges..............And the brother shall deliver up the brother to death, and the father the child: and the children shall rise up against their parents, and cause them to be put to death. And ye shall be hated of all men for my name's sake; but he that endureth to the end shall be saved..........
And fear not them which kill the body, but are not able to kill the soul; but rather fear him which is able to destroy both soul and body in hell..............Think not that I am come to send peace on earth: I came not to send peace, but a sword. For I am come to set a man at variance against his father, and the daughter-in-law against her mother-in-law. And a man's foes shall be those of his very household..........He that findeth his life shall lose it: and he that loseth his life for my sake shall find it."

As Hill read, the faces showed various states of emotion—anxiety, doubt, consternation. It was difficult for some to believe the passages were genuine. The doubt, however, was very evanescent, for when each recalled that Hill was their greatest Bible student, that he was most fervent in his religious zeal, and of unquestioned integrity, they speedily changed their minds. When the enthusiast began to utter the opening prayer and gave his fertile imagination free play, all doubts subsided. Jesus was Christ, and God was Lord of all.

Turner then began to sing, "I want to Be Ready to Walk in Jerusalem just like John." Then followed rhytmic hand clapping, cadenced to the time of the sound. There was likewise a patting of feet to reinforce the joyful emotion, slight at first but later more vigorous as the leader became more enthusiastic. Prayer followed prayer with hopes that God would intervene to prevent the spilling of blood. Then came the song, "Come on, Let's go to the Camp Meeting." This was followed by a number of songs, "I'm Going to Live and Never

Die," "Little David, Play on Your Harp," "Honor, Honor, My Lord." When these were sung the people marcht and shouted, the leader of the song performing many antics, waving his right hand as if a choir master, stooping low, and at times leaning back with his hands to his mouth, as if making a speaking trumpet. He would walk from group to group, waving his hand as if trying to draw forth more powerful sounds from those who seemed to let up from the exahustion of marching or shouting. Then he would place his left hand on his jaw, bend his head to one side and holler or shriek. These gesticulations kept the spirit alive.

In the thralldom of this deep religious emotion, with cares all dispelled, who thot of Thelma? 'The kingdom of heaven was at hand.' Sorrow and sighing had past away.

In the zephyrs of the morning Thelma peaceably slept on, unaware of any plan miscarried. That night somehow, she could not understand, she had had an unusual dream. She saw a hare dart out of a copse and run toward a pack of hounds, which turned from pursuit of a fox to chase this bold little creature. Soon appeared the hunters in fine breeches on fiery horses at great speed. Seeing that hunt had changed, they checked their pace and hallowed to the hounds to retake the scent. The dogs quickly responded, bounding once more for their original prey; but both hare and fox escaped.

When our fair lady awoke, she found herself very much fatigued, she seemed sleepier than ever, and pondered on remaining there longer for another doze. This, however, was only a first thot. She sat up in bed, musing; then she lookt about the room. The sun was well up, as she discovered from the heat and light forcing their way thru the windows. Her attention was now attracted to sweet, harmonious strains joyfully rising in the distance. What could it be? She listened more closely. Where could it be? The words were entirely inaudible, tho the tones were rather distinct. At last came one conviction; the singing was from the colored farmers; for white people did not sing that way. She was eventually reminded, by the minor strains, of the Fisk Jubilee Singers: for she recognized some of the songs those minstrels were wont to sing: "I'm Gwine to Jine de Great 'Sociation," "I Couldn't hear Nebdy Pray," "Go Down, Moses."

She sprang from the bed, happy as a lark, fresh as the dew at early morning. She quickly proceeded to arrange her toilet. While engaged in this, she heard a vigorous knocking. Thinking that it was only the morning call, she shouted, "Mrs. Turner, I'm up." As the knocking did not cease, Thelma observed with greater interest. The sounds did not come from the bedroom door, as she first surmised, but from that room next the kitchen. Upon opening her window and looking down she saw Andy Clarkston and at a little distance from him a motorcycle.

"Do you know where Mr. Turner is? Or do you know where I can find his wife, to learn where he is. I have a letter for him from Rev. Smith which I must give him in person." Such was the inquiry of Andy, who showed signs of eagnerness to execute his business and return to the estate without delay.

"What, are the folks out?" remarkt Thelma with great surprise. "Where can they be? What are they doing? What do they mean by leaving me alone? How long have yott been there?" were her incoherent utterances.

Andy paused awhile wondering which questions to answer, but eventually solved the dilemma by responding to her last. "I suppose I've been here about three minutes. We both seem to be in the same situation. You, as well as I, wonder where are the folks. I had expected to see somebody on guard. Of course the estate is well cared for; but if the other people are defending their farms, it is being done by the old grandmothers. That means that there is practically no protection at all."

Thelma immediately showed signs of anger. For a while she was silent, for the thots that thrust themselves upon her at the very instant would have been uttered but ineffectually due to the absence of those who should hear them. "Mr. Clarkston, can you wait for me a few minutes without arousing the ill feeling of Rev. Smith."

"Miss Haskell, I could wait a life time," he replied bashfully. "To stop for others would displease him, but to remain for your sake I'm sure will give him hours of ecstacy."

Thelma blusht and said, "Excuse me then, I'll be back within five minutes." She hurried to the task. As soon as she reacht the landing she heard strains of "Camp Meeting in the Wilderness." "The people must be there," she thot. She returned at once to the window and said, "Those people I vow, are holding a prayer meeting during these perilous moments. Mr. Clarkston, do you hear that singing?"

"Yes," he said, "it seems as tho it's in the direction of Wendell Hill's. You know he is strong for his religion in season and out of season. The truth is, it should always be in season. Yet there's more ways to serve God than one, one need not pray all the time."

"I dislike to detain you from your errand," she interrupted, "but those people must come back on guard." She wondered why she returned to the window. She had become greatly disturbed.

"By the way," broke in Andy, "Rev. Smith told me to say to you, not to worry the neighbors about him, that he's well protected. And so he is."

"Tell him, 1 understand. I appreciate your kindness extremely," she smiled. And Clarkson felt happy in her sunshine. "I want you to direct me to Mr. Hill's just the same. I'll be with you presently," she spoke and left the window. On this occasion there was no chance for finesse.

Within three minutes she returned ready for the day's work, even tho she had not dined. Andy wondered what to do with the cycle. Seeing the difficulty, Thelma said, "You may go on; I'll find the place. Just give me the directions."

"I'll take you to the place where you will have a straight road to the house. Then I'll go rapidly on. So quickly will I attend to this business, that I shall seem not to have lost any time."

"You're quite obliging, Mr. Clarkston," Thelma smiled again.

Andy was almost frantic with joy. "Don't mention it, Miss Haskell, don't mention it," he said with great embarrassment. "The honor is all yours." He took her to the main road. So Thelma found the place easily.

As soon as he had left the tender visitor, Andy hastened to his motorcycle which contrary to his apprehensions was in front of Turner's door unharmed. Almost in a twinkling, he had started the motor and sped away. He reacht Hill's house at least ten minutes before Thelma. Calling Turner aside he delivered the letter:

"Wait a moment for an answer," said Mr. Turner.

"Rev. Smith said, 'You need not wait for a reply.'" He mounted the cycle and in an instant was out of sight.

Turner read the letter at once. It expressed disapproval of any combining of all the people, urging again that each go to his own home and defend it. What was he to do? What were the others to do? They had given their word to a great lady that they would unite to oppose a common foe. Could they not be mistaken? Was there a common foe? Nobody had come against them yet.

Turner went back to the meeting and, as soon as possible, prayed emphasizing this utterance, "They that use the sword, shall perish by the sword." Several other prayers followed to the same effect. The sentiment was prevailing that God would fight their battles for them.

At the door now stood Thelma, listening to it all, at the same time trying to devise a means of addressing the people. Unwilling to disturb the solemnity of their worship—for. she respected with great reverence the sacred heritage of her people—she determined not to lose her temper. For she knew that once her impetuosity held sway, she would violently disperse the throng. Such an act would only teem with evil consequences; it would destroy at once all her popularity and make her organization of the people absolutely of non-effect.

She thot of getting word to Turner or Hill. This stratagem would have been easy, if singing had been on; but the people were engaged in a chain of prayers. As soon as one finisht, another began. In this way much enthusiasm was kept sustained. There was only one way—it was to be a link in the chain. After there had been uttered several other prayers damaging to her plans, Thelma was able to intervene. She might have interrupted earlier; but she wanted it to be done smoothly, with reverence and perfect accord. There was no delay in grasping this sort of opportunity.

Thelma had not prayed in public for some time. This was one of the first thots to come before her. She knew that, even in praying, practice makes perfect; if one wants to be coherent, fervent, and sincere without vain repetitions. It was useless to engage in extended hesitations. William's safety—

the safety of the man she loved—was in jeopardy, the safety of all those people attending that meeting, whom she now considered warring against themselves, was at stake. Above all, the honor of a loyal race and a grand republic was endangered.

Most important now, a courageous stand by these very people would save everything.

"Our Father," she began, somewhat bashfully, but yet firmly, "who has been our dwelling place thru all generations, help us in this dreadful hour." Heads began to take an erect position and look for the tender voice—somewhat familiar and yet rather strange. This did not last long, for with the remaining thot that they were worshipping Their Maker, the accustomed reverence again prevailed. "Father, I pray for these people here assembled, I pray for the young man who has greatly helped this community, I pray for the good white people of these parts, I pray for the scoundrels who despitefully use us, asking Thee to give us sufficient sense, not to let them despitefully use us any more.

"Father, I pray for this Nation—indeed a great land, a land which will be greater if we use Thy word and fight Thy battles."

"Amen, amen," came from many hearts, "Pray on, sister!"

One brother said, "Father, Those who use the sword shall die by the sword."

"But, Father, Father, Father, Oh Father," she pleaded, "haven't some used the sword, and lived? Did not thy avenging angel use the sword on Sennachrib's host of a hundred and eighty-five thousand men? Didn't Abraham use the sword to drive away the enemy that captured Lot. Didn't David use the sword on Goliath? How did Joshua take the children of Israel into Canaan except by the sword. Didn't George

Washington use the sword and become the first president of this great Nation?"

"Yes, he did, he did, pray on, sister," were the loud acclaims.

"Father, Almighty Father, did your Son not say, 'Whosoever shall save his life shall lose his life; and whosoever shall lose his life shall find it?"

The people at once thot of the scripture that opened the meeting. They especially remembered this passage because Wendell Hill had given it emphasis. "Amen, she is telling truth," came a response.

"Now, Father, just, hear me this time," she continued. "For if you deny me now, I'll find death tomorrow. A prince has come to this community like unto Christ; he has given not his worst, but his best. And as the culprits did unto Christ, so would some do to this kind man—kill him for his goodness. Father, is this to be? He'd give his life for them, for any one of them! Will they not do as much for him? Father, I know they will. They are going back on guard right now. Father, I thank thee for answering my prayer. Amen."

Before anyone could utter a word, Thelma said, "Men return to your posts, maintain the same line of communication even unto the home of Rev. Smith. Let the women and children go on at once accompanied by the advanced guard." All were surprised. Thots of the approaching danger seized them. The meeting had served one good purpose anyhow; most of the participants were ready to die. Few were going to tarry now. All must act with initiative and speed. The men designated aware of this took up their weapons at once and went to the defense. Thelma spoke with the authority of a general; her suggestions carried. "Mothers," she said as they started away, "remember your children. You experienced the throes of death that they might have life. Have no fear ot another. Defend your children with those weapons you possess. You know how, I believe, better than I."

When they had gone Thelma remarkt, "Gentlemen, gentlemen," she spoke curiously, that they considered themselves undeserving that distinction.

"I know you are ashamed of yourselves. Aren't you?" she inquired.

"Ashamed to serve the Lord?" put in Hill.

"Ashamed to serve the Devil," she replied. "Ask yourselves this question, 'Am I my brother's keeper?' If you let those dirty scoundrels harm a hair on the head of Rev. Smith, you're betraying the race. Don't think that they'll stop with him, they won't. When he's out of the way, You Are Next. If you let scoundrels harm innocent men, you're not serving the Lord, you're serving the Devil; and you're as guilty as they. If you compel them to be good, not to harm the little ones of God, great is your reward here and in heaven. If you don't do this, thus offending God—you get no reward either here or there.

"Do you know what happened this morning? No, you don't. Mr. Clarkston didn't stop to tell you. As he started from the post office, having taken the mail from Rev. Smith's private box, he noticed several groups of white men whispering clandestinely. These men, mostly scoundreds and ruffians, were approacht by some individuals you know well: Tom Howell, Robert White, and Sandy James. One group was in the post office. While Mr. Clarkston was there several individuals came in and went out, without attracting their attention in the least. When our friend passed, however, they recognized him and thinking that he must have overheard a part of their conversation they called, 'Nigger, come here. Where you going. What you're doing down here so early anyhow?'

"Mr. Clarkston had started his motor and was enroute speedily for Rev. Smith's estate. They called several times. 'If you don't stop, you're a goner.' Our gallant young man paid no heed. They fired several shots at him, but none hit the mark. He was soon out of range."

Mr. Turner then began, "All the men should know this. Well, we'll see that they get it. They will be ready then for anything."

"How you feel about it, men," he inquired of those present.

"Just fine," remarkt one, "I see now why Dr. Smith had those shooting matches. Men, let's not stay here, let's do our duty."

"Do your duty, don't let all the democracy be in Europe. Let's bring some to America," Thelma smiled.

CHAPTER XXV.

"There comes a time when the souls of human beings, women more even than men, begin to faint for the atmosphere of the affections they are made to breathe. —Holmes

With all determined to resist the enemy if they were opposed, the majority were stationed near William's estate. That thy might aid him and not be killed thru avoidable mishap, Turner seized the opportunity of intense enthusiasm and went to the estate, leaving Miss Haskell as a sort of generalissimo. He was somewhat uncertain as to finding William readily, for he was confident that his friend would not keep in prison. This fear, however, was soon dispelled. He found the distinguisht gentleman, at his desk, busy with papers as if nothing extraordinary had occurred.

Observing who had come, William laid aside the papers and heartily greeted his dear neighbor. So suddenly had he turned from his task that he was somewhat uncertain where to begin. He wanted to know first of all of the security of the people. Were they on guard or were they trusting to chance? Where was Thelma? What could she be doing? Yet his concern for her was less than that for his neighbors, as he was sure of her being sufficiently spirited and equipoised to conquer any situation. The thots of her, therefore, cannot be construed as solicitude, but a curiosity born of a deep admiration for her supreme adaptability to the crisis.

A few minutes past in attention to a plan to operate a community store; then they returned to the matter of most importance.

"Mr. Turner," at length began Rev. Smith after many moments of reflection, "what are the people doing? Are they aware of what is going on or do they, since no one has come against them, regard it as a joke?"

Turner felt somewhat abasht, when he recalled all the circumstances of the morning. More was he ashamed because he regarded himself as having failed in the trust committed to him.

Seeing that his neighbor made no reply, William began to laugh. "You make me think that something's gone wrong. Am I right?" inquired William.

Turner shook his head, yet unable to speak because of his consciousness of guilt. "No?" remarked Rev. Smith. "Then tell me what's going on."

Making a superlative effort to suppress his deep emotion Turner said slowly with hesitation, "Everything's all right now—thanks to Miss Haskell."

"Miss Haskell? What did she do?" his curiosity interrupted.

"She has done everything. The people did well last night, but Hill influenced them to have a prayer meeting. I even listened. When they once started, they forgot the purpose of the assembly and turned it almost into a protracted meeting. Had any one come then, we all would have been lost."

"That was serious. I told them by no means to leave their homes. I wonder if they'll be capable of holding out?" he spoke and then paused, after which reflection he askt Turner to proceed.

"Well, we just listened to Wendell Hill. But thank the Lord, Miss Haskell came among us, prayed a prayer that brot us to our senses. Now we're on guard to stay till the war is over.

"Rev. Smith, we're not going to pay any attention to your

letter at all. We keep in touch with your watchers."

"That's just what I don't want you to do. I want these people to see that I will fully respect the law, even if they do not."

"You're not doing this, Rev. Smith. We're the ones," he defended thus their decisions.

"Those white people will say I'm leading you. Persons so base as to kill an innocent man in cold blood will do anything, will say anything, and their courts will not bring them to justice. I cannot somehow believe that this is your work, for you've generally seen situations as I have. Yet it is possible for differences to occur at some time. And probably this is the parting of the ways." Thus he tried to reconcile himself to the action of his neighbors in behaving contrary to his desire. Yet he had to admire them; for their conduct could have been prompted only by love. "I certainly wish you had not done this. Well, if you will not follow my suggestion, I will partly control the situation anyhow, I can at least keep my men within the law. You may suit yourselves."

"Thank you, Rev. Smith, we're so glad you've given us this permission," came from Turner, who least desired to get the ill-will of the young divine.

"I haven't given you any permission," interrupted William, showing his ire by a sharp grimace. "Do not misunderstand me. You have taken the permission. I merely suffer it." Then as if this were a holiday, he said, "But come, let's go to the garage. I have—"

Turner broke in, "You've forgotten about the folks. I better make my rounds. You know those scoundrels may burst in at any time. And I'd better be going, unless you need me particularly."

"No, you go on. Whatever you do, do not fire the first

shot. It may mean the death or the wounding of one of our
race, but be willing to make that sacrifice. Are you well supplied with arms?"

"Yes, sir. We can handle the situation."

"All right. Success." When Mr. Turner had gone, William returned to his papers. He lookt at them for a while,
then went to an opposite window and watched Turner slowly
crossing a field of corn. He followed him as if in a revery,
until the beloved gentleman was out of view. Then he moved
along the side of the room toward the next window. After
having gone a few steps, he stopt and gazed at a picture in
a frame of ebony. It was the sphinx. As he lingered beholding it, for the first time he noticed its Negro features? "Certainly 'tis because that was the dominating race of that land,"
he thot. It was indeed an inspiration. If that structure which
has been a mystery to all subsequent ages, could be the work
of his ancestors, he himself would be also a mystery. His
foes would not fathom his whereabouts more than they could
solve the riddle of the Sphinx. He pondered long on Africa
and allowed his mind to drift with sweet orientation to his
forebears. He saw it as a land of gloom and then of pure
delight—with the end of exploitation on the part of other folk.
Nations were not greedy for gold, nations were not there to
mutilate. The savage had become cultured; the jungle was
only a dream. Stately schools and buildings, churches in the
grand style, resplendent avenues and vistas had made a paradise. Then how sad he was that his ancestors could not enjoy
it!

While thus his thots moved on like the song of a bird at
the return of spring, his attention was distracted by the call
of "Rev. Smith, Rev. Smith." As it was a sudden awakening
and since he was not at first composed, he ran quickly to the

desk, seized his rifle and started out. When he reached the parlor, he met an outburst of laughter. It was Thelma who had come to wish him "Good morning."

"Put down your gun. You know I wouldn't harm you for the world. Don't you," she smiled.

He did not speak at once, but wiped his face, as if trying to restore emotional equilibrim. Thelma continued to smile in her winning way. "Have a seat, tell me the news. I was thinking what an ideal day this would be for a picnic. Those wickd men had to spoil my dream. You haven't told me about the letter for Washington. You haven't been hospitable a bit this time. I think I'd better go back to Williamsburg at once." She arose to go.

William took her by the hand and courteously bowed her back to her seat, at the same time saying, "Thelma, you know it would have broken your heart to go. You know you wouldn't leave me now."

She rusht to the door and said, "Now I cannot stay. Good bye." William stood silent admiring her august presence, the sweetness of her speech, the gracefulness of her steps. He heard her open the hall door, then he called, "Thelma, Thelma," very softly. She heard. "Thelma," he called again. "Who let you in here any way? I told Mrs. Brown to call me in case of any danger. That surely was her voice awhile ago and not yours."

Miss Haskell returned, moved close to him, with a vindictive stare and began reproachfully, "I came here—I came here." Then she said tenderly, "William, why do you ask? I was—I was just dying to see you." She went quickly to the sofa again.

William blusht, then sat in a chair near the center table ornamented with a Japanese vase of flowers.

"Now you have it. I suppose you're satisfied. Open confession is good for the soul. At least they say so," was her taunting remark. She lookt at William mischievously and started to move towards him.

He waved his hand for repression and said, "No, remain where you are. I'm glad to see you anyhow but you ought to be in Williamsburg."

"I was going, but you called me back."

"You know you must not go now. Besides your going was only pretense?"

"Do I pretend, William?"

"Certainly, everybody pretends sometimes. That was one of your instances."

"I better go back to—no, I won't."

"I thot you wouldn't."

"But, William!"

"Thelma, you must tell me what you have done to my neighbors. They have actually refused to do my bidding. They have rebelled against me," he affirmed. He took a rose from the vase and offered it to her with a bow. "I have no rosemary for remembrance. I wish I did. We have been friends so long and may have to part. Something is going to happen before the sun goes down, I feel; hence I speak. Accept this rose for remembrance. My foes will spare you; but I may have to go."

Thelma held her head as if abasht, then lookt at him appealingly. Turning to one side she noticed a pillow covered with a design after the seal of his alma mater. She put it from her and moved to the other end of the sofa. "Now there is room, William. Come, sit down." He accepted the seat. Then she took a pin, and gave it to him with this remark, "Take this; pin it here." She pointed to her left breast. "Not for remembrance tho. Don't think you will go and leave me here."

"Thelma, you must not be this way. Men, it seems, must die but women must live," he remarkt with resignation.

"No," she said impatiently, "That has been true long enough. Either men and women both must live or both must die. I can shoot. I'll show you." Quickly she had seized his rifle. But he was soon at her side.

"No, Thelma, you must not fire that. My helpers would think I was attacked. I believe you. So you see proof is unnecessary." He placed the rifle on the table, where it was. Then both returned to the sofa. "You have not told me what you did to my neighbors."

"You did not permit me."

"Well, I'm listening now."

"You said the people had rebelled against you. It isn't so. They have rebelled for you. Do not scorn them; scorn me. They were obeying your commands, but I shamed them into rejecting them. They were about to let their religious enthusiasm leave them defenseless. But they are determined now. I was asleep when they played that joke on me; but I'm awake now. Besides, I have foresworn sleep, until we have fought this thing to a finish." She wanted him to be pleased with what she had done, yet she feared to go into details

"To be frank," he put in, knitting his brow, "I'm sorry. Yet you have taught those people a valuable lesson. The sight of a woman, sensible and fearless, calm and resourceful, was something new to them. Clarkston says they almost worship you."

"I rejoice in the fact that they appreciate the situation. You must know tho that I was selfish in doing so," she pleaded.

"I can't understand you," he remarkt appealing, insisting upon an answer. How could you have been selfish?"

"Don't you see, William, I did it for myself?" she continued pleaded, anxious concerning the effect of her admission. "I thot of the people, I thot of the Nation and our race. Overwhelmed with the impulse that we should be willing to give our lives rather than have either the Nation or the race humiliated, I determined on this course."

"That does not make you selfish, it enables you; you were moved by the strongest pulsations of generosity. That's why the people almost worship you," he declared and waited her response.

She paused a while, then lowered her head; but soon it was erect again. Now her entire being pleaded. She lookt at him inquiringly then took his hand. William was thrilled. He tried to push her hand away, he wanted to get up and leave the house. He had to stay. He had not toucht her hand since childhood. How easy it was then; how difficult during the last years! As her hand pressed his lightly, he held her firmly. New impulses, new ideas, and hopes seemed to rush from her to him, and permeate every fiber of his being. "William, William, do not despise me. I have not done this for people, race, or Nation. True, I thot of them; but I did this for myself."

"Thelma! Thelma!" This was all he said. Great was his emotion.

"I love the people, but first of all I love you." She now more firmly pressed his hand, nimbly tossed her head and quickly leaned towards him.

He took her in his arms and kissed her twice; then broke away. "Thelma, I am too happy," he said, when he had reacht the center table.

"Come, William, sit down. Be happy again," she said, and

smiled triumphantly. "I am not going to harm you. You're not going to harm me. Certainly you're not afraid of a woman, especially of her who made you happy?"

"It's not that, Thelma," came forth with a sigh from his true breast. "I shouldn't have sat on the sofa beside you."

"I wanted you to, William, and you came willingly," she said cheerfully.

"Yes, I know I did; but I wonder if I haven't done you wrong and probably someone else wrong."

"Susan?" Thelma remarkt when she noticed his wavering.

"Yes. What would she say? How would she feel, if she knew this?"

"Do you love her, William?" askt Thelma with great sangfroid.

"Yes, I do. That's the trouble?"

"Why not end it by marrying her? I know she's wild about you."

"It's not easy for a conscientious person to make a decision about a matter so serious as this," he replied, beginning to defend himself. "I wanted to marry until those dastardly outlaws sent me that threatening note. I had thot of going to Susan—" Here he broke off.

"You're not hurting my feelings," put in Thelma, suppressing her emotions. It was not perfectly pleasant to listen to the disclosure, but she had staked her all on this interview. If she lost, it would not be her fault. When she saw him pause, she knew that she could not be successful unless she thoroly understood his attitude. Accordingly she urged him on. "We're old friends anyhow. You can tell me anything." she put in.

"I believe I can. I was about to say," he continued, taking her into his confidence, "I had strongly contemplated going home and asking Susan to be—my—wife. Several times before, I had thot of going only to say, I have plenty of time yet." Then when I was threatened, I rejoiced that I was single. Thus I put it entirely out of my mind. Now you come and force my thots in that direction again.

"I had refrained from asking, because of the life I lead— ostracised by the ministers of the state and now attacked by gangsters and felons. When I began this work, I lookt forward to this. I believed that some day my life would be in danger. I'd marry, if I thot I'd have some days of pleasure; but why marry to make a widow and probably an orphan? It is not my wish to make my wife miserable, but happy."

"I am afraid, my dear, you don't understand a woman's heart. We must take life as it is. Many things are done for us anyway and we must be resigned," she affirmed.

"But Susan is a home girl. Her child would need a father. If I were to be killed as her husband, I fear she would die also. True, I have called upon her more than any young woman I've met; but I have made no overtures. For us to part single would not be so calamitous as for us to part married," he said, sitting down by the table which supported the vase of roses.

"Have you allowed her to answer you on this point?" she inquired, made hopeful by his last remarks.

"No, I haven't askt her point blank, but our conversations on varied matters have sufficiently convinced me as to this," he said.

"William, I'll tell you what to do. Let me help you out of the difficulty. Sometimes I become very unconventional," she said with a smile that had its effect. "If many women had come here, as I have, they would have been seeking you and leading you to a proposal. They would have shown they wanted to marry you by smiling as I have"—here she smiled again—"by coming ostensibly to visit the farm and see the town, by making you thousands of little advances. They would have done all the proposing. And a year after you were married, your wife would have said you wouldn't let her rest until she had married you."

"But, Thelma."

"Don't interrupt me at this moment, please. Please wait until I finish." He nodded assent. "Occasionally I am retiring and conventional par excellence, at other times I am frank and unconventional. This is one of the unconventional moments. William, I can help you solve this problem." She proceeded to move toward him.

"Stay where you are," he cried.

She went on to his side and put her arms about him. He did not repulse her. Then she said with penetrating sweetness, "William, you love me, too—no, you're not going to run away. I'll be your widow and to the child I'll be both father and mother. I pleaded for Susan as long as I could, but I'm a woman. I love you for myself. I came here to tell you this."

William arose, drew her to himself and said, "Thelma, I'd like to kiss you. You have made me so happy; but kisses mean so much. When I receive another, it will be from her I must wed."

"And who will that be?" she pleaded.

At this moment the bell rang. As it was not an alarm, he did not respond at once.

"Can you suffer the worries and anxieties of my situation? Can you bear the disquiet of my being subject to attack at any time?" he askt.

"Haven't I already done so?"

"Yes, you have."

"Am I not ready to defend you even at the risk of my life?"

"Thelma, you shall have an answer."

"When, William?"

"Before the sun goes down."

CHAPTER XXVI.

Refrain tonight,
And that shall lend a kind of easiness
To the next abstinence! the next more easy;
For use almost can change the stamp of nature.
—Shakespeare

I say plainly that every American who takes part in the action of a mob or gives it any sort of countenance is no true son of this great democracy, but its betrayer, and does more to discredit her by that single disloyalty to her standards of law and of right than the words of her statesmen or the sacrifices of her heroic boys in the trenches can do to make suffering peoples believe her to be their savior. How shall we commmend democracy to the acceptance of other peoples if we disgrace our own by proving that it is, after all, no protection to the weak. —Woodrow Wilson.

"What you're doing with that rope?" shouted a culprit, disgusted at the very sight of it.

"I thot we might want to swing the coon up to a tree," was the reply.

"Hanging's too good for a nigger. Get those irons there," said the first speaker. "Did you get Tom the plummer's blast? You know we got to heat those irons, if we're goin' to gouge his eyes out right. When it comes to lynchin' a nigger, I believe in doin' a good job."

"I got it all right," was the response.

"Well, let's join the bunch. We're late now. We should have finisht this little job and been back to work," was the cold utterance.

How can they do this? How can they be so devoid of feeling as not to value human life? Some say they do not treat white men this way. Yes, they do; but not so often.

270

The recent years have seen even white men victims of this modern barbarism. Can persons maltreat the Negro and not abuse their own people? A man is a man.

The Court House was the rendezvous for the reprobates bent on this devilish pastime. There were the paved street and granitoid sidewalks before the municipal building with its artistic statuary. There were the many business houses, groceries, notion and department stores, confectioneries, restaurants, hotels, furniture shops, drug stores, hardware stores. There were the pedestrians going in and out; men, women, boys and girls. There were the sheriff and his assistants. While some plied their trades and others pursued the even tenor of their way, the mob assembled with hilarity and profanity; for this was to be a gala day. No colored people were on the streets, except for business; only here and there a few could be seen in the shops, shining shoes, washing cuspidors, hauling trunks, or moving furniture. It seemed well understood mutually that this was an occasion when fiends would dance in triumph.

Tad Temple, Jr., a boy of twelve, evidently the son of a wealthy or well-to-do citizen, passed by the mob. Ben Caldwell, a lad of ten, stepped on his foot. So many had crowded before the Court, that jostling seemed unavoidable. This young fellow did not seek into causes, he yelled, "Damn you, what you doing stepping on my foot. I'll knock your damn block off; I'm no nigger. If you do it again, I'll make dad lynch you."

The other replied, "I didn't go to step on your foot. You curse me because I ain't your size. If I was your equal, I'd treat you worse than a nigger. Your old man can't do nothing to me."

Tad Temple's boy slapped the little fellow, began to choke him. Took some twine from his pocket, and put it around Ben Caldwell's neck. "I'll hang you myself," he said.

Before more could be done, attracted by the cries, several men parted the youngsters. When Tad Temple recognized his boy and understood the situation, he said to Robert White, "Did you see what my youngster tried to do, strangle that little fellow and hang him? When our children start doing this, I think it time we should have stopt. We shouldn't be so public anyway."

"Mr. Temple," said Bob, "you've always been against this fellow's upstart ways. Now that you've got a chance to get him, surely you ain't a going to back out? You know we want an orderly mob, we want some decent folks with us," he pleaded.

"All that's well and good, Bob," put in Mr. Temple, "but when a man sees his child treating another white child as mine did, you know its enough to make a man shiver. If it had been a nigger, I'd enjoyed it; but he was on a white kid."

"What the h--l, what you waiting for? This is a h—l of a mob," said Newton Young. "Are you ever going to get started. That nigger ought to be in h—l by this time."

"D—n it, you're right," remarkt Luke Crabtree. "We don't take all day for just one. Let us have our fun and get back to work."

On the other side of the street stood the president of the National Bank, Mr. Pitts, beside him was the sheriff. "Mr. Simpson, can't you do anything to stop this?" he called.

"Not a thing. You know they will have their way," said the sheriff, with perfect contentment.

"Have you tried?" inquired the banker.

"No, what's the use?"

"This thing is a disgrace to the Nation. It can be stopt. Why don't you order troops of the governor?" persisted the banker.

"He wouldn't take time to send them to save the life of a darkey. If he did, instead of stopping the mob, they'd only join it."

"Well, I suppose you can prosecute them when this is over, can't you?"

"We never can get all the names." Of course, they never tried.

"Mr. Simpson, you and I know at least seventy-five of those men. If you want other names, I'll supply them," said this brave citizen.

"I couldn't get a jury that would convict them; so it's not worth bothering your head one way or the other," declared the sheriff with nonchalance. "Let the darkey die. We won't miss him. We have enough of them anyway."

"Mr. Simpson, you don't deserve your position; you disgrace it." The banker spoke vehemently, for he was both irritated and disgusted. "This is no common Negro these scoundrels are after, it's one of our best citizens, Rev. Smith. The only crime that he has committed is that he has honestly acquired a bank account and helped others to do the same. You know that there have been fewer criminals since he came than ever in our history. If you can get ten men who'll join me, I'll break up that mob. They have well nigh a thousand going to take one man. The cowards! Ten good men can bring them to their senses. Go quickly and see what you can do; if we start in time we can get ahead of them. We don't want it to go all over the country as a big headline of the newspapers, Seaton, a Place of Lawlessness, Mob Lynches an Upright Negro for Acquiring a Bank Account. See what you can do."

"Mr. Pitts, it won't do any good. I'm sorry," he said.

"You won't help to put this down?" he inquired sternly, and paused. "Then I will. Good bye." He went into the throng, then upon the courthouse steps and shouted, "Men, men." Some of the members of the mob paid heed; others were utterly unaware of his anxiety. So occupied were they with cursing and abusing to inflame their passion for dastardly deeds of brutishness and savagery. Savagery? Ah! worse than savagery. Those of the mob who were attentive tried to bring their nearest associates to listen to the banker. "Mr Pitts has something so say," said one.

"H—l, this ain't no time for speeches," said the associate with defiance. "Let's get the nigger and listen afterwards." This attitude was fairly typical.

"D—n it," remarkt another. "Are you goin' to stay here all day? If you don't mean business, d—n it, why don't you say so?"

"Men! Men! Citizens of Great America," called Mr. Pitts, trying to make at least those nearest him take caution. The shouting, fuming, and hubdub of the assembly made his utterances unintelligible even to those nearest. Seeing Sandy James, however, over whom he could exert some influence, he called to him; he even went to him and urged him to quiet the people, in order that he might remind them of their duty in that great hour.

The lawyer, tho a pettifogger, knew he had to obey. Accordingly, without any ado, he spoke to several near him and particularly the leaders, whom he dispatched thru the crowd with these words, "Tell the people they must listen to Pitts, but not do what he says. If he tends to talk long, we'll run off. I'll give the signal. You know my whistle. Remember, you listen, but you do what I say."

The men delivered the communication as directed. It was received, however, with various responses. Some said they would go home and have nothing to do with it; others indulged in prolonged profanity; others received the suggestion kindly. Tho dissatisfaction and spleen ran high in many parts of the crowd, all stayed to listen. The few, who were most ready to rush on without the rest, became somewhat more temperate, when they recalled that they never had fewer than three hundred when such an important job was to be done. They had to have security, you know. Three hundred or a thousand against one. What hideous warfare! Why not a man against a man? Who ever heard of such? The odds would be too great.

When the mumbling, the shouting and the swearing at length subsided and practically all faces were turned to the top of the stone steps, the venerable banker, with his vigorous character lines, and his grizzled hair, somewhat curled up in the rear, with his splendid physique and august look, set off by a penetrating eye, bespoke the honorable gentleman of the New South, the statesman, the twentieth century man. He reminded one of Cicero at the forum, of Demosthenes at the Areopagus.

"Men of the South, American citizens," he began, "and when I say American, I mean all that the word implies; our glorious land, our noble heritage, the honor of our fathers who died to make it free. Do you love this country?"

"Yes, certainly we do," was vociferated in many parts of the crowd, and like expressions. "We hate the niggers tho."

"You ought to love them," he continued. "If you realized that the South never could have developed without them; if you realized how you profit by their labor now, you would be better towards them."

"Is that all you have to say?" burst forth from one embittered by the previous utterance.

"Shut up," came from one near him. "We ain't going to pay no attention to what he says anyhow. We know our business. We're going to get the nigger, d—n it. Ain't that enough?"

The solace, tho crudely put, accomplisht its aims. The mob was soon quiet again. Continuing his remarks, the banker said, "Lynching should never have occurred. Even tho it has been tolerated, we can not afford to have it now. Have you forgotten that our country is at war? Can you not recall that on April 6, 1917, that the President gave us a motive for entering the war by saying, 'Let us make the world safe for democracy.' Gentlemen, that is an awful responsibility. Democracy means that you are as good as I am; that other people are as good as you; that those who govern shall have the consent of those they govern. This is what the President aims to accomplish.

"We have undertaken to make the world safe for democracy while there is very little democracy within our own gates. The Germans oppressed the Belgians and we cry, 'Horror!' The Russians have a pogrom of the Jews and we cry, 'Horror!' The Turks massacre the Armenians and we cry, 'Horror!' Our own citizens murder our most loyal citizens in cold blood and what do we do? Nothing. What do we say? Nothing.

"American citizens, I plead with you to do no wrong. Attorney General Gregory puts this better than I can. Hear what he says in his recent speech before the American Bar Association. He says, 'We must set our faces against lawlessness within our own borders. Whatever we may say about the causes for our entering the war, we know that one of the principal reasons was the lawlessness of the German nation—what they have done in Belgium and in Northern France, and what we have reason to know they would do elsewhere. For us to tolerate lynching is to do the same thing that we are condemning in the Germans. Lynch law is the most cowardly of crime. Invariably the victim is unarmed, while the men who lynch are armed and in large numbers. It is a deplorable thing under any circumstances, but at this time above all others it creates an extremely dangerous condition. I invite your help in meeting it.' Those are his very words, as I read them from this clipping. Say what you wish; but lynching a man in America is not different from lynching one in Belgium or France. For—"

"Ah, h—l, that's enough of that bosh," shouted several, interrupting the speaker. "Let's move where we're going, if we're going."

"Yes, d—n it," shouted another. "I've stood it just a minute too long. I'm so d—n mad; if he don't stop I'm likely to put a ball thru him. Stop your d—n gab or I'll—."

A shrill whistle arose, which was reinforced by similar calls from various parts of the mob. With rifles, pistols, cudgels, irons, ropes and others things, the throng moved at a rapid pace amidst turbulence, shrieking, oaths and vituperation, to seize the great pioneer of race adjustment whose crime was that he served his people and his nation faithfully.

The banker, in great dismay, lookt on the mobile throng as it hurried away. To him it was a calamity,· a man was to be lynched, a soul sent to heaven or hell. He thot of the slaves who defended his mother during the Rebellion, he thot of those that bled under the lash toiling in the wilderness to make it blossom like a rose. He mused how the toil of these humble people had created the wealth of the South, afforded him and others opportunity for leisure, study and enjoyment. These people had become poor making their landlords and employers millionaires. Then he recalled Rev. Smith, who had associated with him on many occasions in improving the lot of the farmer; and had stimulated more friendly relations between the races. "Why is the laborer unworthy of his hire? Why should honest and persistent thrift be unrewarded, even scorned," so he mused, as the spectacle faded in the distance.

At this point, a Negro, very unkempt, a braggadocio and a bully, passed out of the saloon, with an unwrapped bottle of whiskey in his hand. The banker recognized him at once as the shiftless individual, who worked spasmodically on a nearby farm.

"We don't see so many of those now," he reflected. "Rev. Smith has changed many of them to steady workers. They are savers now and work regularly. Some of them are even buying farms.

"I suppose that's the trouble. As long as a Negro is trifling, he's all right. He knows his place.' As soon as he shows himself a man, a valuable citizen, we don't need him. What mockery!" He became stirred to disgust and indignation. He left the steps and started for his bank. "Somehow, I can't give up. That shilly shally sheriff has refused to interfere. Is the case hopeless? I believe I can get ten men who will help me stop this outrage. To get them soon enough is the trouble. The telephone's the thing."

When he had gone a few paces, he was met by his bank messenger. "What is it, Frank?" he inquired.

"There is a gentleman waiting for you at the bank," he replied, with a slight bow.

"How long has he been there?"

"Not long."

"Couldn't someone else look after his business? I have a very important matter to adjust."

"He said he would have to see you."

"Well, I hope it will not be long."

When he entered the bank, he cast about in the lobby to see his caller. As each person there was transacting business, he rang for the messenger. "Frank," he said, when the energetic employee responded, "bring the gentleman to my office, please."

"Yes, sir," he bowed out.

Within a few minutes, Mr. Pitts greeted the visitor. "Davis," he said cheerfully, shaking his hand vigorously, "if I had known you were here, I should have been here long ago. Say, you never told me how much wheat you thresht on your place the other week."

"Five hundred thirty bushels," he remarkt with obvious pride.

"Have a seat," Davis began, "I could say much, but I have only one thing to talk about this morning. As I came down the road I met a mob. Trailing behind them were many women and children going evidently to witness a gruesome sight. And these were dressed in their finest and carried lunch baskets, as if going on a picnic. This thing must stop. We call Nero cruel, but what about our own people?"

"I just left the court house steps. That was their assembly place. I might have been here before, but I watched them out of sight and reflected upon the terrible times in which we live. Think what those scoundreds are hoping to do, while our President is trying to bring peace to Europe," the banker declared with great feeling.

"Pitts, we must stop this."

"That's what I say, Davis. I was just coming here to reach some men over the phone to help me. I believe ten or eleven brave men can turn the trick. I spoke to the reprobates from the steps and they listened; but I alone couldn't do much. If ten or eleven determined men meet them they'll listen, I do believe," spoke the banker optimistically.

"But when you go into a mob like that, to be sure of success talk alone won't do. You must show guns. I shouldn't stop at ten or eleven. I'd get a whole army, Pitts."

"Well, the more we have the surer we are of success."

"To think of having women and children looking on a murder. You know how cruel those fellows are. They don't believe in painless death at all. They lengthen it out; they torture their victims. Then our women and children go to see it; and the cowards pride themselves on taking human life in this way," Davis affirmed with disgust.

"Then they are going to kill an innocent man. If the fellow was some scamp or idler, it would be different. But to kill a man who has done so much for the community," said the banker.

"Yes, Rev. Smith is a very fine man," remarkt Davis. "I can always get laborers now, who will stick right to the job. And I know it hasn't always been so. Besides, if I need extra help and ask him to find some one, he can always get some one there. That means something. These explosive orators who have said, 'Keep the darkey down,' don't know what they're talking about. I believed that stuff once; but I see now that intelligence makes even the Negro a better worker This man has stood by us. Now we must stand by him. Whom were you going to call?"

"Townsend, Hardy, McKinley, and have them mention some others who they think will join us," was the response.

"Call them, see what they say."

Mr. Pitts called the three persons he named and found them ready to co-operate. They were all engaged in important matters, but because the honor of the South was at stake, because the honor of the Nation was at stake, they decided to do the more important thing. As he expected, they suggested others who should be called. When he finisht telephoning he had the promise of thirty-five men, who could call others and come to the bank at once.

"That's encouraging, isn't it?" inquired the banker.

"It certainly is," he replied. "If we can just stop this at once; then prosecute the offenders, we will have made a long advance in ridding the Nation of the lawless. If other towns learn that we have put it down, they will follow suit."

"I found tho that Nailor has been working. He's organizing the farmers who are not with Bob White. He has helping him Henry and James Mitchell, Daniel Martin and Fred Dean. How did he miss you?" the banker askt.

"Well, I have been quite ubiquitous of late—everywhere you know," was the jovial response. "But I'm glad the outlook is hopeful. Did you tell them to bring their guns?"

"No, I did not. It was unnecessary," remarkt the banker. "What fool would come without one in an affair like this?"

"How are we to get there? You know we'll have to use automobiles," said Davis asking and answering his question.

"There will be cars enough," the banker assured him and at once called for all available automobiles to be held in reserve for him.

"How many can you get?" asked Davis.

"More than we need," replied the friend.

The respectable white men of Seaton soon began to pour into the bank, weapons in hand. As most of them owned cars, few had to be ordered. When all who were expected were there, they numbered about seventy-five. No delay was lost in exchanging greetings. The question on every lip was, "who'll lead? Who'll address them?"

"Since Nailor is best as fighter and organizer, let him lead," said the banker. All agreed. "I spoke to the men this morning, so I think it would be better to have a different person." He feared selection.

"Probably you're right," said Davis.

"Then I suggest that Lawyer Jones will address them."

"You handle children. Can you handle men?" the banker askt.

"I think I can. Anyhow, I have to try," was the lawyer's reply.

"Then all is settled?"

"All's settled. Let's meet at Nailor's," said one.

"All right," was the general response.

They boarded the automobiles and sailed off.

CHAPTER XXVII.

Gather ye rose-buds while ye may,
Old time is still a-flying:
And this same flower that smiles today,
Tomorrow may be dying.

Then be not coy, but use your time;
And while ye may, go marry:
For having lost but once your prime,
You may for ever tarry. — Herrick

After William had promised Thelma that he would decide his fate before sunset, he became silent for a while and only lookt at her. Then he began to ponder concerning the wisdom of his utterance; but when the thot came that since he could support a wife, today was as excellent time for a decision as any other, he made himself satisfied. At once he turned to her and askt childishly, "Are you satisfied now? Are you happy?"

She answered with all pleasantness. "William, I'm just as happy as a lark, just as happy as I can be. How are you?"

"Well, I suppose I am happy, too. I certainly have been thrilled by your courage.—But someone rang. I wonder who it can be?" said Smith, becoming practical once more.

Clarkston came in and bowed.

"Pardon me," he said, "but there is a lady who wishes to see you, Mr. Smith."

"A lady? Who can she be?" William questioned himself.

"Well, I know it's time for me to get back to duty," said Thelma, starting to go.

"You know as well as I, Thelma, that you can't go right now. Meet the lady and then go. I always insist upon my guests becoming acquainted. Yet, I wonder what my visitor wants here at this time, when blood is likely to be shed. I shouldn't be surprised at all at your doing such—but for a stranger! Probably it's one of the neighbors. Well, no use wondering about her. Let us look her over," he remarkt flippantly. "Show her in, Mr. Clarkston."

William stood by the table; Thelma sat on the sofa. Each lookt at the other inquiringly but kept silent. While they were in these attitudes, the lady walked into the drawing room. It was Susan. William and Thelma were overwhelmed. Thelma sighed, William was speechless; for a while both had lost their equipoise.

Susan placed her bag on a chair near by and was on the point of extending her hand to William, when she saw Thelma. "You here?" she said. "Well, I expected it." She was rather nervous. "I wanted—I wanted"—here she broke off and sat down. "Oh, it's so hard, so hard!"

"What, Susan?" inquired William, eager for an answer.

"Oh, some day, I'll tell. Some day I'll tell it from the house tops. I'll shout it to all the world," she screamed. "Yes, all the world shall know."

William took her hand and said, "Susan, you're either ill or very nervous. Your hand seems to be feverishly hot and you are breathing very rapidly. Thelma, he entreated, his face showing great anxiety, "go back to the kitchen—you'll find it there—the smelling salts." He indicated the direction. "Ask Mrs. Brown to come here. We can't get a physician at this time, because"—

"William, all that is unnecessary, and if I did need a physician right now, I believe I'd rather die than to have Thelma go seek one. No, you needn't go. It's not necessary. Ha! Ha!

Ha!" she laughed sadly and disquietingly. It seemed as tho she would go into hysterics. Then with a suddenness that surprised them, she stopt. William and Thelma were completely overawed. "I'm all right," she said, rising and moving towards William. "Pardon me for setting your nerves on the rack, but I felt so miserable. Pardon my manners. Shake hands with me, William. How have you been?" William greeted her warmly.

"I've been very well. I'm so glad to see you," he said.

"Are you really," she inquired jubilantly. "I was afraid you wouldn't be—But, I mustn't forget you, Thelma; pardon the hard things I said of you just now. I almost hate you for some things, but we've been playmates and classmates and friends so long. Then I didn't shun you, but you avoided me. Shake hands with me, Thelma." When the townslady showed hesitancy, Susan went to her, took her hand and greeted her warmly. They then embraced. Thelma felt ashamed. "I want to be good now, even if I have to be wicked later on. I want to love you now, even tho I may have to hate you tomorrow. I wish we could be permanent friends again, that we could run to see each other once more each evening; but there are some things we must understand first. Are we friends now?" she askt. "William, Thelma, are we?"

"I am your friend, you may rest assured," William affirmed.

"And you, Thelma?" inquired Susan.

"Susan, I don't know what to say. I have certainly tried to be," she said honestly.

"I ask this, because what we are to settle can not be adjusted by enemies. We must be friends to do it. You can be my friend," she pleaded, "for a half hour, can't you?"

"I—I, yes, Susan; yes, Susan, dear, I can, I can," she remarkt with great effort. She could not throttle the impulse of her heart with its womanly instincts that a few minutes since had gained the mastery, had forced her to reveal her soul to the man she loved without affectation or arrogance. She loved Susan, but she loved William, too. She could act a part even in real life, but not that of a hypocrite. Therefore to say she was a friend and at the same time a rival seemed to Thelma a little inconsistent. As every woman desires the man she loves, so Thelma longed for William. There was to be no concealing it. Yet if he chose her friend, she would suffer, but she would live.

Interpreting Susan's plea as a bid for calmness, she could consent.

"We're all childhood friends. We played and grew together; but now we live apart. In view of the fact that fate or providence has thru the heart brot us once more together, let us be joyful," she said, and laught wholesomely. The others reflected her sunshine with broad smiles. "Sit down, Thelma." Thelma went to the sofa. "Sit down, William," she resumed. She lookt about mirthfully and said, "Are all seated?" She sat abruptly and remarkt with equal brusqueness, "Yes, we are."

"Susan, I can hardly understand you today," spoke William. The various moods, rapidly shifting, were a new sight to him. The calm, equipoised Susan Lee, quiet and patient, had given place to an aggressive personality not easily labeled.

"Sometimes, I can hardly understand myself," she remarkt as one confessing sins to a priest. "I'm nervous William ,and you Thelma. Have I made you nervous?" Taking for granted that she had been the cause of all the trouble, she exclaimed. "I wish I hadn't come. I started not to."

"Why did you come, Susan?" inquired William, thinking of the crisis that would have to reach a head that day, if the blackmailers kept their word.

"Why did I come? Why would a woman steal from parents and friends, and risk abuse and calamity to see a man? Why did Thelma? Has she told you? I came for the same purpose," was the outpouring of her troubled soul. Thelma's heart throbbed violently as Susan spoke. Childhood memories flasht across her mind, and even days of youth and early womanhood. Each had been the life of the other. Was each now to be the death of each?

"Your parents don't know you are here, Susan?" pleaded William.

"I suppose they know now. I left a note within easy reach, but I could not let them know I was coming. Mother would have come along whether I wanted her or not. And I knew she would be entirely out of place. This is a matter for us three. Do you blame me for coming? If you do, I know what that means," declared Susan.

"No, I do not condemn you," he remarkt. He was condemning himself. In all other matters he had acted with tact and expedition. This matter alone of all the interests that had absorbed his mind he had bungled, he thot.

"Can you praise me?" she askt, not satisfied with what seemed a subterfuge. Her question was the prompting of her womanly instincts.

"I must admire you, Susan. You have come thru timidity, I'm sure." Thelma squirmed. What did he mean? Had he not used the wrong word? Was it not supreme courage in the supreme hour of a woman's life that brot her there. Neither Thelma nor William had deemed her capable of it. When crises arise in human affairs, we all may change.

Susan observed and was glad. "I wondered just how I could get away; I found it so difficult. The chance came at last, when mother went shopping. It was my long-sought opportunity. So I am here."

"You little thief!" exclaimed William affectionately. Thelma heaved a sigh. Should she go or remain? She would **remain.** Should she speak or keep silent? She would speak in her turn, but in the main she would say nothing. These were incruciating moments tho. How she had prided herself on having been unusually blest, possessing the best of the **womanly virtues with a** strong admixture of the masculine. Many hard situations, for some women, sad predicaments, many of which would have had no solution at their hands, were for her, but as ordinary difficulties and embarrassments. This **dilemma, however, was** entirely new and in handling it, she found herself only a woman. For the first time in eight years she sobbed. Then tears began to flow.

When she took her handkerchief and wiped her eyes, William and Susan noticed her. "You're crying," he said, "Shame on you."

"I can't help it," she sobbed. "Go on and talk. Don't bother about me. I'll be all right soon."

This was another of the surprises. Thelma had carefully planned what she was to do, but as she had not at all expected Susan; she was disconcerted. Affection for both Susan and William made her distress more intense.

"I'm sorry I came and made you nervous, Thelma. I had it, and you had it. Watch out, William, you'll be next," she said with a taunt.—"By the way, I haven't moved my hat. I mustn't be formal. I'm at home, am I not, William? At least I may pretend so, may I not?" Already she had removed her hat and placed it on the table, near which William sat. "Now, I feel all right."

Now Thelma became more composed. To help the situation she took up a magazine and examined the illustrations. She was trying to remain out of the conversation.

"I'm glad you're feeling fine now. I hope you won't be-

come excited again, for as you said, you may make me lose
my equilibrium," affirmed William.

"Of course, I'm a little fidgety at times. And occasionally I'm impulsive, but don't blame me for it William, please
don't. My nervousness today has been due to several circumstances. You know when I was here two days ago, I wanted
to talk to you alone. You wanted to do so, too. But we were
never to ourselves. You could not run away from your
guests. So there I was. Your intimation, however, gave me
hope that I was not waiting in vain, that soon you would
come to me and at least end suspense one way or the other,"
she spoke rather energetically.

"I meant to come right after the wheat harvest," he put
in by way of corroboration.

"William," said Susan tenderly, "I meant to wait; but
you remember my letter stating that I might come. I was
going to wait; but Thelma came to see you—I'm not blaming
you or abusing you, Thelma. Rather, I rejoice that you
highly value what I also admire. You have paid me a compliment in loving William." Thelma was rather uneasy, only
with quite a struggle in this instance could she refrain from
speech. "Returning to the point, Thelma told different people
about the farm. She did not come to see me. I divined that
she was not visiting the farm, but you.

"Then the other day, I came home from the excursion
here without having accomplisht my purpose, which was to
have a talk with you that would reveal our very souls. When
I learned the following morning that Thelma had left town
again, I thought she would be only around Seaton. I'm not
angry now, but I was almost mad then. I veritably raved.
Mother couldn't understand me. She had Dr. Holmes to come,
who said I was on the verge of a nervous breakdown. So
he recommended a week's rest there, then several weeks in

the country. I tried to urge mother not to have him come, but she would have her way."

"Of course matters will arise at times to displease us all, but we need to be calm. We can't tell what the end may be," he spoke tritely.

"Well, I couldn't be calm when I wanted to. Finally I did become somewhat resigned. Then I determined to be my own physician. So I came here for my health," she smiled. "Shall I live or die? If I am the physician, I suppose I ought to know."

"And what's the remedy?" William askt, of course, only to tease.

"You know as well as I," she affirmed carelessly. "Another thing which unsettled me was this. I feared I might not find you, or if I did, I would find you dead."

"Do you know all?" he inquired.

"Yes—no, I better not say all. Yet I read in the newspaper of your being threatened and that you went to the mayor. Here's the paper in my bag." A few moments were enough to obtain it.

"Knowing this, you came here?"

"Yes, but it almost carried me to the ditch. I don't believe I could do it again. That's what made me so upset when I came. Then to find Thelma here, as I had suspected—What else was there for me to do?" she fondly askt.

"You have suffered much," he said with a sigh.

What enigmas crowd themselves upon us requiring a solution! What questions we must answer! What sacrifices we must make! What sadness we must know! What deaths we must die!

William obviously loved both these women. Each was beautiful and noble and accomplisht. Each loved him solely. He would have chosen one almost as soon as the other, if

"Knowing this you came here?"

both had not absorbed his life very early and for a long time. Tho they were more alike than different, yet the dissimilarities and not the likenesses would decide the issue. He would make an analysis into their characters; he had already done it thousands of times. He knew them as he knew his books—very thoroly.

Yet he must choose. An equal friendship with them, he deemed impossible; for it is characteristic of love to make a claim, in order that, when it will, it may shut the world out and have the object of its affection all to itself. Likewise, he thot their merely being friends would not evoke the highest qualities of his own nature. To reach human perfection man and woman must wed and become one life. To have never too much harshness and never too little tenderness, he knew he had to come into the most intimate relation with one woman. He reflected that a man can never thoroly know even his wife. Human life changes so rapidly. How can a man then thoroly comprehend two women? It just can not be done. He was thinking strenuously.

"Yes, I've gone thru much. But I'm paid. I've seen you, William, I've seen you. Medicine could not have accomplisht these results. Oh, I feel so happy," she said. Her heart was quite full and free. "Now, William, one other question I have to ask. You must answer. Come here, Thelma," she said tenderly. "There are only two women in this world that you love—Thelma and me. Am I wrong?" she askt.

"You're right." He knew what she was coming to, but would not interrupt her.

"Thelma, don't be bashful, come here," she said. "When I command, you obey." She stamped her foot playfully. Thelma came to her hesitantly. "Stand here, William. Now, you have us both; one on either side. You know you're going to marry, and we do, too. It's no use having both of us suffer." Looking across to Thelma, she said, "Old friend, can you suffer?"

"Yes, I have learned how," she said, "but I'd rather die."

"So would I," said Susan, "yet I believe I can suffer. You understand. I waited for you to ask." All the events of his courtship swarmed before him. As he now comprehended it, both he and Susan had proposed and each had rejected the other. This situation he desired ended as well as Susan. Tho the decision would be painful, he should no longer delay. So to some extent he was glad when she said, "You men choose anyhow. Make your choice now."

"You know that I am not happy. I'm suffering more than ever before in my life. I thot the censure I bore from the ministers and the people of Williamsburg was the greatest ordeal of my life. Oh, Father, may I choose properly?" he prayed.

"You're not going to make any mistake," said Susan.

At this point Mrs. Brown rushed in exclaiming, "Rev. Smith, Rev. Smith, the mob is coming. Andy brought the news and hurried back. So I'm doing as you said. I brot you word."

"Thank you, Mrs. Brown. Will you watch over the ladies?" he said, taking his gun and starting out. "Girls, I cannot answer the question now, but if I live; I'll keep my word I'll tell you before the sun goes down."

"What's this, William?" cried Susan abruptly. It was to her as if the malefactors had already done their mischief. Tho she expected such when she was in Williamsburg, she came. Yet, when the danger anticipated was at hand, she could not make a stand against it. Her former self now held sway. "Is it really the mob? You must not go, they will kill you. You have men scattered all around the place, they'll protect you."

"I know they will, Susan; but I'd be a coward to remain behind. I must inspire my men. I'm not going off my estate. I'm going to wage the battle entirely in self-defense. If the enemy doesn't fire, I'll not fire. If the enemy does fire," he declared, "heaven only knows when I'll stop."

"Good bye," he said, starting out again, but Susan clung to him.

"Oh! William, ah!—ah! William, I could stand your refusing me, but not to see you any more," she wept bitterly. "Oh! William, ah—ah," she sighed. Then she began to laugh hysterically. "Thelma, Thelma, you're not going to let him go, are you? Stay, William, stay!"

"I must go, Susan! The men are waiting for me. Try to be calm; see, your nervousness has returned. They're not going to kill me," he said firmly.

"Kill you, kill you," she spoke somewhat wildly. "No, no, no, no—ah." She gave a long sigh. "Don't kill him, don't kill him, don't kill him." Then she fainted in his arms.

"Mrs. Brown, look after her please," he said, and placed Susan on the settee. "Thelma, you'll help, too, I know."

"Certainly," she replied. "If she soon becomes composed, however, I don't promise to remain here." Understanding William thoroly, she knew he would stay upon his estate. Besides, she believed that his neighbors needed the soft import of her spirit. She might fail in an amorous interview, but not in a public activity. She was resolute.

"But you must, Thelma," he spoke with alarm. "You must not go out."

"I heard you say you were going to remain on the estate; but what's to be done concerning the other people?" she inquired.

"They'll come here first, Thelma. Stay with Susan and Mrs. Brown," he said, rushing out.

"As long as possible, anyway," she replied. "But William," she called. He turned and listened. "Give them only justice. We don't get even that."

"You may depend upon me," he remarkt. In an instant they heard the door bang. He was en route to face his foes.

While William and Thelma were talking, Mrs. Brown went for water and remedies. Within a few minutes, she had returned and started to work. Thelma was fanning her friends. By applying smelling salts and bathing Susan's head with cold water, they were able to hasten consciousness. At first she was perfectly still, save for the heavy breathing. As she began to breathe with more ease, she tossed her head from side to side and rolled. Then she uttered unintelligible sounds, groans and sighs. Not long after this, however, she became quiet and then opened her eyes. A few moments later she sat up and lookt dazed.

"Sue, Sue," said Thelma in the old childish way, "how are you?"

"Has he gone?" she askt pitifully. "Has he gone?"

"Yes, Susan. He couldn't stay. The only manly thing to do was to meet those scoundrels," she declared with a sympathy that did much to calm her friend.

"But I fear that they will kill him yet. It would be so great a pity to take our best. Generals remain behind in their quarters. William should have stayed here," she said slowly, more and more gaining composure. At this point she arose.

"Where are you going," inquired Thelma.

Susan lookt at her friend a few moments and said care-

lessly, "Oh!—just to the parlor window. I was wondering
if I might see—see—William. Do you suppose I could?"

"I think not from our location," put in Mrs. Brown.
"You might try, tho." This was said more to give the young
woman satisfaction.

Susan tried, but in vain. "Well, I suppose I must wait."
She went to other windows on that floor, but in each instance failed to see anyone. Returning to the drawing room,
she said desperately, "I give it up." She stretched out on
the settee. "Is this a quiet place to rest, Mrs. Brown? Of
course, today I'm allowing for what may occur on the outside."

"Yes, it is generally very quiet here. I'd suggest, however, that you go to my room. You will be more comfortable,"
she replied.

"I have not slept at all for several nights. I was thinking that a little sleep would do me good. If I keep awake,
I shall become probably more disquieted. For should I feel
that the mob was very near, I'd be entirely unnerved," she
continued. She wanted to throw attention from herself, in
order that the energies of all the fighting forces could un-
swervingly be devoted to the one aim—to help the Nation
maintain the law.

"Come this way, please," requested the motherly Mrs.
Brown. "I'll give you a very mild opiate. When you awake
I'm sure you will be better. You'll be yourself once more."

"You're coming with me, aren't you, Thelma," inquired
Susan, somewhat childishly.

"Yes, I'll come," said the friend.

They all went upstairs to Mrs. Brown's commodiously
furnisht room. Susan took the opiate and lay down. Within
a few moments she was fast asleep. Her rest was quiet.

As soon as Thelma saw this, she took Mrs. Brown aside

and askt, "Are you going to remain here till the men return?"

"Yes, be they white or black," she replied.

"Then I must go out to see what's going on," said Thelma.

"Miss Haskell, the idea! Don't think of it," declared Mrs. Brown.

"Mrs. Brown, I must go. Take care of Susan." In an instant she was gone.

CHAPTER XXVIII.

Germany has outlawed herself among the nations because she has disregarded the sacred obligations of law and has made lynchers of her armies. Every mob contributes to German lies about the United States, what her most gifted liars cannot improve upon by the way of calumny. They can at least say that such things can not happen in Germany except in times of revolution, when law is swept away. *** It can not live where the community does not countenance it. —Woodrow Wilson.

What tho the field be lost?
All is not lost; th'inconquerable will,
And study of revenge, immortal hate,
And courage never to submit or yield. —Milton.

When the mob left the courthouse grounds, it proceeded very much as would a parade, except for the boisterousness, the profanity, and general disorder. There were the spectators, who stopt their work to look from the doors and windows of the shops and homes. Cheering of women and children, however, was absent, for these were not along the line of march, but trailing the column of the chief actors. Thus they proceeded until they were quite near to the outskirts of William's estate.

As they walkt out of town into the country, they also spoke of various things; but chiefly of being an "orderly mob," of doing a "good job" and getting back to work. Some, however, were condemning Mr. Pitts and the entire moneyed class.

Tom Howell, on the other hand, reporter of the "Seaton Gazette," as soon as he could maneuver his way to Newton Young, began to discuss lynching as a means of keeping the

297

Negro in "his place." "Well, what do you think of the mob?" askt Howell, looking here and there with profound admiration.

"Quite a lively bunch, I should say," Newton Young replied with evident satisfaction, "very decent and genteel."

"Well, they certainly are orderly," remarkt Howell. "I'll have to congratulate these men and prepare a fine write-up for the paper. By the way, I saw a lynching at Hollow Plains the other day. It was one of the finest things I ever saw in my life. A darkey named Sam Addams was given six months for shooting a rabbit on forbidden land. He broke from prison and went into some woods."

"I wonder how they could be so lax as to let a nigger escape. It wouldn't happen down this way," declared Young with great sectional pride.

"Well, I must go on," interrupted Howell. "This nigger shot the constable and a deputy in his 'break' for freedom. They succeeded, tho, in wounding the coon. Finally he was captured by a posse.

"When the town learned it they stormed the jail, even tho there had been a quick trial and the nigger sentenced to hang."

"What satisfaction does hanging give, when it comes to a nigger," Young sneered.

"Well, I'll tell you, those people knew what to do. A crowd of something like two thousand saw it. Of course, many of these were women and children. Addams was so badly wounded that he couldn't walk, but not too heavy to be carried," he laught.

Young was enjoying it immensely.

"So they carried him gently almost to the very spot where he shot those fellows and prepared for him a funeral pyre. When this was ready, they chained him to a hickory tree. A short distance away they made another fire with which to heat some soldering irons. As soon as these attained red heat, two of the men took them out and went for the coon. They jabbed these towards his body; as his hands were not tied he grabbed hold of them. He soon released them, but not before the odor of burning flesh filled the atmosphere. The scent was nauseating. For the first time the murderer's will was broken. He was scared to death. He gave away absolutely. At once he began to scream hideously.

"They ran the irons to various parts of his body. The nigger continued to grab fiendishly. Then he shriekt so mournfully, that for a time the children and women were frightened.

"Did they stay there?" askt Young, now extremely curious to seize every detail.

"Yes, indeed," said Howell arrogantly. "They remained thru the entire scene. Some people say women can't stand to see this and that. Women can stand anything." At this point his attention was called to a little altercation between two members of the throng who were to be among the chief actors in the contemplated performance. As soon as he had adjusted this, he resumed his narrative. "When it seemed once that the murderer would get an iron and probably hurl it into the crowd, one of the men plunged it into the fellow's eye; the other followed suit. Then the coon did shriek and yell.

"After these few minutes of torture," he spoke with sangfroid, "men piled the wood about him. Then they poured coal oil on his feet and trousers, not forgetting to sprinkle some on the wood. The nigger begged to be shot or hanged; but the men applied the match. Yells and shrieks of scorn and derision were hurled at him. The flames, as if in pity, speedily singed his hair and destroyed his clothing. The nigger shriekt no more, he didn't even groan. He writhed and soon he was dead."

"Well, I'd like to have seen that," said Young.

Thus they talkt until they came within two hundred yards of the most outlying farm on William's estate. Here they halted to decide on the leaders and the direction of their attack. Some wanted to rush ahead, but Luke Crabtree said that they should wait; that every man should know his business and nobody be in anyone's way. After a brief consideration, they decided upon Bob White, who had always been the chief promoter, Silas Jones, and Hugh Granville—all farmers. Others of the conference were to help where it was necessary. All the remaining members of the mob were to obey these. Young, Howell, Sandy James, and Luke Crabtree slunk to the rear to keep the women and children back. They planned to join the fray later.

It was at the time the conference began that an outpost reported the approach of the mob to Turner, who quickly got word to those on William's farm. He had, in accordance with Thelma's plan, prepared to keep the mob even from setting foot on William's estate. It might mean death to all of them, but Thelma had steeled them to do it and they were not going to turn back.

As soon as Turner had sent word to William, he rallied those who were to resist the mob. "Do you think we should rush out?" inquired Moses Lampkins.

"Not until I give the signal, fool," Turner affirmed. "But they must know we are here and understand that we mean business."

"When must I shoot," askt another.

"Wait for the signal," replied Turner impatiently. "And when I give it don't stop." Then looking about to see if all were there, he askt, "Is there anyone here who doesn't know what he is to do?" He paused a while for an answer. "All understand? All right. What's the slogan?"

"Rev. Smith shall live, our lives for it!" was the acclaim.

"Add this to the other! The Negro stands at bay!" he remarkt. "Let's hear you say it."

"The Negro stands at bay!" they shouted.

"Say this and then the other as loud as you can, say them thus," he commanded, and gave the order of the slogans.

The men responded with vigor, "The Negro stands at bay. Reverend Smith shall live, our lives for it."

"Once more," commanded Turner, "and once again." He called for it several times. "They haven't heard us," he said, for there had come no response of shot or voice.

"Let's move on towards them," said Wendell Hill, who now was ready for any venture.

"There seem to be about a thousand of them," Jim Lane declared with some degree of fear.

"What, are you afraid?" said Hill, absolutely disgusted with Lane. "Take God with you. What does He say? He tells us if we take Him along, one *man* can chase a thousand and two can put ten thousand to flight. Do you believe the Scriptures?"

"Every word of it," replied Lane, now consoled. "If God says 'Go,' I'll kill myself trying. I'm ready; let's go ahead."

"Some folks say never give the first lick, but Roosevelt says, 'If you see a man going to hit you, strike him first in self-defense and when you hit, don't play with him; put him to sleep,'" said Turner. "There they stand arguing, making up their minds, I suppose. Let's go nearer," he continued, "and keep up the slogan till they take notice."

The mob did soon notice the sounds. All were inquisitive. The sounds became louder and more distinct, until they were very intelligible. What had happened? "Where you coming?" came a shout from the woods. "You may shoot if you wish, but thank God we can shoot, too." About five men appeared behind trees with rifles, which flasht plainly before those in front.

The mob was disconcerted. Some hastened to carry the word to the women and children that they should hurry away, lest some of them be killed. "The niggers had arms," they said, "and are scattered in the woods. There's no telling what they'll do."

The mob was furious, because it had met opposition; yet not so furious that its members could not keep their presence of mind. The rifles aimed at the attackers presented the sufficient reason. Meanwhile, Wendell Hill, who somehow, seemed to consider himself the wearer of a charmed life, protected by God, and who was therefore foremost, said: "If you move another step, you'll sleep tonight in hell with your master. We don't care to shed any blood, but as surely you touch that fence, some of you will go back corpses."

"D—n it," fumed Crabtree and others like him, "this comes of waiting so long."

"Let's go after them anyhow? What do I care about dying?" shouted a bully.

"Come on then," responded the defiant Hill. "If you're seeking a grave, we'll give you one in double quick time."

"Man, don't be foolish," urged Crabtree. "What's the use of white men getting killed?"

The situation is easily understood. Hundreds and thousands had been wont to murder one helpless individual. There was no questions of the attackers being killed, because their victim generally was in prison or already deprived of arms by the sheriff. Now for the first time the victims were armed and in ambush. How many were there, they did not know. Yet they were well aware of the numbers that workt his farms and the hosts he had brot to theirs. They began to wonder whether all the people were in arms. When a coward knows his life is not in danger, he can fight like a devil incarnate. When, however, he thinks that he may be killed, likewise his friends, relatives and children, he is less ready to take human life.

While the mob was thus unsettled, automobiles began to sound on the crossroad, the clicking of the motors suggested they were coming at a very rapid rate. Then the horns gave a blare which was, being so discordant, instinctively construed as an important warning. Heads were turned in various directions, to localize the noise and be prepared to avoid any calamity. It was not long before the vehicles were upon them and the faces of the occupants clearly discernible. These were their own friends and associates, even members of their own race. What did this mean? Why were they there?

The manner of approach had been carefully workt out. Nailor, who had been chosen as leader, was in the first car. As he was a man of much initiative and great adaptability, he modified his plan somewhat. His party was armed to stop the mob from carrying out the attack. However, when he saw the mob disconcerted, he was convinced that it had already met resistance. He inferred this from the conference of the group that comprised the chief promoters. The first part of his plan was therefore not necessary. Accordingly he instructed his men to keep their rifles out of sight, tho near them, where they would be readily accessible in case of need.

Nailor then turned to one of the men and said, "Drive that car"—the one in which he came—"right into the crowd."

With considerable maneuvering and at a very slow speed, this instruction was accomplisht.

When the car was in place, he had Lawyer Jones stand in it for the purpose of addressing the crowd. Then he bade his associates who were trying to prevent lawlessness to surround the car. Other persons arranged themselves as they wisht. This done, he clapped his hands to get attention. Here and there distemper arose; and much swearing, but this he did not hear. When he had the attention of the majority, he said, "Men, I know some of you're sick."

In different parts of the mob there arose cries of "Shut up!"

Bob White, however, a well meaning individual, who took everything he did very seriously, who believed in demanding what he thot was his and was always ready to profit by whatever the well-informed had to say, shouted, "Men, this is no way to act. We understood this was to be an orderly bunch. Let's hear what the other fellow has to say— that's my word all the time. When you do that, you don't make no mistakes. When he has finisht and all of us want the nigger, we can get him. But you have to count the costs. Let's listen. It ain't going to do you no harm. Go on, Nailor."

The crowd ceased to show signs of being disgruntled. Then Nailor said, "Men, I'd like to tell you how I feel, but I'm not. I don't pretend to be a speaker; but I have here a *man,* one we all love, who does a lot of talking every day. When people fly up in anger, they need some calm person to talk to them. I can't do it; what I might say might anger you. So I turn this matter over to our distinguisht friend, Lawyer Luther Jones. You know him. Hear him."

Had Lawyer Jones arisen upon a platform to speak in an auditorium, these very persons, who were urged to listen would have greeted him with prolonged applause. When the

issue was of unparalleled moment they gave him a Chautauqua
salute. On this occasion all this was absent. They merely
awaited his utterances in silence. When an individual becomes expectant of an accustomed demonstration and fails
to get it, even if he is an orator of matchless eminence, he becomes somewhat disconcerted. If he has had long experience,
he is ready for any mood of his audience. So was Lawyer
Jones on this occasion. He was not certain of success; but
he was confident, he was brimful of optimism.

In this spirit, he approacht his audience, and said, "Gentlemen, fellow-citizens, isn't this a beautiful day? Isn't it fine
to have such pretty days here, while rain is falling constantly
in France. Isn't it fine to be living at this time, fine to have
others living about us, while in France each day that passes
makes hundreds and thousands of widows and orphans?
Aren't you glad you're not suffering those things; that such
does not exist in America? Aren't you happy that we are
not murdering children, violating women, and torturing men?
Shouldn't we rejoice that such is not among us? I tell you
I myself am overjoyed. This is the happiest day of my life."

The suggestion carried. They had not listened to Banker
Pitts, but they were listening now. They began to see what
their wives and children would suffer, and to wonder if they
would not be criminal to carry on their premeditated mischief.

The speaker continued: "Some of you have sons in
France and want to see them, should they return." By this
time a number of the colored farmers, emboldened by Thelma,
went into the open to hear what was being said. Turning in
that direction, he saw those gallant men and a stately woman
among them—all armed. Then he said, "Friends, you want
to see those; and I want you to have that pleasure. Notwithstanding this natural desire, without thot, as it were, you were
going to expose your lives, some even to die, to lynch an

innocent man. I say to die, because the colored people are armed and ready to resist any attack. If you go against them, what would be the result? You might probably lose your own lives and make many widows and orphans.

"If Rev. Smith has wronged you, bring a case against him in court. I'll offer my services free to plead your case. Besides, you know Judge Randall is a fair man and he will give you justice. Consider the urgent request of President Wilson, that matchless son of the South. He says, 'No man who loves America, no man who really cares for her fame and honor and character, or who is truly loyal to her institutions, can justify mob action while the courts of justice are open and the governments of the States and the Nation are ready and able to do their duty.'

"At present so far as I can see, this man you would attack is no enemy, but a friend. You know yourselves that you would not send your sons to agricultural schools, tho we urged you on many occasions. This man whom you sought to destroy, has been and profited. You, too, have profited by his going. Because of his minding his own business and working his farm successfully for big yields, you wanted to know how he obtained his results. Many of you, who now would do him a malice, he showed how to increase your dollars, yet the man who has made your pocketbooks swell, who made it possible for you to accomplish more than you have for many a day, you would string up and torture.

"Were you able to get even laborers so easily as you have since this man came?"

The mob was listening very attentively. And as they listened, they weighed the speaker's words and thot strenuously of the significance of what they were doing.

"We arrived somewhat late," he continued. "We meant to end any violence because your victim is innocent and our

Country at war. But let us be thankful that those people had sense enough to make a stand and prevent the disgrace to democracy.

"We should praise these people. They take many insults from us and yet they are always loyal. While on this point, let me remind you that what they have done this day is no disloyal act; for the law permits a man to defend himself.

"Do you remember when France was being harassed with trip-hammer blows by the Germans, when she was war-weary, needing instant relief and we had not time to train our men? It was then that the Government called for volunteers to go into the breach at once, if necessary, tho she hoped that the moral effect of their presence would inspire sufficient endurance in the French to have them hold out until our men could be well seasoned. In that crisis the call came to Camp Washington, which received many of our boys. You know the story. Those colored boys who went from here, offered their services, tho they had been but two weeks in camp. Don't you remember when they passed by? Didn't you cheer them? Yes, you did. You honored them then. Honor them now by not assaulting their brothers at home."

Then he paused a moment, waved his hand to the right. This was the signal for Davis to make his appearance. Within a few moments, Davis came forward and planted a large American flag in the car and stood beside it. Lawyer Jones wiped his face during the interval and then continued: "Fellow countrymen, this flag is flying in France. All the world is watching it. Will you hold it up? Will you keep it from trailing in the dust?"

"Yes," they shouted, "stand by the flag!"

"I wish we could sing 'The Star-Spangled Banner' " he said, thrilled with the greatest throbs of emotion. "Let's try it. He led off with his beautiful tenor. The people listened for a while and then joined in. As they uncovered and sang this grand anthem in the grand style, there returned that old respect and love for the Nation.

When they had finisht, he askt, "Will you do something for me—repeat a flag salute?"

"Yes, yes, certainly," were the replies.

"Then repeat this: I pledge my allegiance to the flag, to do no lawlessness in the land; one Nation, indivisible, with liberty and justice for all."

They obeyed. All faces were brighter than they had been all day.

"Noble countrymen, I close with an utterance of our gallant President. I deem it most befitting. He said in making his public appeal that mob action cease, 'We proudly claim to be the champion of democracy. If we really are, in deed and in truth, let us see to it that we do not discredit our own.'

"Now let us go to work," he urged, "and let the world know how well we have behaved ourselves. When all the nations learn, especially when our own native land learns what Seaton has done, multitudes will praise us always."

The people turned and orderly went home.

CHAPTER XXIX.

Why doth fate that often bestows thousands of souls on a conqueror or tyrant, to be the sport of his passions, so often deny to the tenderest and most feeling hearts one kindred one on which to lavish their affections? Why is it that Love must so often sigh in vain for an object, and Hate never? —Richter

When Susan awoke late in the afternoon, she heard a noise of mingled voices that seemed to come from the drawing room. There was so much laughter and hilartiy interspersed that she was at a loss to fix the cause of it. "They are happy," she thot. "Am I so, too? At least I'm feeling very well. How fine it is just to have a sound sleep and not to dream!" Raising herself and looking toward the door, she saw Mrs. Brown absorbed in a book. She called to mind how she enjoyed a good story and desired to remain undisturbed while perusing it. She did not want to interrupt her; but more than this, she did long to know what had happened while she slept. "I'll call softly," she said, for it hurt her to disturb the dear lady. "I'll call softly. She won't mind." Susan then lookt away, as if trying to banish the idea; then spoke gently, "Mrs. Brown." The lady did not notice. "Mrs. Brown," she called louder.

"What is it, Miss Lee?" now was the reply. "Do you mind laying your book aside for a moment to talk to me? I hate to interrupt you—is the story interesting?"

"Yes, very, it is Dunbar's 'Uncalled.' Have you read it?" she said, and then lookt away somewhat abasht. "How silly of me! Of course, you have."

"Mrs. Brown," she broke in, for she did not care at this

time to discuss the book. "I'd like to know what has occurred today. Why all that hubbub downstairs? Where is Rev. Smith? Where is Miss Haskell? She was here when I lay down. Why did she go away?"

"I tried to keep her here for her own sake, Miss Lee. When shots are flying, I'd rather be indoors; but she said she had to see for herself what was going on," was the reply of Mrs. Brown, unaware of what emotions might be stirred in her hearer, and so unconsciously indifferent.

"Thelma went out?" said Susan with astonishment, and with such sad feeling as marks one's beholding a calamity. "How long did she stay? Did she come back?"

"Yes, she returned about half an hour ago. She has been so busy talking of the affair with the others downstairs, that she has become upset, too, I'm afraid. You should have seen the big white men from town shaking hands with Rev. Smith; and they askt to be introduced to Miss Haskell. She did something for which they were praising her. I don't know as yet what it is."

"That's enough," replied Susan, leaping from the bed, "I must go down and gather up all the details." With dispatch, she proceeded to dress. "Help me, please, Mrs. Brown," she requested anxiously, "some day I'll do as much for you." With all her solicitude and haste, she remembered every article with an accuracy and acceleration that caused her assistant frequent moments of amazement; for she was comparing the Susan of the morning with the Susan of the afternoon. Such moods to her were unexplainable; she tried to analyze the situation, but as increased thinking brot only additional complexity, she soon acknowledged herself baffled.

While Susan was dressing, the hilarity did not cease, it seemed to increase and at times to border on boisterousness. These outbursts put her in a reflective mood, which at those

"I'm glad to see you happy."

moments retarded her *preparation de toilette*. It was not long, however, before the task was done. Prepared at last to meet her friends, she lost no time in going to the drawing room.

William had wisht that Susan was there to share in the jokes and tales that were related. Learning, tho, that she was asleep, he would not disturb her. He had told his guests to subdue their voices and had practically decided to go outdoors; but the visit of Lawyer Jones, Nailor and Davis, together with others who had shown a fine spirit in the affair, kept him on the inside.

When Susan reacht the drawing room, William was on the point of going upon the lawn. Indeed many were already there. Seeing, however, that Susan had appeared, he became promptly aware that he must yet remain within. At once he greeted her warmly.

Susan was thoroly a woman. Keenly discerning in matters feminine, she knew that Mrs. Brown had not thot of her at all and her ambitions towards William. To be not temperamentally, but physically asleep, when your rival is on the *qui vive,* to be forced to step aside, while your competitor runs, is not in the nature of things desirable food for a healthy, mental digestion. Thelma was on the outside, while she was securely entrencht within. The idea was not at all inspired. What had Thelma done to merit praise? At least she had left the house.

"William," she said, as soon as they had exchanged greetings. "I'm so glad to see you. I feared so much that you would suffer harm that my nerves were completely unstrung. But I'm all right now," she smiled. "Am I not gay?" she askt abruptly.

"I'm glad to see you happy," he responded, with keen enjoyment. "You must try to keep composed now. Have a seat." He offered her the one he had occupied in the morning, then seated himself in the one she chose at that time. His action was purposed; he wanted not to suggest those strenuous emotional moments. "Would you like to go outside?" he requested, thinking that thus the affair would take a new aspect. Already the guests were going out and grouping themselves on the lawn.

Seeing this, Susan said, "No, I think I prefer to be in here right now." She wanted to talk to him alone and this was her opportunity. In a few moments they were left alone, save for the lively suggestion of a presence behind the lively conversation in progress outside.

Susan now thot of the task she had to perform and wondered how to begin. At length she commenced, not with perfect calmness, nor yet with an uneasiness that might cause alarm. She thot why she had come, then she mused upon the recent events that gave everything a new coloring. "I was just wondering what to say first, William," she uttered in a very mellow tone, which attracted one by its very loveliness. "But I suppose I might as well start at one place as another."

"Certainly."

"Then here I start," she remarkt playfully. "Tell me, sir," she pointed her finger at him as if reproaching, "tell me, sir, all that has occurred since you left me this morning. And don't you dare to omit anything."

"May I not omit just one insignificant incident?" he askt merrily.

"No, not one."

"Well, this is how it was, to be brief. I had organized my helpers to defend this farm; but never had a chance."

"Why was that?"

"Knowing that I was in a delicate situation and that I

might be misunderstood even if I started an attack in self-
defense, I decided to fight only when my assailants had set
foot on my property, or had fired upon us. That this might
be carried out, I had instructed my neighbors not to interfere.
I believe in remaining within the law. The people, however,
at my suggestion, were defending their homes. This was
all they were to do.

"The plan didn't work, not because it might have failed.
It could not; for we easily could have destroyed them from
ambush, as they would pass along the lanes. To my displeas-
ure, the plan was not permitted; for Thelma somehow convinced them that they should defend me even against my
wishes. This they did. I didn't even see the mob. The report
came from some of my neighbors and my white friends who
had formed a sort of counter mob to uphold the law and keep
disgrace from the Nation. Before they could get there, however, my neighbors had made a stand. Then followed my
white friends who poured in reason and finisht the job. But
during the speech of Lawyer Jones, Thelma, with some of
the men, was within hearing distance. Now I've told you all,"
he smiled. "Are you satisfied?" As William reviewed the
events which had just occurred, Susan felt as if she were
upon the wrack.

In reply to his question, she said, "Quite, quite." She
spoke carelessly and knitted her brow.

"I tell you that was something wonderful. How proud
I am of my people! I didn't want the people to do this, because the Nation is at war. Some might have said we were
stirring up strife. But I tell you I feel happy in that they
made the stand they did. I even reproacht Thelma, but I
could not help greatly admiring her courage. She could make
the people dare, and she braved as much as they." He did
not notice the change that had come over Susan. She lookt

at the roses upon the table and proceeded to enjoy their fragrance, in an effort to shake off her wretched feeling.

William now spoke almost absent-mindedly, "When a man walks erect people look up to him; they look down upon the man who stoops. And any man respects a person who is ready to die for his rights. Are we radical to seek these things—life, the right to property and justice in and out of the courts? These things were radical seven hundred years ago, but not now."

"But where is Thelma?" inquired Susan, who had hardly heard the latter part of William's remarks. Her soul was permeating the universe to get all possible help to meet a supreme test.

"Oh!" said William, collecting himself, "really, I don't know. She said she was going to some of the neighbors, but would return very soon."

"She's getting her congratulations, I suppose; but I musn't be jealous. I shall congratulate her, too," she remarkt with difficulty.

"By the way," exclaimed William, now that the excitement had worn off, "Are you hungry? I am. I haven't had a bite since early this morning. You must be hungry, too."

"On the contrary, I'm not," she replied almost monotonously.

"Any way, we must have dinner soon. Excuse me a moment, please, while I see Mrs. Brown and have everything arranged, if she hasn't already done so."

"You're excused. Don't be long," she said plaintively.

What perplexities confront us! We start and all is gay We utter commands and all the world listens. We say we want to live, that we must live, and all the machinery of man is shaped to accomplish this end. Why do we have to leave this period of rapture and innocence? It is not without some sorrows; but our wants in the main are satisfied. We live as king or queen.

Soon, however, we become impulsive, indifferent or dream dreams. A man or a woman becomes the chief friend, we no longer live entirely within ourselves. We need a mate; a mere friend will not suffice. How deficient we are! It was not always so; but so it is now. And often it is a sad truth. Where can I find the golden complement of my existence? East or West? North or South? Knowing best what is right about us, we look next door. We see the gold, we adore it, we take it even in our hand; but can we have it, now and always? That remains for others to say.

Such were some of the thots that ran thru Susan's mind as she waited for William. When he returned he said, "Everything is being prepared. Dinner will be ready within half an hour. I was thinking we might meanwhile take a walk. Won't you go?"

Before she could answer, Thelma had come in. "How are you, Susan? I hope you rested well," she said, friendly embracing her. Susan now arose.

"I slept too well, Thelma. I didn't even dream," she remarkt seriously. "Accept my congratulations, Thelma. You are a brave, brave girl. Will you lend me some of your courage? I'm afraid I'm as timid as a deer."

"You're just saying that. You could have done it, too," she replied. "You came here after reading what was said in the paper. You are just belittling yourself unnecessarily."

"I want to go home tonight, William," said Susan somewhat abruptly, with a sigh. She lookt at him and then at Thelma to glimpse the effect of her remark.

"Don't think of it," replied Thelma.

"No," came from William, "It isn't wise. With the disturbance which came today, we should have been taught to

be cautious. Tho confident that a permanent adjustment has
been made between my people and those who came this morning to work us ruin, we can not afford to be off our guard.
We're not looking for trouble, but if it comes, it must not find
us unprepared. But of course if you insist upon going, we'll
see you off. You know, however, that you should avoid excitement at this time or anything which might give it birth."

"Stay here with me," requested Thelma, "we'll have a
jolly good time."

"Don't you see it's impossible?" Susan said firmly. "I
believe I must go home tonight, *tonight.*"

"I shouldn't have had you come during this crisis. But
as you're here, I wish you wouldn't hurry away. At least
you should stay until—we know this storm is over," urged
William. "Write a letter or better still, send a telegram. I'll
get it off for you at once. Besides, the country is generally
recommended for persons suffering from nervous strain."

"Well, that depends upon the particular country," she replied. She arose and started to ask for a pencil. "Let me
have a—no, I believe I should go."

"Susan, I can't understand you," Thelma interrupted.

"You don't understand? Well, now you shall understand,"
she said, with sad affection. For a moment she was silent.
Then she took Thelma by the hand and called, "William, come,
let us be confidential. Come, join us." He approacht sus-
piciously. As he was at her side, she said, "Here we all are,
whose souls throb for one answer. When, William, will you
decide?"

"Would that I had said nothing," he replied with bitter
anguish. "Before—the sun—goes—down."

"It is far on its decline now," Susan remarkt, "don't you
see already the streaks of red and purple?"

"Don't, Susan, don't," he cried.

Thelma started toward the window. She was beholding the sunset.

"Don't go, Thelma," Susan spoke sorrowfully, when her friend proceeded to put on her hat. "We must have it out. Put down your hat, Thelma, and come here just for a moment." Thelma obeyed. When Thelma had come quite close, Susan said, "See what maturity brings? Here, William, take her. I will not ask you to choose, for you have done so already." She took Thelma's hand and put it in his. "You won him this day. 'What God hath joined together, let no man put asunder.' Take her in your arms and kiss her sweetly." He followed her request. "Now, will you kiss me once? You never have. Since I'll love none but you, will you do that much? May he, Thelma, for he is yours now?"

"Yes, Susan," said Thelma, in tears.

William kissed her gently; for he was thrilled. He got the burning message of her soul.

"Now, I'm going, William," she affirmed, overwhelmed with the burden of her grief. She took her hat and bag.

"Stay, Susan," they both cried.

But Susan left, to ease her troubled breast.